LEGACY

OF THE

DEAD

LEGACY
OF THE
DEAD

—————— ◆ ——————

AN INSPECTOR
IAN RUTLEDGE
MYSTERY

—————— ◆ ——————

CHARLES TODD

BANTAM BOOKS

This edition contains the complete text
of the original hardcover edition.
NOT ONE WORD HAS BEEN OMITTED.

LEGACY OF THE DEAD
A Bantam Book

PUBLISHING HISTORY
Bantam hardcover edition published October 2000
Bantam mass market edition / June 2001

Library of Congress Catalog Card Number: 00-036076

ISBN 0-553-58315-8

Published simultaneously in the United States and Canada

Bantam Books are published by Bantam Books, a division of Random
House, Inc. Its trademark, consisting of the words "Bantam Books" and
the portrayal of a rooster, is Registered in U.S. Patent and Trademark
Office and in other countries. Marca Registrada. Bantam Books, 1540
Broadway, New York, New York 10036.

PRINTED IN THE UNITED STATES OF AMERICA
OPM   10   9   8   7   6   5   4   3   2   1

For L.
with love . . .

1

1916

GLASGOW

THE TWO WOMEN SAT HUDDLED TOGETHER IN THE small carriage, looking around them in dismay, staring at the filthy, closed-in street, the drunken old man sprawled in one of the doorways, the tall tenements ugly and bleak and perilously ill-kept. There was no grace here, only an air of despondency and gloom and poverty.

"It's a horrible place!" one said at last. She was the elder, but not by much. They were both young and very frightened.

"Are you quite sure this is the street we want? I can't believe—" Her companion, the reins lying in her lap, let the words die.

In answer, the passenger dug in her purse for the tattered piece of paper, pulled it out, and read it again. Her lips were trembling, and she felt cold, sick. "Look for yourself. *Oh*—" The paper slipped from her fingers, and she caught it just before it tumbled into the fetid running gutter beneath the wheel.

It was the street and the house they had searched over an hour to find.

There was silence, only the rain and the whistle of a train somewhere in the distance making any sound at all. The horse waited patiently.

"You'll remember, won't you?" the older woman went on breathlessly. "I'm Mrs. Cook. And you're Sarah. My mother had a housekeeper called Mrs. Cook. And a sewing woman called Sarah. That makes it easier for me—" She stared at the house. "It's a cursed place, dreadful."

"I only have to remember who you are. And I've called you that all day. Mrs. Cook. Don't fret so—you'll make yourself ill!"

"Yes." She smoothed the rug across her knees, felt its dampness.

The horse blew, shifting uncomfortably in the rain.

Finally the older woman squeezed her companion's hand and said, "We must go in, Sarah. We're expected. It must be nearly time."

They climbed stiffly out of the carriage, two respectable young women looking as out of place here as they felt. The stench of bad sewers and boiled cabbage, overlaid with coal smoke and dirty streets, heavy in the dampness, seemed to wrap itself around them. A miasma of the city.

They made their way up to the door, stepping over old newsprint and brown sacking that had been turned to the consistency of porridge by the downpour. Lifting the latch, they could just see down a dark, awful tunnel that was only a rubbish-littered hallway but seemed like the final path to hell.

The door they were after was the second on the left, a barely discernible *Number Three* on a grimy card marking it. Someone shouted "Come!" to their tentative knock, and they found themselves in a bare, high-ceilinged room with a half-dozen broken-down chairs and no windows. It was cold with damp, smelled of cigars and stale beer, and to their fastidious eyes hadn't been cleaned in years.

They could hear someone crying in the next room beyond a second door.

The older woman caught her friend's hand and said, "F—Sarah—I'm going to be sick!"

"No, it's only fright. Here, sit down." She quickly found the best chair and brought it forward, then took another one for herself. It wobbled, one leg uneven.

A nondescript paint, peeled from the walls and ceiling, gave the floor a dappled look, and the old brown carpet in the center seemed to be woven of all the hopelessness that had been brought here.

The older of the two began to tremble. "I'm not frightened—I'm terrified!"

"It will be all right—wait and see." It was a comforting lie, and they both recognized it for what it was.

They sat there for a time, not speaking, their hands gripped together, their faces blanched with the thought of what must lie ahead. The crying went on and on, and overhead there was the sound of furniture being shifted, first this way, then that, an endless screech that seemed half human, half demon. Somewhere in the hallway a man's voice shouted, and they both jumped.

Watching the inner door, they could feel the minutes drag into the half hour. "Sarah" found herself wishing it would open, then dreading that it would. They'd been here a very long time—why had no one come out to speak to them? They had been expected at two sharp—

If only the crying would *stop*—

Suddenly the older woman stood up. "No, I can't do it!" Her voice was thick, unnaturally loud to her own ears.

"You must! He'll kill you if you don't!"

"I'd rather kill myself. Oh, God, I can't carry the memory of this place around with me for the rest of my life, I can't—! It was a mistake, I want to go home! Sarah—take me home, for the love of heaven, *take me home!*"

Her friend, compassion in her eyes, said, "You're sure?

It's not to be done again? I can't borrow the carriage again without questions being asked."

"No, just take me home!" She was shaking in earnest, cold with dread, cold with fear, cold with the decision she knew she dared not make. Her friend put an arm around her shoulders, and in the hallway, she was sick, leaning there for several minutes in such pain that she seemed to collapse in on herself, frail and helpless. Weak to the point of fainting, her breath a sob, she pressed her forehead against the drab, dirty paint, grateful for its coolness.

They could hear voices behind the other doors, barely muffled—children crying, a man swearing, a woman singing something mournful and off-key. A cat meowing impatiently, pans banging, and thumps, as if somewhere someone was beating a carpet. But mercifully no one came out into the hall. Still—they might—at any moment—

"Can you walk as far as the carriage?" her companion asked softly.

"I must *try*—" The older woman straightened herself with an effort and pressed a handkerchief to her lips. "I wish I'd never come here—I wish I'd never heard of this place, much less seen it! If I died, how would I have faced *him*, with this place on my soul!"

"He would understand. He would. It's what made him special, poor man."

"Yes." They linked arms for comfort and walked unsteadily back to the outside door. It swung open as they reached it, and a man smelling strongly of sweat and too much beer grinned knowingly at them for an instant, eyes raking both of them. The tenants here must be aware of what went on in Number Three. "Sarah" felt herself flush with embarrassment. But the man held the door wide and let them pass unmolested.

It was all the older woman could do to climb back into the carriage. Once there, she slumped to the side, clinging to one of the braces that held the top in place. Her companion gently wrapped the damp blanket around her and looked pityingly at her.

What were they to do? *What were they to do?*

She took her own seat, remembered she hadn't untied the horse, and climbed down again. Several people were coming down the street now, hurrying past, heads bowed, their shoes splashing in the puddles. Three children, grubby-faced and thin, stopped to stare at her, knowing her for a stranger, before running on. A sudden gust of wind sent skirts whipping, and two houses away a man's hat blew off, to roll down the street like a top. The rain began in earnest and she barked her shin climbing back to her seat. Close to tears herself, she lifted the reins and spoke to the horse. "Walk on."

It was a very long drive back to where they'd come from. Long and cold and wet and dreary. She glanced at the other woman from time to time, saw that she was silently crying with her eyes closed, her lower lip caught between her teeth. Her pale face reflected misery and exhaustion.

I don't know how I'd feel, "Sarah" said to herself despairingly. In her shoes. Bleak of heart. Afraid. But I'll think of something. God help me—*I must think of something!* We can't come back here again. We haven't the *strength*!

It was very late when they reached their destination. The town was dark and still, a dog howling somewhere, the wind whispering around the church tower and swooping among the gravestones of the churchyard—as if confiding the latest news, "Sarah" thought, turning the old horse toward his stable.

I'm so weary, I'm imagining things.

She glanced for the hundredth time at the woman beside her. Her eyes were still closed, but she wasn't asleep.

"We're home," she told her friend gently, trying not to startle her. They were wet through, hungry because they'd been reluctant to stop along the way at the rough pubs or places where decent travelers stayed. They had been afraid of being seen, of being recognized. Of someone remembering that they'd been on the road from Glasgow, where they weren't supposed to be.

"Yes." She opened her eyes, saw the churchyard, and shuddered. The cold white stones seemed to be pointing fingers. "I wish I were dead too!"

Following a path through the stones with her eyes, the younger woman murmured with infinite sadness, "So do I."

2

1919

DUNCARRICK

THE LETTERS BEGAN TO ARRIVE IN THE MIDDLE OF June, hardly more than a few words scribbled in cheap ink on cheap paper.

Fiona never discovered who had received the first of them. Or even—in the beginning—what had caused the coldness toward her. It seemed over the course of the month that one by one the women who were her neighbors found excuses not to hang out their laundry or weed their gardens when she worked in the inn yard. The friendly greetings across the fence, the occasional offer of flowers for the bar parlor or a treat for the child, stopped. Soon people no longer nodded to her on the street. And failed to speak in the shops. Custom fell off at the bar. Men who often came in for a pint in the long summer evenings avoided her eyes now and hurried past the inn door. The coldness frightened her. She didn't know how to fight it because there was no one to tell her what lay at the bottom of it. She wished, for the hundredth time, that her aunt were still alive.

Even Alistair McKinstry, the young constable, shook his head in bewilderment when she asked him what she had done to offend. "For it *must* be that," she told him. "Someone's taken a word wrong, or I neglected to do something I'd promised. But what? I've tried and tried to think of anything!"

He had seen the looks cast her way behind her back. "I don't know. Nothing's been said in my hearing. It's as if I'm shut out as well."

He smiled wryly. Half the town must know how he felt about her. "It may be a small thing, Fiona. I'd not take it to heart." Which was no comfort at all. She had already taken it to heart, and wondered if that was the intent, to give her pain. But *why*?

On the first Sunday in July, the old woman who invariably sat in the back of the church hissed at her as she came in with the little boy, leading him to their accustomed place. The single word was lost in the first hymn, but she knew what it was. *Wanton.* It made her flush, and the woman grinned toothlessly in grim satisfaction. She had meant to hurt.

The shunning had been supplanted by attack.

The sermon that morning was on Ruth and Mary Magdalen. The good, faithful woman who had kept her place at her mother-in-law's side and the wanton whose sins Christ had forgiven.

The Scottish minister, Mr. Elliot, made no bones about which he'd have favored, in Christ's stead. His harsh, loud voice made it clear that good women were jewels in the sight of God. Humility was their shibboleth—such women knew their place and kept their hearts clean of sin. It would take Christ Himself to forgive a sinful woman—they were beyond redemption, in his personal view.

You'd have thought, Fiona told herself, *that Mr. Elliot knew better than God Almighty what ought to be done about sinners—stone them, very likely!* He had a very Old Testament view of such matters, a cold and self-righteous man.

She had never been able to like him. In three years, she had not found an iota of generosity or compassion in him, not even when her aunt was dying. He had thundered at the ill woman, demanding to know if all her sins had been confessed and forgiven. Reminding her that Hell was full of horrors and demons. In the end, he had had no comfort to give. Fiona had simply shut him out. She found herself wondering if Mr. Elliot had forgiven her for doing that.

As he warmed to his theme now, she felt eyes moving toward her surreptitiously, a merest glance cast from under the brim of a hat or from under pale lashes. She knew what they were thinking. The point was being made publicly that in Duncarrick she herself was Mary Magdalen. A wanton. Because of her child?

That made no sense: they'd all been told when she brought the boy here that she had lost her husband in the war. Even her aunt, a stickler for propriety, had held her and cried, then taken her around the town to meet everyone of consequence, lamenting the tragedy of a lad growing up without his father, and the wicked fighting in France that had killed so many good men.

Fiona wasn't the only young widow in the town. Why had *she* been singled out in this fashion? Why had people suddenly—and without explanation—turned so strongly against her? She'd never so much as looked at another man since 1914. She had never *wanted* another man in place of the one lost.

On the following Monday morning, outside the butcher's shop, someone shook a letter in her face and demanded to know what Fiona meant by walking boldly amongst decent folk, putting all their souls in danger.

Managing to reach the letter in the red, waving fingers of the woman who did washing for a living, she took it and smoothed it enough to read it.

Have you taken in her washing? The sheets soiled by her wickedness and the linens that have touched her foul flesh? Have you no care for your own soul?

It wasn't signed—

The shock turned Fiona's heart over in her chest. She read the lines again, feeling sick. Mrs. Turnbull was watching her, something avidly nasty in the set of her face, as if she relished the pain she'd caused.

"You don't do my laundry—" Fiona began, bewildered, and then realized that it didn't matter.

But who could have written such a thing?

It was *vicious*! She was speechless with the cruelty of it.

. . . *sheets soiled by her wickedness* . . . *her foul flesh* . . .

There were no names mentioned—

Then how had Mrs. Turnbull settled so quickly on Fiona as the intended target of such venom? She wasn't a clever woman, nor one overly endowed with either imagination or vindictiveness. How had she picked *Fiona* out as the evil woman? Because Fiona hadn't lived here all her life? Because her aunt was dead now and she had to run the inn alone, without proper chaperoning—it hadn't occurred to her that she needed any! Was that it, the impropriety of a respectable young woman serving men in the bar? Since the war, the inn hadn't paid well enough to keep a barmaid. . . .

"This is malignant nonsense! Where did you get it?" Fiona demanded.

Mrs. Turnbull said, "It was under the mat by my door. And I'm not the first. *Nor* the last! Wait and see!"

. . . *not the first, nor the last* . . . There had been other such letters. Fiona tried to absorb that and couldn't. Had all the people who shunned her now received malicious, unsigned messages like this one? But how could they believe such things? Surely someone could have warned her—a friend, a neighbor—

The washerwoman snatched the letter from Fiona's hand and strode off, self-righteousness in every line. She was a simple woman known for her stringent faith and her narrowmindedness. Both had given her the courage to speak out in her own anger. And fear.

Like the old woman at the back of the church, Mrs. Turnbull had found the bravado of the mob.

IN LATE JULY there was a policeman at Fiona's door. Constable McKinstry stood on the step, uncomfortable and flushed, stiffly in uniform.

"Don't shut the door in my face," he said placatingly. "I've come to ask— It's about the lad. There's— Well, there's been talk going around, and I don't know what to make of it."

Fiona sighed. "You might as well come in. I've seen one of the letters myself. They all say the same, do they? That I'm a fallen woman?"

Alistair said, remaining where he was on the step, casting a swift glance up and down the quiet street, "Those letters? Nasty piece of work, they are. I've just been shown a number of them. You don't want to hear what's in them! Cowardly—unsigned— meant to be cruel. Mark my words, a woman's behind it, a woman with nothing better to do than stir up trouble with lies."

"But people are believing these lies, Alistair, and I don't know how to put a stop to it. They're talking about me behind my back—they must be—but no one will speak to *me* about it. I'm shut out, treated as if I'm invisible."

"The best thing is not to try stopping it. It'll wear thin in another week or two." He cleared his throat. "No, it's not the letters that've brought me here. Not directly. Fiona—now it's said that the boy's not yours."

"Not mine?" She stared at him, frowning. "If I'm a fallen woman, how can he not be mine? It's the sin I'm *accused* of! Wantonness."

"I told you, it wasn't to do with those letters. They're no more than wicked nonsense. No, what's brought me here is another matter. Serious enough for the police to be looking into it." He hesitated, searching for words, awkward with his discomfort. "There's a suspicion that—er—that you killed his mother—and took the child."

He could see the shock in her eyes, the draining of warm color from her face. It cut him to the heart.

"I don't believe you!" she whispered. "No, I don't believe you—it's all part and parcel with the whispers!"

"Fiona," Alistair said pleadingly, "Mr. Robson sent me here, I didn't want to come. He said, 'No need to make a fuss. You'll do it best.' But I don't know how to do anything of the sort—"

Mr. Robson was the Chief Constable. Serious, indeed.

She became aware that they were still standing in the door, where all the world could see. "Come in. There's no one about. There never is anymore."

Fiona led him down the narrow passage that connected the inn to the little wing built into the side of it a hundred years earlier. She'd lived there since before her aunt died. And run the inn as well, from the time her aunt fell ill until custom dried up in June.

He followed her, staring at her straight back and her trim waist. And felt sick. Removing his hat, he tucked it under his arm. His boots clattered heavily on the wooden floor. His uniform seemed to choke him.

In the small room that served her as parlor, she gestured to the best chair and said, "I haven't harmed anyone. It's *barbarous* to say that I have!"

"I'm not liking it myself, to tell you the truth!" He turned away to stare at the tall clock that ticked quietly in the corner. He didn't feel like sitting down, nor did he want to stand there and hear his own voice speak the words. But it had to be done. "They're saying that—" His throat seemed to close.

"That what? You may as well tell me the rest!"

He flushed darkly and said, "—that you've got no marriage lines. You call yourself Mrs. MacLeod, but it isn't true, you've never been married." It came out in an anguished rush. "Could I please see your marriage lines? It will stop the talk, it's all I need."

Alistair had liked her for years. She'd had a suspicion that he was in love with her. Now she knew it must be true.

The cat came in, twining herself about his legs, leaving a blur of hairs on the dark fabric of his trousers. White on blue. She could hear her purring. She had always been partial to Alistair. If he sat down, she would be in his lap instantly, head stretched up to rub his chin, an expression of serene self-indulgence on her face.

Dragging her thoughts back to the policeman, away from the man, Fiona said, "And what difference does it make to anybody if I did have the child out of wedlock? I've done no harm to anyone. And I wouldn't be the first to have loved a man while I could! The war has butchered them without compunction—so young that most of them cried out for their mothers. Tell me why it's the world's business, and not my private affair?"

It was a tacit admission. Alistair recognized it and felt a great sadness for her.

Gently he said, "Well, then, could you prove the boy is your own? Could a doctor examine you and say with certainty that you've borne a child?"

She stared at him. Her face answered him before she could prevent it.

After a moment, he went on. "If you haven't had a child of your own, then how did you come by this one? That's the question, Fiona! They think the mother's buried here in the inn—under the floor, most like, or in the cellar. That you killed her and took the child and buried her where nobody would find her."

"In the inn—!" She blinked, disbelieving. "*This* inn? I had the boy with me when I first came to Duncarrick. How could the mother be buried here? It's preposterous!"

"I told them that. I told them your aunt was alive then and would never have been a party to such a thing. They don't want to listen."

"Who is this 'they' so full of accusations! I have a right to know."

"Mr. Elliot has seen several of the letters sent to his parishioners—"

"And done nothing about them! He didn't speak to me once about them!"

"I know, Fiona. It was wrong of him, he should have scolded half the town for paying any heed to them. He's a man of some weight—"

"I didn't want him to scold the town, I wanted him to call these things *lies*! To tell me he didn't believe what they said. To come here and sit with me, as proof that I am a decent woman! It would have been a *comfort*, Alistair! Instead he's turned his back on me too."

"Aye, but listen to me, Fiona. Three days ago a letter came for him, this one mailed, not left on a doorstep. It wasn't like the others. It wasn't accusing; in fact, it tried to defend you. It said that you couldn't be—er—a fallen woman, that you'd never been wed and you'd borne no children of your own. The letter didn't intend to cast doubts, it was meant to show the rumors and whispers were false. It went on to say that it wasn't possible to produce the lad's true mother, to prove these claims. She'd died after giving birth, and you'd taken the lad away, keeping him for yourself. The writer swore she didn't know where you had buried the woman's body and ended by saying your aunt had been told lies, she hadn't taken any part in what was done."

Fiona swallowed hard, the lump in her throat threatening to choke her. Keeping her voice steady by sheer effort of will, she asked, "Was this—this letter anonymous, like the rest of them? Or was it signed?"

"No. It claimed that the writer was fearful to speak out. She'd held her tongue for your aunt's sake, knowing Ealasaid MacCallum had been told lies. And she's afraid she might be brought up on charges now."

Fiona caught her breath. "The address? *Where did it come from?*"

"There was a Glasgow postmark, but that's not to say it was written by anyone living there. You'd only have to drop it in a post box, wouldn't you? The writer might live in Lanark—Inverness—" He looked down at his boots, missing her expression, bent to touch the cat, then thought better of it. Straightening up again, he went on earnestly. "Mr. Elliot went to the Chief Constable. The Chief Constable is not a man who likes anonymous letters and innuendoes. He told Inspector Oliver to get to the bottom of it. Inspector Oliver has sent me to have a look around. Mind you, only to see if any work's been done in the last few years. To see if any of the flagstones have been taken up or the walls repaired or the cellars changed."

"No one has done work here—not since 1914, the start of the war. Peter, the old man who was my aunt's handyman, can tell you no work's been done—"

"He has that. Inspector Oliver asked him. And your neighbors as well. But it would have been a secret business, after all. You'd not have told Peter, would you, if a body was being hidden? Nor your aunt, just as the letter said."

"It's not true! And it doesn't make sense—if I brought the child here with me, how could I bring its dead mother, to bury her here! In a trunk—? In the back of the carriage—? Over my shoulder?" She was feeling desperate, frightened.

He winced at her bitter humor. "Mr. Robson addressed that. He said the mother might have recovered from the birth and wanted to keep the boy after all. And you stopped her when she came here to find him. I've had my orders—"

"This is my inn now. I won't have anyone tearing it apart to search for a body—*there's no body here!*"

"I must look, Fiona, or they'll send someone else with a search warrant and an ax. Will you at least let me walk about and see with my own eyes that there's nothing to find?"

"No!" Startled by her cry, the cat tensed and then vanished behind the heavy draperies at the side window.

"Fiona—"

"*No!*"

It took him a good half hour to convince her that he was the lesser of evils. That for her own sake she must agree to lead him around the premises. That he would look only where Fiona allowed him to look, move only what she allowed him to move. When, stiffly, she finally gave her permission, he said gently, "I'm sorry. I'm so sorry."

But she ignored him. With a coldness he'd never felt in her before, she led him through the small wing, room by room, even where the child was sleeping in his crib, one hand tucked under his chin, and then through the aged building that had been her great-uncle's inn and then her aunt's, and now hers. Through the common rooms and the bars, through the kitchens and the cellars, and through the few bedchambers that could be taken by occasional travelers and marketgoers. Through the attics where old boxes and trunks littered the dusty floors amid the broken or outgrown furnishings stored there, the long-forgotten belongings of a family that had lived under the same roof for generations. To the cellars where there was still wine on the shelves but very little beer or ale—nobody came to drink it, and like the kitchens, the pantry, and barman's little cubbyhole, the cellars were nearly empty. No sacks of flour or potatoes or onions, no tins of fruit or jars put up from the garden.

He looked as thoroughly as he could without insulting her. He sounded walls and stamped on the floors, peered into the chimneys and moved the largest chests and dressers, opened the tops of trunks and sniffed at their musty contents. Kept his mind and his attention on his task without letting his own misery show in his face.

When Alistair left, she accompanied him to the door and shut it almost before he'd thanked her properly.

Behind its solid oak, where no one could see her, she leaned her forehead against the cool wood and closed her eyes. And then the child, rousing from his sleep, began to sing off-key to himself, a Highland song she had taught him. She made an effort to collect herself, and called, "I'm coming, darling." But it was another minute before she could turn and ascend the stairs.

Whatever Alistair McKinstry told his superiors, a fortnight passed before there were other policemen at her door, demanding to inspect the premises: Inspector Oliver, Sergeant Young, and both Constable McKinstry and Constable Pringle. In his anxiety not to offend her, McKinstry had not properly examined the outbuildings, she was told.

Fiona, torn between fear and disgust, told them to search as and where they pleased, then shut the door in their faces and kept the child out of sight.

It was in the stables in the inn yard that they found the bones, well hidden between the back wall and the little room the liveryman had lived in. Inspector Oliver had been the one to notice the unusual thickness of the plaster in one place. He tapped it with a hammer, found that there was space behind it, and tapped again, watching with interest as a spider's-web crack ran across it. A suspicious man by nature, he went into the dusty room on the other side of the wall and found that a cupboard was not as deep as it ought to have been.

They had the wall down, then, and the skull rolled out before they had even seen the rest of the bones crammed into the long, narrow space. As it came to a stop, grinning up at them, Constable McKinstry smothered a curse.

The long hair still attached in places to the dry bone surely marked it as a woman's.

IT WAS NOT until late August that they arrested her.

The bones in the stables had catapulted the investigation into a dozen new directions. Inspector Oliver, with grim thoroughness, had scoured Fiona's past, had followed every lead that came his way, and had succeeded in bringing new information to light—damning information that supported the theory he found so compelling. The procurator-fiscal had seen fit, after speaking with the Chief Constable, to order a trial on the charge of murder.

Fiona found someone to care for the boy and went to jail with an aching heart. She couldn't be sure who her enemy was, or how he or she had tightened a noose about her neck so cleverly. But she did know one very important thing about this person. The planning and the execution had been quite shrewdly done. Someone had carefully arranged her death, and left it to the law to do the deed for him—or her.

Which meant that someone hated her very deeply.

But who was it?

The only living person she might have asked was the one person she could never turn to for help. Even if she went to the gallows.

She had made a promise, and she dared not break it.

It was the boy she wept for in the night. She loved him completely and without shame. What would he be told now about the woman he believed to be his mother? Who would care for him and keep him safe if she was not there?

The loneliness was nearly unbearable. And the idleness. She wasn't used to sitting in silence the day long, with nothing, neither a book nor a needle, to make the time pass. Even as a child in her grandfather's house, there had been books. A basket of mending. Letters to be written. Now there was no one to write to. Where were the many people who had claimed to be her friends, who had welcomed her first for her aunt's sake and then for her own? She had been visited by none of them, had had no word of encouragement from them. She felt abandoned and wished with all her heart that her aunt were here to comfort her.

And she had no faith in the lawyer who came to speak to her. There was something in his narrow eyes that warned her to be very careful. He was not the sort of man who trusted women.

3

1919

LONDON

HE WAS STANDING ON THE ROAD, LOOKING BEYOND THE low stone wall and down into the churchyard, where the slope of the land evened out. There had been rain in the night; the stones were drenched with it and stood out blackly in the pale morning light.

His heart was pounding. The stones drew him like a magnet drawing iron, and he found himself trying to make out the name on each, searching for one he knew must be there. Then, with an effort of will, he turned to stare at the church tower, still swathed in low rain clouds, and at the tall windows above the door. He wanted to believe it was the church in Buncombe—Cornwall—but he knew it couldn't be. He told himself it was a churchyard in France, but that, too, was a lie.

A flicker of movement distracted him, and then he saw the girl in the shadows of the church door. She was carrying flowers, her arms full of blossoms and long spears of greenery, and as she stepped into the light, he saw that she was looking at him. As if she'd expected him to be standing there. As if she knew he would come, in the end.

He couldn't see her face clearly, but he instantly recognized her. And the grief in her eyes shamed him, cutting through his defenses.

Terrified, he tried to turn away, and couldn't. His feet were rooted to the spot, his body paralyzed by her eyes.

She was coming toward him now, up the church walk. She was saying something to him, then she pointed to the side of the churchyard and the grave there. Only there wasn't a body lying beneath the bare brown earth. He knew that at once.

There were tears on her face, but no hatred. He thought he could have borne the hatred, but not the pity in her eyes.

He began to walk toward her, not of his own volition but of hers, drawn to her, drawn to the drift of flowers she held, drawn to the grave they were destined for. She had brought enough flowers for the two of them to spread over the earth, to cover its ugliness. He could see it now, raw, without beauty or grace or the mercy of time, and he couldn't face it—one more step and he would read the name on the stone, and that would be intolerable—

IAN RUTLEDGE WOKE with a start, breathing harshly from shock.

He was sitting upright, knees raised, head flung back, drenched with sweat and with horror, terrified of the heavy, suffocating blackness that surrounded him, that made him blind.

Frantic, he put his hands to his face to claw the viscous mask away and touched—not the thick mud of the trenches but his own flesh.

Surprised, confused, he tried to think. If he wasn't in France, where was he? His hands floundered, found sheets—a pillow. The clinic?

As his eyes grew accustomed to the impenetrable darkness, he was able to pick out the ghostly shape of his surroundings. A door—a mirror—a bedpost—

Rutledge swore. *I've been asleep—I'm in my bed—I was dreaming—*

But it was several minutes before the vivid dream faded enough for him to shake off the overwhelming sense of doom it had left behind. In the back of his mind he could feel Hamish rumbling like heavy thunder—or the guns—trying to tell him something he didn't want to hear—over and over again.

Fumbling for a match, he lit the candle on the table by his bed, then got up and switched on the light. It blared down at him from the high ceiling, garish and stark after the darkness, but he was grateful for the reality it provided, pushing back the last remnants of sleep and of his nightmare.

He pinched out the candle flame, looked at the watch lying beside the brass candlestick, and saw that the time was close to three o'clock. In France he'd often slept with a stub of candle clenched in his hand. Unlit—it would have been madness to light it—but a symbol of light all the same. He still kept one beside his bed, a talisman.

This was London, not the trenches, and there was no mud— He repeated the words, listening to their sanity.

Around him were his own belongings: the carved armoire by the door to the sitting room, the mirror where he put on his tie every morning, the chair that had been his father's, the tall posts of the bed he had slept in as a boy, the dark burgundy draperies his sister had helped him hang. All of them familiar, and in their own way, unexpectedly comforting. They had been his before the war, just as this flat had been, and returning here had been a bulwark against the intervening hell of the trenches. A promise that one day he would be the same man again.

I've been working too hard, he thought, moving between the bed and the tall chest and coming to a halt by the table set beneath the window. He pushed aside the draperies.

Outside, rain clouds were hanging heavily over the city. Gray and depressing. He turned away, letting the heavy fabric fall again. *Frances is right, I need rest. It will stop when I can rest.*

His sister Frances had put it in no uncertain terms. "You look terrible, Ian! Tired and thin and still very unlike yourself. Tell Old Bowels to give you leave, you've worked as hard as ten men since you came back to the Yard, and the doctors told you quite clearly—"

Yes, they'd told him. But in work was—sometimes—forgetfulness.

Hamish, tireless at the back of Rutledge's mind, said, "It's no' true, you canna' forget. There's only emptiness, sometimes."

"I'll settle for that. When I'm weary enough to sleep, there's peace—*was* peace," Rutledge corrected himself. From long habit he answered the voice only he could hear, the voice of a dead man. It was as clear as his own in the silent room, with a Highlander's soft accent, and so real it seemed to come from just behind him. As if the speaker might be standing there if Rutledge turned his head. But there was no one behind him—although the dread of being wrong about that was nearly as real as the voice.

He tried to shove the dream back into the far reaches of despair, refusing to remember any shred of it, refusing to believe any part of it. Then realized that he was standing in the middle of the floor, frowning, remembering.

He shook himself and went back to the window to look out again. Hamish said behind him, "It's no' so gloomy in the Highlands—the rain's clean, sweet."

Rutledge, grateful for the distraction, nodded.

What we call shell shock for lack of a better term, said the doctor at the clinic—Frances's friend, the one who'd brought him back from the edge of insanity—is not fully understood. "I can't tell you how it will progress. Whether one day you'll find it gone—or whether it will stay with you for the rest of your life. Whether it will get a little better with time or a good deal worse. We don't know, you see. A few of the men like you I've treated have managed to find a way to live with it. You must do the same. Don't worry yourself about the medical aspects of it, just get on with your life and make the best of the fact that you can reason and think and act quite normally."

Rutledge was no longer certain what "normal" was. He hadn't been since early 1916.

His war had not ended in triumph and rejoicing.

By the time guns stopped firing in 1918 at the eleventh hour of the eleventh day, he'd been locked in such desolation that he hardly knew where he was.

A month later he'd been found dazed and incoherent, wandering the roads of northern France. Wearing a German greatcoat, unable to give his name or even his nationality, he'd eventually been sent back to the British command: a major in the French army had recognized him as a liaison officer he'd met in 1915.

The British had promptly clapped him in hospital. Shell shock, the diagnosis was. Outlook: uncertain.

And it had been. Nothing had brought him out of the bleak and accusing silence in which he'd been found. He had begun to remember who and what he was—Ian Rutledge, British officer, former Inspector at Scotland Yard. He had recognized his sister Frances, and been allowed, briefly, a meeting with his fiancée.

It had not been a success. When he reached numbly for Jean's hand, she'd snatched it away. She had been carefully coached by the doctors, but her eyes had been filled with fright as she made inane conversation in a trembling voice. He'd seen her only a few times after that, before she'd broken off their engagement.

It had been his sister who had got him out of the hellhole that was a hospital for shell-shock victims and into a private clinic.

And the doctor there, Fleming by name, had mercilessly broken him.

Rutledge had fought him every step of the way. But bone-weary and ill, he'd been no match for the tall, raw-boned doctor who had seen in the shambles a man worth saving and so refused to admit defeat.

The truth about Corporal Hamish MacLeod had come out, raggedly at first and then relived so vividly that Rutledge had believed he was in the trenches again.

Afterward, Rutledge had nearly killed Fleming, a last desperate defense of an inner self so unacceptable to a conscious mind that he'd hated the doctor, blamed him for bringing him out of his silence and back into awareness. . . .

THE SOMME OFFENSIVE of 1916, a disaster from its inception, had begun in July and dragged on through the summer. So many men had died that the bodies corrupted and rotted where they lay and the survivors lived with the stench. Weeks into the battle, they were none of them quite sane, but when Corporal Hamish MacLeod cracked, the shock of it left Rutledge and his men staring.

There had been no sign, no warning. Taking over from a gut-shot and dying sergeant, MacLeod had led his men with extraordinary skill and bravery, an example to them all. When he abruptly refused to make another assault on the machine-gun nest that was their objective, there was stunned disbelief.

Orders had come down that the gun had to be silenced before the entire line went over the top at dawn. Artillery fire, laid down in earnest during the night, had deafened them, battered them until they were all on the ragged edge of despair. And still the machine gunners survived, because they were well dug in and no one could reach them through the hail of bullets.

As the weary, white-faced corporal shook his head, refusing a direct order, saying only "I willna' kill any more of our own. I willna' go back again. It's madness," the eyes of the men at his back were grim, disheartened.

Rutledge didn't know how he and Hamish had come through each assault unscathed. He didn't know where he himself would find the strength to go back through the wire a sixth time. But there was no choice. One machine gun had the firepower of forty men. It could take down an entire line. It had to be put out of action.

Rutledge reasoned with Hamish, threatened him, called on his patriotism, and the silent Highlander had merely shaken his head. But his face pleaded for understanding even as it reflected the grief and torment in Rutledge's.

In war there is no time for compassion. No time for mercy. To save a thousand lives, one had to be sacrificed. Rutledge gave Hamish an ultimatum. Be ready in an hour's time for the next attempt, or be shot for cowardice.

Hardly cowardice. But that was the name the Army gave it when men broke under fire.

In the end, Rutledge had had to carry out his threat. In the darkness before dawn, a hastily drawn-up firing squad had shot Corporal Hamish MacLeod. And as Rutledge had delivered the coup de grâce to the badly wounded Highlander, the salient had been blasted out of existence by a German shell. Buried alive, blinded, and deaf, Rutledge had lived only because Hamish's body had protected him. A bitter irony . . .

And the machine gunners had died as well, for which Rutledge, disbelieving, had been given a medal and sent back into the fighting as a bloody example. Without rest or respite: the war needed men.

As the hellish summer of 1916 dragged into agonizing stalemate for two more years, Rutledge had carried out his duties barely aware of anything except the incessant voice of Hamish in his head. He had wanted to die, had tried to die, and in spite of war and pestilence, he had lived. To come home a hero. To come home a man hardly able to speak. Bringing a dead man with him.

The doctor, Fleming, had done his work well. In June

1919, Rutledge had returned to the Yard, declared fit for duty. His secret went with him. Not even Frances knew how much it had cost Rutledge to struggle back to his former skills. A murderer standing in judgment of murderers. Nor had Hamish made it easy, standing constantly at his shoulder and condemning him. They had worked out, in time, a relationship that was more a stalemate than anything else. It was only that when he, Rutledge, was most vulnerable, Hamish was the first to sense it. As if, Rutledge sometimes thought, the dead man had taken his revenge.

Not even Fleming, with all his medical skills, could wipe out memory. Or guilt.

Cold comfort on a dark, rainy night of bad dreams and a haunting voice from the trenches.

After a time, Rutledge made himself go back to his bed, draw the sheets over his shoulders again, and close his eyes.

But when the September dawn broke grayly over London, he hadn't slept.

IN THE LIGHT of day, Rutledge could pin down with some certainty what had precipitated the dream. It was the letter that had arrived in the previous morning's post. He hadn't opened it for several hours, knowing who it was from and what it demanded of him. Finally, after it had seemed to burn a hole in his coat pocket as well as his conscience, he had taken the letter out and broken the ornate seal.

His godfather, David Trevor, had written from Edinburgh, saying,

You've made a dozen excuses. Don't make another one. Come to see me. I miss you, Ian, I want to see for myself that you're alive and well. If that grim devil Bowles won't give you leave, come anyway. My doctor will tell him you need a rest. And for that matter, so do I. Loneliness is the very devil!

But Scotland was the last place Rutledge intended to go. The love and duty he owed his godfather were very real, but so was his reluctance to go north of the border, which seemed in the clear light of day an almost superstitious dread, but in the dark seemed an unbearable, unspeakable burden. Not because he hated the Scots but because so many of them had been under his command in France—and he'd led so many of them to their death. He could name every one of them, even the raw recruits he'd known for less than a day.

And leave was the last thing he wanted. Tired as he was, idleness was worse. When a man was idle, his demons marched like ghostly armies in the forefront of his mind.

CHIEF SUPERINTENDENT BOWLES would have been glad to grant Rutledge leave if he had asked for it. The less he saw of the Inspector, the happier Bowles was. The closed door of his empty office was like a benediction when Bowles passed it each day that Rutledge was away from London. Rutledge underfoot was a constant reminder of things best forgotten. Clever men always disturbed Bowles's peace of mind, and clever men with good accents, men who'd been to university or moved comfortably in circles where Bowles, for all his authority, felt stiff and clumsy, were intolerable. Bowles made it a point to rid himself of such men as fast as he could. There were subtle ways to convince a clever man that it was in his best interests to ask for a transfer.

But Rutledge, damn and blast him, seemed to lead a charmed life. He had survived the bloodbath of the Somme, he'd survived wounds, he'd survived months in hospital. And if Bowles's informant was telling the truth, Rutledge had been half out of his head, broken and silent, hardly a promising future. Yet for four months now he'd survived Bowles's concerted attempts to show him up as inept and lacking his pre-war skills.

To Bowles's way of thinking, England would have been better served if Rutledge had died with the rest of what the writers were now calling The Flower of English Youth. Dead "flowers" could be swept up with the rubbish and forgotten. Live challengers to his ambition were fair targets.

Bowles had climbed the ladder as far as his ability allowed, buoyed by some small success hunting German spies during the Great War. But it appeared he was destined to retire as a Chief Superintendent. Climbing higher was out of the question for a man of his station. And that knowledge was a constant goad to his anger and frustration.

He found himself this gloomy morning walking into Rutledge's office and dragging the other chair from where it was usually kept near the wall, out of the way of the door. Sitting down heavily, he slapped a file on the desk.

"There's a spot of trouble in the north, close by Durham, and it seems you're wanted to handle it." He opened the file, reached for a sheet of paper with a dozen paragraphs scrawled across it in heavy ink, and scowled at it. "Here's the long and short of it. And the reports to confirm it."

The Scottish police—with permission from their counterparts in England—had come to a village some miles west of Durham to tell a woman that it was possible her daughter's remains had been discovered on a Scottish mountainside in a place called Glencoe. Lady Maude Gray took exception to the Scottish Inspector's manner and insinuations, and she had her butler throw him out. This didn't sit well with his Chief Constable, who complained to the Chief Constable across the border. Neither of them could persuade her ladyship to give them so much as the time of day.

"You're being sent to smooth troubled waters, in a manner of speaking, and to find out whatever you can about this missing girl. The Scottish police will be grateful. As far as I can tell, reading between the lines, her ladyship is highly thought of in certain circles and she's strong-minded enough to do as she pleases. You'll need every ounce of diplomacy you possess to get through the door, much less into her presence. But failure is unacceptable. Do you understand me?"

Rutledge understood very well. If he annoyed her further, Lady Maude could crucify all of them. If he left without seeing her, it would be viewed as his incompetence.

He took the papers Bowles thrust at him and, when the Chief Superintendent had gone, read them over. The facts of the case itself appeared to be simple enough. The problem lay in Lady Maude Gray's refusal to discuss her daughter with anyone. The local police had noted: *"She has never reported her daughter missing, but it is understood in the neighborhood that there was a rift between them that resulted in the daughter leaving early in 1916. When the young woman came into a large inheritance in 1918, the family solicitor advertised throughout the country for her to contact him directly, and the girl failed to do so."* Further discreet inquiries by the solicitor discovered that none of her acquaintance had had word of or from her either. The solicitor reported his concern and asked for police help in locating her. That search was inconclusive as well. *"It may well be that the remains found in Scotland are those of Eleanor Victoria Maude Gray—height and age appear to be a close match, and the time of death (thought to be autumn 1916) appears to be consistent with the last time anyone saw her. Her mother refuses all comment."*

The Scottish police were convinced that the mother's refusal had to do with the fact that the daughter had been pregnant. The English police were reluctant to conclude that that was the cause of the quarrel between the two women. Some stiffness between the two jurisdictions had developed—the Scottish police believed they had already identified Eleanor's murderer, while the English police were unsure that the girl was in fact dead.

Rutledge looked out the window at the rain streaking the grimy panes and the wet pigeons huddled in whatever shelter they could find. He'd hated the rain in the trenches, it was a torment of body and spirit. Wet wool, the stench of urine or vomit, the heavy sweetness of rotting flesh, the stink of dirty bodies, the slick, black, filthy mud that weighed down boots and caked faces and hands and matted hair under the helmets. The low clouds that hid the gas—

The drive north ought to be pleasanter than the weather here, he mused. And Hamish, a countryman at heart, found that thought agreeable as well. Rutledge took out his watch, realized that he might reach York before nightfall. He stood and stretched, set his current files in order, then walked out of his office and closed the door behind him.

Down the passage, walking toward the stairs, Bowles heard the faint sound and smiled with contentment.

4

LADY MAUDE GRAY LIVED IN AN IMPOSING HOUSE THAT
could be described as palatial. It sat in a vast acreage of park-
land that gave it privacy and offered fine views from all its
windows. The village of Menton, which lay on the main road
a mile and a quarter beyond the massive stone pillars that
flanked the long drive, had been moved to its present location
in the eighteenth century. Not even its church steeple was visible from the attics of the house. Where the village had once
stood, a very fine allée of trees and grassy lawns led to a re-
flecting pool that mirrored a cloudless sky.

It had once been, Rutledge thought, glimpsing the sun-
washed house in the distance as he made his way up the
drive, a fortified abbey in the Middle Ages, but later architects had created a country house in the ruins, with the
choir and apse of the abbey church, presumably the family
chapel now, comprising one wing. The arched buttresses
flowed smoothly upward toward a pinnacled roof, and the
gray stone of the house fabric matched them to perfection,

giving a sense of great age to the entire dwelling. The west front, the main entrance, boasted a graceful spread of steps rising from the drive; a formal garden set with an ornate fountain gave human dimensions to the spectacular view across the countryside that spread out beyond it. Hamish, regarding the view, grumbled, "A lonely place, this. You can hear the wind and feel the emptiness."

To his Calvinist soul, the house itself was ostentatious and unwelcoming. For a man used to the crofts of the Highlands, often a heap of stone in the lee of a hillside, there was no room for display in the struggle for survival.

As Rutledge climbed the steps, he found himself wondering what his godfather would think of the effect achieved here. David Trevor felt the power of stone and mortar in his blood, a man whose eye and taste were trained but whose natural response to building had made him one of the most successful architects of his day.

He felt a sudden surge of guilt that he hadn't replied to the invitation from his godfather, but there was no way to explain why the prospect of leave was anathema. The press of work would have to be his excuse.

Hamish said, "It's no' a lie, is it? Though ye've chosen it yoursel'. And I'd no' care to come home now . . ."

The knocker, shaped like a pineapple—the symbol of hospitality—fell back on its plate with a heavy *throm* that seemed to echo through the house.

Eventually, a majestic butler opened the door, staring at Rutledge with cold disdain. His white hair, brushed to silver, and his height would have done honor to the lord of the manor. Lord Evelyn Gray, however, had been a short, stocky man with dark, curling hair and an iron-gray beard. Rutledge had seen him in London on a number of occasions before the war.

"Inspector Rutledge, Scotland Yard," he said briskly into the silence. Hamish bristled in the back of his mind, an angry counterpoint to the icy regard. "I wish to see Lady Maude Gray."

"Her ladyship has no business to conduct with the police," the man replied, preparing to close the door in Rutledge's face.

"On the contrary. The police wish to express regret for past misunderstandings, and I have been sent from London to offer this apology in person. It would be rude of her not to hear it."

The butler looked Rutledge up and down. Rutledge smiled inwardly. If the intent had been to intimidate, it was a signal failure. Haughty the butler might be, but it was a reflection of his mistress's importance and not his own. Sergeant-Major MacLaren, on the other hand, had been a different matter. A glance could quell an entire battalion. No one dared question his authority; it came direct from God. It was said that even officers walked in fear of him, and most certainly Rutledge himself had deferred to the man's wisdom and experience on a number of occasions.

What the butler saw was a tall man with a thin face who was clothed in a well-cut suit and a firmness that matched his voice. Something in the dark eyes moved the butler to change his mind and say at last, "Wait here, if you please."

He returned after nearly ten minutes. "Lady Maude will receive you in the library," he informed Rutledge, and stepped aside to allow him to enter.

Rutledge walked into a columned hall that reminded him of a Greek temple. The floor, paved in marble, was smooth as cold ice, and the staircases—a pair—flaunted their airy grace as they rose like swans' necks on either side of a niche where an exquisite Roman copy of a Greek Apollo was subtly lit. The stone face, slightly turned and limned by the light, reminded him all at once of Cormac FitzHugh. He buried the memory as swiftly as it had risen.

Hamish said, "Pagan, this is. Like the mistress, no doubt!"

How had the missing Eleanor Gray seen it? Rutledge wondered. Had she played here as a child, sliding across the shining floor, peals of laughter echoing among the columns? Or had it seemed cold to her, forbidding?

A long gallery led off in either direction, with French carpeting, busts on pedestals, and dark paintings of ancestors in massive gold frames.

"There's space enough here to hold half a regiment," Hamish said, his voice disparaging. "Aye, and a military band to sit and play on yon stairs."

The library was a vast room down a passage on the first floor and was undoubtedly chosen to overawe a mere policeman. Its windows rose floor to ceiling, and books filled glass-enclosed shelves. The cream-and-rose carpet on the floor was so old, it had the sheen of antique silk, and the woman waiting for him in the center of it knew that it set her off like a jewel.

Hamish fell silent, in its own way homage.

Lady Maude was a tall woman with silver-gray hair and the carriage of an empress. Her afternoon dress was dark blue, austere in contrast to the handsome double rope of pearls that fell nearly to her waist. In her day she must have been quite beautiful, for the vestiges of beauty were clear in the bones of her face, her violet eyes, and the long, slender hands lightly clasped in front of her. She barely acknowledged the butler's quiet murmur. "Inspector Rutledge, my lady." The door closed softly behind him.

"Inspector," she said as he inclined his head. After a moment, regarding him coolly, she added, "At least this time they've had the sense to send me someone who is presentable."

"I haven't met Inspector Oliver, my lady. His sense of duty, however, is something I understand, as you must yourself, having been born to it."

"I will not listen—" she began, but he cut lightly across her words.

"I am not defending him, I assure you. I am merely pointing out that for any policeman, one of the most painful duties is to inform someone of a loved one's death. If it was not your daughter the Scottish police have found, the sooner they know it, the sooner they can find her true parents. Another mother will have to bear that grief. If you were fortunate and this is not your child, then spare a little pity for the woman who has lost hers."

She stared at him in astonishment, something moving behind her remarkably expressive eyes. He thought, *Her daughter* is *missing*— Then she said, "You came, as I understood Kenton to say, to make an apology."

"Yes. For the fact that Inspector Oliver did not handle this matter as well as he might have. That was unfortunate. I've come in his place to tell you that if you can give me assurances that this young woman discovered on a Scottish mountainside is not your affair, then we can move on to other names on our—"

"She is not my child. My daughter is alive and well."

"And you have heard from her within the past—er—six months?"

"My relations with my daughter are not open to public scrutiny!" She scanned his face again, noting the tiredness, the thinness. Beneath them, she realized suddenly, was a will as strong as hers.

Rutledge listened to Hamish for a moment, heeding the warning that patience was not Lady Maude's long suit. A change of tactics was in order.

"Very well. I accept that. Perhaps you can help us answer a puzzling question: Why has your daughter not contacted her solicitor to sign papers relating to her inheritance? I've read his statement. He expressed some concern that she failed to appear at the time set in 1918. In fact, his last correspondence with her was in 1916. He has made a concerted effort to locate her in the past year, and failed. It was his anxiety that was communicated to the local police, and this year, when a query about a missing person was circulated by the Scots, it seemed prudent for them to speak to Miss Gray. If only to reassure everyone that she could be safely struck off the list. If you could provide me with her direction, I have the authority to close this matter immediately." His attitude was cool, as if Eleanor Gray was of concern to him only if she was dead.

"I might have guessed it was Mr. Leeds's vexatious passion for meddling that lay behind this business. He shall hear from me!" Anger flared in Lady Maude's eyes, deepening the color to dark violet.

"I'd no' like to be in his shoes, then," Hamish reflected.

"He, too, is required by law to carry out his duties to the best of his ability."

"Indeed. Involving the police is an entirely unnecessary course of action."

"I cannot believe that a young woman of your daughter's rank would neglect *her* duty." Rutledge paused and then repeated, "It is cause for concern."

"Nonsense. Eleanor is young, contrary. She has had some ridiculous notion that she wanted to take up the study of medicine. It was the war; it unsettled all of us. But she insisted that she was well suited to it and that her goal was to become a physician. I hoped that with the Armistice and an end to the dying, this absurd dream would be seen in a different light. My daughter is something of a romantic, I must confess. Very like her late father."

Rutledge, still standing, thought to himself, *We'll have to contact the teaching hospitals*— Aloud, he asked, "Would she have settled for nurse's training instead?"

"A nursing sister? Hardly that!" Impatiently, Lady Maude said, "Sit down, young man! That chair, to your left." She crossed to the desk and took the chair behind it. As if putting a solid barrier between them. "When my daughter sets her heart on something, she's single-minded about it. And I must tell you that she doesn't cope well with disappointment. Eleanor has always been rather impatient of impediments and usually finds a way around them." Lady Maude gave Rutledge a space to digest that before continuing. "Now, as for this business of climbing in Scotland—or having an illegitimate child—it's so out of character that I am at a loss to understand how your Scottish policeman arrived at such a conclusion. The man's an idiot. I won't allow him in this house. Nor the local man; he's as great a fool as they come."

"Your daughter never expressed an interest in climbing?"

"Not at all. She's not one of these robust women with an enthusiasm for athletic pursuits. She enjoys a game of tennis. And she's very fond of riding. Before the war, she spent some time at school in Switzerland, and never indicated then or afterward that she cared for climbing. As for the other business, she has far too much respect for herself and her family to find herself in trouble."

The words were spoken with absolute conviction. Women of Eleanor Gray's class were taught from birth what was expected of them. They were to be married off to the greatest advantage, social and financial. Lovers taken after marriage—with absolute discretion—were another matter. Never before it.

The more he heard, the more Rutledge found himself agreeing with Lady Maude that the dead woman found in Scotland was unlikely to be her daughter, Eleanor. None of the facts matched. Still—height and age did. And possibly timing?

"Would it be possible to see a photograph of your daughter, Lady Maude?"

"She'll no' allow it," Hamish told him. "But yon solicitor might have one."

She glared at Rutledge. "To what end?"

"Merely to give me some feeling for the person you've described. I have found that faces tell me more than facts sometimes."

She hesitated. Rutledge was certain he'd given her the wrong answer, and had lost. Then she opened a drawer in the desk. From it she drew a silver filigree frame and passed it across to him without looking at it. He rose to take it from her hand, and sat down again before turning it over.

The face staring back at him was smiling, one hand on

the horse at her side, the other holding a trophy. Beneath the riding hat it was difficult to see her features clearly, but she was an attractive young woman with her mother's bearing. There was something familiar about the face all the same, and he frowned as he studied it. All at once he made the connection.

She reminded him quite strongly of one of the royal princesses—

As if his thought reached her at the same time, Lady Maude extended her hand imperiously, and he had no choice but to return the photograph to her.

Hamish, following his thought, was scandalized.

His sister Frances would know, if anybody did. But looking at the woman in front of him, and remembering the photograph she'd taken from him, Rutledge found himself wondering if Eleanor Victoria Maude Gray was—possibly—the child of a liaison between Lady Maude and the late King Edward VII. The king had had an eye for beautiful women. It wouldn't have been surprising if she'd come to his notice.

Small wonder, with that heritage, that Lady Maude refused to believe that her daughter had come to die on a desolate Scottish mountainside, or that she had borne a child out of wedlock.

Eleanor was destined for greater things than a career in medicine—if she was the daughter of a King, and heir to this house and the fortune that apparently maintained it, she could take her pick of wealthy and titled men.

But if she was as contrary as her mother wanted him to believe, might she not have rebelled against this golden future and found instead some perverse pleasure in making her mother's nightmares rather than her dreams come true . . . ?

LADY MAUDE SAT at the broad desk long after the man from London had gone, staring blindly at the closed door.

How had he tricked her into speaking of Eleanor? She

had told a *policeman* what she hadn't revealed to anyone else—that Eleanor was headstrong, contrary, that her daughter's heritage had meant so little to her that she had walked away from it and never looked back. She had chosen a common *profession* instead, one that dealt with poverty and squalor and hideous diseases. It was unspeakably cruel and headstrong.

She would call London straightaway and have that man broken in rank—

Instead Lady Maude went on sitting where she was, reviling him, refusing to acknowledge pain or guilt. Eleanor was *not* dead. The police were incompetent and stupid. She would not allow them to trouble her again.

Something the Inspector had said came back to her. "Another mother will have to bear that grief . . ."

Then find *her* and be satisfied. *And let there be an end to this!*

Sunlight cast long, narrow shadows across the carpet, and still she sat there. She did not need the photograph in the closed drawer to see her daughter's face, feel the strong presence of her spirit. A mother would *know*—if anything untoward had happened—

They were trying to frighten her into helping them, these policemen, rather than doing their duty as it should be done!

Finally she stood up, took a deep breath, and walked firmly to the door. By the time she had reached the small room where the telephone had been put in, she had made her decision.

5

───────◆───────

RUTLEDGE TURNED OUT OF THE DRIVE BACK ONTO THE main road.

Hamish, reacting to the lessening of tension, spoke after a long silence. "It wasna' a verra useful interview. But sufficient. A formidable woman, that. I wouldna' care to grow up in her shadow."

Was that how Eleanor Gray had felt about her mother?

"My own grandfather was her match," Hamish was saying, "he could have led the clan into battle, anither time and place. But he had anither side as well, he could recite in a voice that kept the room silent. Verse, and the Old Testament. When it came to the Prophets or Robert Burns, there was none to hold a candle to him. I ken many a night when I lay awake in the loft, listening. Does this one have anither face?"

Thinking it over, Rutledge came to the conclusion that Lady Maude did. If she had been mistress to Queen Victoria's son, her husband had been willingly, knowingly, cuckolded. Unlike Henry VIII, Edward had chosen his married lovers with great care, to prevent gossip or scandal. And his friends had known which woman to invite to which social engagement. Or had been quietly informed of royal wishes. Still, it must not have been easy for Edward's wife, Alexandra, or the current favorite herself to live with such an open secret. Or for the favorite to return to her marriage when the Prince's fancy moved elsewhere.

The problem was, a child seldom recognized a parent's strength; it saw only stern discipline that couldn't be easily manipulated by childish whims or caprice. Rebellion was natural—and sometimes dangerous.

Wherever Eleanor Gray might have gone, if she was determined to punish her mother for whatever it was she felt she'd lost or lacked in that grand and cold house, it became a police matter only if she died.

Rutledge found himself hoping that she had not, though Hamish was of two minds about it.

Retracing his route to the town where he had spent the previous night and left his luggage, Rutledge considered his choices. If he made the journey directly back to London today, it would be late when he arrived, far too late to report to Bowles. And this was a Friday. It might be best to find a telephone and make his report orally so that it could be passed along. Inspector Oliver would also be waiting to learn what had transpired.

There was a telephone in the hotel and Rutledge put in his call to London.

Bowles was not in his office, and the sergeant answering the line said, "Rutledge, is it? A moment, sir, I think there's a message that I'm to give you. Ah! Here it is. You're not to return to London, sir."

"Not to return?" Rutledge asked blankly. Hadn't he finished his business here?

"No, sir. The message reads 'Tell Rutledge to stay where he is. He's to call me at nine o'clock on Monday morning.' That's all, sir. The Chief Superintendent didn't explain."

Even for Bowles it was an odd message. But Hamish was quick to remind Rutledge that the man was vindictive and often intentionally bloody-minded. Rutledge asked the sergeant to repeat the message to be sure he'd been given the whole of it, and then said, "Meanwhile, will you put some men to finding out if an Eleanor Gray is enrolled in any of the teaching hospitals? It's likely she's chosen one in London, but be as thorough as possible, will you? I'm told she had a strong interest in becoming a doctor, but if she's studying anywhere, it's important that we find her."

The sergeant laboriously wrote down the particulars and promised to get someone on it right away. Rutledge had a feeling he'd just spoiled the weekend for several unfortunate constables who were on the sergeant's blacklist for some minor infraction or another. But they'd be more likely to pursue their inquiries with diligence, if only to see their names removed from it.

Rutledge thanked him and hung up the receiver.

He sat there in the tiny, smotheringly stuffy room that had been turned into a telephone closet.

Stay where you are—

Was Bowles sending him back to the Gray house because there were new developments in the Scottish investigation and he'd been chosen to handle it at this end? Or had something else come up? But if that was true, Bowles would have left full instructions, telling him where to report and what his duties would be.

It was also possible that Bowles was being perverse, making the assumption that Rutledge would fail in his attempt to reach Lady Maude, and ordering him not to retreat until he'd succeeded. He'd brought only a small case with him; he'd need more shirts, shoes, and another suit if he was ordered to stay beyond two or three days.

Hamish said, "For all you know, he's sacked you and is letting you dangle in uncertainty until he tells you himself—" Rutledge shut out the cutting voice.

And meanwhile?

He was free to spend the next two days in Lincoln or York. Before the war, he'd have leapt at the chance, having friends he could call on, houses where he knew he was welcome. But two of those friends were dead now, and a third was blind, in hospital, struggling to learn a new profession while his wife waited for him to come home. Still, there were hotels where he could stay—

At loose ends, alone and with only his thoughts and Hamish as company? It wasn't a prospect Rutledge relished. He found himself preferring to be called back to London immediately, with another investigation to be handled, keeping him busy, keeping him from remembering that he had ever had a past beyond the last week or even the day before today.

Two days . . .

Guilt stirred again. He owed his godfather a visit. Or an explanation. He was going to find it hard to do either.

Hamish said, "Why does he no' come to London?"

David Trevor had turned the London architectural firm over to his partner in the last year of the war. His son's death had taken the heart out of him, and he had retired to Scotland to heal. He was, according to Frances, writing a book on the history of British architectural style, but it might be no more than an excuse to bury himself in the past until he could face a bleak future.

"For him Scotland offers sanctuary." *But not for me.*

Hamish made no reply.

After a moment, Rutledge picked up the receiver again and put in a call to David Trevor. His intent was to make his excuses, to satisfy his conscience. To explain that the press of business made a journey to Scotland in the foreseeable future unlikely. To put off what he could not face yet.

Surely David would be willing to meet him in Durham or somewhere else for the weekend! A compromise to suit them both—on ground that held no memories for either of them.

As Rutledge waited, Hamish said, "He willna' come—"

"He will. For my sake."

But twenty minutes later, Rutledge was driving north once more. This time toward the Border. Something in his godfather's voice, a relief at hearing from him, a need that wasn't spoken—a surge of warmth when he thought Rutledge had called to give his time of arrival—had made it nearly impossible to refuse or suggest any alternative. It had been taken for granted. As if nothing had changed.

Better to return to the rain of London and the empty flat—better to go to York or Lincoln or Carlisle rather than Scotland, where voices at every turn would remind him of Scots he'd commanded. Men he felt he'd betrayed . . .

There was hardly a town of any size in the Highlands that he didn't know by name, because one or a dozen of the men under his command had lived there.

How many lies had he told frightened boys facing battle for the first time? How many lies had he written to grieving women who had just lost a son or a husband? And yet his men had trusted him. He'd listened to them talk about families, crofts, the land, small victories won in short lives—lonely men leaning against the wall of a trench in the dark watches, wanting to remember home, or lying on a stretcher, trying to die bravely. The Scots had made good soldiers and they'd died hard. Not in their tens or hundreds, but in their thousands. Rutledge felt a duty to them still, and it was a burden he hadn't healed sufficiently yet to put down. It wasn't easily explained—but it was there, that sense of duty to the dead.

He was going to Scotland now, there was no turning back—

It's not as if I'll be driving as far as Edinburgh, he argued with himself. *The Lodge is in the country, for God's sake! Once there, I could be anywhere—in any part of Britain. It will have to be done sometime. I can't hide from the past—somehow I must do this—*

It would be arrant cruelty to call again and say I've changed my mind—

But in the deep recesses of his mind, he could feel Hamish refusing to accept any justification Rutledge might offer. For Rutledge this was a hurdle of the spirit. For Hamish it had been the unacceptable horror of dying in France—his permanent exile from the Highlands. He had not come home then. He would not come home now.

The strain of traveling with that stiff, solid wall of refusal began to take its toll.

APPROACHING NEWCASTLE, ON a whim Rutledge took a side turning and drove west for a time, toward Hexham. When he stopped the motorcar in the middle of nowhere, he got out and walked nearly a mile to where the Great Wall that Hadrian had built across the top of England so many centuries before snaked still across the green land. A rampart of earth and stone to keep the Scottish barbarians at bay, supported in its day by forts and garrisons, shops and sentry posts, long since crumbled and covered by time. He had come here as a boy, and the memory of it had stayed with him.

Soldiers had lived and fought and died here, but that was not the odd pull of this place. It was the rolling green land, the high bowl of sky—the vast *stillness*.

There had been no peace in France. Men standing cheek by jowl in the trenches had had no privacy. The guns, even when silent, could be heard in the bones, that ache of thunder that dulled the brain and deafened the ears for hours afterward. The aeroplanes passing overhead, horses struggling through the mire, the lorries moving up, voices swearing and singing and talking day and night. Or screaming and cursing in pain after an attack, and the barking of dogs searching for the living among the dead.

There had been no stillness in himself either, with Hamish rampant in his mind. He was never truly alone.

But here it was palpable—the quiet—

He stood there, looking up at the empty blue sky, his

head tilted back, his arms out from his sides, his fists unwittingly clenched. And drank in the stillness.

Even the wind had dropped off. Hamish, for a mercy, was silent. And there was no birdsong; the birds had turned south to winter in another climate. The beating of his heart seemed muffled beneath his coat.

Stillness.

It seemed to spread through him, it seemed to wrap him about, it seemed to fill him full.

For nearly a quarter of an hour he stood there alone and listening.

When he turned away to walk back to the car, there were tears in his eyes.

But he had found the strength he needed.

6

MORAG GILCHRIST GREETED RUTLEDGE AT THE HEAVY front door of The Lodge almost before he'd knocked.

She had looked after this house just south of Edinburgh for nearly three generations of the Trevor family, and nobody seemed to know just how old she was. If anyone asked, he was given short shrift. Morag's back was straight as a sergeant-major's, her eyes as bright as a crow's, and her hands as soft and steady as a girl's.

"Mr. Ian!"

He thought for an instant she was going to embrace him. There was such warmth in her face that it seemed to reach out to him. He put his arms around her instead, and she let him, then pushed him away with a "Pshaw! You'll muss my gown, lad! Give o'wer!"

Her black gown, to the floor, was nearly as stiff as she was, Victorian and a badge of honor, like the heavy ring of keys at her waist on a silver chain.

David Trevor came out of the room just off the passage

where they stood, and gripped Ian's hand hard, with something in his face that made them both feel deeply the loss that neither spoke of.

Trevor's son had died at sea in the third year of the war. Ross had been as close to a brother as anyone Rutledge had known. It was still a raw grief.

He was led into the sitting room, small and low-ceilinged and old-fashioned, with comfort apparent in every cushion and a fresh fire on the hearth. The dogs, after their first joyous welcome, curled themselves at his feet with sighs of contentment. The tick of the clock was steady, peaceful. A glass of good whiskey seemed to appear in his hand before he'd settled in the chair opposite the one he knew his godfather favored. The stiffness and fatigue of the long drive vanished. He was, in a sense, home.

Hamish, after hours of angry turmoil, seemed to find his own peace here too. Or was it the fact that Rutledge himself had crossed a border in his mind as well as an invisible line on the landscape? He thought it might be both.

"How was your journey—?"

It was the beginning of a long and undemanding conversation that lasted until Trevor heard the clock on the mantel chime the half hour.

"We'll be late to our dinner and Morag will scold me for keeping you here when you want to change. Go on, it's the old room, under the eaves."

But large enough not to be claustrophobic. Rutledge knew it well; he'd stayed there on his visits, boy and man, since he could remember.

At the door, Trevor clapped him on the shoulder. "It's damned good to see you. I hope you'll stay as long as you can!"

Then his eyes slid away toward the fire. "Mind Morag, will you? She hasn't been the same since—well, since the news came. She's showing her years now, and it's a pity. But she loved him, you know. . . ." His voice trailed off.

Rutledge managed to say, "Yes. I know," and made his way down the passage to the stairs.

His throat felt thick with grief. Ross had been clever and handsome and destined for a brilliant future in his father's architectural firm. And now he lay at the bottom of the sea with tons of metal strewing the seabed around him, one more Navy man with only a memorial to mark his death. Rutledge had received the news in France, one soft spring morning that heralded another gas attack. There had been no time to mourn. There seldom was.

Morag came out of the room that was his, having brought him hot water and fresh towels. She stood with hands clasped in front of her until he reached the top of the stairs and walked toward her. Her eyes were on his face, a woman who had known him from childhood, who had scolded him for mischief-making, saved him cakes left from tea, dressed his scrapes, and mended shirts torn by tumbling out of trees. He couldn't turn away, and so he smiled.

"Were you hurt, then? In the war?"

"Nothing that hasn't healed," he told her, lying for her sake.

But her eyes read more in his face than he realized. "Aye, that's what the letters said, but letters aren't always the whole truth, are they? I wanted to see for myself." She paused. "Do you dream, is that it?"

Wordlessly, he nodded.

"Aye. I thought as much. Well. That will pass. In God's good time."

She followed him to his room, smoothing the towels on the rack, twitching the curtains, moving the chintz-covered chair a quarter of an inch. Then she said quietly, "Mind Himself, lad. He's still grieving. You saw the terrible change in him now."

Rutledge had—the hair grayer, the new lines about his mouth, the dark circles under his godfather's eyes. Trevor had aged—but not from age.

"Aye." She nodded. "Don't let him sit and remember—"

"No. I won't."

"Come down to the kitchen in the morning."

"I will that," he said, and she grinned at him.

"I'll have hot scones for your breakfast, come Sunday." It was a treat, a remnant of childhood. She walked on down the stairs to put the finishing touches on the dinner she'd made.

The two men sat late over their port that evening, and Trevor took out the book sent to him by a young architect who'd joined his firm in 1912. Edward Harper had been killed in 1917, blown to bits with half a dozen other men, when an ammunition wagon went up in their faces.

"Tell me what you think of this." The way he unwrapped it and handed it to Rutledge showed clearly how he himself treasured it.

During his months in France, Harper had managed to finish a collection of watercolors—cameos of men of every rank and unit he'd come across. African chausseurs, Malay coolies, a French dragoon, a cocky Australian grinning cheekily. A Sikh of an East Indian regiment wearing a gas mask, his flourishing black beard framing it like a giant ruff. A range of pugarees—turbans—each identifying the district Indian troops had come from. Spahis, native Africans in French service, who collected trophies. Scots in kilts and a Belgian infantryman in his odd helmet. These were indisputably individual portraits, each vividly captured. It showed a remarkable talent.

"It's wonderful," Rutledge said, and meant it. It also showed the public face of war, cheerful and colorful, without the casualties and the horrors. Safe to send home. But he said nothing of that to Trevor.

Rutledge sat there, turning the pages, thinking of all the men he'd watched die, and all the skills that had died with them. And for what? He wished he knew.

"I'll frame them for the office," Trevor was saying. "A memorial of sorts." Then with intense anger, draining his glass, he added, "A waste. God, it was all a bloody *waste*!"

And Rutledge, watching his face, knew that he was thinking of his son.

THE WEEKEND WAS, oddly enough, healing for both men. They walked in the early morning, they sat and talked by the fire, they took the dogs out to flush game, by common consent leaving the guns at home. There had been enough killing.

Hamish, his presence always there, kept silent for the most part, as if he, too, had taken some pleasure in Trevor's broad interests and quiet humor. Rutledge wondered if the two men would have liked each other in life. Or if his own precious and precarious sense of peace had held Hamish at arm's length. But when Rutledge was alone, it was as it had always been, a trial of the spirit.

When he arrived in the kitchen on Sunday morning, Morag wasn't alone.

In the big room with its iron stove and old-fashioned hearth, the scent of fresh scones was warm and delicious. But the thin, fair man who stood up from the table, pink with embarrassment and determination, was wearing the uniform of a policeman. A Scots policeman.

Morag, fetching the teapot from the stove where it had been steeping, told Rutledge, "He won't go away. His name's McKinstry, and he's the grandson of my late sister's husband's cousin. He wants to see you." In Scotland, kith and kin cast a wide net.

"McKinstry," Rutledge acknowledged, taking his accustomed chair and moving his cup closer to Morag as she turned to pour. "What brings you here?"

"Inspector Rutledge," the young Scot said with formality. "I'm not sure, sir. That is to say, it's business, my own business, I've come about."

"Just as well. I have no jurisdiction here. I'm on holiday."

"Aye, sir. I've been told that." The constable glanced uneasily at Morag. She, apparently, had made it quite plain that no kin of hers would disturb Himself's guest. "I'm from near Jedburgh. The town where I'm stationed is smaller and not on the main road. I doubt you've ever heard of it until now. Duncarrick, sir."

Hamish, who had been on edge since crossing the border, was already busy speculating and not liking the answers he found.

It was the town that Inspector Oliver had come from, the policeman who had so enraged Lady Maude Gray. "Yes. I've heard of it." Morag had set the plate of hot scones in front of him and a dish of butter. He wished McKinstry to the devil but listened politely as he reached for his knife. The man, unwittingly, was an intrusion of things Rutledge had deliberately put out of his mind for these few days. Hamish, stirring as Rutledge himself felt an upsurge of tension, was an undercurrent half heard.

The constable's face brightened. "It's not a troublesome place. I know the people well enough, I can't say they're any worse than people are in the next town or the next—"

"Get on with it, McKinstry!" Morag said.

The scones were excellent. Rutledge had dreamed about them at the Front—the food had been unspeakable, and after a while nobody paid any heed to what he was swallowing, but there were other times when a sudden memory brought back a taste so vivid, it seemed to linger on the tongue. He found himself thinking of Ross, who had always sat across from him, grinning as they put away one after another until the plate was empty.

McKinstry cleared his throat, unaware that he was standing behind Ross's chair, his hands touching the worn wood of the back, infringing on a memory.

"Inspector Oliver informed me late yesterday afternoon that there was a man coming from London to help us in the matter of Lady Maude Gray's daughter. Rutledge, the Inspector said the name was. I came this morning to ask Morag Gilchrist if it was one and the same man she knew.

She said you were here on holiday, but if I was brief, I could ask—"

Rutledge, another scone halfway to his mouth, stared at the young constable. *A man coming from London . . . Rutledge, he said the name was . . .* He turned sharply to look toward Morag, but she was working at the oven, her back to him.

When he'd spoken to the Yard Friday morning, nothing had been said about continuing to Duncarrick. Was he now expected to report his conversation with Lady Maude to the Scots in person? It would be very like Bowles to throw a subordinate to the wolves, if the Chief Superintendent saw unpleasantness ahead. The man had a knack for taking cover at the right time! Or had some new information come to light at the teaching hospitals? Whatever it was, Rutledge had a sudden nasty feeling that he was going to be the sacrificial lamb—

He was aware that McKinstry was still talking. ". . . and it's what London may have given you that worries me, added to the fact she's incarcerated, awaiting trial—"

Who was incarcerated? Rutledge said, "We were speaking of Eleanor Gray—"

"Yes, sir, that's true, but it's only circumstantial evidence at best. All the same, I've a feeling that's sufficient to hang her. In Duncarrick, any jury picked will be ready to vote guilty before they've heard a single word. Overturning public opinion is the hurdle, and I've not got the skill to do it," McKinstry told him earnestly, an undercurrent of severe strain in his voice. "But surely there's a way? I've come to ask you to keep an open mind, and search for it. To my way of thinking, if we fail her, we've failed ourselves as policemen!"

It was a heartfelt appeal, and very near to insubordination. The constable stood there, young and determined, knowing that he'd placed his job in jeopardy by questioning the decisions of his superiors in Duncarrick, but believing strongly enough in what he saw as duty to put his trust in a stranger. There were a number of people at the Yard who would have had McKinstry up on charges. A constable was not allowed opinions.

But his appeal was wasted on Rutledge, who knew only the English side of the investigation. "I haven't any idea what you're talking about," he said flatly. "So far London hasn't told me anything. I came north to speak to Lady Maude Gray, and I have had no orders to continue to Duncarrick." As Morag set a plate of eggs before him, he went on, "For God's sake, man, sit down and eat some breakfast, so that I can enjoy mine!"

McKinstry said, flushing, "I've had mine, sir, if it's all the same to you!"

"Then sit down and drink a cup of tea. And start at the beginning."

The constable pulled out a chair and glanced at Morag. She brought him a fresh cup and set it before him without a word. She didn't need words to convey the message that he had overstepped his bounds. He could read it clearly in her face.

Hamish, moved to comment, said, "He believes what he's come to say."

McKinstry poured himself a cup of tea, added milk and sugar like a condemned man determined to show courage eating his last meal, and then, without tasting it, began rather stiffly. "There's a woman in my district. A good woman—but she's been the subject of anonymous letters. Not mailed, you understand, just stuck in the corner of a door or left pinned to a clothesline, wherever they'd be noticed first thing in the morning."

"All right, anonymous. What did they say? There's usually a theme."

"Not to put too fine a point on it, sir, they called her a whore. And as word spread, the rumors followed. No one confronted her with the accusations. That's what I find hardest to accept. No one gave her a chance to explain. Instead they turned their backs on her. It appeared she'd lied to people, you see, and they saw it as a betrayal of trust." He stopped, frowning. "At least that's what they must have told themselves to excuse what they were doing. I can't see any other explanation. Then, to make matters worse, it came to light just after the letters began that she might have murdered the mother of a child she'd claimed was her own. She was taken up on that charge. Inspector Oliver will tell you the case against her, and about the bones. My concern is that the jury will hang her if they can, because it's human nature to want to believe you can't be fooled for long."

McKinstry recollected his tea, sipped it, and scalded his tongue. Then he said, desperate to make himself understood, "It reminds me of the days when people believed in witches. They sent innocent men and women to the stake or drowned them, in a mad effort to prove that witchcraft existed. A kind of hysteria that took the place of reason. Is that what's happening here? I don't know why I'm not infected by it myself—" But he did know, and couldn't bring himself to say it: he was in love with Fiona and saw her as a victim, not a killer. It was, perhaps, his own hysteria. . . . The thought frightened him suddenly.

"You were one of the investigating officers? Then you should know how sound the case is against her," Rutledge answered. "Does she have a good barrister? From what you're telling me, she needs one."

"Yes, she does—though I don't care for him myself. I've tried again and again to get to the bottom of this business, because I don't think anyone else has. We may have evidence that points in her direction, but is there more that points away from her? And I don't know how to go about searching for that properly. I don't even know where to begin. We don't have much in the way of crime in Duncarrick."

Rutledge said, "But that's what you're trained to do. What's difficult about it?"

McKinstry ran a finger through sugar that in his nervousness he'd spilled beside his teacup. "I can find a man wanted for robbery, I can stop a man from beating his wife, I can tell you who's the likely culprit when the MacGregors' house is broken into, and I can look at the old man out in the bothy by the stream and judge if he's killed himself somebody else's fat lamb and cooked it. That's work I know. This isn't. It's whispers and gossip spread in passing, and nobody knows by whom. That's what sits ill with me, the way it began. It's a word dropped here, a look there, a shrug—and I can't find out who's behind it. Inspector Oliver claims it doesn't matter, that we've done *our* work, and proved the fact of murder well enough for it to come to trial now. But to me it seems to be important to find out how and where the whole business began. The truth is, it appears to be having a life of its own! Like a ghost running about and whispering in people's ears. That's fanciful, too, but I can't explain it any better."

Fanciful or not, it evoked a clear image in Rutledge's mind.

"Rumor," Rutledge agreed, "can be deadly. Especially if people are prepared to believe it. But surely if there was no more to it than gossip, the fiscal and the Chief Constable would never have allowed the matter to come to trial!"

McKinstry shook his head mournfully. "I've lain awake nights asking myself that. I can't see the Chief Constable being taken in, he's not a gullible man. What does he know that makes him so certain there's a case?"

McKinstry gave the matter some thought. "Anonymous letters are a coward's tool. Keep that in mind. And find out who bears a secret grudge against this young woman. It might not be the kind of thing you or I would think to hold against her. It will be something petty. Personal, certainly. And it needn't be a sin of commission. Omission will do just as well."

"The worst complainer in Duncarrick is a neighbor of hers. An ill-tempered man, but he's not likely to go about writing anonymous letters. He's more the sort to use his fists than hide what he feels."

"Could he have taken a fancy to her—and been rebuffed? It may be that he believed she was giving favors to others and refusing him."

There was a comical expression on McKinstry's face. "Hugh Oliphant in the role of rejected lover? He's over seventy! His wife watches him like a cat at a mousehole, but he'd choose a pint over a pretty face any day!"

"Well, then, his wife. Or any other woman who might have suspected her husband of taking too great a personal interest in the accused."

"There's Molly Braddock. Well, Molly Sinclair, that was. Tommy Braddock's good with his hands, he'd done the odd job for the accused. Fixed a window sash when the weight rope broke, and cleaned the chimney when birds nested in it last spring. He's a happy-go-lucky man, the world's his best friend. But Molly is possessive." McKinstry shook his head. "I can give you names, that's easy enough. What I can't do is picture in my mind any of these people sitting down, day after day, to write such wicked nonsense."

Hamish said, "He's a conscientious policeman, aye, and a good man who doesna' ken hate."

Rutledge agreed. He buttered the last of the scones. "Let's take another direction, then," he said aloud. "Were the letters Biblical in tone?"

"Yes, sir! How did you guess?"

"It isn't uncommon for anonymous letter writers to clothe their acts in Scripture. 'It's God chastising you, not me! His judgment of you, not mine.' "

McKinstry sighed. "That would fit half the town. We're a dour lot eager to spy sin around any corner. Aye, and find it as well."

"You do realize," Rutledge said, studying the young man, "that these letters may have had nothing to do with the crime she's accused of. It may simply be that the letters drew attention to facts no one had considered until then. And once the police took notice, the truth came out."

"No, sir," McKinstry said, torn between defending his own beliefs and possibly alienating the man from London he'd pinned his hopes on. "I can't accept that without better evidence. Sometimes"—he hesitated, glancing at Morag—"sometimes there's such a fever pitch of belief in guilt that nobody looks for the *fallacies* in the evidence. I'm saying that because of the letters, Duncarrick was eager to see her blamed. That the letters set the stage for all that followed."

It was easy to shape evidence to fit a theory. . . .

"Yes, I understand," Rutledge answered patiently. "And that's the purpose of a trial—to weigh the evidence openly and fairly."

Hamish grunted, as if challenging Rutledge's words.

"If the jury listens," McKinstry argued. "Then it works. But what if the jury doesn't want to hear anything to the contrary because they've made up their minds? That's what I fear, sir, because I do know my people. And I'm ashamed to say I have no faith in a jury when the mind's shut." He took a deep breath. "And what's to become of the child? There's the other worry. As far as I know, it has no father." He looked out the window, not at Rutledge. "She's a good woman. She's a good mother. If she says the babe is hers, I want to believe it. But the police have said the contrary, that she killed the mother and took it, then told her aunt and the rest of the world that it was hers."

"The child isn't the law's responsibility," Rutledge replied, thinking of Lady Maude Gray. Would she claim it if there was any possibility that the child was her daughter's? Even though she refused to believe her daughter was dead? Stranger things had happened. He felt Morag's eyes on him and turned. The old woman shook her head, as if denying that she hadn't cared for his answer, but he knew she had been disappointed in it. So had Hamish.

His mind busy with Lady Maude, Rutledge said, "How did Oliver connect this young woman living in Duncarrick with a corpse found up in Glencoe? There's the problem of distance, if nothing else!"

McKinstry, much more comfortable with a straightforward report than his own feelings, lost some of his intensity. "Once it was clear the boy couldn't be hers, we went looking for the child's mother. We sent queries as far as Glasgow and Edinburgh, and across the border into England. The lad's going on three, we didn't expect it to be easy. It was Inspector Oliver's belief that we ought to search where the accused had come from, before coming to live in Duncarrick. That eventually led us to the glen. Human remains had been found there just last year, a woman's bones. And they hadn't been identified." He stopped, looked at his teacup, then met Rutledge's eyes. "The Glencoe police were nearly certain that she hadn't been there in March of 1916, when they'd scoured the glen searching for an old shepherd who'd gone off his head and disappeared. And the locals claim it must have been late summer or early autumn, as anybody moving sheep in the spring would have noticed the corbies collecting there. We sent around a description, adding what we suspected in Duncarrick to what little the Glencoe police had in their files. The next thing we knew, an inspector in Menton contacted us for more information. Duncarrick has eaten up the news, taking it as fact. And Inspector Oliver was not disposed to question the connection—" He stopped, suddenly uncomfortable.

Rutledge didn't press. After a moment, McKinstry went on.

"At any rate, the three jurisdictions accepted the possibility that the missing Eleanor Gray was the mother of the boy in Duncarrick and had died in suspicious circumstances in Glencoe. There's similarity in height, for one thing, and the timing fits. If she'd quarreled with her mother in the spring, and then carried a child to term, she'd have been delivered in late summer. And that's when the lad was born. What's more, none of the other inquiries Inspector Oliver received matched nearly as well." He drew a deep breath. Even he, convinced as he was that Fiona was innocent, saw that there was a logic about the evidence that was inescapable.

Rutledge said, "Even if I'm assigned to the case, I can't see what I could accomplish that you haven't." And it was clear that McKinstry himself was not objective. Rutledge found himself wondering what his relationship was—had been—with the accused.

"Show me," McKinstry pleaded, "how to prove she's harmed no one. How to stop the whispers before this case comes to a trial. I'd not like to think my failure has sent her to the gallows. But it's going to happen. I'm helpless to prevent it."

WHEN MCKINSTRY HAD gone, Rutledge turned to Morag. "He shouldn't have come. It was wrong."

He could hear Trevor running lightly down the stairs, opening the door, whistling for the dogs. The weekend had given his godfather a new energy.

"What harm did it do?" She reached for the frying pan. "Alistair's an honest lad with a wish to do what's right. Should I have sent him away without a hearing? As if I couldn't trust you to be just?"

"No. But it isn't my case, you see. It's Inspector Oliver's. And McKinstry doesn't know me. I could have made trouble for him, reported him for going over the head of his superior. Or put him in jeopardy for trying to influence my actions." Bowles would have done so, for one. Another thought occurred to him. "Could the child be his?"

"He was in France. And he does know you. He met you at an aid station behind the front lines. He'd been shot in the leg. He said you were one of the bravest men he'd ever met. You'd just brought in three men who'd been gassed and left for dead near a German outpost. Somehow you found them and got them out. Alistair was glad to shake your hand."

Trevor was striding down the passage, speaking to his dogs. The big kitchen suddenly seemed small, close, and overheated. Hamish, alive in his mind, was as loud as a voice in the room. Rutledge could barely remember that day at the aid station, and certainly not the face of the sol-

dier lying on a stretcher close by who had shaken his hand.
As the doctors cleaned a cut on his wrist, he'd stood there
grimly, unaware of pain. It had happened not too long after
Hamish's death, and Rutledge had purposely taken risks,
wanting to die. It hadn't been courage, it had been despera-
tion—anything to silence the voice in his head. Even death.

Morag was talking, but her words failed to register.
Trevor was greeting him, and the dogs frisked noisily about
his feet.

Trevor said, "Ian, are you all right?"

Rutledge shook his head to clear it. "Yes, I'm fine. Morag
was telling me about a relation of hers. It brought back
some memories, that's all." To Morag he said, "I'm sorry. I
don't seem to place him."

But afterward, as he walked down to a stream with
Trevor, talking about his work, he found himself thinking
again about McKinstry. What the young policeman had
wanted from him was some semblance of hope. The promise that if he took over the case, he'd be objective, not swept
up in the conclusions already drawn.

It didn't matter. There was no reason for him to be involved. He'd finished his business with Lady Maude, and the
rest of the case would be in the hands of the courts. He
didn't want to stay in Scotland.

ON MONDAY MORNING, Rutledge put in a telephone call to
London from David Trevor's study.

Bowles, summoned to the telephone, answered
brusquely, "Rutledge, is that you?"

"Yes." He quickly summarized his conversation with
Lady Maude and ended with his own view. "It's hard to say.
In my opinion, she doesn't know where her daughter is
presently, and it's quite possible that she's at one of the
teaching hospitals—"

"I've already had the report on that. There's no Eleanor
Gray wanting to become a doctor."

"She might have used another name—"

"Yes, yes, I'm aware of that, but there's no one who matches the physical description you gave Sergeant Owens. I'd say at a guess that whatever the quarrel was about, it was not medicine that the young woman left home for. She might not have told her mother the truth." There was a pause. "One thing we did learn. She was a suffragette. Independent young miss, arrested a number of times for chaining herself to fences and making herself a public nuisance in whatever fashion got her the most notice. A young woman likely to find herself in trouble of one kind or another, I'd say. Sergeant Gibson remembered her from before the war, and he says she hasn't been in trouble with the police for some years now. Could mean she'd learned her lesson. Or that she is dead."

Bowles took a long breath, indicating a change of subject.

"We've had a call from Lady Maude. You're to go to Scotland and find out what you can about this corpse. She's insisting that you take over the case, and her family's not to be dragged into it, no speculation about her daughter, public or private, until you are absolutely certain that the corpse is Eleanor Gray's. *What the hell did you say to her?*"

7

---◆---

BY TEN O'CLOCK THAT MORNING, RUTLEDGE HAD ASKED directions from Trevor, accepted the generous packet of sandwiches that Morag had put up for him, and turned south and west toward Jedburgh and Tweedesdale. It was a day of mixed sun and clouds, with a brief shower or two that raised the damp smell of earth. Long shadows were cast across the countryside when the sun came out, vanishing and reappearing like magic as the clouds shifted across the sky. There always seemed to be more sky in Scotland than in England, a different sky. Vast and empty, as if God weren't at home.

He had come to Scotland for a weekend owed to his godfather, and now duty was keeping him here. He felt misgivings, his mind unsettled, the peace he'd found at Hadrian's Wall worn off. And Hamish, in his accustomed place behind the driver's shoulder, was as disturbed by the turn of events as Rutledge himself. He could hear the voice as clearly as if there *were* a passenger. Blaming—stubbornly refusing to accept the change in plans.

"And I'll no' go to the glen again—"

Rutledge tried to shut him out and then fell prey to another kind of haunting, awakened grief.

For the motorcar also carried the "ghost" of Ross Trevor. Rutledge had felt the dead man's presence so strongly at The Lodge. In France he had arrived at an acceptance of Ross's death, but in the house where Ross had spent every summer for twenty-five years or more, it seemed that he must surely be somewhere just out of sight—down the passage—upstairs in his room—out riding and expected soon—talking to Morag in the kitchen. His laughter preceding him, his swift, energetic footsteps approaching the door. Ross Trevor had been a powerful presence, and Rutledge had found himself watching the doorways, listening over the ticking of the grandfather's clock or the wind in the eaves, for some sign of it. It seemed impossible that such a man had vanished so completely, swallowed by the sea—

Over the last four months, Rutledge had begun for the first time to realize what the civilian population had endured during the long, dark days when casualties mounted and there seemed to be no end to the fighting. It was different from the way that soldiers saw the dying. But no less terrible. A time for mourning . . .

He wondered if David felt that same sense of anticipation, and if he did, how he lived with it—and then realized that for Ross's father and for Morag, it might be oddly comforting.

Hamish said, as if picking up the thought, "They never saw him dead. They never closed the lid over his coffin and watched the earth shoveled down on it. Like me, he never came home. And so they're still waiting—"

JEDBURGH, LIKE ITS neighbors from Berwick to Dumfries, was not the Scotland of kilts and pipes and Bonnie Prince Charlie. These were the Marches that ran on either side of the frontier between Scotland and England, the border towns of the Lowlands, where a different kind of war had raged for centuries, raids into England for cattle and sheep and horses, shaping generations of hard men.

The English had raided north too, with equal vigor and cunning. It had been a way of life until the 1600s, sometimes condoned and sometimes condemned, but always profitable enough to be a main local industry. Union between Scotland and England had finally put a stop to that.

And the legacy of John Knox had narrowed the Borderer's wild soul into a primmer mold where business and righteousness walked hand in hand: The Sabbath was holy, women knew their place, and the Kirk was a stronger influence in daily affairs than Edinburgh, much less far-off London.

Legends had grown up around raids and raiders. Ballads and tales celebrated reivers named Sim the Laird, Jock of the Side, and Kinmont Willie. After all, this was land where the shifting sands of policy, war, feuds, and alliances had often redrawn the border to suit the times. What was mine today might be yours tomorrow, and taking it back again became a popular sport.

Rutledge drove into Jedburgh through another shower and found the turning that led to Duncarrick. It was a small town in the green, rolling country between Air Water and the Tweed. A tall hedge of houses, shops, and one hotel formed an irregularly shaped nineteenth-century square with a worn monument at the top, commemorating the burning of the town three times in thirty years during the early 1500s. The pillar stood at the high end of the square, a lonely sentinel of the past surrounded by the town's newer image. Other houses, some much older, straggled west beyond the square, and there was a modest inn among them. The wooden sign over the door read THE REIVERS. Barely a dozen streets bracketed the heart of Duncarrick and gave it an isolated feeling, as if it had been stranded in the middle of nowhere, an agricultural community untouched by the woolen tweed industry that had crowded its neighbors.

"It's no' a Highland town," Hamish reflected, "but it's no' Sassenach either." Not English. And he was right, there was indeed a different air here from the small English border towns no more than a hard ride away.

Where Jedburgh had once boasted walls, towers, a castle, and an abbey, Duncarrick had been burned to the ground so often that little of its past remained. A pele tower, the tall half-house–half-defensive-fortress of the raiding years, stood in a field about a mile past the last dwelling. It was little more than a tall rubble of stone and shadow now, with perhaps two floors still intact and the door slanted ajar. He passed it and then turned around in the next farm lane.

Rutledge got out to stretch his legs, leaving the motorcar parked on the grassy verge some one hundred yards from the pele tower and going the rest of the way on foot.

Such towers were a part of Rutledge's own heritage, and he found them of absorbing interest—an architectural as well as a military solution to what must have been wretched years of constant danger. The Routledges, his own ancestors, had once been Borderers on the English side, raiding with the best of them, until a widow with three young sons had moved south in search of a more peaceful climate in which to raise them. Shrewd and capable, she'd found prosperity there as well. The Borderer had proved to be a match for clever, sophisticated Tudor London. In more ways than one.

There was a painting of her in the London house, with an impeccable ruff like a halo behind her head, a firm chin, and lively, intelligent eyes that the Elizabethan painter had captured so well that they seemed to follow the viewer about the room, staring directly, knowingly, at him wherever he stood. As a small child, Rutledge had understandably confused her with God.

He tramped across the fallow field that surrounded the tower base and heard the clamor of sheep somewhere in the distance, even before he smelled them on the damp air. Standing at the foot of the massive stone walls, looking up at the broken top where birds had nested and wind whipped through the empty windows, he became aware of someone moving toward him. Turning, he saw a man in the rough clothes of a farmer, his face reddened by the sun, his hat jammed on his head like a fixture.

"Good morning!" he called as he saw Rutledge turn. "Looking for something?"

"No, just interested in the stonework." Rutledge waited until the man was nearer and added, "It's amazing, the craftsmanship of the people who built this. It's stood here what—four or five hundred years?"

"About that. Fine workmanship, I agree. Desperate times calling for desperate measures, if you like. It belonged to my wife's family. She knows the history of it better than I do." He took off his hat and wiped his forehead with his sleeve. "God, everything smells of sheep. I'm a horse breeder by preference. Draft horses. But the Army took nearly every animal I had, and I've got to start again. Meanwhile, the sheep are tiding me over." He grinned. "It's a near thing whether I'll kill them first or they'll be the death of me. Stupid beasts, they are. Even the dogs find them irritating."

He spoke well for a farmer. An educated man.

"I'd have as little to do with them as possible," Rutledge agreed.

"Here on holiday? There's some good walking in the district if you know where to look. The rule is, close gates you find closed and leave open gates you find open. There's a nasty-tempered ram here and there, but you'll see him before he sees you."

"Thanks, I'll keep it in mind."

The man nodded and walked on, whistling to his dogs, who ran, tongues lolling, some distance ahead. Their ears pricked, and they obeyed his signals instantly. Rutledge watched them. Clever animals, he'd always admired their intelligence, their speed, and the way they could drop to the ground, nearly invisible, when the command came. Working dogs these, not pampered house pets, and very good at what they did. In the Highlands especially, sheep couldn't be run without them. He had met a man once who trained these dogs, an old rough-edged rogue who had taken his skills and his eye for instinct to New Zealand, where sheep were still king.

Rutledge went back to the motorcar and, starting the engine, headed into Duncarrick again.

HE DROVE SLOWLY through the main square, studying it, before he came back to the hotel and asked directions to the police station. The clerk told him, "But I doubt there's anyone there at this time of day. And Inspector Oliver is away to Jedburgh on business. Constable McKinstry's to home. It's his day off."

Rutledge left his motorcar at the hotel and walked the short distance, following the clerk's careful instructions.

McKinstry lived behind the square, a three-story house with a fresh coat of cream paint. The buckets and ladders stood to one side, in the narrow alley between it and its neighbor, waiting for the sun to reappear. Down the same street, some twelve or thirteen buildings to the left, was the police station, its sign affixed to the door, a neat black square with white letters. As the clerk had foretold, no one was there. Rutledge turned back to McKinstry's house. There was a fair amount of activity in the street—soberly dressed men and women going about their business. Two carters carried on a loud conversation at the next corner, then moved on as a lorry came rolling slowly past, looking to make a delivery at the apothecary's shop.

Hamish, who had been observing the town with some interest, commented, "There's enough money here to keep up appearances. But no' enough to be grand. Plain people, with plain souls."

It was, Rutledge thought, a fair verdict. McKinstry had been right—the police here dealt with the ordinary. And even murder could fall into that category.

Constable McKinstry, concealing his surprise at finding

Rutledge on his doorstep, welcomed him into the parlor and waited for him to explain his visit, although there was a glint of hope in the blue-gray eyes. The paint-spattered coveralls he wore were loose-fitting, as if he'd been a stouter man before the war.

"I understand that Inspector Oliver is in Jedburgh," Rutledge began, taking the chair McKinstry had pointed out. "Let's be clear about that from the start. I came to see him. You were right, the Yard has put me in charge of a part of this case, and I need to know the rest of the details as soon as possible. Can you tell me when he's expected back?"

McKinstry said, "Not until dinnertime, so I'm told, sir. The Inspector said he was attending to a private matter." Or tactfully out of sight. "Would you like me to take you to the Chief Constable instead?" He looked down at his coveralls and grinned. "As soon as I change out of these."

"No, I'll speak to Oliver first. In the meantime, I'd like to hear something about the town and the people here. You've given me a fairly comprehensive picture, but now I need more."

"I was just having my tea, and I'd be honored to have you join me."

Over tea and a lemon cream cake that had come from the baker's, McKinstry chose his words with great care, trying to see Duncarrick through a stranger's eyes.

"You'd call it provincial, coming from London. We don't have broad horizons. But most people have known each other all their lives, depended on each other in hard times, seen each other through the worst and the best that happens to them. Weddings. Funerals." He passed Rutledge a wedge of the cake on a delicate china plate. "If I fell ill tomorrow, I'd have the neighbors bringing me tea and soups and fresh bread. My washing would be done, clean sheets for the bed, someone would think to bring me a few flowers—a book to read. And not because I'm the constable. It's our way."

He cut himself a slice of lemon cake, savored it, then said, "Sorry, I don't have any sandwiches—"

"No, this is enough," Rutledge said. "Carry on."

Hamish had been listening, commenting on the examples McKinstry had given, agreeing with most of them. "In my experience, it would be the lassies, with the flowers! Hoping to be noticed."

"But there's the other side of the coin too, sir. We're a rigid lot when it comes to sin. It's black and white, no gray in between. We can be small-minded. We know each other's business. That's a help to me, as I told you at Mr. Trevor's house. I can guess who's chasing the Youngs' cat or borrowing Tim Croser's horse when he's drunk and not likely to notice. That would be Bruce Hall, who is courting a lass between here and Jedburgh, and hates walking when he can ride. But his pa won't give him the loan of a horse because he doesn't approve of the girl."

"And yet you can't put your finger on the author of these letters."

McKinstry frowned and set down his cup.

"And that's what I find most disturbing," he said, considering it. "Why can't I go and knock on a door and see guilt written in the face answering it? I walk down the street on my rounds, and I look into the eyes of the people I meet. I stand and talk to them for a time. I watch them go about their daily business. And there's nothing about them that I can put my finger on and say, 'Now, that's the action of a guilty woman.'"

"Why are you so certain it's a woman?"

"Because why would a man think to warn a laundress that her soul was in danger, washing a whore's sheets? Or warn a young mother that her small daughter had a bastard for a playmate and was likely to see goings-on at the inn that weren't fit for an innocent child's eyes?"

Hamish was already there, but Rutledge set aside his plate and finished his tea before saying, "A man might write such things to throw you off the scent. Or he may recognize that it's the women in Duncarrick who form public opinion—"

McKinstry's face darkened. "Then he's a bloody coward. Begging your pardon, sir!"

Rutledge asked for a chronology of the case, and McKinstry painstakingly gave it to him, this time leaving out nothing that he considered important. Rutledge paid close attention, noting facts as well as listening for nuances. When McKinstry had finished, he said, "Well done." Hamish, silent in his head, stirred uneasily. Rutledge found his thoughts straying for an instant, then went on.

"My guess is that whoever wrote such letters knew they'd be believed. And that's the next point. *Why* would people so readily believe them? Why didn't the first person to find one on his doorstep march straight to the police or to the accused and make it clear that this wasn't going to continue?"

McKinstry took a long breath. "You are asking me to answer you that she's guilty. The accused. Where there's smoke, there's fire, they say. But I'm not prepared to believe that. I'd rather believe that the letter-writer chose her—his—targets very carefully. Some people relish gossip if it's shocking enough."

"Will you make a list of all the people who have admitted to receiving these letters? What they do for a living. What reason they might have had for disliking the accused. How well they might have known her?"

"Yes, sir, I'll do that today. But, begging your pardon, sir, I don't see how that will help you find out the truth about the bones said to be Lady Maude Gray's daughter's." He shook his head. "And that's another whole kettle of fish."

"It is," Rutledge agreed. "But in my experience, where coincidence dovetails so perfectly, it becomes suspect. First we have these letters, apparently accepted as truthful. And now you tell me there was another one, from here—or from Glasgow, depending on how reliable the postmark may be—only this anonymous writer stoutly defends the accused, and in so doing puts her in even greater jeopardy. A charge of murder, not mere wantonness. There's a search of the inn—where a body turned up. Only it isn't the boy's mother. Now, who knew enough about the history of The Reivers that he or she sent Inspector Oliver on such a wild-goose chase? But it does whet Oliver's appetite for the hunt, and he begins to search for missing persons. The upshot of that is a set of unidentified bones and a connection with a woman in England whose daughter has not been seen since 1916. Now we have larger questions to answer than who wrote the letters. I wonder, was someone counting on just that?"

There was confusion in McKinstry's eyes. "I don't follow you, sir."

But Hamish did. He said, "Is the woman in yon cell a murderer—a victim—or a scapegoat?"

As RUTLEDGE TOOK his leave, McKinstry said, "The worrisome thing in all of this—to my way of thinking—is that no one has lifted a hand for Fiona. No one has spoken up for her. Not Mr. Elliot, not Mr. Robson, not Mr. Burns—the fiscal. Not Inspector Oliver. It's as if she's been found guilty already, and the trial's a travesty that'll put a stamp on it for the world to see: *We were right in what we did. A jury has said as much.* And the truth will be buried with her. That keeps me awake at night." He ticked the words off on his right hand. "Minister, Chief Constable, procurator-fiscal, policeman. And what if she's innocent and they hang her?"

WALKING BACK TO his motorcar at the hotel, Rutledge went over again the information McKinstry had laid out for him. What intrigued him was how skillfully balanced each scrap of the puzzle seemed to be.

Like a game of chess, where the player knows in advance the moves of each piece on the board. In chess there were two players. Attack and counterattack. In life, there would be no certainties about the outcome. . . .

Before Rutledge left the house, the constable had taken out a copy he had made of the letter that had been addressed to Mr. Elliot, the minister. He read it aloud. As Rutledge listened, he found himself thinking that Elliot would have been better advised to go directly to the woman herself and ask for some explanation. Instead he'd chosen to involve the police, indicating that he had already half believed the malicious accusations brought to him by his parishioners. That would be worth exploring. . . .

Taking the copy from McKinstry, Rutledge had scanned it. It was untutored, apparently the work of a woman who earnestly tried to defend—and instead unwittingly pointed a finger of guilt. If it was a hoax, it was very cleverly devised. There was a ring of sincerity in the simple wording.

I have heard horrid gossip about a young woman in Duncarrick . . . It is sad that no one has spoken a word in her defense . . . I will lose my place if I tell you how I met her . . . Her given name was Fiona . . . It was the late summer of 1916 . . . She was traveling with a very young baby and had no milk for him . . . It struck me that she could not be the mother, and indeed, I learned that the mother had just died and she had been given the baby to raise as her own . . . I was distressed for her, because she was unwed and had no family except for an elderly spinster aunt . . . When I asked her if the mother had any family who could help, she began to cry, and wouldn't tell me how the poor creature had died or even where she had been buried . . . She told me fiercely that she would be a good mother and would not allow anyone to take the boy from her . . . I could see that she was very agitated . . . She was always looking over her shoulder as if expecting to see someone there. But there was no one . . . I soon gave up trying to reason with her . . . What struck me was her unshakable belief that she could bring up this poor orphan as her son . . . I cannot be convinced that she would turn wanton and betray the trust that had been placed in her . . . Please, do what you can on her behalf . . . It isn't right for her to be tormented in this way . . . I would as soon believe that Fiona was a murderer as believe she has become a whore . . .

He had even read it a second time, finding the wording and the sense of it more interesting than the content. "And you never discovered who'd written this?"

"No, sir, though we made every effort. It came from Glasgow, but there's no telling who had put it in the post box there. It doesn't quite say that the mother of the boy was murdered, you see. But if the death was natural, surely there would have been a doctor in attendance—relatives notified? And Fiona should have been able to tell us where to find such witnesses! Instead there's a mystery about where and how the child was born. She won't say. She won't tell us where the mother is buried, if it's true that she's dead."

"But that's knowledge after the fact. What convinced the Chief Constable that there ought to be some investigation into the matter? Merely the letter? Or was there more?"

"I've never been offered an answer to that." McKinstry tugged at his earlobe, uncertain. He'd never considered the question himself. Orders were orders.

Rutledge had said, "After all, it began as a moral issue. Whether or not the accused was what she claimed to be, a decent widow with a child to raise on her own. And Mr. Elliot chose to do nothing about it. An admission that he had reason to believe the first letters were telling the truth?"

It would be damning.

McKinstry shook his head. "I can't say. The Chief Constable summoned Inspector Oliver, and then Inspector Oliver sent me to search the premises, and I did. There was nothing out-of-the-way in the living quarters or the inn. The stables were a public place, I couldn't see a body being buried out there, even in the dead of night. Any work would have been noticed straightaway by the handyman. But Inspector Oliver prides himself on being thorough, and he had the place apart. That's when he found the bones in the back of a cupboard that had been walled up. It dumb-founded the lot of us, I can tell you!"

"And he believed he'd found the body of the child's mother?"

"Oh, yes. There was long hair on the skull. I was sent to summon Dr. Murchison, and he came at once, then told Inspector Oliver he'd been brought out of his surgery on a wild-goose chase. The bones were not a woman's. They belonged to a man. And they were all of a hundred years old!"

8

―――――◆―――――

WALKING BACK THROUGH DUNCARRICK'S MAIN SQUARE, Rutledge stopped and considered the shops and houses lining either side of the road. These townspeople were prosperous enough, as Hamish had pointed out, but without obvious signs of wealth. Surely a small inn on the outskirts of town would offer neither problem nor competition. If The Reivers provided extra rooms to people on market day, so much the better. As for competing with the only hotel, Rutledge doubted if it could hold a candle to the amenities offered there. It would have served a simpler class of person who couldn't afford the grandness of The Ballantyne. And any success it had enjoyed would have been modest in comparison to this part of the town. A good living for the owners, yes, but hardly extravagant.

He moved on, watching people going about their daily lives. Women entering and leaving the shops, a nursemaid with a pram carefully maneuvering it through the door of a house, a woman sweeping her front step, a small boy playing with a top, men in dark suits coming out of offices, others in work clothes, carrying the tools of a trade, a crocodile of schoolgirls marching in the wake of a schoolmistress wearing a thick coat and unbecoming hat.

Ordinary people, their eyes avoiding those of the stranger passing them. No curiosity about his presence or his business. As if once burned, twice shy . . .

Hamish said, "McKinstry was right. They're a dour lot!"

There was one other common feature among them. Unsmiling faces and thin, tight mouths. As if life was a burden, and they were used to enduring it.

A woman stepped out of a shop close to where he was standing and cast a surreptitious glance in his direction.

Hamish saw her before he did, commenting that she could have studied him just as clearly from the front window. A tall woman, pretty in a severe way, with her hair in a tightly confined bun, her sweater and skirt a very prim gray with only a touch of color in the silk shirtwaist, a paisley of peach and gray and white.

She made a fuss over the potted plants that stood on either side of the shop door. They were pretty, a mixture of rose geraniums and something lavender and white, like pansies. Satisfied, she turned and went quickly back inside. He looked at the neatly painted sign above the door. A. TAIT MILLINERY. He filed it away for future reference. If she had been interested enough to inspect a stranger, she might also be a gossip. . . .

Rutledge retrieved his car from The Ballantyne's yard and drove out past the church. He found The Reivers again and stopped across the road to look at it. Yes, he'd been right. Comfortable, decent—hardly a blot on the conscience of Duncarrick. Neither a wild tavern nor a seedy lodging.

Small and long, no more than two stories with an attic above, the inn was one of those old buildings that survived because they were in nobody's way—no one wanted to build a square here, or shops, or a large house.

Duncarrick's main square, on the other hand, had

probably seen the demise of a whole street of houses to widen the space to suit nineteenth-century builders with Progress on their minds.

The houses on either side here and down the lane by the inn's stables were neither picturesque nor ugly, more a reflection of the straightforwardness of the people who lived in them. Only the house to one's left facing the inn was by any measure grand, boasting three stories and an extension toward the rear, as if it had grown over the years with the family living there. The windows had been set with some eye to symmetry and style, lending a faint touch of grace.

The inn looked rooted in its earth, tidy, freshly whitewashed in the past year, the door to the bar hidden behind a climbing rose that had spread with age to cover the porch it had been intended to adorn. It was a hardy rose to survive in this climate, and the small garden at its feet showed some care for the impression the inn made on passersby. The bar parlor, on the side facing the narrow lane into the inn yard at the rear, had a green door, and crisp white curtains showed behind the windows next to it.

Time could have turned this into a rowdy pub on the outskirts of town, but the inn had managed, somehow, to retain a certain dignity. Because two women had had the care of it?

"I canna' think why they'd persecute a lass with such a dowry as the inn," Hamish was saying. "They'd be more likely to want their sons to wed her."

And that, too, was a question worth considering. It all kept coming back to that: Why had the town united so easily against this woman?

On impulse, Rutledge shut off the engine and got out, crossing the road and walking down into the inn yard, where the stables and outbuildings stood.

They were in a fair state of repair. With little work done during the war and no money after it to tackle major improvements, upkeep spoke well for the management.

He was poking about in the stable, looking for the cabinet where Inspector Oliver had discovered the first set of bones, when a loud voice said, "Here! What do you think you're doing!"

He turned to find a tall, heavy-shouldered man of middle age standing in the doorway, arms akimbo, staring at him with harsh dislike. Shadowed by the doorway, his face was dark and ugly but had a strength to it as well.

Rutledge, well aware that he was trespassing, replied peaceably, "I'd heard that the inn might be for sale."

"There's no decision been made to sell or not sell," the man said.

"I see." Rutledge turned, having found what he was looking for, the part of the wall pulled down to bring a skeleton to light. The cupboard, deep enough to start with, had been made shallower to conceal the grave behind it. A careful bit of work—a hundred years ago trouble had been taken to make the spot seem ordinary, unsuspicious. It must have been quite a shock for Inspector Oliver to discover that his "corpse" was nearly as old as the inn.

Rutledge began to walk toward the man blocking the exit. It made him uneasy to have his way closed—even in the relative spaciousness of the stable, he could feel the claustrophobia it invoked. The air seemed thick, suffocating—

"Tell me about the owner—" He broke off. After being buried alive in the impenetrable mud of a shell crater, weighed down by Hamish's body, Rutledge had come to hate being shut in—confined in any fashion. Traveling on trains, sleeping in a small room, seeing himself cut off from escape through a door or down a stair—the need for space was so urgent that it ignited a rising panic. Even here he could feel the sudden dampness of sweat on his face, the difficulty breathing, the awareness of hideous danger—

"You'll be wanting to speak to the police, then," the man told him bluntly but didn't elaborate. His stance was intentionally threatening now, belligerent, as if he sensed Rutledge's sudden uneasiness. Rutledge felt his own muscles tensing.

Rutledge replied, "A woman, I understand. What has she done to find herself of interest to the police?"

"None of your affair, is it?" At last the man moved out into the sunlight, and Rutledge followed, his breathing still uneven.

Damn this, he swore, fighting the claustrophobia. *Keep your mind on what you're doing, can't you?*

But Hamish, too, was responding to the man's aggressive stance, asking if he had believed the innuendoes and the letters—or was incensed by them. Rutledge thought, It was difficult to tell. He was a man who showed little in his face; he would not be easy to interrogate.

"Does she have any family? Heirs?"

"None." Uncompromising. Cold. Then, grudgingly, "None that I know of."

No mention of the boy. But he would inherit nothing . . . would he?

"Then I'll be on my way." Walking back toward the inn, Rutledge could sense the man's stare boring into his back between his shoulder blades.

If this was any example of how the townspeople felt about the woman who owned this property, it was evident that she had somehow made abiding enemies.

Which didn't fit into the picture of her that McKinstry had so glowingly painted.

Who was the woman in the eye of a controversy that might well end with a hanging?

Rutledge realized suddenly that he didn't even know her full name. Not that it mattered, he thought, but it was an indication that whatever crime she had committed—from lying to murder—she had somehow lost her identity because of it. As if, by refusing to call her by name, Duncarrick could finish what they had begun back in June—shunning her until she was without reality and finally disappeared.

What had this woman done to stir up such dark passions?

It was odd, he thought, crossing the quiet street to his car. First the venomous letters and then the one to the minister—Elliot? The finding of one body that didn't match the crime, and another that did. Persistence, patience—and what else? Luck? Or persecution?

It smacked of the latter. Hamish, in the back of his mind, agreed.

Rutledge stopped before turning the crank and looked back at The Reivers. The accused owned this inn. Did someone covet it? She had a small child to provide for, never mind whether it was rightfully hers or not. Did someone covet the child? Or want it taken away to punish the accused, a twisted revenge for a real or imagined grudge? And these were the more obvious reasons for wanting the woman in prison and out of the way. What others might there be? Was there something in the inn that no one knew about, which mattered to another person? Or was it something in the past of the accused that put another person in jeopardy? Hanging was a certain way of silencing her.

He found himself thinking of the child again. Torn away from its mother, from the only home it had known, put to live with strangers. There was a cruelty in that.

Then why hadn't she lied to protect the boy? "I don't have my marriage lines—my husband took them, to show the Army. . . ."

Why hadn't she left the town as soon as the shunning had begun? But he thought he had the answer to that—the shunning had reduced custom at the inn to the point that she might not have had the money to go away. Had that been the intent of it—?

The woman's voice behind him startled him. "Are you looking for someone?"

Rutledge turned and removed his hat. Hamish, responding to his surprise, was suddenly alert, watchful. She was tall and plump, dressed in black but young, perhaps twenty-four or -five. A little girl of six or seven held her hand.

"I was admiring the inn. I'd heard it might be for sale."

The woman shook her head. "Early days to know that!" She turned to the door of the house in front of which he'd left his car. A neighbor, then . . .

"I understand the owner is to stand trial on some charges."

Her face hardened. "She is."

He found himself asking, "Do you know the name of her barrister? I might speak with him."

"Armstrong's his name, but he doesn't live in Duncarrick. Jedburgh, I think I was told."

Rutledge smiled down at the little girl. She smiled shyly back. He wondered if she'd played with the child living in the inn but couldn't ask in front of the mother. And as if the thought had sprung from his mind to hers, the girl said in a soft, sweet voice, "I used to play with him. The little boy at The Reivers. But he's gone away. I miss him."

"Hush! You were told never to speak of that again!" the woman commanded, and the child turned her face into her mother's skirts, flushing with shame, as if she had transgressed horribly.

The woman opened the house door and went inside, shutting it firmly behind her. Shutting out Rutledge and his questions. Unwilling to gossip—to speculate—or to defend.

9

RUTLEDGE DROVE BACK TO TREVOR'S HOUSE RATHER than take a room at The Ballantyne, unwilling to move himself into Duncarrick until he'd spoken with Oliver. It was a courtesy, but often small courtesies lubricated the wheels of change. The long drive gave him time to think. That evening over dinner, he told David Trevor how he had spent his day.

Trevor smiled. "Once a policeman, always a policeman."

Rutledge grinned in return. "Blame human nature. Curiosity is man's besetting sin."

"The Garden of Eden," Trevor agreed. "Eve is always blamed for offering Adam the apple, but it's my view that he had been looking for an excuse to see how it tasted. He would have bitten into it on his own in a day or two.

"What I find interesting about the situation you described," Trevor went on, "is that I know the Chief Constable in that district. Robson. A good man. So is the fiscal, by reputation. I can't quite see Robson railroading a young woman if there was no real evidence against her. You know that Scotland is different from England in that we don't have a coroner's inquest. The procurator-fiscal and the Chief Constable, together with the officers involved, discuss the evidence and come to a decision as to whether or not there should be a trial. It isn't based on a coroner's jury that might be prejudiced for or against the suspect. And it's often decided on several levels—whether, for instance, the woman would be better off having a jury establish her innocence for all to see. Have you considered that aspect of a trial, Ian?"

Rutledge finished his soup and set down his spoon. "I have, but it seems to me that bringing her to trial—assuming of course that she's innocent of the charges—has hardened feelings against her. In the upshot, the jury might prefer to hang her."

Trevor nodded to Morag to take away his empty soup plate and said, "They'll work it out, Ian, but I'd watch my back if I were you. I've never met this Inspector Oliver, but he's certain to resent your interference—that is, if he's still smarting from his encounter with Lady Maude. And *she* could be trouble, come to that. There's a very complex relationship between parent and child, and I have a feeling you'll be damned if you do—and damned if you don't— prove conclusively that Eleanor Gray has nothing whatsoever to do with this business."

"If women sat on the jury, there would be no doubt that this young woman would be convicted—and the question is, will they bring such pressure to bear on their menfolk that the results are the same?" In his own cases, Rutledge made it a point to be absolutely certain that his evidence, clearly presented, left no room for doubt. In his mind or the jury's. But jurors were often contrary—convicting where there was only circumstantial evidence and acquitting where proof seemed indisputable.

"Burns—the fiscal—is too good a man to allow a prejudiced jury."

But was he? The woman was already set for trial on purely circumstantial evidence. What if, Rutledge thought, he himself proved that the bones on the mountainside were Eleanor Gray's and that she had borne a child before she died? The assumption would be that it was the child the accused was raising. A natural assumption—but not necessarily a true one. Would there be justice—or a miscarriage of justice? And for the child's sake, it was imperative that Rutledge got it right. He could feel tiredness seeping into his shoulders and into the muscles of his neck.

"Are ye up to it, then?" Hamish asked.

Rutledge let the subject drop. At the end of the meal, David Trevor studied him for a moment, then said, "It's still on your mind, isn't it? That problem in Duncarrick. You'll be leaving for good in the morning, I take it." There was a note of regret, barely concealed, in the pleasant voice. "I'm glad you came. You don't know how much it has meant to me to have you here."

Rutledge looked down at his plate. "I wasn't sure I could face coming back to Scotland. It seemed insurmountable, just thinking about it."

Trevor said, "Yes, it's different, isn't it?" With a sigh, he added, "I suppose a time will come when I don't listen for him in the late afternoon, just before tea. Or lie awake at night, thinking I've heard his key in the lock. Or look for him at breakfast in the morning."

But Rutledge hadn't been thinking of Ross Trevor. His mind had turned to the dead Scots soldiers who had not come back at all.

ON THE BRINK of sleep that night, the nagging doubts began.

Hamish, listening to the questions that Rutledge was mentally cataloging, said, "You canna' know the whole of it. You havena' interviewed the prisoner nor looked at where they found the victim. You havena' spoken to the neighbors nor even seen the child. You've heard only yon constable's view of the matter, and he's prejudiced in the woman's favor."

Rutledge said in defense of his doubts, "I've investigated too many murders, I know something about the way evidence comes to light. The facts here don't fit awkwardly, as they should do. Who could have known that the skeleton was in the back of the cabinet in that stable? Someone did, I'll wager! Because Oliver came back a second time to search. If he didn't know, who did?"

He turned over, feeling sleep slipping away from him.

"The inn is closed, the child is taken away, and the woman is sent to prison to stand for her trial," he went on to himself, unable to stop his mind from working. "With no impediment."

Hamish countered, "Aye, but there was no way of knowing the Yard would be brought into the case."

"Why did Lady Maude change her mind? I was nearly certain when I left there that her daughter was alive and well. *Why did she change her mind?*"

Hamish said, "She didna' strike me as frivolous or foolish."

And that, Rutledge thought, finally on the verge of sleep, was an extremely insightful analysis of Lady Maude.

THE NEXT MORNING in the rain Trevor helped Rutledge carry his luggage out to the car, then shook his hand warmly. Morag, a shawl over her head, came to embrace him, shamelessly reaching up to him. Rutledge found himself wishing that he needn't leave after all. He had found ghosts here—and affection. The ghosts he was accustomed to. Affection he was not.

The rain fell in a heavy downpour that seemed to presage winter, a coldness in the air that touched the skin as he drove back to Duncarrick.

Inspector Oliver wasn't at the police station. The constable on duty, MacNab by name, stood up warily as Rutledge introduced himself, and offered to send for Oliver. "For he's out at a farm west of town. There's been a rash of small fires that were probably set on purpose."

"No, let him finish his business. I'll be at the hotel—The Ballantyne. Tell him he can find me there." He left, wondering to himself if Constable McKinstry could put a name to the arsonist.

The hotel offered an old-fashioned but comfortable elegance that breathed Victorian respectability. The young woman behind the desk looked up as he came dripping in and smiled. "Good morning, sir! In a manner of speaking!"

He took off his hat and looked ruefully at the wet brim. "Indeed. I think I could use a drink. Then I'd like a room."

"I'll be glad to see to that for you, sir." She indicated the door to his left. "The bar parlor is through there."

"Thanks."

He went through the door and found the room filled with other refugees from the rain. The atmosphere was muggy, as if the dampness each had brought with him had settled in a cloud around them, like fog. The smell of wet wool mingled with wood smoke. Someone had lit the fire on one side of the paneled room, and it struggled to assert itself, adding measurably to the gloom. But no one paid any heed, lively conversations holding their attention instead.

Rutledge found a table by the windows that overlooked the street. He could hear the laughter from the bar, rough and male, workmen who had taken advantage of the rain to stop in for a pint.

He wondered how many of them had once patronized The Reivers.

A man with a fierce mustache came in, looked around him, and saw Rutledge. He came striding across to the table, nodded, and said, "I'm Oliver."

Rutledge got to his feet and offered his hand. Oliver's grip was strong but brief. He took the other chair at the table and beckoned to one of the barmaids. She came over, took their orders, and was gone.

Oliver stretched his feet out, looked ruefully at his wet shoes, and sighed. Then he turned to Rutledge and said, "I won't beat about the bush. It's not my way. I don't like London sending someone up here to mind my business. But it's done. I'll cooperate in any way I can."

"I'm afraid this is not my doing either. But there we are. I'd like to discuss the evidence with you when you have the time."

The barmaid brought their orders, and Oliver drank his ale, savoring it. Then he said, "The evidence isn't the problem. It's the bones. Did you learn anything at all from that termagant in Menton? I've need of it, if you have."

"Lady Maude refused to acknowledge that she'd quarreled with her daughter," Rutledge answered, "but if I were a betting man, I'd give you good odds she did. The question is, where is Eleanor Gray now? And no one seems to know. Lady Maude swears her daughter had no interest in or enthusiasm for walking in the Highlands, that there's no explanation that might put Eleanor in Glencoe or anywhere else in Scotland during 1916."

"Yes, well, mothers are like that, they shut their eyes to a good deal that they find it unpleasant to take notice of. Look at it this way—if a handsome young soldier told the daughter he'd like to spend his leave walking about in the Scottish hills, do you think she'd refuse to go? War does strange things to women—put a man in uniform, and they trust him with their virtue and their lives!"

"She'd hardly go walking in the mountains when she was nine months pregnant. Or, for that matter, find a soldier willing to take her there."

Oliver grunted. "I'm just saying that mothers don't always know their daughters. Lady Maude may think what she pleases. The fact is, it's not proof of anything."

"Why were you and the authorities prepared to arrest this local woman? London gave me the outline of the case, little more."

Oliver thought it over, then said, "It was this way. The anonymous letters started in June, as far as we can tell. And what I found curious about the dozen or so brought to my attention is that people believed them. At any rate, her neighbors began to shun Mrs. MacLeod, as she called herself then. A few of them finally stepped forward, taking the letters to the minister, Mr. Elliot, but not to ask if the accusations were true or not. They were more concerned about their own souls. And after some thought and prayer, Mr. Elliot came to the police."

"The letters fell on fertile ground, then. Why? Was this woman not liked or accepted in Duncarrick?"

"If you'd asked me just a few months ago, I'd have said she was well liked. I never heard of any problems—moral or otherwise. And I hear most things. The general feeling seems to be that the young woman must have lied to her aunt, because Ealasaid MacCallum was an upright woman who would never have countenanced a falsehood told to her acquaintance. She'd have been the first to say 'My niece has gotten herself into trouble, but I've brought her here to give her a chance to repent and atone. It's my Christian duty.' And people would have respected that, you see."

Hamish said, "Aye, that's the way it would ha' been done."

But without compassion, Rutledge responded. *A cold and judging second chance.*

Oliver went on. "Mr. Elliot then told me privately that a number of people had spoken to him about the young woman. Before the letters started. One man found himself tempted by her and was afraid for his soul. A young woman saw in her an instrument of the devil because she had turned the head of a young man who frequented the inn. Another woman found her far too warm to the child, saying that it was no way to bring up a lad. 'Spare the rod' was the message. And Mr. Elliot had already tried to speak to Miss MacDonald about her attendance at services. She'd told him that her duties at the inn sometimes kept her up late and she'd found it hard to be prompt on those Sunday mornings. He had thought at the time that it was not a proper excuse."

"I see," Rutledge commented into the silence that expected a response. But what he saw was a judgment, a sense that the accused had not lived up to the high standards others had set for themselves and, by extension, for her.

Oliver looked across the room at another table, something else on his mind, then picked up the thread of his narrative. "On the heels of the anonymous letters came another correspondence, and that damned more than it exonerated. I thought, as did the Chief Constable, that it bore looking into. Where there is a pattern—"

Where there was smoke . . .

"And that's when I sent my constable—who knew her well enough to question her gently—to ask for her marriage lines. She as much as told him there weren't any, and when he asked if she'd submit to an examination by a physician in regard to the birth of the child in question, she adamantly refused. McKinstry had no choice but to conduct a search of the premises but failed to carry it out to my satisfaction, and I came back. Instead of a buried woman, I came across a man a hundred years dead, and it made me a laughingstock, I can tell you. Dr. Murchison had more to say than I cared to hear on the subject."

"Aye," Hamish remarked, "it touched his pride." Rutledge thought that that was possible and might account for Oliver's unflagging determination to find answers to the questions raised about the woman.

"I sent out a request for information on any missing persons, and that's when I heard about the corpse found up the glen. I'd just come back from viewing it, when Menton contacted me with the information they had on the Gray woman. And fool that I was, I set off to England with the feeling that I was bringing the loose ends tidily together, and got my head bitten off instead!"

He regarded Rutledge for several seconds, as if weighing

how his view of the situation had been received. Apparently satisfied, he asked, "Can you tell me what you're considering as the next step?"

"I don't know," Rutledge replied with honesty. "You've most certainly done all that was required of you, and more. What has the accused told you?"

"Precious little. Only that she's committed no crime, and she's worried for the child. I'm not surprised she feels an attachment there. Women have a natural mothering instinct whether they've borne a child of their own or not. It's to her credit that she's raised him to the best of her ability. Mr. Elliot has closely questioned the lad, and he appears to know his Bible stories. The boy's particularly fond of Moses and the bulrushes, it seems. And Joseph's coat of many colors." He smiled. "Ealasaid MacCallum, the accused's aunt, made the lad a bathrobe in multicolored stripes, and he's very fond of it. We let him keep it. And the little stuffed dog the accused made out of one of her great-uncle's wool socks. There was no harm in that either. It seems to comfort him. He's cried more than a lad going on three should. But then, he believes the woman to be his mother. It will take some time to convince him otherwise."

Rutledge found himself thinking of Morag and the expression on her face when he'd said that the child was not the concern of the law. The words had been spoken in another context, that of dealing with a woman charged with murder. But Morag had taken them to heart and let him know it. She'd always had a warm feeling for young things, children and puppies and kittens—even an orphaned lamb that Ross Trevor, age seven, had insisted on hand-rearing. Rutledge wondered what she would have to say about Oliver's remarks. *It will take some time to convince him otherwise.* Left unsaid was the corollary: By the time she's hanged, he'll not be mourning for her.

Would anyone?

"Why do you think she took on the responsibility of this child in the first place? A single young woman? Surely it would have been simpler to carry him directly to the nearest hospital for foundlings."

"Who can say? She might have known the father. I'm told that when she wanted to represent herself as a married woman, she took the name of a soldier of her acquaintance, one dead on the Somme. Easy enough to do if he can't come back and deny he wed her. She might have been jealous of him and wanted the child she couldn't have by him."

Changing the subject, Rutledge said, "Is it possible for me to speak to the accused?"

"To what end?" Warily.

"She might—without realizing it—have more to tell us. No one has brought up the name of Eleanor Gray in her hearing?"

"No." Oliver drained his glass.

"It's a place to start," Rutledge told him, his voice reasonable.

"Then finish your pint. I'll take you there."

AS HE FOLLOWED Oliver out to his motorcar, Rutledge had an odd sense of foreboding. It was something he couldn't explain either logically or emotionally, just a sense of—foreboding. For no reason at all, he remembered the dream he'd had in London, and felt cold. Hamish, reacting to the tension in Rutledge's mind, was there, a fierce presence that seemed to walk at his shoulder and condemn.

It wasn't until the door of the cell swung open, and the scent of lavender reached him, that he turned his mind toward the woman he had come here to see. His thoughts in a turmoil, he had nearly forgotten about her as an individual.

"It's remembering that poor devil in his cell in Dorset— Mowbray," Hamish offered in explanation.

But was it?

The woman in the room had risen from its single chair and turned to face them. She was pale, circles beneath her eyes, her shoulders braced as if anticipating a blow. The dress she was wearing, a soft gray, enhanced the paleness and made her seem almost invisible against the grayer walls.

Even as Inspector Oliver made the introductions, Rutledge had lost the thread of everything. And Hamish in his mind was railing like the banshees of hell, a cry of grief and torment and repudiation that rent the soul.

Rutledge had seen her picture many times in France. She was the woman Corporal Hamish MacLeod had loved and expected to marry. The woman whose name Hamish had cried in the last instant before the rifles fired and he fell dying in the mud. Fiona. Fiona MacDonald. Who now called herself Fiona MacLeod.

Rutledge was unprepared, defenseless.

How could he have known? How could he have connected a Fiona MacLeod of Duncarrick with the face of a woman he'd thought lived far from here? It was a common enough name in the Highlands—

How could he have known—?

Fiona MacDonald. Who would in truth have been Fiona MacLeod if he hadn't shot the man she loved.

The woman in the dream he'd had in London . . .

10

───────◆───────

SHE WAS LOOKING AT RUTLEDGE, A SADNESS IN HER face.

Hamish had told him so much about this woman during the war. It was hard to imagine her now as the girl haying on a hot August day in 1914. Or walking through a small Highland village beside a tall man dressed as a soldier, saying good-bye. Hamish had cried out her name over the roar of the guns as the firing squad shot him down. He had wanted to die—but not to lie in France, far from the ancient churchyard where his ancestors rested. He had not wanted to live—but he had wanted to come back to her.

Rutledge's mind was whirling. Did Fiona MacDonald sometimes feel Hamish's presence, just as Rutledge had felt Ross Trevor's in The Lodge outside Edinburgh? It was odd how some people left their stamp so vividly on a time or a place. And she would know, better than most, how profoundly Hamish had loved the Highlands. Had she wept into her pillow because there was no marker where she could take her grief? Or had she walked the hills and felt closer to Hamish than she could have in any churchyard?

This brief, silent, strained confrontation affected Rutledge's perception of Fiona MacDonald. Of the crime she'd committed—was alleged to have committed. Of the debt he owed to Hamish MacLeod for being the instrument of his corporal's death. It magnified the burden he'd carried back from the war in the dark reaches of his mind.

He turned around and walked out of the room without a word, and Oliver, startled, was left standing in the doorway, staring uncertainly at the woman Rutledge had come to see.

Rutledge, breathing hard, his heart pounding, his mind a blank, blundered into the corner of a desk and then somehow found his way to the outside door. He flung it open and stepped out into the rain, oblivious.

It was some minutes before he realized that Oliver stood just behind him, sheltered by the doorway, saying something to him—

"I'm sorry—" He kept his back to Oliver, afraid of what could be read in his face. He added lamely, realizing it was expected, "Suddenly I needed air—" He could feel the rain wetting the shoulders of his overcoat, and his hair felt heavy with it, matted flat to his skull. How long had he been standing there—for God's sake, how long—! He couldn't remember; he couldn't think; he couldn't clear the horror out of his mind.

And Hamish, after that first cry, had gone silent, a black weight on his spirit, like the weight of the dead.

Rutledge forced himself to swallow the sour taste in his throat, and after another minute turned to Oliver. "I'm sorry," he said again. And then, slowly taking a grip on his emotions, "I—It must have been something I ate—"

"I've never seen a man turn so white. I thought you'd seen a ghost."

"No . . ." Fiona MacDonald was no ghost.

What am I going to do? he asked himself silently. *I must call Bowles, tell him I want to be relieved—*

But that was addressing his own needs. What of hers?

What, in God's name, of hers?

What if he failed her and she hanged? He'd have no choice but to kill himself: he couldn't add that burden to the other guilt he carried. It would be a bitter defeat, after all he'd striven to recover of his own past, to fall prey to Hamish's . . .

It wouldn't be a German pistol. It would be his own.

Oliver was asking him something. About going back to the hotel? A glass of water? He couldn't remember.

"No, I'll be fine—"

"Then come in out of this rain, man! I'm getting wet through, standing here!" The door slammed shut.

Rutledge turned, opened it again, and walked back into the front room of the police station. He said, "I'm all right."

"You don't look it. Here, sit down."

Rutledge took the chair shoved his way and tried to sit, but his muscles seemed taut and stiff, and he had to force them to obey his command. Oliver thrust a glass of water into his hand. Rutledge made a pretense of swallowing it, afraid he'd choke, making a worse fool of himself, his throat too tight to get it down.

And slowly his wits seemed to come back to him. The room took shape, the four walls painted an ugly brown, the desks and chairs older than he was, the single lamp in the ceiling casting glaring shadows over everything. Oliver's face, expectant and watchful, waited for him to make a decision.

Rutledge took a breath. "All right. Let's return to the cell." In the back of his head, Hamish was a thunderous roar, and the ache that was swelling in its wake was nearly blinding.

"You're sure? Frankly, I've no wish to have you casting up accounts all over my floors!"

Rutledge came close to laughing, a wild reaction to his own tension. Nausea was the least of his troubles. "I won't do that."

He followed Oliver down the passage that led to what Rutledge saw now must have been a kitchen in its day: a large room with no furnishings except for a narrow cot, a chair, and four bare walls. The chimney that once stood against one of them was closed off, the iron plate that had lain on the floor before the hearth now turned up and bolted over the opening. Behind a screen were the chamber pot and a table for water and towels. The room was cold, and Fiona MacDonald had pulled a shawl around her shoulders.

Her own face was white as Oliver made some apology for their abrupt departure some ten minutes earlier. Rutledge realized that she must be expecting some news of her trial. Or—of her child. The tenseness in her shoulders betrayed her as she waited for Rutledge to speak.

"Inspector Rutledge has come from London to look into the identity of bones discovered up the mountainside in Glencoe. He has questions he wishes to put to you."

"Yes, very well," she said, her voice soft, hardly more than a whisper.

Rutledge had no idea what he had expected to learn. His mind was a blank wall of nothing. He found himself looking away from her, not wanting to meet her eyes. But he managed to speak to her, feeling his way. "You've been asked before, Miss MacDonald—but can you give us any information that might help us find the child's real mother? Or failing that, if she's dead, her family? Surely you must be concerned for his well-being, and he'd be far happier with a grandmother or an aunt than in a foster home."

"Will he?" she asked. "I've killed no one. I expect to return to my home and to my child." Her voice was resolute, but there was fear in her eyes.

"If he's not your child," Rutledge said gently, "I doubt you'll be allowed to keep him, even if you're found not guilty. A young woman having to make her own way, with no husband or family of her own, could be considered unfit to make a suitable home."

"Then I'll marry," she said with resignation. "I'll make a home, give him a father!"

"You have no claim upon the boy. The law has its own views on the care of orphans." He tried to keep his voice quiet, without condemnation.

Fiona bit her lip. "I don't believe you!"

"Everything has changed, you see. When you first came to Duncarrick, you were thought to be a married woman, a widow. No one had any reason to question your right to the child. Now there is every reason."

"No, I'm the only mother he's *known*—!"

Changing his approach, Rutledge asked, "Did you write that letter to Mr. Elliot? The anonymous one mailed from Glasgow?"

Oliver stirred behind him. He hadn't thought to ask that.

But the shock in Fiona MacDonald's face answered any doubts Rutledge might have had.

"No!" There was passion in her voice, not mere certainty. Why? Then she added, as if to cover it, "The letter damned me."

"You might have realized that those notes were bearing fruit. You might have wanted to protect yourself."

"Then surely I'd have gone about it with more wisdom! I—I can't—this letter is something I dream about in the night. It frightens me. I have been shown it and cannot recognize the handwriting. I have asked Mr. Elliot if he knew who had sent it, and he claims he doesn't. But he tells me to throw myself on the mercy of the courts and save my immortal soul. I've asked the police if they've discovered the sender, and they tell me they don't need to know who it is. But surely the author matters to them as much as it matters to *me*!"

"Do you suppose Eleanor Gray might have written it? With the best of intentions, unaware of the use to which it might be put?"

The name failed to register. "Why should a stranger defend me? I don't know any Grays. Certainly not an Eleanor Gray. Ask her, not me."

He hesitated. His head was aching so severely, he could

hardly breathe, much less think clearly. "There's very good reason for us to believe that Eleanor Gray gave birth to the child you have been raising and called your son."

There was a flicker of something across her face, gone so quickly that Rutledge wasn't sure he'd seen it. Humor? No, it was something else.

"What do you want from me? Lies? I don't *know* this woman."

"Perhaps you didn't know her name. Was her death an accident? Or an illness—the result of childbirth?"

She smiled sadly. "If this Eleanor Gray is dead, how could she have written to Mr. Elliot or anyone else?"

Touché! "The Grays have money. They are able to give the boy far more than you ever can. It would be possible, I think, for arrangements to be made to visit him. You'd not lose touch entirely. In a crowded asylum for orphans he won't receive the love and attention he needs. Surely that weighs with you?"

"It weighs with me, Inspector," she said tiredly, "but not enough to lie to you. I don't know Eleanor Gray. I know nothing about when or how she might have died, and I can't tell you if she gave birth to a child. There is nothing I can do for her family except tell the truth. And I have." There was disappointment in her tone. "Is that what you wanted—what brought you here? The need of a comforting story to take to a grieving woman? I also grieve, and no one will tell me about my son. Whether he's well or ill, whether he remembers me or has been made to forget me." Her face nearly crumpled, but she fought for and won composure. He could see the tears in her eyes.

"He's well," he answered, ignoring the smothered protest behind him. She had a right to know. She might be a murderess—

The thought stopped him cold.

RUTLEDGE COULDN'T REMEMBER returning to the hotel and picking up the key to his room.

The woman at the desk, true to her word, had chosen well. Cream walls and white lace curtains were set off by the sea blue of the bedding, the patterned carpet, and the chintz-covered chairs. Stiff silk flowers stood in a blue-and-cream bowl, and there was a blue-trimmed cream shade over the single lamp on the corner table. He hardly noticed. But there was a pair of windows looking down on the square, where rain-wet pavement glistened and shop lights cast gaily colored splotches across the puddles.

He lay on his bed, staring at the ceiling and trying to remember what he had said to Fiona MacDonald—and how she had answered him. His mind refused to give him what he wanted, and in the background, Hamish was such a force that the voice in his head seemed to scream louder than the sounds of people or vehicles outside or the nearby church clock sounding the hours one by one.

THE NEXT MORNING, when Rutledge arrived at the police station, Constable Pringle was there alone. A ruddy man with sandy hair and the freckles that matched. He stood and formally introduced himself as Rutledge gave his name.

"Inspector Oliver isn't in—"

"I've only come for five minutes. Oliver and I interviewed the prisoner yesterday. I have a question or two that arose while I was reading over my notes."

"I shouldn't leave my desk," the constable said, uncertain.

"No, that's all right. I can find my own way."

Pringle went to a cupboard and took down a ring of keys. "This one." He handed Rutledge the lot, singling out a heavy one in the middle.

"Thank you."

With Hamish ominously silent, like a dark cloud foretelling a storm, Rutledge walked down the passage to the room where Fiona MacDonald was kept. A plump woman in a blue uniform was scrubbing the last few feet of the passage, her face red with effort. She moved aside as Rutledge passed and went back to her task as he set the key in the lock.

He found that his hands were shaking.

Opening the door, he saw that Fiona had risen to meet him, the wary expression on her face changing to surprise. "Inspector," she said carefully.

He closed the door to give them some privacy.

"Last evening—" he began, and then dropped the pretense that he had been going over his notes. He said instead, "I've come to clarify a point or two. Do you wish to have your barrister summoned?"

"I'm more afraid of Mr. Armstrong than of you," she answered. "The way he stares at me, I feel . . . unclean. He despises women, I think. We are weak vessels in his sight, better left uncreated." She tried to smile and failed.

There was a brief silence. She studied him, and he wondered what she saw in his face. But he didn't want to know.

"Did you ask for this case?" The words seemed drawn from her against her will.

"No. I was summoned to deal with the missing Gray woman. Until I came through that door—" He stopped. Something had altered in her face. A tightness, as if to protect herself from hurt. Had she expected, when he arrived with Oliver the previous night and she recognized his name, that he had come to help her? That somehow he had learned she was charged with murder and felt a duty to look into the matter?

A frail strand of hope—

Hamish must have written to her about his commanding officer and what Rutledge had done in civilian life. And Rutledge had written to her, too, giving her the news of Hamish's death, offering empty platitudes of sympathy and concern: "He spoke of you often. You were his bulwark and shield throughout the fighting, and he would have wanted you to know how bravely he died for his country—"

She had believed the comforting lies. She had cherished them—

He added quickly, "No one told me—the Yard, you see, didn't know who you were. My superior was concerned with the Gray family."

"Would you have come—if you'd known?"

He didn't answer that directly. He said, "It wouldn't have been my choice—to come or not. It has to do with protocol, not personal decisions."

"I still have your letter," she told him. "Did *he* write, before the end?"

Hamish had written a letter that last night, but afterward it had been stained with his blood and with Rutledge's. The Army had not seen fit to send it. Someone had told Rutledge as much a month or more later.

Heavy censorship kept the people at home ignorant of the suffering and despair in France. The expectation was that loved ones would offer encouragement and hope to the brave men they'd sent off to battle, and bolster their courage—if they didn't know the truth. The men themselves wrote home what they thought their families could bear to hear. It was a vicious circle of lies that was classified as military necessity: "Good for morale."

In that last letter, had Hamish told the woman he loved so deeply the truth about his death? Or had he told her sweet lies that would prepare her for the news that would be brought to her? A condemned man was not always circumspect. He wrote what he felt and believed in in those last dark hours. And Hamish had been torn apart—he had wanted to die, before he was forced to lead more men back into the face of certain death.

Rutledge said, "Our sector was heavily shelled. Letters and the like are hard to find in the mud, afterward." He didn't add that buried men disappeared in the stinking black depths as well, eaten by rats, used as lumber underfoot until someone could retrieve the decaying corpses.

Rains that last autumn had brought to light a private from Skye, listed as missing for weeks. Even the dogs hadn't found him. As the water sloshed thickly about the trench, something had tripped up a sergeant, sending him cursing and sprawling. As he got dripping to his feet, he reached out for what he thought was a piece of shell and realized too late that it was a shoulder blade. The rest of the rotting corpse had come up bit by bit, like an overdone chicken falling off the bone. The smell had been unbearable. But they had had to stand there in the snaking line of the trenches for another thirty-six hours before they were relieved.

Rutledge could hardly tell Fiona MacDonald the truth. His letter to her, as Hamish's commanding officer—like so many others—had been a tissue of lies devised to comfort and to heal and to offer pride of sacrifice in the place of loss. A tissue of lies . . . They had come back now to shame him.

He could feel Hamish's anger, could feel the torment he carried within himself, like a second soul.

"My son is named for you," she said into the silence. "Have they told you? Ian Hamish MacLeod. Hamish would have liked that. He spoke so warmly of you—he admired you."

Rutledge, his mind reeling, heard Hamish cry out. The words were lost, but he thought for an instant that she had surely heard the voice and recognized it. The strength of it was echoing off the walls around them.

"What's wrong?" She stepped forward, reaching out to touch him. "Are you ill again? Yesterday, I thought—"

"No." It was curt, an effort of will without embellishment. In the silence he could hear her quick breathing and the *chunk* of the cleaning woman's brush scrubbing outside the door. His heart pounded in his ears. With fierce determination, he got a grip on himself. "I'm sorry," he said. "I try not to remember the war."

And Hamish said quite clearly, "You remember it every hour of every day. You always will. It's the cost of surviving."

And it was true.

"I CAME TO talk to you about the child's mother."

Rutledge picked up the thread of what he'd come to say, forcing himself to shut out everything else. Neither Fiona nor he could afford to lose track of the police inquiry again. "You must surely see that you are condemning yourself by refusing to give the authorities any information about her. If she's dead, explaining why and how she died can save your life."

"The police said that to me. How can they know? What if I tell them I choked the life out of her? Or pushed her out a window? Or gave her a drink that muddled her wits and left her to die in the cold?"

"Did you do these things?"

"No!" she cried. "If I had, how could I have loved the child so deeply? Every time I look into his eyes, I see his mother's face. How could I hold him and remember *her* dying by my hand? She trusted me with the most precious thing in the world to her. You went to war," she went on, tears filling her eyes, "and you suffered horribly. But do you *ever* think about what it must be like for *us* to love a man who will never come back, never give us the children we might have borne, never hold us in the night, never watch our sons and our daughters marry? Never carry a grandchild in our arms or grow old together? Do you know what it is like to want someone so terribly that you ache, and dream, and wake up to find that it's over?" The tears fell and she brushed them away angrily. *"I have given this country my future too.* And all that was left to me, another woman's child, you've taken as well."

It seemed to be an admission that the woman was dead. But as he looked into the dark eyes and saw the anguish there, he read something else too—fear. Not for herself, he was sure it wasn't that. Nor was it guilt.

He struggled to concentrate, called on his intuition to bridge the gap between what he had seen—and what it meant.

Silence came back to him. Nothing but silence. And then—

The woman, he realized suddenly, must still be *alive*. The child's mother. And for some reason, even to save her own life, Fiona MacDonald dared not name her.

11

———◆———

LOCKING THE CELL BEHIND HIM, RUTLEDGE STRODE
past the woman collecting her brushes in the emptied pail
and went out into the main room, where Constable
Pringle sat reading through a stack of reports. He looked up
as Rutledge handed him the key ring.

"All settled, then?" he asked.

"For the time being," Rutledge answered.

He thanked the man and went out into the street. The
day was fine, and there were people everywhere, attending to
whatever business brought them out on a fair morning.
Carts and wagons and lorries vied with motorcars for space
on the roadway, and he heard a vendor shouting as a passing
horse snatched at an apple from the baskets piled high on a
trundle. Rutledge felt alone.

Hamish railed on in wild fury, begging, cajoling, pleading for Fiona, obsessed with what had been done to her. And
helpless to change it.

As the warmth of the sun touched his face, Rutledge took a

deep breath, willing the tension to subside, willing Hamish into silence, closing his mind to the harshly sharp image of the woman he'd left in the comparative darkness of the small room at the back of the police station. Walking helped, each stride seeming to keep pace with the rhythm of Hamish's voice, forcing it to remain just out of sight behind him.

What had appeared to be a search for Eleanor Gray had become a complex confrontation with the past and a young woman who might be cleared—or damned—by what Scotland Yard found out about both women.

It was a grave responsibility. It was also a professional conflict.

Rutledge turned toward the hotel, seeking sanctuary without realizing it, seeking the peace and quiet to think. Everything he'd learned here had changed its shape, throwing evidence and emotion and belief into a maelstrom of doubt. And then something Hamish was saying caught at his attention. He found himself listening now.

"It began as a moral issue," Hamish told him. "That's what you told yon constable. And who better to ask than the man who didna' ken what to do about it?"

Mr. Elliot. The minister.

Rutledge reached the main square and went away from the hotel toward the church rising tall and dark from the pavement. Bare of ornament, it seemed to thrust heavily toward the sky, built by men who found in their faith a strong and abiding force but very little beauty. There was no churchyard here, but he thought it must lie behind the building. He'd noticed a wedge of green grass surrounded by a low wall of the same stone as the church, broaching on the street behind. And when he came to the corner of the church, he realized he was right. Headstones marched in tidy rows almost to the apse.

He paused to read the board by the main doors and at the same time saw the small wooden sign on the Victorian house just beyond the church. "Pastor" was written there in Gothic lettering.

He walked on and knocked at the house door. A woman opened it to him. She was young and frail, but she answered briskly enough, "Yes, sir?"

"I'd like to speak to Mr. Elliot if I may. Is he in?"

"He's just come back from the kirk," she replied. "Step in and I'll ask if he's receiving visitors just now. May I give him your name?"

"Rutledge."

"Thank you, sir." He could almost hear her mentally adding, *You must be the policeman from London.* She disappeared down a dark passage, the wood paneling there and where he stood in the high-ceilinged hall bare of decoration but highly polished. It offered a modicum of brightness in the general gloom. The only portrait was a formidable man with a graying patriarchal beard, wearing the garb of a churchman of two hundred years or more before. The eyes were dark and very stern, but the mouth was soft, almost gentle. A face that offered both judgment and compassion.

From down the passage Rutledge heard a light knock, and a door opened. After a moment, the young woman returned.

"Come this way, sir, if you please." She led him toward the back of the house, where he found himself in a large room so crowded with furnishings and shelves of books that it seemed on the brink of collapsing in upon itself.

The man at the cluttered desk was of medium height and build, but he possessed a hatchet nose and the eyes of a fanatic—hot with the belief that he had answers to whatever questions confronted his flock. He was stony-faced, but the eyes were alive with his righteousness. Hamish, a Calvinist to the core, muttered, "He'd burn heretics at the stake if he could. . . ." And there was no praise in the words, only warning.

Elliot held out his hand to Rutledge but didn't rise. Rutledge took the dry, stiff fingers and shook them briefly.

"What may I do for you, Inspector?"

"I've been sent to Scotland to look into this business of the woman who called herself Mrs. MacLeod," he began easily. "The child's true mother may have been English."

"I see." Elliot frowned. "It could be possible. Yes."

"Miss MacDonald, I understand, attended services in your church. Have you visited her since her arrest? As her pastor?"

"Only once." His eyes moved around the room. "Nor has she asked for my counsel and guidance since."

"Surely even she is worth saving?" Rutledge spoke quietly.

The fierce pale blue eyes came back to Rutledge's face. "Redemption is not granted. It is earned. She refuses to confess her sins."

Plural. "Sins?"

"They are many. Arrogance. Pride. Wantonness—"

It was noticeable that murder was not listed among them. Hamish pointed that out, growling. He had taken an instant dislike to the minister. Rutledge made an effort to maintain his own objectivity. But he found himself thinking that this man had used the anonymous letters to punish the recipient, not the sender. Which seemed an odd choice for a man of God . . .

"If the child is not hers, how can she be accused of wanton behavior?"

"I have watched a man sink to his knees and beg God's forgiveness for the desire she had aroused in him, and agonize over his soul's danger. He is a decent man, and he cannot bear the guilt."

"Surely that is his sin to expiate, not hers."

Elliot smiled coldly. "Women have always been temptresses. Adam ate the apple at Eve's behest. He fell from grace with God, and our own Savior came to redeem that mortal sin. Redeem it on the cross with His flesh. Fiona MacDonald is a weak vessel. The spirit does not move in her. Such women are to be pitied."

"From what I hear, no one has accused Miss MacDonald

of being a poor mother. She loves the child she called her son." He found he couldn't speak the boy's name.

"All the more reason to keep the lad from her. A God-fearing family will soon wipe away all memory of her and bring him up as he should be brought up. She has no claim upon him, after all."

"Do you believe she's guilty of the charges brought against her?"

"Oh, yes. Beyond any question." Elliot rubbed his chin. "I have seen the faces of my flock turn against her. One by one. It is a judgment."

"Then she will surely hang."

Elliot looked him up and down. "Very likely. Why are you convinced of her innocence?"

Startled, Rutledge said, "Am I?"

"Oh, yes," Elliot said again, steepling his fingers. "I haven't been pastor of my flock these thirty-two years without learning how to read the men and women who come to stand before me. You are a guilt-ridden man, haunted by the war. And you believe you have seen the face of evil on the battlefield and learned to recognize it. Have you, indeed! You watched *bodies* shatter and minds breaking, in France. But I have watched souls destroyed."

Rutledge unexpectedly found himself remembering Cornwall, and Olivia Marlowe. "It must be far worse, in its fashion," he agreed evenly. "But since I am not God, I don't presume to judge my fellow human beings. I want to find out the truth about Fiona MacDonald. It's my duty as a policeman. To her. To you. To society."

"Examine your own motives first, Inspector, and the truth will become clear. Wishful thinking is not the truth. Be careful that your own loneliness does not become a trap of error."

Rutledge could hear Hamish, a rumble of hostility. Whether against him or against Elliot, it was hard to say. He said, in response to Hamish, *I see her as you saw her—*

Aloud he said carefully, "We've wandered from the purpose of this conversation. I'm here to ask if you can give me any information about the accused that will help me find the boy's mother."

"The boy's mother is dead. Otherwise she would have come forward to take her child. There has been widespread publicity. By now she would surely have come."

"What if—for very good reasons—she can't step forward?"

Elliot picked up a book and put it down again, signaling that the interview was over. "Then she is an unnatural mother. A tigress will defy death for her young. No, I am satisfied beyond a shadow of a doubt that the poor woman died at Fiona MacDonald's hands, giving her son life. May God rest her soul!"

As the young woman—the housekeeper, he thought—saw him to the door, Rutledge paused on the threshold and asked, "Do you know Fiona MacDonald?"

She hesitated, casting an eye uneasily over her shoulder and down the passage before saying, "Yes, indeed. She and Miss MacCallum—her aunt—were very good to me when I was ill. It was—I nearly died. Fiona sat beside me and held my hand through the night, until I was out of danger the next morning."

It was on the tip of his tongue to ask what she had been ill of. But the pleading look in her eyes stopped him. She had taken her courage in both hands to put in a good word for the accused—a kindness for a kindness.

"Do you know her—um—child?"

"Oh, indeed. Such a pretty lad! And well-mannered. I worry what's to become of Ian now. But no one will tell me."

"He'll be well cared for. I'll see to that." The words came out of their own volition. He hadn't meant to say them.

Hamish growled something that Rutledge didn't catch. He let it go.

"I'd like to think so. Such a shame that Miss MacCallum

isn't alive. She'd have set this all to rights. She was that sort of person. It was Miss MacCallum who found this position for me. Mr. Elliot's housekeeper had died of pleurisy."

Rutledge would have liked to ask Hamish about Ealasaid MacCallum. But there had been no mention of her the long night that he and the condemned man had spent talking in the guttering light of a candle.

"Is Mr. Elliot a good man to work for?" Rutledge asked instead, curious.

The young woman's face flushed blotchily. "He does God's work. I try to be as quiet as I can. But I'm sometimes clumsy and in the way."

Which no doubt meant that Elliot was a demanding bastard on his own turf and made her life wretched. Rutledge found Hamish agreeing to that. Hamish, apparently, had seen very little to approve of in the minister.

"Do you live here?" Rutledge asked, concerned for her.

"That wouldn't be fitting! Mr. Elliot is a widower. I have a room at the top of the road there, above the milliner's shop. Miss Tait offered it to me." She pointed with a small, thin finger.

"Were you surprised when the rumors began about Miss MacDonald?"

"I never was told them," she said naively. "Not until much later. People don't confide in me, not often."

No, this writer of poisonous letters appeared to have chosen each recipient with an eye to inflicting the most damage on Fiona MacDonald's reputation. The thin, frightened housekeeper to the minister was not likely to sway the citizens of Duncarrick with her views on any subject.

"Thank you—I'm afraid I don't know your name . . ." He left the sentence unfinished.

"Dorothea MacIntyre, sir," she told him shyly. "Will that be all, sir?"

"Yes. If—er—Mr. Elliot should ask, I wanted to know only if you'd received one of the letters."

"I'm grateful, sir!" She closed the door softly behind him

as he stepped out into the street. The sacrificial lamb, he thought. Too poor to be anything but dependent on the generosity of others, afraid of her shadow, and well aware of her duty, having had a lifetime of charity to teach it to her.

RUTLEDGE WENT BACK the way he'd come, passed The Ballantyne without stopping, and searched out the milliner's shop he'd seen the day before. Where Dorothea MacIntyre lived.

A silver bell rang genteelly as he opened the door. The woman arranging hats on a stand in the back looked up, then walked briskly to meet him. "May I help you, sir?" She cast a swift glance over her merchandise, and then waited with folded hands for him to speak.

It was a woman's shop, intimate and yet vividly decorated with almost Parisian flair, oddly out of tune with Duncarrick. Orange and peach and shades of lavender, with a strong pink thread drawing it all together.

Hamish said, "I'd no' like to hear what Mr. Elliot thinks o' the colors." He himself seemed to be of two minds about them.

The shop carried lace collars, gloves in kid or cotton, stockings, some twenty or so hats in every style from drab to elegant, handkerchiefs with dainty edging, shirtwaists, and what Rutledge took to be undergarments, discreetly folded into brightly painted boxes set along one wall.

The woman herself, tall and boldly attractive, seemed the antithesis of Dorothea MacIntyre. Rutledge wondered if Ealasaid MacCallum might have found a haven here for the girl, someone who would play dragon at the gate.

"Inspector Rutledge," he said, "Scotland Yard. I won't keep you. I'm searching for the mother of the child Fiona MacDonald calls"—he hesitated—"Ian MacLeod. I'm asking young women who might have known her if she had at any time confided in them."

"Are you, indeed?" Her eyes were angry suddenly. "Well,

if Fiona had seen fit to confide in me, why should I rush to tell you whatever might have been said between us? It's ridiculous to expect anything of the kind. You're a policeman. You should be able to do your duty without my help!"

Hamish said, "Aye, but then, she doesn't know you, does she? Or how well or ill you do your duty!"

"I'm not," Rutledge said gently, "looking for evidence to convict her. Only for evidence of the child's parentage so that he can be returned to his mother's family. Or, failing that, to his father's."

She turned away. "I have better things to do with my time than provide you with local gossip. I don't particularly like Fiona MacDonald. Anyone will tell you that. On the other hand, I think she's been wretchedly treated, and I'm not going to be one of those throwing stones."

"Why didn't you like her?"

"I thought we might become allies. We were alike in one thing, at least. We didn't squeeze dutifully into the rigid mold of Duncarrick. Silly notion, as it turned out. She kept to herself. I suppose that's understandable in light of what's happened since, but at the time I felt—betrayed. As if she'd turned her back on me, preferring instead to ingratiate herself with her aunt's friends. Apparently, she didn't succeed very well, did she? In the end they turned their backs on her!"

"Did you receive one of those anonymous letters?"

Her laughter pealed out, harsh and startling in the ambiance of the shop. "I am more likely to be the subject than the recipient of such things. In point of fact, I've sometimes wondered why they targeted Fiona rather than me. There are people in this town who would gladly see the back of me." She gestured at the walls and the hangings that shut off the back room of the shop for privacy, their flamboyance almost a defiance. "But I'm trapped here. I inherited the shop, and I don't have the money to walk away from Duncarrick and start again elsewhere. I lived in London for a time— worked there before the war and for two years of the fighting, learning my craft from a Frenchwoman who had come from Paris to design hats in London. She closed her shop—no one had a taste for extravagant hats, no one wore them anymore, the war changed that. Women made do with what they had or refurbished them themselves. And I came here. This place had stood empty for nearly three years—it had been a haberdashery." With an angry shake of the head, she added, "Why am I telling you this!"

Hamish said, "It's the way you listen, I'm thinking. People forget you're a policeman—I did mysel' many and many a time!"

Rutledge asked, more as a shot in the dark than with the expectation of an answer, "In London, did you by any chance know Eleanor Gray?"

She shrugged. "I knew who she was. But we moved in different circles. I had no interest in becoming a suffragette. I didn't find it an attractive prospect to be dragged off to prison and force-fed by beefy matrons with a taste for sadism."

"Is she still in London? Or has she gone elsewhere?"

"The Honorable Miss Gray was as unlikely to confide in me as Fiona MacDonald is. Why, is she a friend of yours? Is that why you're looking for her?" She studied him with interest, deciding that he was a very attractive man despite the thinness and the haunted eyes. "Men did seem to interest her more than women did. It was odd, she could collect them by the droves if she was in the mood to talk. Women bored her. Eleanor Gray was one of those people others gossiped about. What she did, what she wore, where she went. I doubt if a quarter of it was true, but it was fun to pass along. But you haven't answered my question."

Rutledge smiled. "No, I've never met her. Did you ever hear gossip that she was preparing to become a doctor?"

"No, but I wouldn't have been surprised if I had. She was a very handsome woman, she had more money than she knew what to do with, and her bloodlines went back to William the Conqueror—or Alfred the Great, for all I know.

And yet—there was something that burned in her. A passion. I was never told what it was, but she seemed to waste a good deal of energy on makeshift enthusiasms. Like suffragism. And then the war itself. She was always manning one of the canteens for soldiers, always visiting the hospitals, writing letters for the wounded, always pushing for better care, better conditions. I've heard she was a superb horsewoman, too, and was rabid about the treatment horses received at the Front."

"You know a great deal about a woman you've never met."

She shrugged again. "I was envious, if you want the absolute truth. And so I listened when people talked about her. If I'd had her money and her breeding, I'd have married well and never set foot in this shop. Now, I have a hat that must be finished by this afternoon. Is there anything else you want to know?"

"I understand that Dorothea MacIntyre lives above your shop—"

"She does, and you'll leave her alone, do you hear me? She goes in lively terror of half the town as it is, and it won't help to have the police harassing her. She thinks Fiona and her aunt Ealasaid walk on water. Well, that's as may be. In my humble opinion, Ealasaid should have been taken out and shot for putting that girl into Mr. Elliot's vicious clutches!"

"In what sense, vicious?"

"Dorothea is a silly goose who never did any harm to anyone, and all he can think of is whether she has unconfessed sin on her soul. On the subject of sin, he's worse than the Inquisition, that man! And she's driven to despair thinking that nothing she does is worthy of him. That's why I offered her a room here—I thought it would be the ultimate cruelty for her to live under Elliot's roof. It has been an inconvenience and a hardship, but I take great satisfaction from the fact that when she's here, she isn't scrubbing and hauling coal and cooking and washing up and fetching the laundry back from Mrs. Turnbull's, not to speak of the other heavy tasks he puts on her. All because he's too miserly to hire another girl. He took her in, you see, when she had no work, and he never lets her forget the duty owed him for that *kindness!*" Her eyes blazed.

He was on the point of asking if Fiona MacDonald's child could have been Dorothea MacIntyre's, and then stopped himself. Mr. Elliot's housekeeper was no guardian of secrets, her own or anyone else's.

12

———◆———

THE BEDROCK OF POLICE WORK WAS THE STATEMENT, A record of every witness questioned, scrupulously preserved in evidence.

Rutledge walked back to the station and asked Constable Pringle if he might read statements taken down when Inspector Oliver interviewed everyone who had received one of the letters denouncing Fiona MacDonald.

Pringle handed him a thick file box and said tentatively, "They're in proper form, sir."

"I'm sure they are." He smiled, took the box, and moved one of the chairs nearer the door, giving himself a semblance of private space. Sitting down, he untied the red string. Pringle went back to his own work, glancing up from time to time. As if, Hamish growled, Rutledge were not to be trusted.

Ignoring that, Rutledge lifted out the papers inside and began going through them.

Mrs. Turnbull, laundress. "I'm a respectable woman. I

don't have anything to do with the likes of *her*." Question: Have you ever done her washing? "No, I have not, and I thank God for it!" Question: Why, then, would someone send you such a letter? "Because they know I'm a good Christian, that's why. And I'd lose custom if it got around that I was taking in washing from whores!"

Hamish, incensed, swore.

Mrs. Oliphant, neighbor. "It was a warning to mind where my husband was of an evening. But I didn't need it, did I? Hadn't I seen her slipping out of the inn late at night, while her aunt was still alive?" Question: Did you speak of this to Miss MacCallum? "I did not. She was ill, dependent on Fiona. It seemed a cruelty." Question: Do you know where Miss MacDonald went when she left the inn so late? "I'm a decent woman, I don't go prowling about in the dark." Question: How often did she do this? "I saw her with my own eyes four, or maybe even five times." Question: What direction did she take? "It was always the same, away from the town." Question: How can you be so sure it was a lover Miss MacDonald went to meet? "Because I went out to that pele tower the very morning I found the letter on my doorstep. To see for myself if it was true. I found a bed of straw where a part of the roof had tumbled down and left a dry corner behind a heap of stone. And it smelled of lavender—that's *her* scent!" Question: But you wouldn't have thought to go to the tower if the letter hadn't suggested it. "Oh, I'd wondered, right enough! Where else might a whore have some privacy?"

Hamish said bitterly, "Can ye no' see that it's what they want to believe?"

Or someone had been a step ahead of Mrs. Oliphant, and set the scene she was expecting to find. . . .

Mrs. Braddock, neighbor. "I've seen how my husband looks at her! He's often offering to do work at the inn. But he isn't eager to keep up his own house, is he? I've been after him to paint the kitchen for six months." Question: So you believed the letter you found? "When it said my daughter was playing with a bastard and learning nasty things at the inn? Yes, I did. I had sometimes watched Ian while Miss MacDonald was out, and she'd returned the favor. He'd been no trouble at my house, but how was I to know what went on in hers?"

The silence from Hamish was thundering.

Mr. Harris, shoemaker. "She'd come in for her shoes, and was polite as you please. I never guessed, until the letter came! I'd known Ealasaid MacCallum for fifty years—she was a good woman, a good Christian. *She* wouldn't have allowed such things to go on. It's a disgrace, that's what it is!" Question: Had you visited the inn? Before the letter came? "Aye, that I had. It was a respectable place for a pint of an evening. There was always good company, and a man could sit and talk with his friends. The Ballantyne, now, it's all well and good, but crowded. You can hardly hear a word said to you!" Question: And while you were sitting in The Reivers, there was no indication—as far as you knew—that Miss MacDonald might be using the upstairs rooms for indecent purposes? "I should have guessed when Fiona took over tending bar herself. None of the MacCallums ever had! I said to Mrs. Harris, it's not right, mark my words, no good will come of it. Ealasaid would never have agreed to it. Fiona blamed it on the war, and necessity, help being so hard to find, but it still wasn't proper." Question: Did Miss MacDonald ever offer you an opportunity to visit upstairs? "I'm a married man!"

"Aye," Hamish commented through clenched teeth, "and sorry for it!"

The writer of these letters, Rutledge thought, thumbing through a dozen more statements, had been very clever indeed. Possibly too clever? She—or he—had known Duncarrick well, to choose the letters' recipients with such unerring accuracy. The seemingly untutored handwriting and the cheap stationery were no more than carefully thought-out trappings. This could not be, in his opinion, the work of a jealous wife or a jilted lover, driven to striking out.

The widow whose husband had died in the war: "I thought she might be more sympathetic to *my* suffering, having lost her own husband. But she wouldn't talk about Corporal MacLeod. Now I doubt he ever existed!"

The elderly woman who cleaned the church: "I went to Mr. Elliot, I was that upset! That she should be sitting among us, a two-faced harlot. And Mr. Elliot said he'd prayed over her from the start—she hadn't worshiped with what he believed to be sincerity—"

"Is it likely yon Mr. Elliot has written these abominations?" Hamish demanded. "He claims he sees the weaknesses of people—"

It was something Rutledge had been considering. To teach Fiona a lesson? If so, it had gotten out of hand. . . .

Another woman with small children: "Young Ian had lovely manners. I never guessed that he was what he was—but blood tells, doesn't it? In the end, blood tells! I'm so grateful that dear Ealasaid never lived to see this day. It would have been horrid. She was so happy when Fiona came—"

A woman who had been close to Ealasaid MacCallum: "I can't sleep at night thinking how this would have hurt dear Ealasaid. I've known her since she was a girl, and it would have broken her heart to find out how she'd been—used—in this fashion. It won't surprise me at all if Fiona *is* a murderess! Look how she treated her own flesh and blood—she knows no *shame!*—"

Hamish railed, "The shame's *hers*—"

"It's human nature we're dealing with here," Rutledge answered. "Don't you see? The first stone has already been cast. When the police interview the next person, he or she wants to be counted among the righteous. It doesn't prove anything except that people as a rule are easily led."

Rutledge put the statements back in their original order and set in the box. It had been unpleasant reading. Someone—Constable McKinstry, he thought—had likened

Fiona MacDonald's situation to the hysteria of witch hunts in the 1600s. And so it was. Fiona's sin—if there was a sin—had been to keep to herself. Many people had held that against her and at the first test showed neither generosity nor trust.

In choosing so carefully, the writer of the letters had been successful in destroying Fiona MacDonald's good name.

But were there other people, reluctant to step forward in the face of overwhelming public opinion, who privately might help?

RUTLEDGE WENT BACK to the square and at random stopped several women doing their day's marketing. The first one was red-faced, with graying hair straggling out of the tight bun at the nape of her neck.

Introducing himself, he explained that he was searching for anyone who could give him information about Fiona MacDonald's history before coming to Duncarrick.

The red-faced woman assured him that she had no knowledge of "that person."

He thanked her and moved on. His next choice was a middle-aged woman in a neat blue coat and a hat with a modicum of style. A schoolmistress, he thought, walking the narrow line of decorum required by her position.

She was flustered by his question, and he wondered if she had known Fiona better than she wished people to remember.

"No—no, I really didn't know her well. A passing—acquaintance. I accepted her for her aunt's sake, of course, believing that Ealasaid's family must be above reproach. It was a terrible shock when I heard—my first thought was 'Oh, I'm glad her aunt isn't alive to see her taken up by the *police!*'"

"You knew nothing about where Miss MacDonald lived

before coming here? Her aunt never spoke of her niece in your hearing?"

"Well—that is, I believe—er—Miss MacDonald lived with her grandfather until his death. Ealasaid must have said something about that. I—I seem to remember that she—Ealasaid, of course!—thought very well of *him*. A good man—well-respected in the Highlands. Which made it all the more shocking that his granddaughter should—well, disappoint the family so horribly."

She had managed to appear totally ignorant of any facts—aware only of hearsay and half-remembered gossip. Her pale brows and lashes fluttered as she asked plaintively, "Is there anything else, Inspector?"

He shook his head and thanked her.

Hamish was pointing out, "That one hasna' the courage to stand alone. She's too afraid of people turning their faces fra' her."

A harried young woman with boisterous twins dragging at her heels blushed when he stopped her, and turned her face away to speak to the boys. They were just old enough—three? four?—to have been playmates for Fiona's son. "I saw her sometimes on the street, and for her aunt's sake tried to be nice. But she wasn't a woman I was likely to be friends with."

"Did your children ever play together?"

"Oh—! Well—sometimes, when I called on Miss MacCallum. That is, it was not a usual thing, you understand. But young children—they don't *play* very much at this age, do they? They— It was more a matter of sitting and staring at each other across the room and—um—sometimes passing a toy back and forth."

"Did you feel that the MacDonald child was not a proper companion for your children? After all, his mother worked at The Reivers."

"It was a very *respectable* inn! Miss MacCallum would never have allowed any impropriety there. No—it's just that

we live on opposite ends of the town. It was not convenient. . . ." She let the words trail off.

Rutledge asked again, "Do you know where Miss
MacDonald resided before she came to stay with her aunt?"

The woman scowled, and disentangled one boy's chubby
hand from the edge of her coat. "No, Donald, you mustn't
pull at me. We'll be walking on presently." She turned back
to Rutledge. "I remember she said something about a family
she'd lived with. How much she'd cared for the children."

"Can you tell me who her friends were in Duncarrick?"

"No—of course I wasn't close to her—she—I have no
idea."

Which was another way of washing her hands entirely of
the matter. Hamish said, "She's repeating what her husband
has told her to say."

Rutledge tended to agree with his assessment. There
was neither warmth nor anger in her responses, only a
determined effort to keep clear of the tangle of Fiona
MacDonald's affairs.

He let her go and crossed the street. Outside the
milliner's shop he met a tall, thin woman coming from the
other direction. She had an air of fragility, as if she was recovering from an illness, but she moved with grace. When
he removed his hat and spoke to her, she stopped with courtesy and waited for him to ask his question.

"I'm sorry," she answered in a pleasant voice. "I've been
unwell, and find it difficult to go into society as I used to. I
don't believe I have met Miss MacDonald. I can tell you Miss
MacCallum was both respected and admired. She was very ac-
tive in charity work and had a reputation for honesty in all her
dealings. And as far as I knew, Miss MacDonald was a very fine
young woman. The charge of murder against her is beyond
belief."

Hamish said, "Aye, it's guid to hear the truth!"

This woman's appearance and manner indicated that
she might have been educated at one of the better schools.

Or perhaps lived for a time in England. Rutledge asked, "Did you—do you know anyone by the name of Eleanor Gray?"

She frowned, considering his question. "Eleanor Gray? No, I can't say that I ever met anyone by that name. I did know a Sally Gray."

"Where did you meet her?"

"In Carlisle at a party given for my husband. But that was before the war. I haven't seen her in years. Her husband was something in shipping, I think."

A dead end. He thanked her and walked on, immersed in his own thoughts.

Realizing that he'd arrived at the stone monument at the top of the square, Rutledge stopped there for a time, listening to Hamish comparing this town with the scattered houses that comprised his own small village. Like most Highlanders, Hamish had been used to the silences of the mountain glens and the long, smooth mirrors of the lochs. These had given him, as a soldier, a resilience and a strength of mind that had raised him from the ranks.

Idly watching the medley of activity that gave life and color to the street, Rutledge considered the townspeople of Duncarrick. If anyone here had had close ties with Fiona MacDonald, they were busy now burying them as deep as possible.

It also seemed unlikely that Fiona had confided in her aunt.

But then, it was two secrets that Fiona held close. That the boy was not hers—and that she knew the identity of the child's mother. For some reason, the latter must have been the darker of the two. Fiona had taken the very grave risk of going to trial for murder to protect it.

And if the mother was still alive—

As Mr. Elliot had so cleverly pointed out, she hadn't stepped forward.

Why not? And where was she?

Hamish sighed. "Anywhere in England or Scotland, for starters."

Rutledge turned toward the monument, one hand reaching up to touch the surface. This face was cold at this time of day, waiting for the sun to reach it. Like the town itself in some ways. Waiting for enlightenment.

The stone was a rough-hewn monolith set in the pavement. Links of heavy iron chain attached to four short iron posts encircled the stone, marking it as a shrine of sorts. On the side of the monolith that looked down the length of the square was a relief carved coarsely but tellingly into the stone. Houses, buried nearly to their rooftops in flames, jutted from the surface, and around the scene reivers sat on their horses, dressed in trews and leather jerkins, hats jammed on their heads as they watched the town burn. At the feet of the horses lay sacks of plunder and sheep milling about in fright.

Beneath the relief, three dates were incised in the stone—the three times Duncarrick had gone up in flames at the hands of English raiders. It was a powerful memorial, and Rutledge made a rough guess at the number of dead.

Or had the inhabitants been warned in time and found sanctuary somewhere in the fields or behind the stout walls of the pele tower, watching the night sky as their homes and possessions went up in black smoke, filling the cold air with choking ashes.

Small wonder the people here were a different breed from the citizens of southern English towns that had settled into quiet prosperity centuries before—where the tread of armies and the threat of fire and sword were a far distant memory. Small wonder that a stranger was welcomed for her aunt's sake—and not her own. Small wonder that suspicion was so easily aroused, and trust was snatched back so readily.

Someone had known how to use Duncarrick's entrenched character to reach out and anonymously destroy Fiona MacDonald. But to what end?

For what purpose?

Hamish said, "When I went to France, she was living with her grandfather. But when he died, she left the land and went to Brae—her last letter was fra' Brae."

It was where Rutledge had sent the only letter he had written to Fiona MacDonald. To tell her of Hamish's death. He said, "Then I'll have to go to Brae. . . ."

He had come here to search for Eleanor Gray. If Oliver was right, she must be somewhere in Fiona MacDonald's past. He had to find out where their paths had crossed—and *if* they had crossed. And why something that had not even happened in Duncarrick—the birth of a child—should cast such a long and deadly shadow over the lives of two women who should have had nothing in common. Oliver wasn't going to like Scotland Yard meddling—

As if conjured up by his thoughts, down the square Rutledge saw Oliver coming toward him, in the company of a man in a well-cut gray suit. A second glance identified Oliver's companion as the sheep farmer Rutledge had met that first day close by the pele tower. They were speaking earnestly, and then Oliver looked up, lifted a hand to hail Rutledge. He excused himself and, leaving the farmer, strode toward Rutledge.

"You look like a man in need of his lunch," Oliver said.

"I feel like a man in need of a drink. But what I need now is to learn more about Fiona MacDonald's whereabouts before her arrival in Duncarrick."

Oliver studied him. "I should think the logical place to begin would be with Eleanor Gray's movements after the quarrel with her mother in 1916."

"Logical, yes," Rutledge replied patiently. "But that's a wider investigation and will take far more manpower. Why not narrow it by starting at this end?"

"Yes, I see. Well, the best person to tell you what you need to know is Constable McKinstry. But I've already been to the town of Brae, and I've been to Glencoe. There can't be much left to find in either place!"

"You didn't know to ask for Eleanor Gray."

"No, that's true. But I did ask about any other place the accused might have visited about the time the boy was born. For I can tell you this much—a woman with the Gray name and money would never have chosen backwaters like Brae or Glencoe to live in. The two must have met in Glasgow—or Edinburgh. And there's your needle in the haystack again!"

Rutledge said thoughtfully, "If you were the daughter of Lady Maude Gray and expecting a child out of wedlock, a backwater might offer obscurity as well as seclusion. The larger the town, the greater the risk of being recognized."

Oliver took a deep breath. "You may be right, of course. It's possible. But not likely. Still, talk to Constable McKinstry. Tell him to let you read my notes." Then, echoing a remark Rutledge had already heard that day, he added, "Too bad, in my view, that her aunt is dead. Or convenient—who's to say?"

He walked on.

CONSTABLE McKINSTRY WAS on duty at the station, his chair back on two legs and a book in his hands. It was on Scottish law.

McKinstry, closing the book and lowering the feet of the chair to the floor, looked wretchedly at Rutledge as he listened to his request. "Fiona never confided in me. I'll tell you what I can, sir, and what Inspector Oliver wrote in his report." He put the book on a shelf behind him and added, "Did he send you? Aye, I thought so." Wryly, he confessed, "It's my punishment to be made to talk about her! The Inspector hasn't forgiven me for the fiasco with the first skeleton. If I'd been thorough, it would have been my embarrassment, not his."

"I need dependable facts. You're most likely the only inhabitant of Duncarrick who isn't afraid to admit you knew her. Man or woman."

"That's true enough." McKinstry sighed. Considering how to begin, he looked at the ceiling, smudged with smoke from the stove, and arranged his thoughts.

"I was in France when Fiona arrived in Duncarrick. I remember my mother writing that Ealasaid MacCallum was having trouble with her right arm shaking and had sent for her niece to come and help out at the inn. Later she told me that in her view Mrs. MacLeod was a respectable young widow with a baby to care for, but strong and capable for all that. She'd lived in Brae, and if I should hear any news of men from there, my mother would be glad to pass it on."

He stopped, squaring the blotter and moving the ink pot to the other side of the desk. Then, absently, he moved it back again.

"To be honest, I never asked Fiona about her life before she came to Duncarrick. I was jealous, if you want the truth, of her husband. Only he wasn't, was he?" He sighed. "Fiona left her grandfather's croft in the spring of 1915, I do know that. She couldn't run the farm on her own. It's inhospitable country at best, but the old man had made it pay."

"Aye," Hamish said unexpectedly. "He knew the land better than anyone I ever saw." There was a wistfulness in the voice at Rutledge's shoulder. "Fra' him I learned how to handle a team and to find water, when we needed to dig a well. I took a forked willow stick, skinned and dried. He said I had the gift—I could feel the stick stir and bend in my hands. And it was sweet water I found!"

McKinstry had gone on, unaware of the interruption. "Some cousins were willing to take it over—they were too old for the war, but still able-bodied. She said once that she wished the lad's father could have been buried there in the glen, because he loved it so. At any rate, Fiona was glad of the position she found in Brae. It took her mind off the war. A Mrs. Davison was looking to hire a nanny for her children." He paused. "Brae's south of Glasgow. Just above Lanark."

"Yes, I have a general idea where it is. Go on!"

"When her aunt wrote asking Fiona to come to Duncarrick, she was sad to leave Brae. But she promised to come as soon as Mrs. Davison found a replacement for her. She and the boy."

"Miss MacCallum said nothing to your mother about the boy's—history?"

"Her only worry was that Ian was so young and might distract Fiona from her duties at The Reivers. I thought it was a selfish view, but then, no one knew just how ill Miss MacCallum was."

Rutledge made a note of Mrs. Davison's name and asked, "What did the people in Brae tell Inspector Oliver?"

"Not much. That Fiona minded her own business, was friendly enough, and worked hard. No one was aware that she was expecting a child when she left there. And we've traced all the children born to residents in 1916. A woman named Singleton had a child in Glasgow that spring, but it's accounted for, and the three born in Brae are accounted for as well. I never knew Fiona to mention any particular friend there—though she spoke often of Mrs. Davison and her children."

"I'm considering driving on to Brae. To see if there's any connection to Eleanor Gray to be found there."

"Begging your pardon, sir, it's a waste of time. I've seen Brae. A woman like Eleanor Gray would stand out like a sore thumb. It's not the kind of place she'd be hiding herself away in."

"Still, we must begin somewhere," Rutledge answered. "All right, is there any other name you can give me?"

McKinstry took out a folder and opened it. When Rutledge had finished taking down two or three other names, he closed his notebook and said, "I'd like to speak to the accused again before I leave."

"I don't know—" McKinstry began doubtfully.

"It will take less than five minutes."

And McKinstry, capitulating, took out the keys and handed them to Rutledge.

He unlocked the door for a second time and walked into the cell. Fiona MacDonald was sitting in the chair, her hands folded in her lap. But her eyes flew to his as he entered.

"I'm driving to Brae today," he said, watching her face. There was a very slight tightening of the skin, as if she was not happy with the news.

"You will be seeing Mrs. Davison. Please tell her—" She stopped and shook her head. "No, I don't suppose she'd want a message from me now." Her fingers folded and smoothed a pleat in her skirt. "I forget, sometimes, that a murderess has no past. But if the children should ask about me—please, will you tell them that I'm well and think of them often?"

"I will."

She managed a smile. "They're too young to know about murder. They'll be glad to be remembered. And I do think about them. It takes my mind off other—other things."

He said without stopping to think, "I wish you could trust me and tell me the truth."

"It isn't a matter of trust," she answered quietly. "It's a question of love."

"Love?"

"Yes." She looked away. "I can't explain it, except to say that there are many faces of love, and sometimes they can be cruel. My mother loved my father so deeply that she grieved herself to death for him. And left me with only a grandfather and an aunt to care for me. I was the child of that love, but it didn't matter enough to her to want to live. I never understood that. I still don't. I didn't want to die when Hamish did. I wonder, sometimes, if that meant I didn't love him enough." Her eyes searched Rutledge's face, begging for reassurance.

"It isn't a question of loving him enough. The man I knew in France wanted with all his heart to come home to you—"

He caught himself in time, before he'd destroyed the comforting lie of a hero's death for King and Country. Clearing his throat, he said instead, "—and he'd have wanted you to live. Above all, he'd have wanted that." For once he knew beyond question that he spoke for Hamish. "And if you lost your own mother when you were very young, you must see that it's wrong to leave the boy unprotected, as you have."

"You've told me yourself that I'd not be allowed to keep him!"

It was true. But he said, "You were wrong to allow yourself to be taken up on a charge of murder—wrong to allow the evidence to go on pointing to your guilt. Wrong to accept the fact that you will surely hang! There may come a time when the boy will need you and you won't be there."

Hamish cried out that it was wrong to use her own words to force her to surrender whatever truth she had hidden so long, so well.

She seemed fragile and alone in this ugly cell, but Rutledge did not make the mistake of underestimating her strength. She squared her shoulders with a courage he deeply admired and replied, "It must be a painful way to die. I've made myself try to imagine what it's like—"

Harshly, caught up in his need to bring her to her senses while there was still time, while they were alone in this cell and there was no one to stop him, ignoring his own conscience hammering at him over the anguish of the voice at his shoulder, he said, "I've watched men hang. What happens to the body as you die is not something a woman would wish for herself."

She had flinched as he spoke, and he instantly regretted the words, cursing himself. Wanting to recall them. But they seemed suspended like a wall of coldness in the air between them.

He took a single step forward, then stopped short, forbidden by who he was—and who she was—from offering any measure of comfort. "I'm sorry—"

She said only, "I won't be alive to know, will I?"

But as he left the room, he could see the tears filling her eyes.

13

───────◆───────

DODGING A LORRY, THEN A DOG SNIFFING THE PAVE-
ment with intent interest, Rutledge walked back to the hotel.
He encountered Oliver just coming out the door.

"Found McKinstry, did you?"

"Yes, thanks." He was on the point of walking on, and realized all at once that Oliver had something he wanted to
say. Rutledge stopped and waited.

Oliver looked over Rutledge's shoulder at the square beyond, as if surveying his domain. "I've thought a good deal
about our Eleanor Gray and what might have brought her to
Scotland. The father of the child might have been a Scot.
Women can be sentimental about such things as their time
draws near, and she might have decided the child ought to
be born here. Or perhaps it was the father's last wish in his
last letter. Who's to say? But there's our reason for coming
north! Lady Maude's daughter or not, she's still a woman,
and apt to go mawkish. Do you agree with me so far?"

Rutledge thought of Eleanor Gray, the suffragette chaining herself to fences and letting herself be dragged off to prison. "Mawkish" wasn't a word he'd have chosen to describe her. Still, Oliver had a point to make. Rutledge nodded.

"Next question, then. What happened between crossing the border and meeting Fiona MacDonald, as she must have called herself then? Did our Miss Gray, for sake of argument, leave too late and never make it to her original destination? Women have been known to be wrong about their time!"

That was true. But Eleanor Gray had wanted to be a doctor. Would she have got it wrong?

"Yes, I can see the possibilities. That she felt ill and stopped for help. Or that something else had gone wrong with her plans." He looked down at Oliver. "Glencoe isn't necessarily where she died. If she is dead."

"Oh, she's dead, right enough. And those are her bones out there in the glen. Who would know better where to hide a victim than someone who'd grown up in the district? If I had a corpse on my hands, I'd take it to such a godforsaken place no one was likely to stumble over it until it was clean bones. And that's just what the MacDonald woman did. The local police didn't have any luck at all identifying the remains last year when they were discovered. If we hadn't come along, she'd be without a name still."

Hamish, angry, described Oliver's ancestry and future destination in some detail. Highlanders were, as a general rule, creative in their cursing.

"A dangerous choice, wouldn't you say?" Rutledge found himself defending Fiona MacDonald. "I'd have taken the body miles from where I lived."

"How far could the accused go, burdened with a newborn child and a dead woman?" Oliver said thoughtfully. "Or turn it upside down—she might have felt a little safer with each passing year, when the body didn't come to light and there was no hue and cry for a missing child. Knowing it was there, if she ever had to devise an account of finding the mother dead. But herself safely out of the picture here in Duncarrick, otherwise."

Words that would come back to him later—but Rutledge said now, "No, I don't see that. Why didn't she tell you those clever lies when you first became suspicious of her?"

"Because she misjudged me. She thought we'd be satis-fied tearing the inn apart and coming away empty-handed." Oliver smiled. "She failed to see, didn't she, that making a fool of me was a blunder! I'd stake my hope of promotion on that. And now all that's left is to put a name to that corpse. Which is why you are here." It was a friendly warning not to cross the lines into Oliver's own patch. The smile faded. "If I were a vengeful man, now, I'd look forward to presenting the haughty Lady Maude with proof that her daughter is not only dead but bore a child out of wedlock to some unknown soldier. First time that's happened in *her* family tree, I've no doubt."

RUTLEDGE ATE A hurried lunch, then informed the woman at the hotel desk that he might be away for several nights but wished to keep his room.

Morag had seen to his laundry for him, but he had writ-ten a brief note to Frances in London asking her to send a larger case north. He handed that to the clerk to be mailed. It appeared that he was going to be in Scotland for some time. Like it or not. But he was damned if he'd go any far-ther north than the borders!

Heading west from Duncarrick and then bearing north, Rutledge made first for Lanark. There was no direct road to Brae. It was only a small village on the way to somewhere else. The browns and golds of September already colored the landscape. The open land, with few of the hedgerows that the English used to set off fields, had been made suit-able for sheep rather than agriculture. The cramped and compact towns, so different from the picturesque villages farther south, seemed to be locked into a harder past. The people here, independent and far less class-conscious, shared a different history from the English, and it had marked them. *Set me down on either side of the border,* he told himself, *and I would know instantly on what ground I stood, English or Scottish.*

As Rutledge settled into the long drive, Hamish turned from his annoyance at Inspector Oliver's obtuseness to his memories of Fiona MacDonald before the war. Rutledge tried not to heed them, but the words kept pushing aside his own thoughts.

They had known each other from childhood, Fiona and Hamish. She had been lively and intelligent even then, accustomed to games with her brothers and their friends, running barefoot in the summers, her long, dark hair and her skirts tangled with briars and straw. Her grandfather's favorite, she had learned to read at an early age and to form her own opinions freely. As she grew into a woman of humor and warmth in the summer of 1914, Hamish MacLeod had asked her to marry him. Only he'd marched off to war within a matter of weeks, and in 1916 died in France, far away from Fiona and the Highlands, from everything he held dear.

Small wonder she'd been tempted to take a motherless child and love him as her own, to bring him up as she and Hamish might have brought up their brood. A legacy of the dead, a child with his name if not his blood.

In the trenches, where men talked of home and a lost, safer world, Hamish had drawn a picture of a caring woman, of laughter and trust and abiding affection, that a soldier had carried with him to war.

But Rutledge had seen something else in her—through *his* eyes, not Hamish's.

He had seen strength in her, and the ability to look directly at the world. He had seen courage—and fear. He had seen a fierce longing for something to come out of the ashes of her heart. And now even that had been taken away.

She was everything, he realized suddenly, that Jean—whom

he'd wanted to marry, who he'd believed cared for him—had never been. And for the first time since Jean had broken off their engagement, he was entirely free of her spell. As if scales had fallen from his eyes, he saw clearly how very different Jean's conception of marriage had been from his. She had wanted a future that was protected and secure, accepted by society, applauded by her friends. A man in turmoil, his mind shattered, his future uncertain, was a terrifying prospect.

Fiona MacDonald knew what love meant, and what it cost, and what the war had taken from her. She would have loved Hamish if he'd come home scarred with burns, without his legs or his arms. She would have loved the man he'd become as well as the man he was.

She would even have loved him shell-shocked and consumed by nightmares—

Rutledge refused to follow that line of thought.

But his mind brought back other images, the women like Jean who came to the clinics and stared with horror at the ruins of husband or lover—he had once encountered one of them running out the door, face buried in her handkerchief, moaning in shock. And in the room behind her, a man with bandages where his face had been lay mute with clenched fists, unable to cry. There had been others who had accepted the living shell gratefully, with an intense sense of wonder that they had been among the lucky ones to have their soldier home again.

Fiona would have been among those. . . .

That was the kind of courage she possessed. Was she also a murderess?

Rutledge felt the betrayal even as his mind framed the question. A betrayal of Hamish and of Fiona MacDonald.

HE SHUT THE war out of his mind and tried to concentrate instead on what lay ahead.

Fiona had left her grandfather's home and moved south to Brae.

But why Brae?

"Because it was different from the glen," Hamish answered unexpectedly. "It held no memories. Of her grandfather, of me. Of her brothers who had died."

Rutledge recalled the statement McKinstry had read to him. When she'd been asked if Fiona could have been pregnant when she left Brae, Mrs. Davison had answered unequivocally. "No. I would have known," she'd said. "I kept a strict eye on Fiona—not because she was likely to find herself in trouble, but because she was a young girl, alone and in my care. Come to that, it wasn't hard to do—she seldom took her day off, and even in the evenings, when the children were in bed, she'd sit with me and do the mending or read aloud."

Oliver's comment on Mrs. Davison's character was "I'd take my oath that she's telling the truth. Forthright to a fault, as my sergeant put it."

Mrs. Davison might well have told the exact truth. People often did.

The whole truth was another matter. And how an investigating officer probed for it determined how much of it came out. Objectivity . . .

Oliver was convinced that Fiona MacDonald was a murderess.

If she wasn't, how did she come by the child? That was the stumbling block, and her life depended on the answer. And Rutledge was going to have to find it.

BRAE WAS SOUTH and east of Glasgow, on the outskirts of an area that had suffered from fast expansion and then depression in the previous century. The basin of the Clyde had become a forest of steelworks, factories, and mines, but it had never been a scenic wonderland. All the same, what little beauty there was had been swallowed up long since. Lanark, on the other hand, was a pleasant town with associations with the Scottish hero William Wallace, and it was there that Rutledge ate a late dinner before continuing to Brae.

But there was no place in Brae to spend the night, and he was forced to return to Lanark.

It was early in the morning when he came back, and even Hamish could find nothing attractive in the plain houses, the dull landscape, or the feeling that time had dealt harshly with the little village. Even its few streets seemed tired.

Mrs. Davison lived in a brick house that had been well kept, one large enough to have been a manager's home when industry had mushroomed in the region. The windows were clean, with pretty curtains behind them; there were flowers still in bloom in the sheltered garden to one side, and behind the house vegetables had been grown in long rows that were now brown and untidy except for the dark green of beets and cabbages at the far end. The house stood at the edge of the village, set back from the street behind a low brick wall. A ball, a doll with a china face and no clothes on its white kid body, and a small bucket full of stones littered the walk in front of the door.

She answered his knock herself, a woman with a kind face but very perceptive hazel eyes. She looked him up and down as he introduced himself and then said, "Yes, I'm Penelope Davison. I've talked to the policemen in Duncarrick. Why should London have any interest in going over the same ground? I know nothing about Fiona that can help you in any way." In her own fashion, she reminded him of Lady Maude. The same independent spirit and refusal to be overawed by the law.

"All the same, there are some questions I must ask."

She sighed and opened the door wider, inviting him in to the parlor, on the left side of the entry. It was small with dark furniture, a goodly number of green-leafed plants, and very little frivolity. There was a charcoal portrait of a man with fine mustaches and an air of importance, framed in oak and gilt; a small reproduction from a newspaper of

Queen Victoria's jubilee procession, framed in dark wood; and a bookcase with glass doors holding rows of calf-bound volumes, scuffed from much use, just under the window. The books had been tidily sorted by height, not content. But there was an air of calm and comfort in the room that impressed Rutledge as he took the chair she indicated.

From the back of the house he could hear the high voices of children, and realized suddenly that it was a Saturday and they were not in school. Hamish said, "You must speak to them—you gave Fiona your promise!"

Mrs. Davison was saying, "Well, then, you've come all this way. What is it you would like to know?"

"When Fiona MacDonald first came to live with you, did she have references? A letter of introduction?"

"She answered an advertisement I'd placed in the Glasgow paper in 1915. Her letter impressed me and I asked her to come for an interview. I liked her immediately, but I'm not a foolish woman, and I made inquiries before taking her on. Her grandfather was a respected man, and there were a number of people around Glencoe who spoke well of her. She came to me and I never had a moment's regret over hiring her. I can't bring myself to believe that she has killed anyone. But that police inspector claims she has."

"There is evidence pointing in that direction, yes. It isn't necessarily proven. That's why I'm here. Did she have any friends in Brae? Young women she might have grown to know well?"

"No. She was grieving most of the time, you see, and she went out very little. Her brothers died one after the other, and then, in 1916, her young man. There was another woman here who used to walk with her when the weather was fine. But I wouldn't have described Mrs. Cook as a friend. They were more—I don't know—fellow sufferers. The newspapers pretended the war was going well, but too many people were dying. It's a terrible weight when you worry day and night about someone. And when the news came, and Fiona knew the worst, it was hard for her to speak of it. She didn't tell me for weeks. I think most of us pressed her to cry but she wouldn't. Mrs. Cook didn't press. She seemed to understand what it was like."

"Tell me about Mrs. Cook, if you will."

"She was ill—her lungs. As I understood it, her doctor had hoped that better air would help. The smoke of Glasgow most certainly had not. At any rate, early in 1916 she took rooms in that white house you must have passed coming into Brae. On your left. Mrs. Kerr's sons were off to France, and her husband was away building ships. She didn't want to live alone and advertised for lodgers. It seemed to suit both of them—Mrs. Cook was quiet and no trouble. Mrs. Kerr preferred it that way."

"Do you know anything about Mrs. Cook's background, where she'd come from?"

"Before Glasgow? I have no idea. Her husband was at sea, and Fiona's young man was in France. They seemed to have very little in common other than that. I thought perhaps Mrs. Cook had come from a wealthy home and had been given advantages that Fiona hadn't. Which is not to say that Fiona was common. She was a most unusual girl, and I found her a very pleasant companion. Her grandfather had reared her extraordinarily well!"

"How long was Mrs. Cook here?"

"Seven months, I'd say. Then her husband was invalided home, and she went to London to be with him."

"Fiona had been living here for some time before Mrs. Cook came?"

"Of course. Over a year. And if you're asking me if they might have known each other before moving to Brae, I seriously doubt it. Fiona left only after she'd had word that her aunt was taken ill and couldn't manage the inn on her own any longer. She cried when she left, and my children cried with her. I was not above crying myself! That's why I didn't ask her to work out her time."

Not to work out her time—but Fiona had told her aunt that she must!

"How long after Mrs. Cook's departure was that?"

"Three or four months, I'd say."

Hamish pointed out that if Mrs. Cook had been expecting a child when she came to Brae, then she had had it alone and without Fiona's help. Seven months and four months added up to eleven.

Nevertheless, Rutledge made a note of it. He said, "Did Mrs. Cook leave a forwarding address, do you know?"

"If she did, Fiona never said anything about it. Mary Kerr found a pair of gloves in the bedroom after her lodger had gone—they'd fallen under the bed. Mary wanted to send them along to her but didn't have her direction."

"Forgive me, but why do you think a woman of Mrs. Cook's apparent position should wish to spend over half a year in Brae?"

Mrs. Davison smoothed the white tatted cover on the arm of her chair. "I wondered about that myself. Brae left her to herself. And I think that's what she needed most. I wondered, once or twice, if she might be a married woman who'd had an affair and the man died. Time to heal, you see. Away from everyone who didn't know and couldn't understand." She shrugged. "Perhaps that's an overly romantic view of her. There could be any number of other reasons. Fiona gave no sign of missing her other than the occasional remark that anyone might make. When the cat had kittens, she said something like 'Mrs. Cook told me once that she'd never had a cat or a dog of her own. It's too bad she couldn't have one of these.' "

Hamish said, "I canna' see a child romping with a dog in Lady Maude's house." It was true. . . .

Rutledge said, "Do you recall her first name? Her husband's name?"

"I don't think I ever heard her speak of him by name. It was usually 'my husband.' But her name was Maude. I thought it was rather pretty."

A coincidence . . . it was a common English name.

"Did you say anything to Inspector Oliver about Mrs. Cook?"

"I saw no reason to. I told you, it wasn't actually a friend-ship, it was simple loneliness. I don't suppose they'd have spoken a dozen words to each other ordinarily! But the young women here in Brae had gone away to do war work, and the ones with children, like me, spent a rather dreary war. Fiona and Mrs. Cook, the outsiders, naturally were drawn together."

"I've been trying to locate an Eleanor Gray in the hope that she might throw some light on Miss MacDonald's situation. Has she visited Brae?"

Mrs. Davison shook her head. "We aren't a crossroads here, though it may seem as if we are. There was never an Eleanor Gray here. I'd have known if there was."

WITH MRS. DAVISON's permission, Rutledge sat at the rough kitchen table with the three children Fiona had cared for: a girl and two boys. The girl was shy, but the boys were eager to talk.

The picture they drew was of a young woman who could sit on the floor and play games with them, who read to them in the evening if they went to bed without fuss, and who knew the most fearsome tales of Highland feuds and battles.

"She spent a night once in a haunted house, and there was a man there who carried his head in his *hands*. Fiona saw him, plain as day!" the eldest boy told Rutledge with great relish. "He was a Campbell, killed by a MacLaren, and seeking revenge." He launched into the details of the feud, but his mother, smiling, said, "Yes, that's all very well, but I don't think Mr. Rutledge has time for the whole story."

He spent a quarter of an hour with the children and Mrs. Davison but came away with nothing more. He needed no further reminder from Hamish to pass on Fiona's message to the children. The shy little girl smiled and said "Fiona" in a soft voice. "Is she coming back?"

Her mother looked over her head at Rutledge and replied, "Not for a while, dear."

MRS. KERR, OVER sixty and showing her years, told him what she knew of Mrs. Cook, but there was nothing new in what she had to say.

As he got up to leave, Rutledge asked, "Did Mrs. Cook and Miss MacDonald seem to be close?"

"Not close, no. They'd walk in the evenings sometimes. That was all."

"Where did they walk most often, do you know?"

"Mrs. Cook wasn't country bred, so they didn't go far. About the town, mostly, or in the churchyard. It's protected from the wind, I suppose that's why. I had the feeling that they both felt comfortable among the graves. Odd thing to say, I know, but there you are. As if they drew strength or peace or the like from the quiet there . . . Fiona, now, I knew she'd lost the man she was to marry—she told me once that he was buried in France. Mrs. Cook's husband was at sea. But she never spoke much about herself. At first I put it down to being too good for the likes of us in Brae, then I saw that she was not one to talk. Some folks aren't, are they? It's what makes the world go 'round, differences."

RUTLEDGE CROSSED THE street from Mrs. Kerr's and walked as far as the small, ugly church. The early Victorian brick and stone mixture had not been successful, but it stood apart, among great old trees planted generations before for an older church. There were paths among the graves, white graveled ribbons through the green, hum-mocked grass. A number of bare plots spoke of recent buri-als, and he shivered, remembering his own dream.

He went through the gate and spent some time moving through the wilderness of stone, reading the inscription on first this one and then another.

Not far from the rear wall one headstone caught his eye. It was old, the dates smudged and barely discernible, but the name carved deeply into the gray face was quite legible.

Hamish MacLeod.

Not the man he'd killed—the dates were much older, a century or more older. But Rutledge found himself wondering as he stood there and looked down at it, if Fiona MacDonald had also known about it and in some way had taken comfort from it. A gravestone for a man who had none.

A place to sit on the weedy grass while she remembered a past that had no future. It must have offered consolation as well as privacy to mourn.

He had the oddest feeling that he was right.

But what name had Mrs. Cook found here if her husband was still alive? What memories had comforted her?

He walked through the stones again, searching. There were Campbells and Lindsays, MacBrays and MacDougals, a long list of Highland and Lowland names that had no special meaning to him. He found a Trevor, and thought of Ross, then moved on. Little and Elliot, Davison and Robson, Pringle and Taylor, Henderson and one Gray. Evelyn Gray. He had died as an infant.

It was Eleanor Gray's father's name—the man she had called father all her life.

Had she been closer to him than to her mother in spite of the fact that he wasn't her natural father?

Girls were often attached to their fathers, and if Evelyn Gray had accepted her publicly as his daughter, he would have brought her up to the best of his ability. Even if he had not loved her for her own sake, he would have treated her well for King Edward's sake. The men had been close friends.

And he might have been the only warmth in Eleanor's life. Rutledge could not envision Lady Maude holding a squirming child in her lap to read it a story, as Fiona had done with her charges in the Davison household.

But then, he might be doing Lady Maude an injustice.

He had met her after the quarrel with Eleanor. Her daughter's refusal to acknowledge her duty to her blood and heritage had hurt deeply. There might have been a very different relationship between mother and child before that.

Otherwise, why had Lady Maude insisted that he, Rutledge, take charge of this question of identifying the bones?

"She might," Hamish said, "be wanting to protect her family's honor—"

14

———◆———

RUTLEDGE DROVE TOWARD GLASGOW WITH HIS MIND busy. Hamish was making comments on the evidence as well, but he tried to ignore them.

Such small things—the name on a grave—the Christian name of a woman—the fact that Fiona had told her aunt she was working out her time at Brae . . .

Where had she gone for that brief, unaccounted-for span of weeks?

And did it have anything to do with Maude Cook?

He spent Sunday in Glasgow, asking the police there for any information they might have had on anyone by the name of Cook, but the half-dozen families he was sent to see were unable to help him. They shook their heads when he asked them about a Maude Cook. As one middle-aged man put it, "It's a pretty enough name, Maude, but not one of ours." Nor had relations to their knowledge spent part of the war years in the village of Brae. "It's not likely, is it?" a woman asked him. "So close by? Besides, I'd have sent any daughter or daughter-in-law of mine to our kin, not to live on the charity of strangers!"

But as Hamish pointed out, if Maude Cook's connection with Glasgow was through her own family, Rutledge didn't have her maiden name and would never find her in the welter of people in the city. It would require a door-to-door search. An enormous amount of manpower.

Driving back to Duncarrick on Monday morning, he reached the outskirts of Lanark and stopped the car, rubbing his face. Lanark—

He considered Lanark for a time. That it was close to Brae. That it was large enough that a woman using a false name might not be noticed and gossiped about. Especially if she was already certain there were no acquaintances living there who might see her in the street and recognize her. And it would offer adequate medical care to a woman on her own. . . .

Rutledge continued into the heart of the town, finding the local police station and then searching for a place to leave his motorcar. It was a busy morning; the town seemed to be full of people and lorries, carts and wagons. Men were setting up a pavilion near the church for a fete or exhibition. Others were carrying potted palms from the hotel, walking trees that wove their way along the pavement like Great Birnam wood come to Dunsinane and about to attack the waiting Macbeth.

When Rutledge made his way back through the crowds some fifteen minutes later, he had the information he needed.

The lying-in hospital was in a back street, a small but well-kept building that had potted geraniums in front of its door and a woman in a dark dress at the desk in the small reception hall.

Rutledge asked for the doctor in charge and was soon ushered into a chilly office at the back, where a tired elderly man turned from the window to greet him. On the desk were stacks of folders waiting to be sorted.

"I'm Dr. Wilson. I was up until five this morning with a difficult delivery. If you'll make your call a brief one so that I can sleep, I'll help in any way I can."

"What kind of cases do you take here?"

Surprised, the doctor said, "Difficult ones that can't be safely delivered at home. The well-to-do, who want more comfort than an upstairs bedchamber. And the rest are female complaints where surgery or other remedies are required. I deal with a goodly number of women who are ill. Tumors or excessive bleeding. Miscarriages. Stillbirths. I find that a number of husbands don't heed me when I tell them a wife should bear no more children. I save the woman if I can. I also deal with botched abortions, where infection is rampant and the woman has waited too long to seek medical help. I don't see how any of this is of use to the police!"

"You don't handle lung complaints—"

"Not if they don't bear on a pregnancy or other reproductive problem." He was impatient now.

"Can you give me the names of women who came here in 1916? I can't tell you with any certainty what the date was. But the woman I'm seeking was delivered of a healthy son."

"No, I can't." It was short and curt.

"Then can you tell me if a Mrs. Cook was your patient in that time period? Mrs. Maude Cook. We are investigating a murder that might have a connection with her."

"My patients don't commit murder!" the doctor said indignantly.

Rutledge had heard many people express the same certainty. It was a common reaction, a natural one. *No one I know could do such a thing!* But murderers came in all shapes and sizes, all denominations and races, all social strata. And more often than not, they had friends who were appalled. . . .

"I'm sure they don't, Doctor. In this case, we're speaking of a victim. And of a three-year-old child who may have been orphaned. We need to contact the parents of the woman, or her husband."

"A victim." Wilson regarded him differently. "I don't recall anyone by the name of Maude Cook. But let me check my files."

He went to an oak cabinet against the side wall and pulled out a drawer. It was stuffed with folders and papers. He thumbed through some dozen of them, and did it again, then finally shook his head.

"I don't find a Maude Cook at all. Are you quite sure you have the right name? There's a Mary Cook here. And she gave birth to a male child."

"In 1916? What was the date?"

Wilson gave it to him. It was a month too early. Still—

"Can you tell me where she lives? Or give me the direction of any family?"

Wilson turned back to the files. "She gave London as her home. There's no other information. The father was dead. In the war. She cried when I told her she had a son. She said he would have been proud. A good many women tell me that. I have tried to grow accustomed to it, and failed. Children need fathers. Too damned many of them in these last years had none to go home to." He rubbed his eyes. "Is that all you want of me?"

"Did Mrs. Cook have lung disease of any kind?"

"No. She was young and healthy. There was a complication, however. It was a difficult birth. Long and tiring, and there was a good deal of trouble. Breech birth, you see. Touch and go, but I saved her and the baby. Infection set in. She was quite lucky she was here—she'd have died otherwise. The fact remains, she'll not be able to conceive again. Well, she has her child and I doubt she'll marry again. So many men died. . . ."

It was cold comfort, but all the doctor had.

"Why did she come to Scotland to have this child if she lived in London?"

"She was traveling. Foolishness on her part at that late stage, but she was on her way to London when the bag of waters broke."

But Wilson had no idea what had brought Mary Cook north from London or how long she might have lived in Lanark before consulting him. "I don't have time to question my patients about their private lives. Still, there're any number of Cooks in the neighborhood of Loch Lomond. She might well have been visiting one of them."

IF MAUDE COOK was the mother of Fiona's child, she had had the boy in a clinic, not on some windswept mountainside. And left there well enough to travel.

Was she in fact Eleanor Gray? And had she given Fiona a child she did not want to keep? In exchange for a sworn promise never to reveal the boy's parentage?

It was possible—but not very likely. As for Mary—

Where had they met? Why had the mother so readily given up her son to a comparative stranger?

There was absolutely no certainty that Maude Cook and Mary Cook were the same person—Cook was a common name, as the doctor had pointed out.

Rutledge drove back to Duncarrick feeling the long hours at the wheel of the motorcar and in no mood to confess he'd found only the most tenuous threads to account for the number of miles covered. Or endure the constant hammering of Hamish's questions.

The woman at the desk of The Ballantyne smiled at him as he came into the lobby and then turned to a drawer, where apparently she kept messages for hotel guests.

There was one for him, but not from Old Bowels, as he'd expected.

It was a politely couched request for him to telephone Lady Maude.

She wanted a report of his progress.

And so far he had nothing to tell her.

HER VOICE CAME clearly down the line—imperious and cold. "I expected you to keep me apprised of your investigation," Lady Maude said accusingly. "You have disappointed me."

"I had only mundane details to report until today. Tell me, do you know a Mrs. Cook, Maude Cook?"

"And who is she?" Lady Maude parried.

"I can't be sure," he admitted. "I'm exploring every possibility, and her name has come up in the course of inquiries."

"I have no interest in a Maude Cook!"

"Did your daughter have friends in Glasgow whom she might have visited for a period of time? People who would let her stay for several months?"

"Certainly not. I can't think of any reason why my daughter might wish to go to Scotland at all. It's very unlike her. But I've told you that before."

He said, "Did your daughter know a Fiona MacDonald?"

"I think not. It isn't a name I'm familiar with." She paused, then made—for her—a difficult concession. "The war unsettled accepted social behavior. In London Eleanor must have met any number of people outside our own circle of friends. I can't be expected to know all of them." It was the closest she had come to admitting that for three years she had no knowledge at all of the people who might have been important in her daughter's life. And then, behind the coldness, there appeared a brief glimmer of warmth. "Inspector. I am waiting for news of my daughter. Something that will prove that it's impossible for her to be connected in any way with this sordid business of murder!"

"The police here are still convinced that the—er—remains that have been found must be your daughter's. I'm not as sure, for a number of reasons. But it isn't something I can prove in a matter of days. The woman accused of the murder has been less than helpful. We are having to trace her movements over a period of three years. Until that's completed, I can't promise you any news."

She considered that in silence.

Then she said, "I shall expect regular reports." It was as far as she could go, admitting that she was worried.

"I understand."

He put down the phone and considered going into the saloon bar for a drink. But he thought better of it and climbed the stairs wearily to his room.

Hamish was a dull murmur in his ear as he fell deeply and dreamlessly asleep.

OLIVER'S FIRST QUESTION was "Did you learn anything?"

Rutledge hesitated and then decided on discretion. Oliver was protective of his own investigation, and any evidence that might conflict with his carefully constructed case would immediately be suspect. "Enough to convince me that if the accused met Eleanor Gray in Brae, there is no evidence to prove it."

It was a cool morning, the kind of day that reminded people in the north that winter would be long and dark and dreary. Rutledge hadn't finished his breakfast when Oliver strode in and joined him, going directly to the point.

He said now, "Well, I did tell you that we'd been thorough." He studied Rutledge for a moment, rubbing the menu he'd been given against his freshly shaven chin. "If the movements of the accused are accounted for, then we're left with the time it took her to travel from Brae to Duncarrick. And the road she took. It must have been there that the two women met. A matter of days, surely!"

Rutledge weighed the fact that Fiona had not worked out her time in Brae, though she'd told her aunt she must do so.

Where had she gone for those few weeks? Back to the glen where she'd been born? Or down to Lanark to meet someone?

No, it couldn't have been planned ahead. She hadn't known she would be summoned to Duncarrick by her aunt.

But what if—what if she'd been aware for some time that she was to meet someone on or about a certain date— and the summons from her aunt had given her the perfect opportunity to leave Brae at the right moment, without excuses or explanations? She had loved the Davison children, she had cried when she left them—but leave them she did.

No lies told to Mrs. Davison. No lies told to her aunt. Just the simple fact that suddenly Fiona MacDonald had been given a gift of time.

And therein lay the mystery of Eleanor Gray and the child.

If she wouldn't tell him what she knew, there might be another way of examining her past. . . .

Rutledge said to Oliver, "I'd like to search the inn if I may. Can you arrange it?"

"What on earth for?" Oliver demanded.

"I don't know. Yet. But it's worth looking to see whether—for the boy's protection if not her own—she left something there that might help us. A connection to the child's background that might have been overlooked because at the time no one understood what it represented."

Oliver shook his head. "I've been through the inn. Upstairs and down, the public and the family quarters. There's nothing."

But Rutledge knew more about Fiona MacDonald than Oliver did—and what he wanted to find, if they still existed, were any letters that Fiona had written to her aunt before she came to Duncarrick.

HE WAS GIVEN the key and Constable McKinstry as an observer, and allowed to inspect the inn.

McKinstry moved with nervous apprehension, a man torn between two duties. He showed Rutledge the way the inn was laid out, and then hovered at his shoulder like a

second Hamish, both of them carrying on a desultory conversation with him as he moved from room to room of the
private wing. By the time they'd finished with the small parlor, then walked into the dining room behind it, and the
kitchen beyond that, Rutledge said, "The boy's room. Have
you searched it thoroughly? If I were hiding anything, I'd
put it in among his toys, or perhaps at the bottom of a
drawer filled with outgrown clothes—"

"But what would she have been hiding?" McKinstry
asked wretchedly. "If she's not guilty, what *is* there to
hide?"

Rutledge turned and started toward the stairs. "This
way? Right! The boy's proper heritage is what we're after. If
anything had happened to Miss MacDonald—illness—accident—she had no family of her own to come for him and
take him in. Surely she'd have thought to leave some instructions for the child's protection? A name, or how to go
about reaching a solicitor, perhaps. Eleanor Gray had a solicitor who conducted her affairs for her." But was Mr. Leeds
courageous enough to take on Lady Maude's displeasure a
second time?

McKinstry said, "We've looked—"

"—but haven't found anything. Yes, I know. Look again
for that reason!"

McKinstry led the way up the stairs, where several doorways opened onto a central passage. Rutledge followed him.
The private wing, as he had noted, was small and old but
well-kept and comfortable. It spoke well for Fiona's sense of
duty to the inn and the child in her care.

Hardly, he thought, a den of iniquity, as some had imagined it!

A white cat came out of the room at the head of the
stairs, friendly and curious. She was well-fed, Rutledge saw,
and not frightened. Someone was looking after her—

He went into the room and saw that it must be Fiona's.
There was a round depression on the pillow at the head of

the bed and a thin carpeting of white hairs. This was where the cat slept.

Besides the bed, which boasted a coverlet trimmed in eyelet, there was a chest, a dressing table, and a desk. Two chairs stood beneath the windows, both cushioned in a rose print. He went to the desk first, but left it after a cursory examination. It would be the first place anyone looked. Oliver, for instance, would have gone through it with great care. All that appeared to be left were bills, unused stationery, a penknife, ink, pencils, envelopes, a large book of accounts for the household, and other ordinary items.

Hamish was no happier about his task than McKinstry had been, and reminded Rutledge that he had no right to pry here, police business or not.

Ignoring Hamish's irritation, he went through the drawers of the chest, found them neat and orderly, then looked at the back of each. Nothing.

Behind a curtain, clothes had been hung on a wire, and there was a pair of shelves for hats and shoes, but nothing of interest. A sweet perfume followed him as he let the curtain drop. Then he lifted it again, remembering another time and another place. He examined the shelves closely and found nothing. But a floorboard had moved as he stepped deeper into the small space, which was no larger than a cupboard.

Squatting on his heels, he examined the board and found that it was not loose. But the baseboard behind it, he thought, might be. He took out his pocketknife and, finding a seam, tried to pry out the board.

It didn't come. It was firmly nailed in place, and it had been imagination that had made it appear loose. Wishful thinking.

He moved through the room, searching the dressing table next, then pulled out the bed, which stood against the wall that formed part of the stairs on its other side.

The baseboard here was indeed loose. Eight inches or

more yielded to his questing fingers as he worked his knife into the seam.

He stood up quickly as he heard McKinstry come down the passage from the boy's room beyond.

"Nothing, sir. I've looked at every possible place she might have hidden something. Where else should I try?"

"Where did she do the inn's accounts? Is there an office in the inn proper?"

"Yes, sir, behind the bar. It isn't an office in the true sense—more a small cubby that has a curtain across it. She kept her account books there."

"Then you begin with that area. I'll just finish here and join you when I've satisfied myself I've looked everywhere."

McKinstry nodded, and there was a glint in his eye, as if he was glad that nothing had turned up.

But it should have—Fiona had had warning enough to hide private papers from the police, but would she have risked the child's safety by destroying them?

When the constable's footsteps had reached the bottom of the stairs, Rutledge waited for them to fade along the lower passage, then turned back to his own find.

Squatting on his heels again to reach into the dark and dusty hole, he nearly leapt out of his skin when the cat brushed against his leg. She started away in alarm, then came again for petting. He rubbed her ears and soft throat, then gently pushed her aside.

From the hole he brought a box, tin, he thought, and no more than ten by eight by six inches in size.

There were letters in it, the deed to the inn, several old envelopes of papers that seemed to go back in time to Miss MacCallum's father, and a collection of odds and ends that must have been considered family treasures—a man's pocketknife made of stag's horn, a pocket watch that had an elegantly engraved case bearing the name MacCallum, a pair of ivory crocheting hooks with a matching ivory thimble, and a little medicine flask made of silver with a fine engraving of the Tollbooth in Edinburgh. And a letter bearing Rutledge's own handwriting. The letter he had sent from France to a grieving young woman who had just learned that the man she loved was dead.

He could hear Hamish lamenting in his ear, anguish clear in the soft Highland voice.

"It had to be written," Rutledge told him. "It was kinder than hearing from the Army what had become of you."

"And none of it would ha' happened if we'd no' been so tired and afraid. . . ."

"No. It had to be done. It was done. I had no choice."

"Aye, it must seem that way now. In the safety of a house that was never bombarded for days at a time!"

"You chose to die," Rutledge reminded him, but knew even as he said the words that they were a lie. None of them had chosen to die—though he had tried in the months afterward to put himself in the way of a German shell or machine gunner's sights. They had all wanted to live and come home. . . .

He took each of the other letters out of their envelopes and scanned them quickly. The first came from Fiona, carrying the news that her grandfather had died. The next was also to Ealasaid MacCallum with word of the death of Fiona's brothers. After that, Fiona had written to tell her aunt about her position in Brae, describing the Davison family and how different the countryside around Glasgow was from the beauties of the mountains to the north.

I will be happier here, she wrote. *It is not as lonely, and these people are wonderfully kind to me. The children are a delight. . . .*

But the following letter was very different. It read:

I have sad news to tell you, dear aunt. I've lost Hamish. He died in the Somme offensive, like so many others. I have just had word. I still don't believe it. It seems that if I wait long enough, he will come through the door and take me in his arms again. I lay awake last night, praying that it was no more than a dream, but this morning the letter was still beside my bed. I can't cry, I can't feel, I don't know what to do. The minister here has come to offer comfort and Mrs. Davison has been kindness itself. I ache so, I want to die, but I have every reason to live. When Hamish was home last, we were wed in secret. And I am now carrying his child. It will be born in the autumn, and it will never know its father. But I will have a part of him to hold and love—a living memory of the man I married. I hope you will rejoice for me—and not feel that it is sad to be alone. I am not alone now, and I never will be again. . . .

Rutledge folded the page gently and put it back in its envelope without finishing it. He had seen all that he needed to see.

She had told her aunt that she was carrying a child—but he knew for a certainty that Hamish MacLeod had never been home that terrible year to father it. And it was not until Hamish was dead that she had admitted to it.

In ordinary circumstances, this could have meant that Hamish was not the father. That she was trying to pass off another man's child as his. But these were not ordinary circumstances. The night Fiona had lain awake praying the news was a dream, she had also made some very important decisions.

One of them was to tell her aunt that a child was to be born in the autumn.

A CURSORY READING of the remaining letters satisfied him that they held no secrets. Only the words of a young woman describing her pregnancy as it progressed. How had Fiona MacDonald known the feelings and the emotions and the sickness that a woman in her condition should have experienced?

Because the real mother had told her—and Fiona had carefully written it all down.

Was it from Maude Cook that Fiona had learned such things? Or—had she cleverly asked Mrs. Davison about her own confinements and what it was like to bear a child? Mrs. Davison, mother of three, would have talked to Fiona as one woman to another, prodded by questions, by interest, by the fact that she loved her own offspring and enjoyed sharing the giving of life.

But the letters offered no answers to that. Or to the question of why Fiona had carefully told her aunt lies, and led her to believe that she was with child.

And she hadn't been.

She had been very forward-thinking. She had woven the tissue of lies well before her aunt had sent for her. In the last letter, there were the words, *I must work out my time here, as I promised Mrs. Davison. And Ian shouldn't travel just now, it will be difficult for both of us. But by the end of the month, we shall arrive in Duncarrick and I look forward to seeing you more than you know.*

Fiona MacDonald hadn't come upon a woman lying by the roadside in the throes of childbirth, taken advantage of an opportunity to kill her and steal her baby. She had known for some time that a child would be born—she had made sure that her aunt had known too. And it meant, clearly, that the infant had been promised to her.

But by whom?

And if there had been no need to kill the mother in order to take the child, who was the woman whose bones had been found on a mountainside?

More important from the point of view of Lady Maude, what role—if any—had Eleanor Gray played? And where was Eleanor Gray now?

No one could say.

Hamish spoke the thought that Rutledge had already considered—and did not want to address now: that the child might have been a temporary gift to Fiona, to keep until the mother was ready or able to reclaim him. Until she had done what she had intended from the start to do, study to become a doctor?

And Fiona, already planning for the child, wanting the child, coveting the child forever, might have decided that she couldn't bear to give him up.

Hamish added, pain in his voice, "It's what they'll say. It's what they'll want to believe. Unless the mother is found alive, to bear witness for her!"

15

RUTLEDGE PUT THE TIN BOX BACK WHERE HE'D FOUND it for the time being, and was already on his way to the stairs, when a thought struck him.

His sister Frances had found in a small cedar chest belonging to their mother the carefully preserved christening robes that the two of them had worn. Wrapped in tissue, these were still white and soft, with lacy bodices and a wide band of matching lace at the hem, small caps frilled with lace and the tiniest of tucks, long ribbons for bows under the chin. Little knitted boots with blue or pink ribbons to tie them. Frances, who seldom cried, had said in a husky voice, "She never held grandchildren—mine or yours. It must have grieved her."

As if that was the ultimate wrong to the dead . . .

And in the center of each long skirt, hanging down almost to a grown man's knees, let alone an infant's, had been a large embroidered oval with entwined initials in white satin thread.

His had been his great-grandfather's christening robe, carefully handed down from generation to generation.

Frances had worn their grandmother's. A family tradition that had meant much to people proud of their heritage—

And surely, even if she had abandoned her baby at birth, Eleanor Gray would have seen to it that he was christened properly, and in a long white gown. Not, perhaps, the one that had been passed down through the Gray generations, but most certainly one that was suitable to the occasion. Unless it had been borrowed—

Rutledge turned around at the head of the stairs and walked swiftly back down the passage. While Fiona had had the front room, there were two more at the back, one empty with a neatly made bed covered with clean sheets to keep off the dust, and the other a small boy's realm, with a toy chest, a clothes chest, a dresser, and a crib.

Rutledge went first to the clothes chest. It was nearly empty. Here were only the outgrown dresses and stockings and tiny shoes kept for memory's sake. A small, pretty blanket for a baby that had seen much service. A blue velveteen coat with a matching cap, and a threadbare stuffed horse, one ear chewed off and one leg missing. At the bottom, carefully preserved in tissue and lavender, was a christening gown. He took it out and unfolded it with gentle hands.

Hamish saw it before he did. An embroidered half-circle of entwined letters, this time in the bodice.

Rutledge carried it to the window and examined it closely. Beautifully shaped initials with tiny forget-me-nots in the spaces. MEMC.

But did it stand for Maude Cook—or Mary Cook? Or someone else?

By the time McKinstry had come back to report to Rutledge, he had already put the gown back in the bottom of the clothes chest and dropped the lid.

THE MAN THAT Rutledge had encountered in the barn was standing outside the door as the constable and Inspector stepped out on the pavement. McKinstry, key in hand, turned to greet him. At the man's side stood a small, untidy boy of three or four. He was tall for his age and sturdy, with dark hair nearly the color of Rutledge's, and gray-blue eyes that were darker in the sunlight than they might have been by candlelight.

"I've come to feed yon cat," the man announced abruptly, his eyes on Rutledge in condemnation.

So you know who I am now, Rutledge thought, *and don't like it. I wonder why . . .*

"I didn't know you had a key," McKinstry was answering, surprise showing in his face.

"Aye, you don't leave a house to mind itself. I've had a key since Ealasaid MacCallum took her father's place."

"I don't know—" McKinstry said again, but the man cut him short.

"The cat's to be fed. Are you taking her, then? The lad will grieve for her. And he's lost his ma already."

McKinstry said, "Very well, then, as long as you don't touch anything!"

The man glared at him. "I've no' touched anything of anybody else's since I was *his* age and didn't know better!" He inclined his head toward the child.

Hamish had been saying something, but Rutledge had found it hard to make sense of it—he himself was silenced by the doleful stare of the child.

This, then, was Ian Hamish MacLeod.

Rutledge felt his heart turn over. A handsome child, this was. A small, lost child.

Rutledge dropped to one knee, and the man holding the boy's hand stepped forward, tense and prepared to intervene. But something in Rutledge's face stopped him; he stepped back again.

"Hello, Ian," Rutledge said, trying to speak through a constricted throat. This might have been Hamish's child if he'd lived. This might have been Jean's if she and Rutledge had married in 1914— "Going to see your cat, are you?"

Ian nodded. His eyes solemnly moved across Rutledge's face and then to McKinstry's. McKinstry must have smiled as he said "Hallo, Ian," because the child smiled and it was as if the sun had come out. The eyes filled with light and with warmth, and the sadness vanished.

"Is Mama here? Has she come back?" he asked breathlessly.

"No, but I have seen her," Rutledge said. "She's well, and she misses you." He looked at the man's face and dared him to contradict him. But the man didn't, and although McKinstry stirred at Rutledge's back, he, too, said nothing.

"When will she come back?" Ian insisted, anxious now.

"Soon, I hope," Rutledge answered. "I'll do my best to bring her home."

The boy's eyes swept his face again, as if to judge how truthful he was. Then he nodded, turned to the man holding his hand, and said, "Clarence?"

"Aye, we'll be feeding her. As soon as these gentlemen have gone away."

"Good-bye," the child told them, his voice firm. "Clarence is hungry."

"Clarence?" Rutledge questioned as they walked away and left the odd pair to do their duty by the cat.

McKinstry's eyes crinkled. "Well, there was a litter of kittens, you see, and Peter, the old man who worked in the stables, brought the boy one of them. Peter had named her Thomasina, after another cat he'd once had in the stables. But Ian has called her Clarence instead. I wondered why at the time, but haven't thought about it since."

Hamish, finding his voice, provided the answer. The Davison children had had a fog-gray cat by that name. And

Fiona must have told Ian about the litter that Maude Cook had never seen. . . .

As they walked back toward the hotel, Rutledge asked McKinstry who the man was.

"His name's Drummond. He and his spinster sister live next to the inn, and Fiona chose to leave the boy with them. She said he'd be less frightened with people he knew."

And people she trusted? It was worth bearing in mind. . . .

When McKinstry had gone on his way back to the station, Rutledge retraced his steps and came to a halt outside the house where the Drummonds lived.

It was the house he had noted before, the one with the extension in the rear and the windows with unexpected symmetry.

His instincts told him that Drummond and the child had not come back from feeding the cat. He wondered if Drummond allowed the boy to play with the toys in the chest, or sit on his mother's bed and hold Clarence.

When Rutledge knocked at the door, a woman of middle age answered, her fair hair drawn back and tight curls adding a softness around her face. She brushed these back, as if afraid the caller on her front step might take them for a softness in her as well, and said, "If you've come to see Drummond, he's not in."

"Miss Drummond? My name is Rutledge, I've been sent by Scotland Yard to look into the matter of the parentage of the boy you have in your keeping."

"Young Ian? And what interest has London got in a lad of three?" Her voice was sharp, indignant. But her pale eyes were wary, almost frightened. As if he'd come to carry the boy away.

"If his mother—the woman he calls his mother—is

hanged for murder, it would be best if the child went to his own kin. I think you'd agree with me there."

"I agree with nothing." Her fear made her garrulous. "Ian wouldn't be here if he hadn't been given to us by his mother. And if Drummond hadn't fought against that fool Elliot to keep the lad with us until—until it was all decided. *He* was all for sending him to the Forsters."

"Did you know Miss MacDonald well?"

Hamish said, "She must have done, else the lad would never have been entrusted to her. Fiona would never set a child at risk!"

Miss Drummond had not invited Rutledge in, but kept him on the doorstep like a tradesman. "As to that, knowing her well, I'm thinking now that none of us did. But Ealasaid MacCallum I knew. For her sake I agreed to do what I could. Drummond's reasons are his own. Ian's a likely lad, and has been no trouble. And I expect we can feed and clothe him better than most, if it comes to that," she added with some pride. "Before the war, Drummond made a fair living, working at Mr. Holden's. A good man with horses," she added grudgingly, as if she disliked admitting to better qualities in her brother. "They're great beasts, the shire horses, but when *he* handled them, they were meek as lambs. The Army took the lot of them and brought not one of them back. There's only sheep to be run at Holden's now. And my brother's not a man who cares for sheep. But Drummond can turn his hand to anything asked of him, and Mrs. Holden keeps him busy enough working about the house. He ought to be busy about the needs of his own! I can't do it all alone."

Hamish said, "She doesna' approve of her brother. But they live together like two peas."

"That's most likely the root of it," Rutledge replied silently. He thought the pair must have inherited this barn of a house together, and neither had wanted to move out. Or sell up. It could make for bad feelings over the years.

"Can you tell me anything about Miss MacDonald's family?"

"Everyone knew her grandfather. He was respected. He'd played the pipes for the old Queen in his day, when first she came up to Balmoral. And the MacCallums have owned The Reivers for four—five—generations. We've been neighbors for nearly three, the Drummonds and the MacCallums. Always honest, God-fearing. Minded their own business. Kept the inn in good order, never any rowdiness or drunkenness allowed. Still, all I knew about Fiona was what her aunt told me—that she was a hard worker and tidy and had no eye for the men. Not thinking to find another father for Ian, you understand."

"Then, why," Rutledge asked quietly, "did the town of Duncarrick turn their backs on her?"

"Ah!" Miss Drummond said it as an exclamation and a sigh. "If we knew what was at the bottom of that, we'd be wise, wouldn't we? Is that all you've come to ask?"

Rutledge said, "Tell me about the boy. Is he bright? Does he mind?"

"He does. I will say this for her, Fiona raised him proper. I've told that fool Elliot as much, but he sees only what he wants to see. I'm thinking it's no surprise he's a widower—drove his wife to an early grave, if you want my opinion! Ealasaid gave him the benefit of the doubt, but I had no patience with him! The old minister who was before him, *he* was a man of God, and he preached a mighty sermon of a Sunday. Mr. Hall, his name was, come from Dunfermline and married a Croser from over to Hawick. We went to kirk every Sunday, and were proud of it. But this fool Elliot, now, he's besotted with sin. He doesn't care a whit about redemption, only in setting blame. And what good's that, I ask you!"

"I've been led to believe that Fiona never confided in her aunt—never told her, for instance, that she wasn't the boy's mother. Surely she must have told someone? A woman she trusted—a friend or neighbor—your brother—"

Miss Drummond stared at him consideringly. "Any secret's best kept if it's kept. You should know that as a policeman! Fiona was friendly in a quiet fashion, respectful to her elders. Nice ways about her, as if she'd gone to school to learn them. But all I've ever heard was that she'd loved her grandfather and he was a bonny piper. Oh, and that she'd been happy with her soldier before he died. More than that I never asked and she never spoke of. Now, it's time you went, or Drummond will be home and shout at both of us. He doesn't like anyone prating about Fiona or the lad. 'Least said, soonest mended.' That's his view!"

"There's only one other question before I leave," Rutledge said, holding his ground. "I've been told that men were attracted to Fiona MacDonald. Was that true?"

He was met with stony silence. Miss Drummond's face had changed, the color shifting to a mottled red, as if some emotion had risen swiftly and as swiftly been stamped down. Anger? Or jealousy? After a few seconds, the woman before him, her voice very different, said tightly, as if the truth had been forced out of her, "They say still waters run deepest. I don't know. Fiona's not by nature a talkative woman, the kind you'd sit and gossip comfortably with. I never could tell what to make of her. I never got close to her. Men, on the other hand, they saw something else. I can't put a name to what it was. They'd watch her, and wait for her to smile, and then their faces would light up. I've seen my own brother staring at her, mesmerized by something I couldn't feel or understand. As if he thinks he's found the core of her and wants it. If you ask me, Drummond's besotted with her. And if you want the whole truth of it, Elliot is as well. He raves on about sin like a man who knows what it means to burn with desire at night!"

"But surely the police haven't fallen under her spell—"

"Haven't they now? McKinstry would save her if he could, he's in hopes of marrying her. Oliver used to stop by the inn of an evening before he went home, sitting there like a suitor, and him with a wife. And what troubles the Chief Constable and the fiscal is that she refuses to bow her head and confess to what she's done, and beg for mercy, the way a woman should. They see it as defiance of their authority, and it unsettles their faith in their own importance. I'm not surprised they all want her hanged. Don't you see? It's the best way to be free of her!"

WHEN RUTLEDGE WALKED into the hotel, the man at the desk said, "There's been a telephone call for you, sir. From London."

He took the message and read it.

Call Sergeant Gibson.

One of the best men at ferreting out information of any kind, Gibson had a reputation for being thorough as well.

Rutledge went into the telephone closet, set his hat on the little table there, and put in his call to the Yard.

Gibson came on very shortly to say, "Inspector Rutledge, sir?"

"Yes. I'm in need of good news. I hope you're going to tell me you have found Eleanor Gray."

"No, sir, that I haven't. But I talked to suffragettes she'd marched with and was known to be friends with. They haven't seen her in some three years. What they tell me is that she went off to Winchester one weekend and never came back to London. At least not as far as anyone knows. Most of the women thought Lady Maude had had enough of her daughter's wild ways and sent for her."

"Are they certain she actually went to Winchester? She could have lied about her plans."

"Yes, sir, I thought of that, and took the liberty to call on the people she was to stay with. Miss Gray never got there. She was set to drive down with an officer she'd known in London. But she changed her mind at the last minute and said the two of them would be going to Scotland instead—he was on sick leave and it wasn't up for another week. She promised to call back when she returned to London, but never did."

Scotland! "Did you ask the name of this officer?" Rutledge asked.

"That I did, sir!" Gibson's voice came strongly down the line. "But they've forgotten it. Still, it was someone she'd met before. Not a stranger, or she wouldn't have asked to bring him to Winchester with her. They tell me she was not one to impose on her hostess in that way."

"Well done, Gibson!" Rutledge said. "Do you have a number where I can reach these people in Winchester?"

He could hear down the line the shuffling of papers. "Yes, sir, here it is! A Mrs. Humphrey Atwood. She was the Honorable Miss Talbot-Hemings. Went to school with Miss Gray for a time and stayed friends." There was a pause. Rutledge could hear a door shut. And then with a note of triumph, Gibson added, "The Chief Superintendent told me I wasn't to bother talking to the suffragette ladies. Addled, all of them, he said. A waste of time." There was another pause. "Bit of luck, wasn't it, sir!"

If he hadn't known Gibson better, Rutledge would have imagined him grinning ear to ear. It was there in the voice. But Gibson seldom smiled. He was also seldom wrong in his findings or his conclusions. He was the kind of man who took pride in himself and in his work, and was bulldog tenacious when he wanted to be. Only his eyes warned that inside the beefy, middle-aged body was a brain sharp as a razor. Rutledge had always suspected that Old Bowels and Gibson were enemies from years back.

That didn't put Gibson in Rutledge's column at the Yard. But it meant that an opportunity to blacken Chief Superintendent Bowles's eye was savored by the man, and often produced information that Rutledge found valuable.

As in this case.

Rutledge thanked him and put up the receiver, standing there for all of a minute, thinking.

Here was the first tie between Eleanor Gray and Scotland. Secondhand it might be, but it was better than none.

Why would a man bring a woman some months pregnant from London to Scotland—unless he was the father of her child?

Hamish said, "Unless there wasna' anyone else she could turn to, and he felt sorry for her."

There was also that possibility, Rutledge acknowledged, opening the door of the little room and taking a deep breath of fresher air. But he thought it was more likely that the officer must have known the father, if indeed he wasn't the father himself. He himself would have done as much for a friend at the Front.

He closed the door again and was on the point of asking for the number Gibson had given him, when he realized that he ought to go to Winchester himself.

It would mean a long, fast drive there and back, but it had to be done. A telephone was a device that allowed people to hide behind distance. Nothing said into the telephone could match the nuances of expression and tone of voice that he used so often to judge information and people.

Hamish said, "It's been close to three years. It's likely true they canna' remember the officer's name now."

On the way to his room to pack what he needed, Rutledge answered, "Very likely. But you never can tell what other information they still have."

16

RUTLEDGE SPENT THE NIGHT IN THE MIDLANDS. HE had tried to persuade himself that he was good for another hour or more of driving. But heavy rain caught up with him, nearly blinding him. When he narrowly missed an unlit wagon going in the same direction, he pulled over, waiting for the worst of the downpour to pass. Only then did he recognize just how tired he was. There was an inn on the High Street of the next village, and rousing the owner from his bed, Rutledge asked for a room and was brought a tray of tea and dry sandwiches as well. He was on the road again as soon as it was light. By the time he arrived in Winchester, the stiffness in his back and legs was turning to cramp.

Hamish had spent most of Rutledge's hours behind the wheel earnestly pulling apart the evidence against Fiona MacDonald and quarreling over the role Eleanor Gray might or might not have played.

It had been exceedingly difficult for Rutledge to explain Hamish's existence, the reality of his voice, to the doctor at the clinic. He was not a ghost—ghosts could be exorcised. Nor was he a disembodied voice repeating Rutledge's thoughts like a parrot. What was there was vivid—the nuances of thought and tone demanded answers. And Rutledge in 1916, broken in spirit and mind and nearly in body, had found it easier to answer the voice than to challenge it. He had known Hamish through two years of war— his memory was filled with conversations that had shaped new conversations—new thoughts—new fears.

In the five months since returning to the Yard, Rutledge had slowly found the courage to argue, to refute—to take on the voice in verbal battle. A painful step toward sanity, he told himself again and again—not away from it. But challenging it went beyond his courage still.

Hamish was saying, "It's those bones in Glencoe that gave Oliver an excuse to bring a charge of murder against Fiona. He wouldna' care about them, else. It's no' even his jurisdiction! It doesna' matter to him whose they are."

"True enough, but until we know how that woman died, we're bound to take them into account," Rutledge argued. "As long as her shadow—whoever she may be—falls over the evidence, it will obscure everything else."

Hamish still disagreed. And said so. Rutledge shook his head.

"Eleanor Gray's disappearance gave the police in Duncarrick a name to put to those bones. Identify the corpse— that's the first rule of a murder inquiry. And Oliver is convinced that he has. Once that's established, he has to find a clear connection between the two women. If Eleanor Gray was pregnant and came to Scotland to wait out her term, then the link begins to take shape. If that's *not* true, then there has to be another explanation for her presence in Glencoe. And if it can be proved that the bones aren't Eleanor Gray's after all, Oliver is simply going to search for another identity to give them. Named or nameless, the woman is a stumbling block."

"Aye, I grant you. But can you no' see that named or

nameless, it's happenstance that connects these bones with Fiona in the first place. What if Oliver proves they belong to the Gray woman? What if he proves she was pregnant when she disappeared? It's still a giant leap to prove Fiona killed her!"

"Or any other woman. I agree. But finding Eleanor Gray alive will eliminate her from the list. If she's dead, and Oliver does have her body, then we're back to the problem of *how* she died where she did. Murder—natural causes—even suicide. Whether the answer will clear Fiona or damn her isn't the issue. We have to look for it. By the same token, if it turns out that Eleanor Gray was murdered, then we have to prove that Fiona was the only person who might have had a reason and opportunity to kill her. Oliver may be content to jump to conclusions, but the truth is, Lady Maude won't be as easily satisfied."

"Who's to say that in the end those bones are no' their own mystery—and no' ours?" Hamish countered stubbornly.

"Then you'd better pray that Eleanor Gray left the child with Fiona while she secretly went off to finish her studies. It's the only way to convince Inspector Oliver that he's got no case. Which brings me back to what I've been saying all along. Right now Eleanor Gray is the key to the investigation."

"I canna' say I like it!"

It was odd, Rutledge found himself thinking at one point, how Hamish had coped with the unexpected and sudden confrontation with Fiona MacDonald. He was vigorous in her defense, and he had never questioned her innocence. But far deeper than that ran the knowledge that her life now was separating from his. Not as Jean had left him, wanting to be free of what she feared, but in the very fact that living had drawn Fiona into new directions and new feelings and new places that Hamish would never share. He had not known about Duncarrick; he had not known about the child. The silences that followed his meeting Fiona again had been a painful reminder that time did not wait, that there was no holding on to it. That there was an emptiness in death. And yet in some sense, it was as if she was the one who had died, for Hamish mourned her loss with a heavy sorrow, with yearning and despair. And the burden Rutledge carried grew daily heavier with it.

It was Rutledge who struggled with the reality, the fact that Fiona could be found guilty of murder and hanged. He was the one who dealt with the tired face and dark-circled eyes of the woman in the cell. It was Rutledge who bore the brunt of fear and uncertainty about his own views of the evidence and the case building so tightly. Uncertainty, too, about his personal feelings.

He had seen Fiona through Hamish's eyes for so long that until now she had seemed rather like the Dresden figurines on Frances's bookshelf—gentle and uncomplicated, frozen in time and place, mourning her dead soldier. A woman wronged by what he, Rutledge, had been forced to do on the battlefield. The martyr, as it were, to his own guilt. Even in the dream in London she had been connected to the death of Hamish, with no existence all her own.

He had, he realized suddenly, seen her through Hamish's *memories*. . . .

Now he had his own.

A flesh-and-blood woman, somehow attractive and, right or wrong, displaying remarkable strength in her lonely defiance of the law. Mourning Hamish still and giving that pent-up love to a child . . . The courage of innocence—or guilt? Rutledge found that she had brought out the protective streak in him, and he couldn't be sure whether it was for her own sake or Hamish's that he felt bound to do his best for her.

There was confusion and emotion in his mind fraught with his own bitterness, his own loneliness. It was, he thought, forcing him to think without the clarity and objectivity he tried to bring to every investigation assigned to him.

Hamish, God damn it, was right—

"And where was your objectivity in Cornwall—or Dorset?" Hamish demanded. "Where was your clarity then? Those women touched you too. How can you be sure it is Fiona and not *you* who's on trial here!"

Rutledge had no answer.

RUTLEDGE STOPPED IN Winchester long enough to bathe and change his clothes and then found his way to Atwood House.

It was a small manor house built of mellow stone by a sure hand in the 1700s. The architect had set it on a knoll that offered splendid views to the south and an old grove of trees to the north, offering privacy and a barrier against cold winds. A stream meandering through the property was lined with wild roses, thick with hips now. Rutledge could see a pair of swans swimming regally on a pond created for the rowboat tied to a post. Someone had opened out the stream to fill the pond, and created a lovely effect at the bottom of the western gardens, a mirror of the sky that barely rippled as the swans floated above their own images.

The drive swept him up to the Georgian front with its dressed stone and pedimented windows. He got out of the car, nodding to the gardener trundling a handbarrow filled with spades and hoes and trimmers across the lawn toward the drive, and walked to the door. A brass knocker, which looked to be a more modern copy of an earlier iron one, clanged mightily as he let it fall.

After a proper passage of time, an elderly butler answered the door.

Rutledge identified himself and asked to speak to Mrs. Atwood.

The butler, noting his crisp collar and the set of his suit

across his shoulders, said, "I'll ask if Mrs. Atwood is at home this afternoon."

He led Rutledge to a coldly formal room and left him there for nearly seven minutes. The walls, sheathed in blue silk, shimmered in the light from the long windows, and the French chairs that set off the white marble of the mantel were arranged for elegance, not comfortable conversation. There was no carpet on the floor, and on closer inspection, the walls as well as the fabric covering the chairs were worn. But over the mantel was a wonderful painting of the view he'd seen coming up the drive. It was a younger time, the trees were not yet mature, there were sheep grazing the smooth lawns, and the house did not have the patina of age, but the serenity was there, unchanged.

The butler returned and conducted him down the passage to a sitting room that also showed wear. Well-worn chintz, a faded carpet on which an elderly spaniel slept noisily, and an air of comfortable, genteel shabbiness told him that the house had suffered much use during the war and had not yet reclaimed its former elegance. But the windows faced the pond and the stream, framing the view and bringing in the soft light of afternoon. It was peaceful.

Mrs. Atwood was standing by the empty hearth as he came in. A pale woman in every sense, slim and willowy in pastel green, pale of hair and eyes and skin, as if all the color had been washed away in the long, careful years of family breeding.

He discovered very quickly that the character had not been washed away.

She said with graciousness that was backed by steel, "I have spoken to—um—a Sergeant Gibson. There is nothing more I wish to say to the police."

"That's quite possible," he answered. "Sergeant Gibson was here as a duty. I have come as an emissary of Lady Maude Gray."

Something unexpected stirred in the pale blue eyes. They

were the color of faded lupines, hardly differentiated from the white surrounding them. "I have not heard from Lady Maude in some years." Her voice was neutral, giving nothing away.

Hamish, silent until now in the shadows of Rutledge's mind, said softly, "She doesna' care for yon Lady Maude. . . ."

Making a note of it, Rutledge answered, "It isn't surprising. She quarreled with her daughter. I cannot say she regrets that quarrel, but she has come into information now that has disturbed her. It's very possible that Eleanor Gray is dead. How and where she came to die we don't know. I am doing what I can to find answers."

Surprise flared in the long face. *"Dead!* But your sergeant—"

"—said nothing about that. Yes, I know. On my instructions."

He let the silence fall and gave her time to digest his curt answer.

"I don't see how I can help you. I haven't seen Eleanor since the middle of the war. I thought—Humphrey and I were quite convinced she'd gone to America when she couldn't take up medicine here. It would have been so like her!"

"Why should she choose to go there? Did she have friends—someone who might put in a word for her?"

"As a matter of fact, there was someone." She hesitated and then added, "I called Alice Morton after Sergeant Gibson left. She was in school with Eleanor and me. But her husband is an American—he's at the embassy here. His brother John is a professor at Harvard. He'd written to Eleanor once, in the spring of 1916, at Alice's request, laying out opportunities she might wish to consider over there. Alice told me John had never had a reply. Eleanor hadn't contacted him at all." Mrs. Atwood shrugged lightly. "She was always strong-minded. She might not have wished to be beholden, even to a friend."

LEGACY OF THE DEAD   181

"Why did you call and ask about Miss Gray? If you hadn't tried to find her for three years?"

Mrs. Atwood was disconcerted by the direct question. "I—I don't know why. Not really. It was just—I wanted to be reassured, I suppose. We don't often have the police asking about an acquaintance. It was—only that."

Hamish demanded, "Was it?"

After a moment, Rutledge asked pleasantly, "Tell me about the last time you saw or spoke with Eleanor Gray."

He had made his hostess uneasy. From reticence she had moved to explanations and now apology. "I'm sorry, there isn't much to tell. Not really. She was to come down for the weekend and bring a friend. But she telephoned to say she'd changed her mind. The young man had more leave than she'd thought, and she wanted to go to Scotland with him."

"I wasn't aware that her family had a house there." He deliberately misunderstood her.

"No, of course they didn't! It was the pipers, you see—" Breaking off, she started again. "Eleanor was eager to do what she could for the wounded. I found it rather—depressing—being around them. But she did her best to try to cheer them. Brought in singers, performers, that sort of thing. She became convinced that hearing the pipes might encourage the wounded and help them endure their pain better. Perhaps remind them of the courage they'd shown at the Front."

"She went to Scotland to find them?" Again he subtly twisted her words.

"No, no, you don't understand. She arranged for pipes and drums to visit the manor houses that had been turned into clinics or hospitals. We had about twenty officers ourselves, broken bones generally. She invited the pipers here first, to see what the response might be. And it brought the men to tears. They were so buoyed up! It was amazing. She had two young officers with her who had helped find the pipers. Both were Scottish, and both were quite taken with

Eleanor. I thought she rather liked the dark one. She was upset when he went back to the Front."

"Do you recall the names of these men?"

"Good gracious, no, not after all this time. I do remember that the fairer one spent a considerable part of his day in our stables. The horses were gone, of course, but it was the construction that interested him. The stonework was eighteenth century, and he admired it."

"And the other officer? The one Eleanor Gray seemed to like?"

Mrs. Atwood frowned. "His father was something in finance. I can't tell you what it was. We were so crowded, and there was so much happening. I tried to be polite, but the truth is, I barely listened."

"Please try to remember." It was a command sheathed as a polite request.

She shook her head. "It was so long ago. And you can't imagine what it was like, the house at sixes and sevens, things packed away in the attics, no room to entertain. Though we did make an effort when we had fewer patients."

"But she saw this man more than once? Perhaps having dinner with him in London as well as bringing him here for the pipers?"

"I can't be sure. They're all Mac-this and Mac-that, aren't they, the Scots? And Eleanor was in London, I could hardly keep track of her friends."

"Yet you say she rather liked him and was upset when he went back to France."

She bit her lip. Caught in her own tangle of truth. She turned and walked to one of the windows, looking out with her back to him. After a silence, she said, "I think the dark one, the one she liked, was named for a poet. How odd—I had forgotten that! Yes, I'm sure he was the one. There was some joke about it the first time he came. We asked if he'd read from his works—teasing, of course! And he said he might, after a good dinner. But he never did. A charming man with a charming accent. I hope he survived the war."

So Mrs. Atwood had seen him more than once. . . ."There are a number of Scottish poets," Rutledge said gently.

"Yes, I know. How absolutely maddening! I remember the teasing—I remember his smile as he answered. I remember that his father was in finance—"

It was Hamish who made the leap, quite unexpectedly. "Robert Burns."

Startled, Rutledge repeated the name aloud.

"Yes! They called him Robbie!" she responded, turning back to him, her face brightening with a becoming flush. He couldn't be sure whether it was relief at having the answer handed to her or chagrin that he had caught her out. "He had a small house in the Trossachs. That's in Scotland, I'm told. Though heaven knows where it is. I remember he said he ought to have been named Walter Scott, because he lived in the wrong place for a Burns. How odd that I should recall that so clearly now!"

Rutledge felt a surge of hope. The Trossachs lay in central Scotland, almost halfway between Glasgow to the south and Glencoe to the north. There must be, Rutledge thought, a thousand men in Scotland called Robert Burns. Of every age and station and background. But a young officer with a house in the Trossachs—that could narrow the search enormously. Yes, and with a father in finance.

Finance—banking or— He tried to keep his voice level, his words without emphasis. Hamish was hammering at the back of his mind, almost drowning what he was saying. "Was his father by chance a procurator-fiscal?"

But her face was blank, as if she had never heard the title before. Shaking her head, she gestured to the chairs neither of them had taken. "Please, do sit down! May I offer you tea or a glass of something?"

Buying time, Rutledge said, "Yes, I'd like a cup of tea."

She rang for the butler, who must have been hovering nearby, expecting shortly to show Rutledge out, and gave her instructions.

As Rutledge sat in the nearer chair, he said, "Tell me about Eleanor Gray. As you remember her."

"She knew her worth. But she was never condescending. A dependable friend. Good company as a house guest. Independent. She told me once that she had no real hope of becoming a doctor—her mother would see to it that no one took her seriously. I think that's why she was a suffragette. It seemed frightfully vulgar to me, but Eleanor laughed and called it an adventure. I think it made her mother furious, and that pleased Eleanor. They never saw eye to eye."

"Why?"

"I don't know. She adored her father and would have done anything he asked. But he never told her what to do or not do. He said she should please herself. It was odd how much she loved him. I thought he cared for her, but I could never quite see it as love. Some fathers dote on their only daughters, you know. Spoil them, that sort of thing. But Evelyn Gray was— fond of her. Merely—fond. Perhaps they had little in common. . . ."

She let the thought trail away as the butler arrived with tea. Hamish warned, "It's no' like her to talk so much." Rutledge agreed.

Mrs. Atwood thanked the butler and dismissed him, settling herself to pour. As she handed Rutledge his cup, he said, "Why did Eleanor Gray want to be a doctor? It's an odd choice, given her wealth and social position."

"Ah, that was something I never fully understood. Humphrey—my husband—rather thought it was a passing fancy, with the war and all. But I don't see it that way. At a dinner party once, Eleanor said that doctors were woefully ignorant and uninterested in what caused diseases. She argued with the Army doctors, too, when she felt it was warranted.

She cared intensely about the patients, but it wasn't sentimental in any way. It was practical and realistic. She would have made a good doctor, in my view."

Rutledge said, "And when she didn't contact you for three years, you accepted the fact that she must be in America? If not Boston, then somewhere else there."

She was silent so long, he thought she didn't want to answer the question. Hamish, responding to the odd tension in the air, said, "You made the right decision, coming yoursel'."

Then Mrs. Atwood replied, "You've made me afraid. The police. You and Sergeant Gibson. The last time I spoke to Eleanor she was in London—it was a strange conversation. She said something—I thought she must be a little drunk that night, and I was worried that she was contemplating driving to Scotland in that condition. And she said, 'I could die.' And I took it to mean she was so happy, she could die. But what if that wasn't what she meant—what if she truly wanted to die. . . ." Mrs. Atwood looked at him, pain in her eyes. "Was there some terrible accident? Is that what happened?"

"No," Rutledge told her. "It wasn't an accident. It's more likely that someone murdered her."

She turned so white, he thought she was going to faint, and was halfway out of his chair.

"No!" she said in a strangled voice. "No—I'm all right. It's just—" She tried to breathe deeply and instead her breath caught on a sob. "I've never known anyone who was murdered—that's horrible—*horrible*—"

"If she was driving north with a soldier to spend his leave in Scotland, she must have known him well enough to go with him."

"Of course she must! Eleanor wasn't the sort who—who used the war as an excuse to behave as she pleased. She wouldn't have gone with a stranger, or a man she didn't trust." There was conviction in the low voice.

"Was it Burns that she went to Scotland with, Mrs. Atwood?"

"I tell you, I can't remember! You can ask the servants—they might—"

"Would you have tried to stop her if she was about to do something—silly?"

"I—" She broke off, caught between her own emotional dilemma and his dark eyes watching her face. They seemed to see into her soul.

"You must tell me the truth, Mrs. Atwood. A lie won't serve you or me."

When she spoke, her voice was husky with shame. "I—I was hurt that she wasn't coming for the weekend, I told myself she was *happy*, while I was wretched. There had been no letters from Humphrey for weeks, and I'd just received word that he was being listed as missing. I knew what that meant—he was dead but they hadn't found his body yet. I hadn't even told my mother—I could hardly bear to believe it myself! And to have Eleanor let me down when I'd been counting so on her company—to go larking off with someone, half drunk with champagne, most likely, sounding quite unlike herself—it was—I *couldn't* tell her about Humphrey then, could I? I was angry—angry and upset. I didn't care to know, I didn't want to know what she was doing! I hoped she'd end her week just as wretched as I was—" She stopped and then went on almost against her will. "That's why I refused to be worried when she didn't come back or call me. I was still angry—I told myself she wasn't a friend at all, it was better if she went her own way. She'd gone to Scotland and could stay there forever, as far as I cared. Then I got word that Humphrey was alive and safe, and I didn't want to think about anything else—I didn't want to remember how badly I'd behaved."

She regarded him with hurt, frightened eyes. "If she died that night—it was my fault, in a way. For letting her down. For not worrying when she didn't call at the end of the week, or come down, or write. I punished her for being happy when I wasn't, and then I put it all out of my mind, *deliberately.*"

As HE DROVE toward London, Rutledge tried to set out in logical detail what he had learned from Mrs. Atwood and her servants.

Hamish said, "There's still no name to put with the Gray woman's companion."

"No. But there's a connection now between Eleanor Gray and Scotland. The wrong side of Scotland, but it's a start."

"Aye, but it would ha' been better if there was no connection at all. If she'd gone to America."

"We have to find this man Burns if we can."

"Aye, but there's no proof Eleanor Gray went to Scotland with *him*!"

"He may know the name of the man who did accompany her. He may have introduced them, he may have been a friend of both." Rutledge thought about it. "She wasn't traveling alone. But she went of her own free will. She was alive when she left London."

"Ye canna' know that!"

"But I do—she told Mrs. Atwood where she was going, and with whom. It was planned. It was something she wanted to do."

Yet her mood had been unsettled. "*I could die—*" From happiness—or despair? Had this been just after Eleanor's quarrel with Lady Maude?

Rutledge had asked Mrs. Atwood to put a date to that conversation. It was early in 1916. Spring. The timing fit. If Eleanor was pregnant, she could still conceal it. If her mother had refused to help her, she could still make other plans.

A small house in the Trossachs. A place to hide?

A place to start, most certainly.

Rutledge stopped long enough in London to pack another case. He didn't contact the Yard.

But back on the road, heading north again, he decided it was time to report to Lady Maude Gray.

17

LADY MAUDE RECEIVED RUTLEDGE WITH COOL DISIN-
terest, as if he had come to report on the state of her drains
or her roofs.

She again conducted the interview in the library, but this
time had seen to it that tea arrived shortly after he did.

Pouring his cup, she said, "I knew nothing would come
of this ridiculous business. There is nothing in your face
that tells me you have been successful."

"On the contrary, there have been a number of small
successes. Not yet a whole. But enough to be going on with."

She smiled, lighting the remarkable violet eyes from
within.

"Then tell me. I shall be the judge."

"Your daughter did not go to America to study medicine.
We have that on the authority of a professor who had been
advising her." It was only a patchwork of truth and fiction.
But he saw the small flicker of surprise in her face.

Like Mrs. Atwood, Lady Maude must also have soothed her

conscience with the notion that Eleanor Gray had gone abroad to study. Against her mother's wishes—but surely safely accounted for. Lady Maude had even closed her ears to Inspector Oliver, so certain was she. And then Rutledge had somehow raised niggling doubts. This was news she had not expected to hear. Hamish, who did not care for Lady Maude, was pleased.

"Go on," she said curtly.

"She was last heard from on her way to Scotland with a young officer by the name of Burns. He had a small house in the Trossachs and enough leave to go there."

Her voice was cold. "You are mistaken. Eleanor would not have gone anywhere with a strange man."

"He wasn't a stranger. She had known him for some time apparently, and a Mrs. Atwood believes that Eleanor was—attracted—to him. They had worked together to arrange for pipe concerts at various hospitals, to cheer the wounded. I was given the impression that your daughter had spent enough time in this man's company to grow fond of him. Whether as a friend or more than that, I'm not able to tell you at this stage."

Like a mask, her face remained unchanged. Her hands, holding her cup and saucer, were still quiet in her lap, too well-behaved to indicate by any movement of their own that she was unsettled. But along the firm jawline there was a small nerve twitching.

"When I requested that you be assigned to this case, Inspector, I believed I had chosen a man of intelligence and integrity. I had not expected you to be a listener to gossip and innuendo. You have disappointed me."

He smiled. "For that I shall apologize. But the fact is, I talked to the person whom your daughter telephoned just before leaving for Scotland with Burns. She had been promised to the Atwoods for a weekend, and had—quite properly—called her hosts to explain the change in plan. You had brought your daughter up well. She remembered her manners even in a time of great distress."

He set his empty cup on the tray. Check. And mate.

Hamish, in the ensuing silence, said only, "Well done!"

It was rare praise. Rutledge had no time to savor it.

Lady Maude said, "If your information comes from Grace Talbot-Hemings—now Mrs. Atwood—I'm sure she reported the conversation exactly as it happened. She was a truthful child and has no doubt grown into a truthful young woman. This is not to say that what my daughter told her is to be believed. On the contrary, Eleanor might well have left a false trail if she had found passage to the United States and wished to be absolutely certain that no one stopped her. This would also explain her great distress, as you call it."

Rutledge had to admit that it did.

Lady Maude was not easily broken. She had been the mistress of a king and knew her worth. She had known her daughter's worth as well, and lived to see Eleanor turn her back on it.

Rutledge thought: *Eleanor died in her mother's heart in 1916.* And he suddenly knew why. The daughter Lady Maude had given up her own self-respect to bear to a Prince of Wales had not been worthy, in her mother's eyes, of such sacrifice. Eleanor had neither understood nor appreciated the burden her mother carried, and if anything had, in her youthful rebellion, mocked it.

For the most fleeting instant of time, he wondered if Lady Maude might be capable of killing her only child.

Lady Maude also set her cup on the tray with firm finality. "You must realize, Inspector, that your"—she hesitated delicately—"small successes, as you call them, are proving to be a reflection on my daughter's character that I find unacceptable. You will not pursue them."

"Aye, she doesna' want to learn that her daughter was pregnant," Hamish said. "If it damns Fiona, neither do I!"

"I have no choice in the matter," Rutledge said, "I am trying now to locate this man Burns. He should be able to lead us to the next step. Where Miss Gray went in Scotland. And why."

Lady Maude rose. "I must thank you for your courtesy in reporting your information to me in person. I expect we shall not meet again."

Dismissal. Permanent dismissal, Hamish pointed out.

Rutledge stood as well. "I shall respect your wishes. Would you prefer a written report to a message by telephone when I've completed my investigation?"

Their eyes locked. Hers a deep violet with her anger, and his a mirror of his voice, official and unyielding.

For a full twenty seconds she said nothing, waiting for him to look away first.

Then she snapped, "I can break you, Inspector."

"No doubt," he answered. "But it will not change the truth, nor will it give you great satisfaction. Good day, Lady Maude."

He had reached the door before her voice stopped him.

"You will find nothing connecting my daughter to those appalling bones!"

He turned, and for a moment looked at the room enclosing them with such elegance and formality. "That's my hope as well. It will be a great tragedy if I do. For many people."

As the door began to close on his heels, he heard her voice, commanding and clear but not raised. "Inspector."

He stepped back in the room. Nothing had changed in her face. She said only, "It is fortunate, is it not, that my daughter has found a champion in you. I fear that I have been hurt too often. It is difficult to summon the courage to face another disappointment. But I shall try."

He inclined his head. It was, in its way, a salute. And an apology.

This time she didn't stop him as he left.

Hamish, digesting the last exchange, said only, "I canna' say that walking with the great is the road to happiness."

No, Rutledge silently answered. *That woman has paid a dear price.*

AN HOUR AFTER leaving Menton, Rutledge found a telephone in the next town and put in a call to his godfather.

Morag answered the telephone and went to find David Trevor.

He said, taking up the receiver, "Ian? I hope this means you're coming to dinner!"

"I won't make it to Scotland in time. It's late and I've had three days of hard driving. No, it's information I need, sir. You told me earlier that you knew the procurator-fiscal in the MacDonald case. Well enough to tell me anything about his family?"

There was an instant of silence, then David Trevor said, "Yes, I can give you what I know. He married a young woman from the neighborhood of Stirling. If I remember, her father was a lawyer, and a brother was a judge. I think I met her once or twice at some official gathering. They had three children. Cathy, the daughter, is married to an Englishman and they live in Gloucester. George, the older son, is with a London firm. The youngest, Robert, is dead."

"Did either son serve in the war?"

"George was in the Navy. Invalided out in late '17. Robert was killed in France. Artillery. Early 1916, I think."

"Was Robert married?"

"No, there was a girl in Edinburgh whom he was unofficially engaged to. It was an understood thing, but no announcement had been made. Then she died of appendicitis. I don't know quite when—well before Robert was killed, certainly. In the winter of '15, I think it was. Why this sudden interest in Robert?"

"I don't know," Rutledge said truthfully. "Could you describe him?"

"He was dark, and well set up. And I'm told he had the most wonderful wit. Ross had heard him offering the toasts at a wedding, he had the guests bent double with laughter. He said that Robert could have stood for Parliament if he'd wanted to go in that direction. But he was interested in law or banking, I forget which." Rutledge could almost hear the smile in Trevor's voice. "Have I earned a consulting fee for my knowledge of Scottish social circles?"

"Without doubt! Thank you, I appreciate your help."

"Will you be coming again, Ian? Before you leave Scotland?"

There was a quiet longing in the seemingly casual question.

"As soon as I can," Rutledge promised, and said goodbye.

ANOTHER NIGHT ON the road saw Rutledge back in Duncarrick, tired and out of sorts. He stopped at the police station before he went to the hotel, and asked to speak to Fiona.

McKinstry was on duty, and he said diffidently, "You've been away, I think."

"Yes, there was business outside of London to see to."

McKinstry took him back and opened the door himself, smiling at Fiona. He said wistfully to Rutledge, "Shall I stay and take notes?"

"No, no, it isn't necessary." He waited until McKinstry was out of earshot down the hall before going into the small cell and closing the door behind him.

Fiona, with nothing to say, watched his face. Rutledge bade her a good morning, and then asked, "There was a Scottish officer who was well known to Eleanor Gray. Robert Burns, called Robbie by his friends. Did you ever meet him?"

She answered, "The only Burns I know is the fiscal. He isn't young enough to have been in the war. He lives in Jedburgh."

Rutledge said, "Yes. Well, it doesn't matter." He gestured for her to sit, and she looked first at the cot and then at the single chair, and chose the cot, perching herself stiffly on the edge of it. Rutledge took the chair and said conversationally, "Fiona, why do the people of Duncarrick dislike you?"

"Do they?"

"They must. They believed the scurrilous letters about you. They believe now that you're capable of murder. Would you have picked out, say, the Tait woman at the hat shop as a murderer? Or the young woman who keeps house for the minister? Would you find it easy to believe people who claimed *they* were whores and worse?"

She flushed.

"But people believed these things about you. If I can discover why, I might know who is behind the lies. It will be a beginning."

"I've told you before—I don't know why. If I did, I wouldn't be here, locked away from the sunlight and the wind on my face!"

"I accept that. Have you ever met the father of the boy you call Ian?"

The sudden shift in direction made her eyes widen. But her answer was swift and seemingly honest. "No."

"You're quite sure of that?"

"I have never set eyes on Ian's father. Before God, it's the truth."

"Then," he said with cold reason, "the trouble you are in today must come from the boy's mother—"

"No! She's dead. I have told you that."

The interruption was so swift that she hadn't allowed him to finish what he had planned to say—*the boy's mother's family.*

"She isn't dead," he said gently. "And that's the problem, I think. She's afraid of you. Afraid that you might tell her new husband about the child she bore out of wedlock. Afraid that you might grow weary of caring for the child, and decide one fine day to bring him to her doorstep. She is afraid of you, and she's here in Duncarrick. Or close by. And it is she who has poisoned the town against you."

Fiona was standing now. "Please leave."

"Because I'm too close to the truth?"

"No," she said, her eyes meeting his with firmness. "Because you are so very far from it that you frighten me. I thought—I thought once that you had believed me. I thought you might help me."

"*You* refuse to help me."

There were sudden tears rising in her eyes but not spilling through the thick lashes. "I have done nothing wrong except to love a child that is not mine. If you want my help, you will have to promise that nothing touches Ian. Nothing! I have kept silent for his sake. I have tried to protect *him*, not myself."

"From what? What is there that could harm him?"

"The people who might take him if they knew he existed. Who would want to punish him for what his mother did. Who would make him suffer because of what she had done."

"What had she done?"

"She loved someone. Terribly. Deeply. It was wrong, but she—There were reasons why she did. And there was a child of that love. A woman in her position couldn't go home with an infant in her arms and say 'Forgive me, I couldn't help myself. Let me pick up the pieces of my life and go on as if nothing has happened!'"

"Why haven't you told the police this? The fiscal?"

"They'd demand her name to prove that I was telling the truth! And I was given Ian to guard and love and protect. Not to betray!" The tears spilled, running like quicksilver down her cheeks. "I am lost," she said, "whatever I do. And it is better to hang than it is to fail. At least I would die knowing—*knowing* I had kept my promise to the end."

He fumbled for his handkerchief and handed it to her. "Surely she would come forward if she's alive. And spare you. For the boy's sake—"

"No, I tell you, she's dead. It's her family I fear, not her!" Choking back a sob, she repeated, "I am not afraid of the dead."

While Hamish argued fiercely in his mind, Rutledge said

quietly, "I can see that you might have taken the child and given promises. But what would you have told Hamish MacLeod if he'd come home from the war and found you with a child you claimed to be your own?"

She stared at him, wretched. "He would have loved us both. He would have trusted me and loved us both!"

And for once, to Rutledge's shame, the truth rang clearly in the little cell.

HE WENT TO see the procurator-fiscal late in the afternoon. Jedburgh was busy. The heart of the town was crowded, the shops doing a bustling trade along with the pubs and the hotel, people spilling out into the street in the path of carts and wagons jammed with goods. There had been a cattle market in the morning, and farmers in for the day seemed to be making the most of it. To Rutledge's eye, the population of Jedburgh had nearly doubled, and no one seemed to be in any haste to go home again. Finding a place to leave his vehicle took nearly twenty minutes, and even then he had to pay a grinning, gap-toothed man for the privilege.

The procurator-fiscal's office, overlooking the center of the town, was dark-paneled and furnished with mahogany and leather. The books lining the shelves above the handsome old desk were a blend of law and science and literature.

Burns was tall, stooped, and thin. A handsome head of white hair was brushed back from his forehead, and gold pince-nez concealed sharp blue eyes. A man used to command and discipline.

"Inspector Rutledge. It's good of you to come. May I offer you tea? A sherry?"

Rutledge, judging him rightly, accepted the sherry, and lifting the golden liquid in its slim glass, he saw that the pattern etched around the base of the cup was of thistles.

"Have you made any progress in the matter of Eleanor Gray?"

"I know more about her now. She was a wealthy young woman with a taste for rebellion and an intense desire to study medicine. She worked with the wounded during the war, providing entertainment for them where possible and taking an interest in their care. She was invited to a house party near Winchester early in 1916 and accepted. But the officer she was bringing with her discovered he had more leave than he'd expected. She came north with him instead, apparently intending to spend a few days at his house. Whether she got there or not no one seems to know. Where she may have gone after that week no one seems to know. But the information I have is reliable, and puts Miss Gray in Scotland in the spring before the child was born. If she had just learned that she was pregnant, she could have arranged to wait for the birth of the child here, where she wasn't as well known."

"Yes, yes, that makes sense to me. Who was the officer, do you know?"

There was nothing in the procurator's face to show that he was in any way prepared for the shock that was to come. Interest and a natural curiosity were there. Nothing more.

"We have reason to believe that the officer she had been friends with for some time was a Scot," Rutledge said carefully. "I've been told by a reliable witness that his name was Robert Burns."

The procurator was startled enough to tip his glass of sherry. He swore under his breath as a golden river trickled onto the papers in front of him, and he took out his handkerchief to stanch the flow. The room smelled heavily of the richness of the wine, and Rutledge set his own glass down, untouched.

"That is, as you may know, my late son's name."

"Yes. But there are, I should think, many men called Robert Burns to choose from," Rutledge replied.

"Where was this house you spoke of?"

"I'm told it was in the Trossachs."

Burns dropped the wet handkerchief into the paper-filled wastebasket at the side of his desk.

"My son had a house in the Trossachs. Not far from Callander. But I have never heard that he was acquainted with Eleanor Gray. If I had, I should have said something to Inspector Oliver and the Chief Constable. Furthermore, my son was to be married. If—if he survived the fighting. He was not likely to be in the company of other women in London. Nor was he likely to bring them to his house!"

Rutledge said soothingly, "If she was a friend, and in need, he might. Whether he was the father of the child or not."

It offered a way out. The fiscal seized it. "He would indeed have given what help he could. But I cannot believe he would allow her to use his house. It was his mother's house before we were married. She had left it to him. Robert was close to his mother. He would not have dishonored her memory." He looked distastefully at the remainder of the sherry in his glass, as if he blamed it for spilling. "Besides which," he said, rather spoiling the lofty effect of his earlier words, "if there had been anyone living in the house, I would have heard. There is a neighbor who looks in on it from time to time, has a key and all that. I would most *certainly* have heard! Mrs. Raeburn is very particular."

Hamish said, "Aye, if the neighbor is an auld biddy who would ha' relished telling his father tales, I canna' think Robert was sae foolish."

"Indeed," Rutledge said aloud, answering both of them. "Then he could have found another place for her to live until she was able to return to London. If it was your son. Did he have an interest in piping?"

"He studied the pipes as a child. But he didn't continue. What has that to do with Eleanor Gray?"

"I recall someone telling me that this same officer was helpful in finding pipers to play for the wounded."

"You needn't play the pipes to like them. Or to know pipers."

Rutledge said nothing.

After a moment, Procurator-Fiscal Burns said, "What, pray, has any of this to do with the young woman in Duncarrick? If the Gray woman came north in the spring, she might have gone *anywhere* in Scotland in the weeks following!"

"That's true, of course. But it is a beginning, and I'm hopeful that we'll eventually trace Miss Gray to Glencoe, if that's where she died." Rutledge paused, then said almost as an afterthought, "I don't suppose we'll ever know the name of the father of the child Fiona MacDonald has had in her keeping. It's a pity, really. He's a fine lad, and if he had been mine and I'd died, I'd have hoped my family would claim him in my place."

Burns regarded him coldly and said nothing.

Rutledge rose and then asked, "Would you have any objections, sir, if I took the prisoner to the place where the bones in question were found?"

"There's no provision in the law for that!"

"No, sir, I'm well aware that there isn't. All the same, I need to find the truth about Eleanor Gray, and what the link is between the two women. In a prison cell, it's very easy for the accused to remain silent and stubborn. Faced with her victim's grave, she might well break down and confess. It would save a good deal of trouble if she did. I think the case as it stands would be difficult to prove in court."

"Nonsense! It's a very sound case indeed."

"Is it? If I were her lawyer, and clever, I would make it very clear to the jury that while there is living proof of a child, there has been no proof of murder. And the jury might well agree with me."

There was a startled look in the blue eyes, as if Burns had never considered anything but a guilty verdict.

Leaving, Rutledge was reminded that Drummond's sister had insisted that the fiscal had been angry with Fiona for refusing to cooperate with Inspector Oliver.

Hamish said, "He didna' want to hear his son was involved."

"Yes, I know. Well, that may be true, he may not be involved. Or the fiscal may have been very good at concealing his own suspicions. Still, I don't think the fiscal was protecting his son when he ordered Fiona held for trial. It would have been the wrong move—if I hadn't come across Robert Burns's name, someone else might have. No, there was more behind the decision."

"Then turn it another way. What's the use of a trial? No' to discover the child's name or parentage but to punish Fiona for killing the mother. To put the blame on *someone* for a woman's death. So that when the body is found, it won't point a finger at the true killer. The likes of the fiscal and the Chief Constable and their friends would protect their own!"

Making his way back to his motorcar, Rutledge shook his head. "No. It can't be that. But the fiscal's an intelligent man, and he should have said 'If someone is claiming my son's involved in this business, I want you to look into it.' And then given me a list of people who knew the son well enough to tell me the truth. But he didn't. And that's what's odd."

As he bent to turn the crank, Rutledge added, "Don't you see? McKinstry is absolutely right. The verdict on Fiona MacDonald is already in."

18

────────◆────────

THE NEXT MORNING RUTLEDGE RECEIVED BY PRIVATE messenger permission to take Fiona MacDonald to Glencoe, as long as they were accompanied by a matron and a constable.

It was not how he had wanted to go there. He had thought of it as an expiation, sitting in the fiscal's office. He had seen it, too, as an excuse for getting Fiona out of that small, dark cell and into the light. A muddle of reasons, none of them wise.

But the sooner he went, the better, before someone changed his mind.

He arranged for sandwiches in a basket to be packed for the journey, and then went out to his motorcar to drive around to the police station.

Oliver wasn't there. Pringle thought he had gone out the Jedburgh road to look into a theft of a lorry's contents. "It seems," Pringle ended wryly, "that the driver fell asleep and ran off the road. When he went to find help dragging the lorry out

of the ditch, someone helped himself to the contents instead."
Pringle shrugged. "The driver's in a rage, but Inspector Oliver
isn't likely to be swayed by that. We had an incident once before where a driver sold off part of the contents and then
claimed he'd been robbed. Inspector Oliver has a long memory. You don't make a fool of him twice!"

Rutledge found himself thinking of the skeleton discovered in the stables at The Reivers. Oliver had gone on from
that embarrassment to find the bones in Glencoe—

Rutledge thanked Pringle and decided to drive out the
Jedburgh road himself. But he had hardly reached the outskirts of Duncarrick when his engine spluttered, caught, and
then died.

Swearing, he got out to crank it again, but nothing happened. Taking a look at the engine—and attracting two
young farm lads who came to peer over his shoulder at the
mysteries under the bonnet—he could see nothing wrong.
He asked one of the young men to hold the wire while he
turned the crank and checked the spark. It was clearly not
that. There was fresh petrol in the tank, filled in Jedburgh
just the day before. And he could see no indication that
anyone had meddled with the car.

In the end, Rutledge commandeered a horse and cart to
tow the vehicle (with accompanying humor from the old
farmer who didn't hold with infernal combustion) back into
Duncarrick, where it was left to the mercy of the mechanic
at the smithy.

He wouldn't be traveling anywhere with Fiona
MacDonald this day. Or tomorrow—

"And who will be pleased to hear that?" Hamish asked,
irony heavy in his voice. "The fiscal?"

"Burns gave permission. But grudgingly."

Rutledge went back to the hotel and searched the space
by the shed where he usually parked the motorcar. A precaution.

He walked around the space, examining the ground. The
dust had been scuffed, but no clear footprints were visible

except for his own. The rear of the car had been in the shadows cast by the shed standing no more than ten feet away. Easy to crouch unseen there in the darkness late at night and take an ax to a tire, if someone wanted to disable the car. But the tires hadn't been touched. And as far as Rutledge could tell, the engine hadn't been damaged either.

He'd just driven the car hard for four days—

Everyone in Duncarrick knew whose car sat in the hotel yard day after day. No one in his right mind would touch it.

"Unless," Hamish pointed out, "you've tread on toes."

RUTLEDGE WALKED TO the police station and from Constable Pringle borrowed the key to The Reivers again. The inn wasn't likely to yield more information than it had, but he wanted to go there on his own and be sure.

Clarence, the cat, followed Rutledge soft-footed from room to room, a silent white ghost at his heels as he took his time in each. He couldn't have said when he started what it was he wanted here.

Such a place as The Reivers, he thought, was not made for the morning. The echoes of the night would linger still in the air—laughter and voices—someone singing off-key—and the smell of spilled beer and ale, the reek of smoke would drift down the passages. There would be an emptiness, a loneliness, as if the inn stood waiting for the doors to swing open again and new patrons to stride through them, thirsty for a pint and the companionship that went with it.

Now there weren't even the echoes of the previous night. The inn had stood empty long enough that the only smells stirred by his passage were of dust and old wood, and in the kitchen, the ashes of fires in the great stove.

Hamish, at his back, noted the smoke-darkened beams and the polished wood of the bar; the windows with their starched curtains and the small pewter pots on each table that must often have held flowers; the pretty handmade coverlets on the beds of each upstairs guest room—hardly a temptation to whoring; the tidy row of hooks that held gardening tools in the small stone-flagged room off the kitchen. The cupboard that held linens smelled faintly of lavender and rose petals. The pantry was empty, only a few tins of food standing like sentinels on the long shelves. In the kitchen, dishes were stored neatly in a huge wooden dresser, great iron pots hanging within reach, the sink dry where vegetables ought to be lying, waiting to be scrubbed and cooked.

"I could hae' lived here," Hamish said wistfully, "and been at peace. With her. I wouldna' ache for the Highlands if she was here wi' me. . . . I could rest easy."

Rutledge tried to shut out the soft voice at his shoulder and listen for other ghosts that should dwell here. Ealasaid MacCallum for one. Or the sounds of a small boy as he played with his cat or ran shouting from room to room with his three-legged stuffed horse. Or Fiona's presence as she went about her daily tasks. But he couldn't find them. Especially he could not find Fiona's.

It was as if even the floors had been scrubbed clean of the imprint of her shoe, to remove the last sign of her. Fiona had lived here—and put down no roots that he could see. She had done her duty by her aunt, had kept the inn alive and busy, had nurtured a child there. And let no one inside her heart, not even the building that she called her home.

After a time, to break the heavy silence that seemed to pervade the very walls, he turned to the cat and knelt to pet her. She reared her head under his hand, her eyes mere slits, and began to purr. "What would you have to tell me if you could speak?" he asked softly. "Hmmm?"

A voice said, "She's naught but a dumb animal, man!"

Drummond, Fiona's neighbor and guardian now of the child, stepped into the room, his presence startling the cat. Rutledge got to his feet as she disappeared behind the bar.

Even Hamish had not heard Drummond coming.

"But she has eyes, doesn't she? And no reason to lie. I think it's time that someone told me the truth," Rutledge invited.

"There's no truth to tell. What brings you here again?"

"I'm looking into the past, to see what's hidden there that frightens so many people." And yet he realized now that he'd spent his time at The Reivers trying to find a measure of Fiona MacDonald. Looking not for evidence but for the character of a woman who was as elusive as a wraith with no substance . . .

Why, then, hadn't she sold up and left? If she had not been happy.

Eleanor Gray's words came back to him. "*I could die—*"

"Hummph." Drummond was regarding him with dislike. "You're a stupid man, then. It's not in the fiber of this building. The past. It never was."

"Why are you so certain of that?"

"Do I have to tell the police their business, then? Because the child wasn't born here, was he! That's where a sensible man would look, wouldn't he? Where the child was born. If he can discover it." There was a glint of challenge in his eye. As if he'd offered Rutledge an enigma.

"I've already been there. Where he was born. It's a very ordinary clinic with a doctor too busy with his patients to care who they are. I'm told it was a normal birth, but the mother was very ill afterward."

Appalled, Drummond stared at him. "And how, by God, did you discover any such thing? It's more than Oliver ever did—or wanted to do!"

"I'm a policeman. It's my job."

Digesting the news, Drummond asked suspiciously, "Where might this clinic be found?"

Rutledge smiled. *Interested, are you?* "London. Carlisle. York. Your choice."

Angry, Drummond said, "I won't be taunted, policeman. Or made fun of. If you found the clinic, you found a name to put to that child. And to the child's mother. Is that true?"

"Yes. I was given a name. It isn't one I know."

"And where might she be found now? On a hillside in the Highlands, bare bones with the corbies for company?" Something had changed in Drummond's face. A tightness of the muscles under the eyes. A tension along the jaw.

"In her grave," Rutledge answered, suddenly wary. He could feel the powerful emotion building in Drummond's bulk. Why did Drummond care so much? Or if it wasn't that—if he wanted the information for another reason—why the intensity? He added carefully, "If you know what's best, you'll leave her there. In her grave."

"Why?" It was a growl.

"Because she's safer there. And the child as well."

"Which still leaves Fiona MacDonald in the hands of the hangman!"

"Not yet. Why should it matter to you?" Rutledge asked.

Drummond glared at him in hot, fierce silence.

"I've met no one else in Duncarrick save Constable McKinstry who gives a tinker's curse for what becomes of her," Rutledge repeated. "Why should you?"

Silence still.

Rutledge added, "Is it the tilt of her head when she listens to you? Or the smile in her eyes when she laughs—"

The fury erupted. "I'll rip the tongue from your head!" He lunged, fast for such a big man, his fist grazing Rutledge's cheek. But Rutledge had already stepped aside, catching Drummond's wrist as he went off balance, turning to twist it high behind his back, forcing him hard into the edge of the bar as momentum carried him forward. Drummond was breathing heavily, well aware of the strength he possessed as he struggled against Rutledge's weight—and nearly turning the tables. Rutledge's fingers bit deeper into the man's wrist, and he could feel the elbow strain.

"No, you listen to me, Drummond! If Fiona MacDonald is going to live, it will take more than you or I or anyone else can do to save her. Do you hear me? She's doomed. And that child will grow up in an orphanage, believing what they tell him about her. If he remembers her at all, it will be with loathing."

Drummond roared, swearing to kill Rutledge.

"Then help me, damn you!" Rutledge ended through clenched teeth.

He let the arm go and moved out of reach as Drummond swung around like an angry bear, his other fist just missing its mark. "I'll help you to your *grave*—!"

"*Touch me again and I'll have you taken up for assault!*" Rutledge warned him. "And if you're in a cell, your sister will be the only one left to care for that child! Will she want that responsibility?"

He watched the battle behind the big man's eyes, saw the furious desire to pound his fists into Rutledge's face, saw the driving hunger to hurt. Dammed-up anger, too long restrained, long stored, needing release. And then saw, too, the swift victory of clear reason that overcame the wrath.

Rutledge tried another strategy. "Look, I'm sorry. But I can't trust you if you won't trust me. Do you see that? If I tell you whatever it is I believe I know, how can I be sure that it won't reach the wrong ears?"

"What wrong ears?" Drummond was hardly coherent as he added thickly, "There's a score to settle between us. The time will come when it *will* be settled."

He brushed past Rutledge and went out the door, his breathing harsh and his anger still palpable. The clump of his hobnailed boots echoed through the bar.

Hamish, breathing nearly as hard, said, "It wasna' clever to make him an enemy!"

"No, it wasn't clever. But I think it was useful. He knows something, that man—or is afraid he knows something. And it must be damning, or he would have stepped forward in the beginning!"

"He lives next door—he might have seen what he shouldn't."

Rutledge shook his head. "Whatever it is, he won't be made to talk."

He found the cat, carried her to the bedroom where he had seen the indentation on the pillow, and set her there. She curled herself around, lay down, and began to spin, her purr a heavy sound in the silence.

"Fiona?"

Rutledge said the name aloud. The cat turned and looked toward the door of the bedchamber, ears pricking. But there was no one on the stairs. She went back to kneading the pillow, her eyes half closed.

Suddenly claustrophobic, even in the large, sunlit bedroom, Rutledge turned and left.

RUTLEDGE RETURNED THE inn's key to McKinstry and went back to The Ballantyne. There was still a quarter of an hour before luncheon was served, and he went up to his room. Opening the door, his mind on Drummond, he stepped inside and then stopped. The hackles on the back of his neck rising in warning, he closed the door quietly behind him and stood there, just inside the empty room.

Hamish said, "It's no' the same—"

Someone had been here.

Not the maid. She had come and gone while he ate his breakfast. Even if she'd returned with fresh towels or to close the windows, his mind would have recorded that without thinking about it.

This was different.

And instinct told him it was not a friendly intrusion. Something below the level of conscious thought had pricked down his nerves. The war had taught him to heed instinct. . . .

He moved around the room, carefully searching with his eyes but touching nothing. Whoever it was had been very thorough, going through his belongings with painstaking attention to where each item had been before. But he—or she—had made certain that Rutledge would know his privacy had been invaded. His shirts in the drawer of the chest.

His shoes on the rack in the wardrobe. The way his ties were folded . . . Each had been moved. Each had been put back very nearly where it had been. But with just enough change to catch the eye of a man *looking* for change—

Because the atmosphere had changed. It was alien. Hostile.

Drummond?

Rutledge hadn't survived four years in the trenches without learning the skills of the hunter—and developing the sixth sense that kept the hunted alive.

Nothing had been taken. He was sure of that. The intent had been to show him his own vulnerability, not to steal.

It was, in a way, a gauntlet thrown down.

And not as a challenge.

More a very coldly calculated threat.

I can touch you—but you cannot touch me.

It was the first mistake that had been made in what had been—to this point—a very skillful game.

RUTLEDGE WAS JOINED at lunch by Inspector Oliver.

He made a circuit of the dining room, greeting first this person and then another, once stopping to listen to a man by the window and then laughing quietly as if he appreciated the humor of what had been said.

Hamish said, "There's a man wi' something on his mind."

Finally arriving at Rutledge's table, Oliver pulled out the empty chair on the other side and signaled to the middle-aged woman who was serving this noon. She came over, smiling, and said, "Would you like the menu, then, Inspector?"

"Thanks, Mary." He nodded as she handed it to him, then turned to Rutledge and said affably, "What's that you've ordered? The roast ham?"

"Yes. It's quite good. Who are the people over there—the table by the fireplace?" He had seen the man out by the pele tower. But his interest was in the woman—he had questioned her about Fiona.

Oliver peered in their direction. "That's Sandy Holden. Landowner. Had a horse farm, now trying to get by with sheep. He'll make it. A good man."

"And the woman?"

"His wife, of course. Madelyn Holden."

"She looks as if she might be ill. Lungs, at a guess."

"Good God, no. She nearly died from the influenza last autumn. Hasn't got her strength back yet. The doctor says it will come with time, but Sandy frets about her. It's been almost a year, and she's no better. Shame, really. She was one of the finest horsewomen I've ever seen." He turned to the menu. "It's the ham, then. Or—there's stew. They put turnips in the stew here. I'm fond of turnips." He set the menu aside and added, "I hear you drove to Winchester. On this business or another?"

"On this business. We found someone who remembered Eleanor Gray from her schooldays and had kept in touch. Until, that is, the spring of 1916, when Eleanor was expected to spend a weekend at Atwood House. But she called Mrs. Atwood at the last minute and said that she and a friend were driving to Scotland instead."

"Ah!" Oliver looked keenly at Rutledge. "Friend. Male or female?"

"An officer she'd met some time before. At least we think it's the same man. He had enough leave left to make the journey. She came with him. No one has seen or heard from her since, as far as I can discover."

"Are you certain about the timing? Eleanor Gray couldn't have borne the child in the *spring*!" He shook his head. "This Mrs. Atwood has got it wrong, I think."

"*I could die*— " Rutledge could hear Mrs. Atwood's light voice repeating the words. No, she hadn't got it wrong. Eleanor's mood had aroused her jealousy. And later her guilt.

But he said aloud, "She needed a place of refuge for the

next four or five months. Someone may have let her have the use of a house or flat."

"I see what you're getting at. If she'd stayed on in London, her little secret wouldn't have been a secret very long." Oliver gave the matter some thought. The people by the window got up to leave, distracting him. He said, "I had wondered, you know. How a woman like that could spend dreary months in some out-of-the-way Scottish village. Made no sense. Well, I saw the house she grew up in, it was a bloody *palace*! A flat now, in Edinburgh or Inverness, that's more likely! But surely it would have been easier to find someone in London to rid her of the child."

"She was too well known in London. She was too well known in medical circles particularly."

"There are back streets where such things can be done discreetly."

"At a price. She might have feared blackmail."

"Then why not in Glasgow—Edinburgh—Carlisle? She'd not have given her right name or her direction. Easy enough if she'd had a mind for it. Such things went on in the war. She wouldn't be the first—or the last."

Rutledge thought of the clinic and Dr. Wilson but said, "Perhaps she wanted the child. Or, at the very least, wanted it to live. And as soon as that was accomplished, she walked away from it."

"Then you're saying that the accused had no need to kill the mother—the child was hers for the asking!" Mary came to take Oliver's order, and he settled for the stew.

"Yes. It fits the timing."

"Then why hasn't she turned up since? You're off the mark! Eleanor Gray is dead, and we've found her bones." Oliver leaned back in his chair and scanned the room. Without looking at Rutledge, he asked, "What's this I hear from the fiscal, that you want to take the accused to Glencoe?"

He had finally got to the subject that had brought him here.

"She knows the terrain far better than any of us do. I'd like to confront her with her crime. And watch what happens." There were other reasons. He had not let himself think of them.

"Her lawyer will tell you it's not on."

"Then let him come as well."

"A bloody circus!" Hamish put in.

"Then *I'm* telling you it's not on! I see no purpose to be served," Oliver said angrily.

McKinstry came through the door to the dining room and stood scanning the tables until he saw Oliver.

He crossed quickly to Oliver's side, bent over, and said quietly, "You'd better come, sir. There's a message from the police in Glencoe."

"I'll be there in a quarter of an hour. Damn it, can't you see I'm in the middle of my *lunch*!"

"Yes, sir." McKinstry straightened and started for the door.

Oliver threw his serviette in his plate and got up, swearing under his breath.

Rutledge was finishing his flan. He started to follow, but Oliver motioned him back into his chair.

"No, this is my end of things."

Rutledge acknowledged his barely veiled order and stayed where he was. It never paid to argue jurisdiction with the local man, even when you were in the right.

Hamish said, "He's no' finished what was on his chest."

"Just as well," Rutledge retorted. For an instant he thought he had spoken the words aloud.

TEN MINUTES LATER Oliver was back. His face was grim.

"They've found something up the glen. We're on our way. Where's your motorcar?"

Rutledge explained.

Oliver nodded. "Well, you'd better come along, then. You'll want to hear what's said."

Torn between duty and dread, Rutledge slowly got to his feet.

GLENCOE HAD A long and dark history. The bloody massacre there on 13 February 1692, had left its mark in the very ground. And the great bulge of mountains that overshadowed the valley below seemed to hold a long and bitter memory in their barren rock.

MacIan of Glencoe had failed to take his oath to the King, William of Orange, by 1 January of that year. It wasn't his fault; he had reached Fort William in time, but there he had been sent on to Inveraray. Still, a punishment was held to be in order.

Campbell soldiers were quartered on the MacDonalds.

The Campbells had lived peacefully for twelve days in MacDonald homes and eaten their bread and salt. Then, without warning on that dark, cold February night, the soldiers had risen from their beds and slaughtered men, women, and children indiscriminately. Those who escaped died of cold and hunger and wounds in the bleak, unforgiving hills. And for the handful of survivors, the name of Campbell was ever after anathema.

As Oliver's motorcar passed Loch Leven and took the road south of the river that led into the heart of the glen, Rutledge could feel the press of time and anguish, just as he felt Hamish's unspoken grief. He wished fervently that he hadn't come. He'd planned to drive here with Fiona; he'd seen her as his shield against the glen, but he knew now, beyond question, that it would have been wrong then just as it was wrong now.

Even Fiona couldn't protect him from the images in his own mind.

Not far from here, Hamish had been born, grew to manhood, and went off to war. This was land he knew so well, he had described nearly every inch of it to Rutledge the night before he died. It wasn't imagination that peopled the great empty glen with memories, it was the stored knowledge of a lifetime. And the lasting voice of a soldier who had spoken softly in the candlelight but tellingly, the noisy darkness around the small makeshift hut they sat in notwithstanding, until Rutledge could have recited each and every word in his dreams.

As the miles rolled behind them, Rutledge relived that night with such ferocity that he was back again in 1916, even as he saw every turn of the road.

After a fashion, Hamish had come home.

19

IT WAS A LONG DRIVE. BY THE TIME THEY HAD REACHED the rendezvous point where an Inspector MacDougal was waiting for them, Oliver and McKinstry had fallen into weary silence, and Rutledge, sharing the rear seat with Hamish, was racked by the tension. It was not, by any token, an easy homecoming for either man. Rutledge had never expected to see and recognize landmarks that stood out now with such clarity. Nor had he expected to find here such a barrenness that in itself was beauty to someone who had seen it every day until the death of an obscure Austrian archduke had tumbled the world into war.

Glencoe was haunting—and haunted.

Ahead, where the unpaved road entered a narrow neck of the glen, they could see a motorcar pulled off to one side, under the frowning slopes. A man climbed down from the driver's seat as they approached.

He was square, with flame-red hair and freckles so thick he seemed to be deeply tanned. Grinning at them, he raised a hand and called as Oliver slowed down, "Have ye brought the entire force from Duncarrick, then?"

Oliver pulled his vehicle off the road behind the other motorcar, raising a thick cloud of dust. The only traffic they had seen for miles was a flock of sheep and several carts piled with cabbages and sacks of potatoes. The road in either direction snaked yellow in the sun, like a dry river.

Solitary. But not empty. This place was never empty if you knew its history. Hamish, who did, was silent in the face of it. Rutledge thought, if ever there was a place for the pipes, it was here. Keening a lament on the wind and filling the valley with human sounds to shut out those no one could quite hear.

He forced himself to concentrate. Introductions out of the way, MacDougal went back to his own vehicle to open the door for the passenger he had brought with him.

She was no more than fourteen or fifteen, wrapped against the chilly wind that was blowing down from the heights in a faded plaid shawl that reached her hips. Her skirts whipped and snapped about her ankles. Her hair, in a bun, was a mousy brown, and youth was all that made her pretty.

But she faced the strangers as they were introduced in their turn and seemed to be collected for someone her age.

"And this is Betty Lawlor," the Inspector ended. "Right, shall I begin, or will you, Inspector Oliver?"

Rutledge said before Oliver could speak, "Do you know the MacDonalds up the glen—" He dredged his memory for a name, and Hamish supplied it.

"—kin of Duncan MacDonald, who died in 1915?"

Betty gave him a sour look. "Aye. I ken who they are."

"Are you friends, then?"

"Not friends, no."

"Did you know Duncan's granddaughter, Fiona?"

"I did. Not well. She was older. My sister's age."

Rutledge looked around him at the great expanse of emptiness. "I should think that neighbors here might look out for one another."

Betty stared at him. "My ain grandfather was transported to Australia for sheep stealing. I havena' any dealings with the MacDonalds. It was their sheep."

Rutledge nodded. Oliver, impatient, said abruptly, "What did you find up there, Miss Lawlor?" He pointed to the mountainside above them, a great bulge of rock that seemed top-heavy.

"I was walking up there one day and saw something shining in the sunlight. I picked it up. It was this."

She extended a work-worn hand and in the palm lay a small brooch. Rutledge and Oliver stepped forward to look at it more closely.

It was oval, with a single stone in the center and around it a circlet of smaller stones, set like the petals of a flower. On the back was a simple pin to hold it closed.

The color of the stones was a smoky brown. Smoky quartz.

"A cairngorm." Hamish said it before Oliver did.

A stone found in Scotland and popular for jewelry. In the hilt of a *skean dhu,* in the froth of lace at the throat in eighteenth-century portraits, adorning the necks and fingers of ladies, it was a symbol in its way of the Highlands.

The setting was gold, a dainty filigree.

A pretty thing, and had probably been treasured once.

Rutledge said, "May I?" and took the brooch to examine it more closely.

The stones, well polished, flashed in his hand. The color was striking. He turned the brooch this way and that, to catch the light. Under the pin he noted that something had been engraved. Time had worn whatever it was to a blur.

"See just there. Initials, I think." He pointed these out to Oliver. "Or a name. I can't quite make them out—" Working with the light and shadow, he finally said, "There's an M— possibly an A—a D—surely that's an A—L."

Oliver took the brooch and turned it back and forth

himself, then shook his head. "Is that an M? Are you certain? Or an N?"

He passed the brooch on to MacDougal. "I looked at it earlier," he confessed. "With a glass, before I telephoned you. It's an M right enough." He paused, and then said, "With a glass you can read the whole of it. 'MacDonald.' "

McKinstry moved, denial in the abrupt shift from one foot to the other. In the ensuing silence, MacDougal handed the brooch back to Betty Lawlor. Her fingers closed over it until the knuckles were white.

"How far from where the body was found would you say this came to light?" Rutledge asked MacDougal.

"Possibly a hundred feet downhill. But it could have washed that far. In the rains and melting snow. After all, if you take into account the fact that it was here for several years, it's not surprising at all." He pointed above their heads again, where scree had been brought down the rough face of the peak. "I'd say the brooch must have come from above. There's no other explanation. People don't walk just here. It's too uncertain. Most climbers follow that line over there." He shifted to show them the preferred path. "And there." He pointed across the road to the opposite slope. "It's not impossible someone would be walking in our direction, but I'd say the odds were strongly against it."

Hamish said, "The cairngorm wasna' scratched enough to ha' washed that far!"

Rutledge turned to Betty Lawlor, standing silently as they talked, her eyes moving from face to face. A self-contained child . . . "How did it happen that you were up there?"

She shrugged. "I walk all over this land. Always have. Helping with the sheep. I doubt there's a foot of it I havena' covered at some time or another."

"But you never came upon the body that was found higher up?"

"I might've if the sheep had gone that far up. But

generally they don't just there. Stupid beasts, they are, but not foolish."

He looked down at her shoes as she spoke, thinking of her walking day after day over such rough terrain—a hard life for a child.

Her shoes were new. Sturdy. He could see the leather toes just peeking out at the hem of her gown. The gown was a hand-me-down, the shawl the same. But her shoes were new. Even the edges of the soles hadn't been worn yet.

Oliver said, "Tell me what you told Inspector MacDougal when you brought in the brooch."

She looked at him directly, shading her eyes with her hand. "It was nearly a year ago that I found it. Summer anyway. I saw it in the sun. It was the first day it hadna' stormed in a week or more. I didna' like to think it might belong to— to whoever it was they found. Up there. It was pretty, and I wanted to keep it. But I'm afraid my father will find it and beat me for stealing. So I went to Inspector MacDougal to ask him to set it right!" She broke off, then asked anxiously, "You aren't going to take it away, are you? You can't be sure it's *hers*!"

Oliver said magnanimously, "I'm afraid it must be taken in evidence. But when we've finished with it, I'll see that you have it back again." His eyes switched to Rutledge's face. He didn't have to put into words what was in both their minds. This was the first direct link between Fiona and the mountain. Between Fiona and the bones that might be Eleanor Gray's.

Rutledge said nothing.

MacDougal asked Betty to take them to the place where she found the brooch, and she turned to spring up the hillside like one of the sheep she watched out for. Strong for all her thinness, and agile, she seemed to fly. Oliver, puffing in her wake, swore under his breath, but didn't ask her to slow down. McKinstry turned back to stay with the vehicles.

Rutledge was just behind her, watching the new shoes, watching her almost intuitive knowledge of where there was enough stability to place a foot. She had learned from the sheep—

MacDougal, keeping pace but red-faced, said, "Fra' the top are fine views. I used to climb here as a lad, with my brothers."

"Did you know the MacDonalds?" Rutledge asked him.

"I knew one of them—brother of the accused, I'd guess. A good man. He lost his legs and bled to death before they could get him back over the wire. My brother died the same day. Machine-gun fire. I was lucky—shot three times but nothing that kept me from going back." There was a quiet irony in his voice.

They had come some distance, cutting diagonally across the mountain's face, slipping and sliding here or there, and Betty had begun to look around, as if trying to find landmarks.

Finally she paused and pointed to an area that was perhaps ten feet square. "About here, I'd guess," she told them.

It was a rocky slope that seemed to be no different from any of its neighbors for a hundred yards in any direction.

"Why are you so sure?" Oliver demanded, mopping his face with a large handkerchief. "I can't see any difference between this patch and that one—or that one over there."

"See for yoursel'. I can match that spot just above us with that one across the way—" She pointed to the great bare face opposite, and following her finger, they identified a small outcropping of rock.

If you looked, Rutledge thought, you could find your way easily. But it was always a matter of *seeing*. To the uninitiated, this was barren ground. Above their heads, another tumbled mass of rock stood out against the sky.

Following his gaze, MacDougal said, "It was there we found the remains. In a slight crevice where water has brought down the supporting scree and left a hollow." He paused, then said, "You'd have to know it was there. The hollow. It isn't visible from the road."

In short, no one would think to leave a body there who didn't have some familiarity with these mountains.

"Want to climb up?" MacDougal asked.

Rutledge nodded and they walked on, picking their way carefully. It was hot here in the sun, and feet unused to this terrain found it difficult to know where to step with any certainty.

Carrying a body, Hamish pointed out, would not be easy. And for a woman, very nearly impossible. "Unless the corpse was dragged on a rope."

And there was no one to see such a long, laborious effort. From where he stood, Rutledge could look down at the two motorcars, Oliver standing talking to Betty Lawlor, and a ruined croft some distance away. In the far distance, he saw sheep, but no one with them.

"Hard place for a woman to carry a dead weight," MacDougal said as if reading his thoughts. "But if that brooch belongs to the deceased, it means she's not your missing woman. Eleanor Gray."

"And if it belonged to the murderer, then we have her in custody," Rutledge finished for him.

They had reached the outcropping where three heavy rocks were lying in a heap. Not so large by the standards of these mountains, but beyond a man's strength to tumble together so tidily. And where the smaller fragments had washed out from under, there was indeed a crevice. Put a body here in April, and it might be found. But put it here before the weather turns and the autumn storms begin, and it would still be here in the spring. What was left.

Rutledge squatted on his heels. MacDougal said, "You won't find anything. We were verra' thorough."

"I expect you were," Rutledge said evenly. "I was just thinking that this was a perfect place for bones. What makes you so certain that the body was not here before 1916?"

"Condition, for one thing. And I talked to all the families who run sheep. They were certain it wasna' here in the summer. A fox or dog had chewed the shoes, and what bits of clothing we found weren't of any use. First thought was that we'd found a climber. People climb here who havena' the sense of a beetle! They canna' believe on a fine day like this one that the mists can come in sae fast, you're lost before you take ten steps. And she was doubled up, as if trying to keep warm. Loose stones had washed around and over her."

"Doubled? How?"

"Head on knees, arms around them. Made the body smaller, kept heat in the middle. The bones were still in a huddle, like. The doctor found no injuries, but that's no' to say she hadna' turned her ankle or twisted her knee."

Hamish said, "Doubled o'er, she'd fit behind the seat of a car, out of sight."

Rutledge said, "If she was already dead, rigor had passed."

"Aye, that's right. Or hadna' set in. The birds and foxes must have stripped the body in a matter of days. We couldn't find one hand or the best part of a foot. Other bones had been pulled apart to get at the meat. The skull had rolled into her lap." MacDougal sighed. "We've had a walker or two lost in these parts. But we always ken how they got into the glen. They'd be seen and reported. One left a bicycle. Another begged a lift on a crofter's wagon. With this one, there's no way of establishing when—or how—she came to be here. We don't know the question to ask, do we? And it's possible she came over the top, from the other side."

"What's your opinion of the engraving on the brooch?"

"I have none. It spells out 'MacDonald,' and that's your patch, is it no'?" MacDougal grinned, then shrugged. "It could hae come from the dead woman's clothing, if she was murdered and dragged up here. Climbers don't wear much jewelry as a rule. Or it came from the murderer's, trying to drag up that corpse. We do na' have well-dressed middle-class women promenading up this mountainside, losing the odd brooch or two."

"The center stone of the brooch isn't scratched enough to have been washing down a mountainside since 1916."

"Yes, I ken what you're suggesting. Still, if it lodged somewhere for a time, then came down in the rains Betty spoke of, it might not have tumbled about all that much."

If—if—if— Investigations were made and lost on "ifs."

"We'll have to take the brooch back with us. Oliver will give a receipt to Betty."

"It's a valuable piece to her," MacDougal agreed. "I'm surprised she brought it to me in the first place. But her father's a devil when he's drunk. If he found she had such a thing, he'd beat her for stealing it and use that as an excuse to take it from her. She was probably counting on me to speak up for her if that happened. Betty spends the summer wi' the sheep, as far away from him as she can get. I've seen her out here in all weathers, a small figure with naething but a dog for companionship."

Rutledge got to his feet and looked around. This was a very beautiful valley—and very bleak. "Wild" was the word most often used to describe it. He thought about the February night when the massacre had begun, and how the soldiers had run through the darkness with torches, searching for those who had fled. Driven by blood lust. A nightmarish way to die . . .

"Is there any other?" Hamish asked quietly.

Rutledge shivered in the warm sun.

"Did you come here?" he asked Hamish silently. "You and Fiona? When there was no work to be done on the farm?"

"Aye, we came. With horses. Sometimes we climbed. Or we'd find a place out of the wind and eat the bannocks we'd brought wi' us. She liked the glen. The silence, but for the wind. And the closeness to her kin . . ."

MacDougal was asking if Rutledge had seen enough. He nodded and they started back down, slipping once or twice.

"The Lawlor girl. What sort of family does she come from? Aside from the drunken father?"

"Poor enough. She's the middle girl. They work hard and go hungry sometimes, I've no doubt."

"Why didn't she bide her time and quietly sell the brooch for whatever it might bring? Even a little money would allow her to escape from the glen and her father and her poverty?"

"She's too young," MacDougal said simply. "In another year or two she might have. That's why she wants it back. If you take it, she's locked into this life. There won't be other brooches waiting for sharp eyes to pick them out!"

Joining Oliver and Betty Lawlor, they descended to the road. Oliver bent to brush off his trousers where the cuffs had collected a fine pattern of dust.

Rutledge said to the girl, "I've been admiring your shoes."

There was a flare of fear in Betty Lawlor's eyes, then she said defiantly, "I earned the money for them!"

IT WAS A silent journey back to Duncarrick. McKinstry was wretchedly weighing the damage the brooch would do to Fiona MacDonald's case. Rutledge, in the rear seat, could see the fine lines around his eyes, as if his head ached. But he drove with skill and attention to the road, wherever his mind was.

Oliver, on the other hand, was a satisfied man. His investigation had borne fruit, and he could see the end of it now. There was a smugness in his face, and from time to time his head dropped to his chest, relaxed into sleep.

Rutledge, remembering Betty Lawlor's face when Oliver had offered her a scrap of paper in exchange for the brooch, wondered if she could read.

Fiona MacDonald's lawyer could argue that the brooch was found in a part of Scotland where the MacDonald clan had lived for centuries. The brooch might well have belonged to any one of them.

But a jury could find it damning evidence. . . .

The three men stopped for the night in Lanark, finding a small hotel where they were served a dinner of mutton soup with barley and a roast chicken. Oliver, fidgety and eager to be back in Duncarrick, called it an early night. McKinstry, poor company at best, excused himself as well.

When they had disappeared up the stairs, Rutledge went out for a walk. Relieved to be out of the glen, relieved to be alone—except for Hamish. The night was clear though cool, and the smell of wood smoke followed him out of the hotel. He was restless, thinking of Wilson and the clinic, thinking of the brooch and Betty Lawlor's new shoes, thinking of Fiona.

The town was tranquil, lights shining from windows in the houses along side streets, shop fronts dark, a pub noisy with singing and laughter, a dog scavenging in an alley. Several men passed him, and then a couple arm in arm, intent on their soft conversation, and the sound of a carriage echoed down the main street. He could see the stars overhead, and the first threads of clouds winding among them.

Hamish hadn't relished the journey to the glen. And it had awakened memories that Rutledge had convinced himself he was beginning to forget. Instead Scotland had revived them with a vengeance. He had been right not to want to come here.

Wishful thinking, that time might heal—it seldom healed anything, only making scars that were often tender to the touch, and ugly.

Without knowing how he got there, he found himself outside the local police station. He had come here the last time he was in Lanark, asking for information about private clinics and hospitals. The constable on duty had sent him to Dr. Wilson. He stopped, looking up at the lamp above the door, his mind not really taking in his surroundings.

Cook. Maude or Mary. Two names. A woman in Brae, a

woman in the private clinic here . . . Separated by a matter of miles—

He went up the steps and through the door.

The sergeant on duty, a bluff man growing stout with years, looked up and said, "What might I do for you, sir?"

"Inspector Rutledge, Scotland Yard. I need some information."

"Are you here on official business?" the sergeant asked warily.

Someone was banging a metal cup against the bars of a cell, the clanging echoing through the building like a berserk, off-key bell. The sergeant appeared not to notice the racket.

"Indirectly. I've been trying to trace several families. What can you tell me about anyone by the name of Cook living in or around Lanark in 1916? Late summer, at a guess."

"There's a number of Cooks. Mostly from Loch Lomondside. Tell me what they've done and I'll tell you what matches."

"As far as I know, they've done nothing. We're searching for a missing woman. She called herself Mary Cook. Or possibly even Maude Cook. There's some indication she was in Lanark in 1916 for a period of several weeks. After that we seem to have lost track of her."

The sergeant nodded. "Before the war I could have given you the history of nearly every family in Lanark, and a good bit of the countryside around it. It's harder now. Even a small town like Lanark has seen its changes. But I don't recall a woman by either name going missing. It was 1916, you said?" He gave the matter some thought. "An inheritance involved, is there?"

"Possibly. We won't know until we find her."

"My guess is, there's nothing here for you. Unless someone reported her missing, we'd have no record of her."

A constable came in from his rounds, nodded to the sergeant, and went through a door on the far left.

"Still, if you come back in the morning, I'll have it nailed down. I wouldn't raise my hopes too high if I were you—but I'll look into it."

"Fair enough." Rutledge took out a card and wrote the number of The Ballantyne Hotel on it. "You can find me there tomorrow night. I'd appreciate any help you can give me."

The sergeant grinned. "Duncarrick? That's Inspector Oliver's turf. Good man, Oliver. I worked with him on a case in 1912. A series of murders that were never solved. Took it hard, he did."

"In Lanark?"

"No, Duncarrick. Five women found with their throats cut. There was a scrap of paper pinned to each of the corpses. Right over their breasts. Called them whores. Harlots. They weren't, of course, just young, pretty in a way. Lively. Working-class women. The bodies were found over a matter of months, but always on the same *day* of the month. Odd business. Had Duncarrick in a sweat, I can tell you! But the killer must have moved on. We never caught him."

"What was the reaction of the public to the accusations on those pieces of paper?"

"What you'd expect—where there's smoke, there's bound to be fire. Unfair, but the belief was that such things didn't happen to *nice* women."

Rutledge said, "Can you recall any other details?"

"That's the whole of it. Two were servant girls, one was a scullery maid at The Ballantyne, and the other two worked on outlying farms. Clever bastard, left no evidence behind. None we could use, at any rate. Just words on a scrap of paper. And the bodies out on the western road."

BACK ON THE pavement outside the station, Rutledge listened to Hamish, savagely drawing conclusions of his own.

The five dead women had no connection with Fiona

MacDonald. She had been in Glencoe in 1912, a young girl living with her grandfather. All the same, their deaths had paved the way for her persecution. "Whore" was a charge that the good people of Duncarrick already associated with murder.

20

───────◆───────

BY THE TIME RUTLEDGE REACHED DUNCARRICK THE
next day, there was a message waiting from Sergeant Bowers
in Lanark.

"No one by either name shown as missing in the year in
question. The only Mary Cook living in the district is sixty.
There is no record of a Maude Cook. Sorry."

It had been a long shot, but he'd already taken the advice
Bowers had given him. He hadn't raised his hopes.

FIONA'S LAWYER WAS summoned to Duncarrick and the
brooch was shown to him. He was a dyspeptic man, with
lines incised deeply in a dark face. Even his eyebrows, thick
and wiry, seemed to be set in a permanent frown. His name
was Armstrong, and he seemed more English than Scottish.

Hamish took an instant dislike to him and said so
clearly. "I wouldna' have him defend my *dog*!" Rutledge
winced.

Oliver was inquiring after someone in Jedburgh who was an acquaintance, and Armstrong responded with unconcealed relish, "Not likely to last the month out, I'd say. The cancer is spreading too fast. You'd be advised to visit if you want to find him coherent. Now, what's this nonsense about a brooch found on a mountainside?"

Oliver took it out of his desk drawer and passed it to Armstrong.

The lawyer examined it with care, squinting at it through spectacles he strung across his nose. "There's an inscription, you say?"

With the nib of his pen, Oliver pointed it out. "MacDonald." He rummaged in his desk drawer and came up with a large magnifying glass. "See for yourself."

Armstrong studied the back of the brooch for some time. "MacDonald is a common name in the Highlands. And how do we know that the name wasn't put there by someone other than my client?"

"Well, of course it was put there by someone else!" Oliver was losing patience. He had found exactly what he wanted, and he would brook no opposition to the conclusions he'd drawn from it. "The engraver."

"I meant," said Armstrong, looking up at him with a sour expression, "that the name could have been engraved on the back just before the brooch was put where it might be found, to please the police."

Oliver held on to his temper and said, "Which is exactly why you are here. We want to show it to the accused and ask her its history."

"Ah, yes." Armstrong handed back the glass and took off his spectacles. But he held on to the brooch. "I don't think I can allow that. Her answer might be self-incriminating."

"I should hope it might be," Oliver retorted through clenched teeth. "That's the intention of the police, to prove her guilt."

"It's no' the place of a policeman to worry his head about innocence," Hamish said. "Nor the church either!"

"You may show it to her," Armstrong answered after letting Oliver stew for several minutes as he looked at the brooch with concentrated attention. "But I will not allow you to badger her. Do you understand?"

Oliver got to his feet and retrieved the key from behind his desk. "You'd better come as well, Rutledge. She might have something to say about the dead woman."

They walked back to the cell and Oliver unlocked the door. As it swung open, Fiona rose from her chair to face them. She looked at the three men, then her eyes swung back to Rutledge's.

He could read the silent message she had sent him: *What has happened?*

Armstrong went up to her and took her hand with unctuous courtesy, rubbing his thumb across her knuckles. "There's nothing to fear, my girl. The police want to ask if this object belongs to you. Please answer that question and that question only."

He opened his palm, and the dim light in the cell caught the brightness of the gold but left the smoky stone dark.

Fiona stared at it. "It's my mother's brooch."

"Not yours, then?"

"No, I—"

Armstrong cut her short. "There you are, Inspector. It does not belong to the accused."

But Oliver could read faces too. He could see clearly that while the brooch had belonged to Fiona's mother, at some time it had been in her possession.

"Is your mother alive?" he asked, already knowing the answer to that.

"She died when I was very young."

"Do you remember her?"

"No. A shadowy figure. Someone with a sweet voice and soft hands. I think I remember that."

"Then you were too young to be given the brooch?"

She glanced at Armstrong. "I was too young, yes."

"Who took charge of it at her death?"

"My grandfather must have done. There was no one else."

"Is your grandfather still living?"

"He died in 1915."

"And you were the only daughter of the house?"

"I was."

"Your mother's brooch would by right pass to you, not to your brothers."

Fiona nodded.

Hamish said, "The conclusion is plain! The brooch must have come into her possession in 1915. A year before the body was left up the glen. They've damned her now!"

But Armstrong had nothing to say in her defense.

There was a gleam of triumph in Oliver's eye. "I'll have that brooch now, Mr. Armstrong, if you please!"

Armstrong passed it over to him, then rubbed his palms together as if to rid them of the feel of it.

Fiona opened her mouth, was on the verge of speaking, and caught instead the swift but barely perceptible shake of Rutledge's head. She closed her mouth and looked down at her hands clenched together now at her waist.

As if he'd heard the unvoiced question, Oliver answered it. "This is evidence now. Thank you, Miss MacDonald!"

Oliver turned on his heel and went out of the cell, followed by Armstrong. Fiona looked quickly at Rutledge, but he said nothing, turning his back with the other men and leaving her alone. But before the door closed finally, she saw him look over his shoulder and smile reassuringly.

It was a reassurance he did not feel.

AFTER ARMSTRONG HAD taken his leave, Oliver waited until he had heard the outer door close behind the lawyer and then said to Rutledge, "Sit down."

Rutledge went back to the chair he had vacated to shake hands with the departing Armstrong. He knew what was coming.

Oliver was saying, "Look, in my view, we have all we need to proceed to trial. This brooch is the connection we didn't have before—it provides a link between the woman MacDougal had found up the glen last year and the accused. And it will see her hang. There's no reason I can think of for going back to Glencoe with her. I think you'll agree to that."

The thought of facing the ghosts of Glencoe again, even with Fiona, turned Rutledge's blood cold. But he said neutrally, "We can't be sure we've identified the corpse. There's no proof yet that she ever bore a child."

"But there's proof that the accused never bore one. If the accused didn't conceal the body there, who did? Why was her brooch found so close to the makeshift grave? Not a stranger's brooch, mind you, but one with her family's name on it!"

Rutledge said with infinite care, "Still, it's circumstantial—Armstrong could make the point that she had lived hard by the glen."

Hamish said, "But he won't. He doesna' care enough."

In the silence Oliver stood up and went to the single window. Its glass was dingy—no one had washed it in years. But he stood there with his back to Rutledge, apparently looking out on the street, and went on. "What you do to satisfy Lady Maude is your business."

"Fiona MacDonald is the only person who can tell me if the woman she's accused of killing is Eleanor Gray."

"I doubt she ever will. She's likely to go to her grave with that secret!"

It was the one point they saw eye to eye on.

"I'd like to talk to her. Now that she's seen the brooch."

Feeling expansively generous, Oliver said, "Go ahead. I'll give you as long as you need."

He turned from the window, picked the key ring up from his desk, and passed it to Rutledge. And he repeated, "As long as you need." But there was a final ring to it now.

"Thanks." Rutledge took the ring and walked down the hall again.

Hamish said, "Oliver willna' find it so easy to dismiss Lady Maude. The Yard willna' either!"

Rutledge answered, "But Lady Maude doesn't want to hear the truth about her daughter. She never has."

As far as he could tell, Fiona MacDonald had not moved from where she had been standing when the three men had walked out of her cell a quarter of an hour earlier.

He closed the wooden door and stood with his back to it. She said almost at once, "Why did they take my mother's brooch?"

"You're sure it belonged to your mother?"

"Yes, of course I'm sure! My grandfather let me wear it on her birthday. To remember her. All day I could wear it, pinned to my dress. And I was always very careful, very proud. I felt close to her."

He could see the small child, dressed in her best clothes, gingerly moving about the house so as not to tear her skirts or soil her sleeves. And the grandfather still mourning his dead daughter in his own fashion, instilling into Fiona the feeling that her mother was near—if only for this one day each year.

It was, in its way, a very sad picture.

"Where did you keep it? After you moved to Duncarrick."

"It's in a small sandalwood box with the bracelet Hamish gave me and the onyx studs that belonged to my father. Or it was—why did they go through my things and take my mother's *pin*?" There was anguish in her face.

"Did you have the brooch with you in Brae?"

"Yes, of course I had it in Brae! You can ask Mrs. Davison."

"And it came to Duncarrick with you?"

"Yes, I told you, it is—was—kept in the tall chest in my room at The Reivers. In the second drawer. I didn't wear it often. I was afraid I might lose it working in the bar."

Rutledge said, "Can you think of anyone in Duncarrick who might have seen you wear the brooch within the past year? Constable McKinstry, for one?"

She considered his question, then took a deep breath. "I remember now the last time I wore it. On my mother's birthday in June of this year. Yes, and again in early July, when I attended church. Will that do?" She read the answer in his face. "But it was *there*. I swear it was there when I was arrested!"

"But you can't be sure?"

"I—no, I had no reason to look for it. I wouldn't have brought it here!"

"No." He considered how much to tell her about how and where the brooch was found, then said instead, "How could you be so certain it was your mother's brooch?"

"It has to be—my father had it made up as his wedding gift to her. There couldn't be another like it."

"You didn't need to read the inscription on the back?"

"What inscription?"

"There's a name. 'MacDonald.' Just under the pin."

She frowned. "Are you trying to trick me?"

"Why should I?"

"Because there's no inscription on the brooch. There never was."

"There are six people who could tell you the name is engraved there. I'm one of them."

Frightened, Fiona said, "Will you take me to the inn? Please? Will you let me go there and see for myself? *It has to be there—!*"

"Oliver won't let you go. But I'll look. You're sure that it's kept in the sandalwood box?"

Her face answered him.

"Then I'll bring the box to you," he told her. "Unopened."

He turned and went out the door, locking it behind him and then pocketing the key.

Oliver looked up as Rutledge came down the passage. He said, "Finished?"

"No. I need to fetch my notes. I'd like to read Mrs. Atwood's statement to Miss MacDonald."

"Suit yourself."

Rutledge went out the station door and walked briskly in the direction of the hotel. *Damn*—he had forgotten that his motorcar was not there.

He reached The Reivers out of breath from the brisk pace he'd set himself. *Please God Drummond is at home—! He has the other key.*

Rutledge knocked at the door of Drummond's house, and to his relief saw that his quarry was there.

"Come outside. I need to speak to you."

"What about?" Drummond demanded, not moving from the doorway.

"Come outside, I tell you! Unless you're willing to shout to the world what this is about." A clear reference to his sister. Reluctantly, Drummond obeyed.

"Look, I need to go to the inn and search again. I want a witness there when I do. And I don't want that witness to be a policeman. Or someone who is unfriendly to Miss MacDonald. Will you help me? Will you unlock the door and come with me?"

"I won't."

"Don't be a bloody fool! I need to get into that inn—time's short!"

"Ask Inspector Oliver to lend you his key." Drummond read the answer in Rutledge's face, and it seemed to persuade him. "All right, then. If it's a trick, I'll kill you with my bare hands!"

"It's not a trick." They walked quickly to the inn, and Drummond took out his key. Unlocking the door, he blocked the way.

"Tell me where."

"Upstairs in the wing the family used. Fiona's room."

Drummond grunted and led the way. Clarence came to greet them, stretching and yawning broadly. Drummond ignored the cat and stopped on the threshold of Fiona's bedroom.

"I'm waiting."

Rutledge said, "The tall bureau. Go to it and open the second drawer from the top. Go on, man, this is no time to be fussy about such things."

Drummond reluctantly crossed the room to the chest and then pulled open the second drawer from the top. "I won't touch her things!"

"No. You shouldn't have to. There's a small sandalwood box there. Do you see it? Probably the color of honey now. Perhaps a little darker. Just a small wooden box."

Drummond grunted. "I don't see it."

"Look, man!"

With a rough forefinger, Drummond pushed at the contents of the drawer. "It's here."

"Then take it out. Take it over to the bed."

Drummond did as he was told. The box was no more than six inches long, four wide, and perhaps not quite four deep. The color of the wood was a dark amber.

"All right. Open it. I don't want to see the contents. But tell me, if you will, what is inside."

He could hear the little silvery sound of things falling onto the coverlet of the bed. "Trinkets," Drummond said.

"Name them." Rutledge could feel his heart beating and hear the clamor from Hamish as Drummond pawed among Fiona's jewelry.

"There's a bracelet. Here are studs, onyx, from the look of them. A small teething hoop, silver, at a guess—it's tarnished. A ring or two. Here's a brooch. And that's the lot."

Rutledge could feel his heart stop.

"Describe it. The brooch."

"I'm not one to describe a woman's gewgaws—"

"Damn it, tell me what it looks like!"

"It's gold, three strands twisted into three circles. Like loops. There's a small stone in the center. A pearl. I've seen Ealasaid wear that of a Sunday."

"And that's all?" He was breathing again.

"That's the lot. I told you."

"Then put it all back into the box and close the lid."

"What's this in aid of?"

"I can't tell you. If you'd found what I had hoped was there, it could have saved Fiona from the hangman. Now—" He put the box that Drummond gave him into his pocket and went to shut the drawer in the chest.

Drummond said, "I won't have you taking her belongings!"

"I'm taking them to her. I'll bring them back shortly. She wants to know if her mother's brooch is still there."

"But that's Ealasaid's brooch—"

"Yes," Rutledge said as he led the way down the stairs. "And it isn't enough!"

TWENTY MINUTES LATER, Rutledge was back at the police station. Oliver wasn't there, but Pringle was. Rutledge explained what he wanted and was allowed to go alone to the cell.

When he was sure that the door was firmly closed behind him, he reached into his pocket and pulled out the sandalwood box.

Fiona took it with trembling fingers, then smiled at him over the lid as she lifted it. "It's so good to touch my own things again. Even if it's for just a little while. I hate wearing these dresses, dreary and plain as this room! They are enough to make the angels despair."

She went to the narrow bed and poured out the contents, just as Drummond had done, then gently sorted through them.

And saw that her mother's brooch was not there.

She turned and stared at him, unsure what to say.

"There's a brooch in the box," he said. "Just as you told me there would be."

"It isn't my mother's. It belonged to Ealasaid. I'd forgotten it was there—"

"Did you deliberately lie to me, Fiona? Or have you told me half-truths from the start?"

Her face flushed, and she bit her lip. "I haven't lied. I have only refused to tell you secrets that aren't mine."

"Then what has become of your mother's brooch? How did it come to be found miles from Duncarrick, over a year ago?"

"I don't know. It was *here*! In this box. I will *swear* to that on my grandfather's soul!"

He wanted to believe her. Hamish told him to believe her.

"Can you trust Drummond? Would he have stolen anything from you—would he have considered the brooch fair payment for the care of the child, then sold it?"

"No—he wouldn't do anything of the sort—!"

"Does he owe loyalty to anyone else? Would he have taken the brooch and given it to someone else, not realizing that it might be used to incriminate you?"

"No. No, I can't believe he would do such a thing! Not Drummond."

"His sister, then? Could she take the key when he wasn't looking, and use it—or allow someone else to use it?"

She hesitated. "No. She wouldn't dare. No."

"Are you very sure, Fiona?" Rutledge asked. "The brooch is gone, after all. When you had told me you believed it was still in the box."

Fiona turned away and began to gather up the things on the bed, her fingers lingering over them as she felt the pull of memory. "I'm sure."

"Then someone else may have taken it. Can you think who that might be? A cleaning woman? A patron when he thought your back was turned? Or someone who might want a souvenir of the wicked harlot?"

"There's no one else with a key. Except for the police—"

The police. But Rutledge, standing there, facing her, was sure that the police had not had anything to do with the missing brooch. Except to retrieve it from a young girl who wanted a better life than she had had . . .

21

---◆---

RUTLEDGE SAT DOWN IN THE CHAIR, WATCHING FIONA while she paced, the box clasped tightly in her hands. Restless and uncertain, she asked him several times to tell her why the brooch was important, but he couldn't. Instead he said, "You'd better give the box back to me. I don't want Oliver to see that you have it."

"Why not?" Reluctantly, Fiona brought it to him, and he put it in his pocket.

"Because, my dear girl, I've got to work with Oliver, and I don't need to have him furious with me for interfering in his investigation. But you seem to be the key to mine."

She said nothing.

He went on. "Do you know a Mrs. Atwood?"

"No. At least I don't remember having heard the name."

"What about Robert Burns?"

"He's a poet—he lived near Ayr."

"No. A person you might have met."

She thought about it. "I recall someone saying that the

fiscal lost his son in the war. I don't remember whether his name was Robert."

"I've been searching for a woman called Eleanor Gray. She may or may not be the person you're accused of killing. The bones that were found in Glencoe. Eleanor Gray's been missing since 1916. She had a quarrel with her mother over—money. And just after that she was supposed to spend a weekend near Winchester with a friend, Mrs. Atwood. Instead she came to Scotland with a man, possibly a friend of this Robert Burns, who may or may not be the fiscal's son."

Fiona smiled. "May or may not be—possibly a friend— supposed to spend the weekend. Hamish said you were a clever policeman."

It was the first glimpse of natural humor he'd seen, lighting her face from within. Lighting her eyes.

"Yes, sometimes I wonder myself," he said, returning the smile. "The odd thing about Eleanor Gray is that no one appears to have cared for her. Ann Tait knew of her—and envied her. Mrs. Atwood was jealous of her. Her mother saw to it that she couldn't pursue medicine, which was Eleanor's passionate interest. She may have died in 1916, and the only person who has tried to find her was a solicitor who wanted her to sign papers relating to her inheritance. You are accused of killing her—and yet you don't know her."

"And that's true." She was serious again, resuming her pacing. "Why should I choose a woman at random, kill her, and take her child? A stranger I knew nothing about! It makes sense to the police because they're men; they believe that because I wanted a child, I wouldn't care who or what it was."

"Their response would be, you knew Eleanor Gray was alone and in hiding. The perfect choice. There was no one to come looking for her."

"To learn that much about her, surely I'd have learned her name as well. I don't know how people behave in France or Canada. In Scotland we don't confide in strangers!"

"Perhaps you met her as someone else. Using another name." He paused. "Mrs. Cook—"

She went so white that her knees buckled, and he sprang from his chair to catch her as she fell. Carrying her to the bed, he laid her gently on the rough surface of the blanket. "Fiona—"

Her eyelids fluttered, then shut. Her voice when she spoke trembled. "I don't know a Mrs. Cook."

"Yes, you do," he said, pulling the chair closer to the bed. "You know precisely who she is. She gave birth in Lanark to the child you called Ian Hamish MacLeod. I've spoken to her physician, his name is Wilson. I know that she had a hard birth and a very difficult recovery. I know, too, that it will be impossible for her to bear other children." He stopped, then added the last bit of information that sealed his certainty. "You told your aunt you were expected to work out your notice at Mrs. Davison's. But you didn't. You explained to her why you were being sent for—that your aunt in Duncarrick was ill—and Mrs. Davison, a compassionate woman, released you immediately. She cared enough about you to make it easier for you to leave her family. And so there was nearly a month between the time you promised to come to Duncarrick with your child and the time you arrived here. You spent that time somewhere with the boy and his mother. But you lied to your aunt, you lied to Mrs. Davison, for all I know you have lied to Mrs. Cook. But you can't lie to me, Fiona. I know too much."

She reached out and caught his hands. "Please. I don't know a Mrs. Cook. This woman you've just told me about—*she has nothing to do with me or with my child*! You mustn't—there is no need to search for her. Because she doesn't exist." Her face was earnest now, her eyes wide. "It was Eleanor Gray I killed. I will swear to it! Bring my barrister to me—Inspector Oliver—the fiscal. In front of them I will tell you everything that happened. I didn't mean to kill her—I didn't want to kill her. But she told me I could have Ian, and then she changed her mind. I loved him, I'd held him, I wanted him. And so when she said she intended to take him after all, I pulled the pillows out from under her head and I held them over her face until she stopped struggling. And then I dragged her to the head of the stairs and—"

She broke off, crying, her tears hot against his hands. "Oh, please, I killed Eleanor Gray! Please go back to London and leave me to die in peace!"

"Fiona, listen to me!"

"No, I've listened long enough! I want you to bring Inspector Oliver to me, and Mr. Armstrong. Please—I don't want to talk about it anymore!"

"If you killed Eleanor Gray, what did you do with her body?"

"I buried it. In a field somewhere along the road. It was dark, and I couldn't see to dig, and there was a dog barking somewhere, and I was so frightened. Then Ian began to cry, and I shut my ears and kept digging until I could roll her into the hole I'd made. Someone had piled branches and tree limbs nearby, ready for burning. I pulled them over the raw grave and left them there. It was at the edge of a field, near a wall, where no one would plow—"

"You're lying—!"

"No, I'm telling the truth at last—Mr. Elliot said to me that confession would free my soul, and it has—I'm ready to die . . . *I want to die—!*"

IT TOOK RUTLEDGE nearly ten minutes to stop Fiona's tears and make her listen to him. Shaking her lightly, he forced her to look at his face. Her eyes, rimmed red from crying, were the saddest he'd ever seen. Dark pools of anguish in her white face.

He wanted to hold her and comfort her. Instead he said, "Fiona. If you confess to murder, there is nothing I can do to save you. Do you understand that? You will be hanged. With joy and thanksgiving in Duncarrick. If I swear that I won't speak Mrs. Cook's name again, will you promise me to say nothing to Oliver or Armstrong? *Nothing!*"

She said wearily, "I'm tired. I want this to end. I don't want to remember Hamish and I don't want to think about Ian, and I can't *bear*—" She stopped, shaking her head.

"It will only be for a short time. I have to search for Eleanor Gray. Do you understand that? And if I find her, you won't have to tell anyone about Mrs. Cook. Will you trust me a little longer?"

After a moment, she said, "I don't want to trust you. I don't want to see you again."

"If you won't do it for me, then for your grandfather—and Hamish."

"They are dead. I'd rather be dead with them. It hurts too much to live." Then she pushed him away and said, "Very well, then. As long as you keep your promise, I shall keep mine. But I haven't the strength to sit here in this silence, alone and afraid, much longer! If I am going to die, I want to do it before I disgrace myself!" She caught her breath on a sob. "Courage is elusive in the dark of the night."

He stood up. She seemed very small and helpless. He knew how confinement shredded the soul. But he had seen her strength. And he was touched by it.

"I'll send word as soon as I can. Through McKinstry. You can trust him."

"He's— Yes, I trust him."

Rutledge took a handkerchief from his pocket and held it out to her. She took it gratefully.

He walked to the door, wanting to say something. To offer her courage. Or to tell her she'd be safe. But he didn't turn.

And Fiona MacDonald didn't stop him as he left.

LEAVING THE CELL key with Pringle, Rutledge went to The Reivers, summoning Drummond en route to unlock the door again.

Rutledge took the stairs two at a time, intent on restoring the sandalwood box to Fiona's room.

Drummond lumbered after him, far lighter on his feet than a man his size ought to be. "I did what you asked. Now you owe me an explanation," he said at Rutledge's heels.

Rutledge set the box in the drawer, carefully arranging it among the gloves and the handkerchiefs. Then he turned to Drummond with his answer ready. The man was blocking the doorway. Clarence, half rising from the pillow on the bed, looked at both of them with wary eyes. A sudden move and she would be gone, out of sight.

"Something belonging to Fiona MacDonald has been found near the place where Oliver thinks the body of the child's mother was hidden. In Glencoe. Fiona told me it was safe here at The Reivers. But she was wrong." He let out a breath in frustration. "Oliver has all he needs now to convict."

"Are you telling me something has been stolen from here?"

"The police at the scene think the murderer dropped it while trying to drag the woman's body high up the slope on a mountainside. A sheepman's daughter found it. I don't know what to believe."

"I have the only other key, and it was given me by Ealasaid MacCallum herself. Fiona handed hers to Oliver when they took her away. Are you calling me a thief?" Drummond's voice was dangerously quiet.

"No, damn it. I'm saying that what was found in Glencoe is enough to hang Fiona MacDonald. However it came to be there. And if she's right, that it was here in Duncarrick in July, then someone must have come in here secretly and taken it!"

"Fiona doesn't lie. I've never known her to lie!"

"She lied about the child."

Drummond gestured angrily, and Clarence fled over the

side of the bed in a single fluid movement. "That's not the same thing. You know it isn't the same!"

Rutledge started toward the door. "Drummond. I have to leave Duncarrick for a time. Keep an eye on the inn. It wouldn't do for more—evidence—to find its way to Oliver."

Hamish warned, "It's a thin line you're walking! There's no way to know where *his* loyalties lie!"

Rutledge responded silently, "Call it the Biblical casting of bread upon the waters. I need to find out if he's friend— or foe. He has custody of that child!"

Drummond let him pass. As they went down the stairs, Rutledge said over his shoulder, "If I can put a name and a history to the bones in Glencoe, I will. That's the only way to break the chains tying Fiona MacDonald to murder."

WHEN RUTLEDGE ARRIVED at the smithy, he found that the motorcar was repaired and ready to drive.

The young mechanic came out of the small shed where he worked, rubbing his black, greasy hands on a greasier square of cloth. Grinning, he beckoned to Rutledge. "Come look at something."

"I'm not sure I want to," Rutledge answered, following him. "What's wrong with my engine?"

But the mechanic said nothing. When he got to a workman's bench full of tools and parts and a jumble of odds and ends, he reached for a grimy jar that was sitting behind a coil of rope. Holding up the jar, he said to Rutledge, "Now take a look."

The jar was full of petrol. Except at the bottom, where a layer of something else moved less sluggishly.

"Water!" Rutledge said, surprised. "There was *water* in my tank!"

"When all else fails," the mechanic said happily, "expect the impossible. Yes, indeed, ordinary water. Stopped you as efficiently as an artillery shell. And with greater accuracy, I might add! I drained off the lines, let the jar's contents settle, and there you have it. A mechanical marvel." He put the jar back on the bench. "Been swimming in that motorcar, have you?"

Rutledge paid the inflated bill without comment.

AS THEY DROVE out of the smithy's yard, Hamish said, "This meddling with the car was no' the same as searching your room. And if there's anyone who will ken where to look for whoever is responsible, it's yon constable."

"If it was mischief," Rutledge responded, "then the timing was remarkably opportune. I don't like coincidence."

McKinstry was coming out of the barbershop when Rutledge spotted him and offered him a lift as far as his house. In response to Rutledge's question about malicious property damage, the constable shook his head. "We don't see much of that. Too easy in a town this size to guess who the culprits are likely to be. The Maxwell brats, now, they're a wild lot, and it's only a matter of time before their mischief turns to something more serious. The Army might make men out of them, but their father never will—too quick with his fists." He added with curiosity evident in his face, "Any particular reason for your interest?"

"I wondered about it, that's all."

"It wasn't mischief that lay behind the notes written about Fiona. If that's what you're getting at!"

"Not at all." Rutledge changed the subject.

It wasn't until he'd dropped McKinstry at his door that Hamish said, "He didna' speak of the brooch to you."

"No," Rutledge answered. "He doesn't want to accept what it means. For that matter, neither do I. If no one took it from The Reivers—" He left the thought unfinished.

Hamish told him, *"She didna' kill!"*

But the woman in the back room of the police station was not the same girl that Hamish remembered haying in the summer of 1914, the sun warm on her face and laughter in her eyes. The day war had begun in a small town in an obscure province of the Austrian empire. Hamish had carried that memory with him to the trenches. Time stood still for him. It had moved on for her. In five years, people can change. . . .

LEAVING HIS CAR at the hotel, this time in the open rather than in the shadows of the shed, Rutledge went to the shop owned by Ann Tait.

She was folding lingerie into pale lavender paper, and a box stood ready at her elbow. Lifting the paper, she laid it gently into the box and arranged it a little to make it fit snugly. Then she put the lid on the box and set it aside before turning to Rutledge.

"Have you found your Eleanor Gray?"

"Not yet. But I shall. No, I've come about another matter. I was speaking with a Mrs. Cook. I can't recall her first name. She'd stopped me on the street. A few days ago now. I must try to find her again. Can you help me?"

Ann Tait looked at him consideringly. "As far as I know, there isn't a Mrs. Cook in Duncarrick. At any rate, she isn't among my customers. There was a woman by that name I met in London. She was elderly and impossible. I didn't like her."

"Well, then," he said helplessly, "who was I speaking with?"

"Was this a large woman? Overbearing in her manner?"

He smiled as if relieved. In fact, he was. "Yes. I'm afraid so."

"That was Mrs. Coldthwaite."

"Yes, that's it. Coldthwaite. I'm grateful. Or—should I be?"

Ann Tait nodded sympathetically. "Wretched woman. She comes in and tries on corsets half her size, then complains to me that my stock is ill-made. You'll find her in the gabled house next but one to the baker's shop. And I wish you joy of her!"

Outside on the street again, Hamish was roundly telling him that he had already broken his promise.

"No, I haven't."

"It's no' a name you can use with impunity here!"

"I have a feeling Ann Tait won't repeat it to anyone."

All the same, he paid a call on Mrs. Coldthwaite.

And paid the price for it. Once she had him in her parlor, her sole intent was to pry out of him whatever tidbits of potential gossip she could pass on. It was done graciously, in the name of concern for "dear Fiona." But her eyes were cold and her mouth small, tight.

A "wretched woman," Ann Tait had called her. Hamish preferred "vicious."

She did, unintentionally, give Rutledge one piece of information he had not heard. The question was, should he treat it as dependable?

"We—my husband and I—were at a lovely dinner party in Jedburgh a week ago. The Chief Constable, Mr. Robson, and the fiscal, Mr. Burns, were there too. And I distinctly heard Mr. Burns saying to Mr. Robson that many of Fiona MacDonald's sins would never come to light. 'We shall try her for murder, and leave the other unpleasant facets of her character for God to judge.' And when someone—Mr. Holden, I believe it was—asked Mr. Robson what was to be done with the child once the trial was over, Mr. Robson answered, 'Mr. Elliot has spoken with an orphanage in Glasgow that trains children in various trades. He will go there if the victim's family doesn't care to take responsibility for him.' It's my understanding that they're *quite* well-to-do and might find the child an—um—embarrassment."

Rutledge silently swore. Hamish called Mrs. Coldthwaite "a gossiping auld besom."

She watched Rutledge's face avidly, her smile inviting him to enlighten her further on the subject of Eleanor Gray's family.

Rutledge replied blandly, "I'm afraid Inspector Oliver is your man for word on that subject. Ealasaid MacCallum was, I'm told, a very fine woman. I had wondered if she'd confided to you any concerns she might have felt about the conduct of Miss MacDonald after her niece came to live at the inn."

In a thousand or more words, the answer appeared to be no.

He had the feeling Mrs. Coldthwaite was deeply disappointed to have to admit it.

22

◆

After returning to The Ballantyne, Rutledge went to the telephone room to put in a call to Sergeant Gibson in London.

He got Old Bowels instead.

"Rutledge? Is that you?"

Rutledge closed his eyes. Hamish was still furious with him for breaking his promise to Fiona regarding the name of Mrs. Cook. The angry rumble at the back of his mind, like a headache, had shortened his own temper.

"Yes, sir."

"What the hell are you doing, man! This business should have been cleared up by now."

It was useless to explain the complexities involving Fiona MacDonald and Mrs. Cook. "It's difficult tracing a woman who didn't want to be found."

"I'm not interested in excuses. I'm interested in results."

The receiver was slammed down.

Hamish said, "You've lost your skills—"

"You're wrong—"

It was an old argument. The sting of it hadn't faded with time. Rubbing the bridge of his nose between thumb and forefinger, he tried to think. Gibson . . .

He called the Yard again and this time reached the sergeant.

"I need to know who might have had a brooch engraved—" He described the brooch in minute detail, the letters on the back. "It could be very important."

"Where do you want me to begin?"

"Edinburgh. Glasgow. Not the fashionable shops." The engraved letters had seemed worn, their shapes elegant but their depth shallow. "A middle-class shop, where a cairngorm brooch wouldn't cause comment." He paused, considering all the possibilities. "It's going to be the proverbial needle, Sergeant, but I need the answer. And I know for a fact that the engraving was done within the past five weeks." He remembered the water in his petrol. Not vandalism— time bought? "Possibly within the past two or three. That should help."

Gibson sounded dubious. "It's a tall order."

"Yes." Rutledge tried to think. Hamish wouldn't let him. He said, "Gibson—try England first, will you? Just over the border from Duncarrick. I have a feeling—"

"Feelings are all very well, sir, but they don't help very much, do they?"

"This time, Sergeant, I think they just might!"

EARLY THE NEXT morning, Rutledge pulled out of Duncarrick with his luggage in the boot of the motorcar.

But he had kept his room at The Ballantyne, and made it clear to Constable Pringle, whom he met in the hotel yard, that he would be gone no more than a few days.

Heading east, he reached David Trevor's house in time for dinner, and Morag greeted him with the warmth lavished on lost sheep. Lost black sheep, Hamish corrected him.

Trevor was also happy to see him. "I was looking forward to a lonely meal and only Morag's company," he told Rutledge. "Have you finished your work in Duncarrick? Is this visit a farewell before leaving for London?"

"No. I haven't found Eleanor Gray. And Ha—" He was about to say, "Hamish is giving me no peace!" But he stopped in time, and instead ended lightly, "—and I'm not going to be very pleasant company in this mood!"

"Nonsense. You're always good company, Ian."

As they sat in the drawing room after dinner and drank whiskey that Trevor had stocked before the war, Rutledge waited until a comfortable silence fell, and then said, "I've come for a reason. I need to talk to someone sensible who isn't connected with the investigation that's under way."

"I'll listen. I might not have sensible answers."

"Listening is enough." Rutledge launched into the events of the past week, and in the process of putting them into coherent order found himself thinking more clearly as well.

"And that's where it stands."

Trevor said, "Yes, I see your point. There could be two separate investigations here. Or only one. And if there's only one, then Fiona MacDonald will be found guilty of the charges brought against her. If there are two, then the woman on the hillside may have nothing to do with Duncarrick. And you won't be able to answer that until you find out who she is. It's going to be nearly impossible after all this time, isn't it? I don't envy you the hunt! But it seems to me that you've come a long way in establishing that Eleanor Gray reached Scotland."

"Yes. If I weren't a damned stubborn policeman, I'd have concluded yesterday that Oliver is right, it's finished, and gone back to London satisfied."

Trevor looked consideringly at him. "You like this Mac-Donald woman. You would like to see her proven innocent."

"You're telling me I'm not objective," Rutledge answered, feeling himself flush. "Is that a fair judgment?"

"Oh, I think you are objective. What I see from my own vantage point, not knowing any of these people well enough to be anything but objective, is that you may well be in danger. Have you considered the possibility that from the start of this business, Fiona MacDonald was going to be sacrificed? And your questions are getting in the way of that. Take care that you don't threaten someone who believes he—or she—is well hidden behind the scenes."

"That's an odd warning." Rutledge rubbed the bridge of his nose. His head still ached. But Hamish had fallen silent. "I can't find any reason for someone to hate Fiona MacDonald deeply enough to concoct such a mound of evidence against her. I've searched."

"Yes, I'm sure you have. Which leads me to believe that the girl is a scapegoat for someone else."

"The child's mother. I've considered that, yes. Fiona won't tell me who she is. If the woman is dead, then surely it doesn't matter?"

"Turn it another way. Who is that child's father? Is he alive? If so, why mustn't he be told he has a son? Or, if he's dead, his family. Why should it be so important to keep someone in ignorance? So important, in fact, that Miss MacDonald is willing to hang and leave the child to the tender mercies of an orphanage."

Rutledge said tiredly, "If the mother is alive, she's sacrificing Fiona and the child as well. Willingly. And that makes no sense either!"

"Then that's where the secret lies. The one you have to dig out."

He had left Mrs. Cook out of the story. He said, "Before I can find the father, I have to find the mother. And before I can be sure I've found *her*, I must track down Eleanor Gray."

"Then walk carefully. I don't have a good feeling about this, Ian. Walk carefully!"

IN THE MORNING, Rutledge left to drive north to the Trossachs. Sir Walter Scott had used the district's great beauty for the setting of his poem *Lady of the Lake,* and again in the novel *Rob Roy.* Whether Rob Roy MacGregor was a bandit or a Scottish Robin Hood depended on who was telling the story. But between them, he and Scott had made that stretch of lochs and hills famous. Even the Wordsworths, William and his sister Dorothy, had walked there.

Rutledge spent most of his second day searching for a Robert Burns. Ordinarily, he'd have asked the fiscal for his son's direction, but he wanted to avoid any interference with the neighbor, Mrs. Raeburn, before he got to her.

He didn't distrust the fiscal; he thought the man was probably honest and by his own lights dependable. But when it came to family secrets, even the most honest of men fiercely protected their own.

On the third morning, he found what he was looking for. Driving into a ring of spectacular barren hills, he reached a town called Craigness. It lay in a tree-rimmed bowl, east of where two rivers joined and a bridge wide enough to take motorcars crossed them. Its tall, slender church tower gleaming in the morning mists, and its houses looking far more English Georgian than Scottish, gave it an oddly graceful air, but north of it spread out the Highlands. Here Rutledge located the law office of Burns, Grant, Grant, and Fraser. It was an old building in a line of old buildings, with a first-floor bay window that jutted into the street. The brass handles and doorknob shone with polish against the dark red door.

"With prices to match the furnishings," Hamish commented as Rutledge opened the outer door to the smell of beeswax, good leather, and better cigars. An aura of respectability, timelessness, and good taste hung in the air.

Neither Mr. Grant Senior nor Mr. Grant Junior was in, he was informed by a young clerk. But Mr. Fraser would see him.

Rutledge walked into a paneled room filled with books, floor-to-ceiling shelves, volume after volume spilling over onto chairs and tables and every other flat surface, even jostling for space on the windowsills and cluttering the beautiful old carpet on the floor.

The man behind the desk rose to greet him, offering his left hand. His right arm was missing. "Inspector Rutledge! I'm Hugh Fraser. I hope there's a grisly murder under our noses. I'm sick to death of wills and deeds and title disputes." The fair face beamed at him, but the blue eyes were sharp.

"No such luck. I understand from the local police that one of your partners was a Robert Burns."

"Yes, Robbie died in France in 1916. We've left his name on the door out of respect. Although I must say, I would welcome his ghost as a partner to help me sort out this tangle." Fraser waved his left hand at the chaos.

No, you wouldn't, Rutledge silently replied. Aloud, he said, "Do you know when he was killed?"

"In the spring of 1916." He gave Rutledge the date. It was the same week Eleanor Gray had told Mrs. Atwood that she was going north to Scotland. "I heard it almost at once, actually. From a supply sergeant I was dealing with. He wasn't aware that Robbie was my law partner. He just said he'd been told one of the Trossachs men had bought it that morning and thought I might know him. Hell of a way to find out. Robbie was a good man." The smile had faded. "We lost too many good men. Were you out there?"

"On the Somme," Rutledge answered, his voice cold enough to ward off friendly reminiscences.

Fraser nodded. "That was the worst of a bad lot. Why is

the Yard interested in Robbie? Is it to do with any of his personal affairs? We handled everything. The will was straightforward, as you'd expect. I can't imagine that three years later it might interest the police."

"Not the will, no. I'm looking for the property that Captain Burns owned here. A house, I think."

"His father hasn't sold it. As I remember, it was a family property and Mr. Burns Senior was not prepared to part with it. He hasn't changed his mind, has he?"

"Not to my knowledge. During the war, did Captain Burns's friends use the house from time to time?" If Burns was killed the week she came north, he hadn't driven Eleanor Gray to Scotland. Someone else had.

"I have no idea. I wouldn't be surprised. Robbie was a generous man; he often did such things. You'll have to speak to Robbie's father. But I can tell you how to find the house. Craigness is small. You'll have no trouble."

"There was a young woman Captain Burns met in London whilst on sick leave. Eleanor Gray. Did he ever speak of her to you?"

"Eleanor? Oh, yes. Often. Robbie had helped her find pipers to entertain the wounded. Quite an undertaking, that was. He sent me a witty account of it, and it reached me in the middle of a push. It was a bad time, and the laugh did me good. At any rate, he and Eleanor went on to spend a good deal of time together before he was sent back to France. Showed me her photograph, in fact, when we crossed paths the last time. I got the feeling it was fairly serious. Robbie had enormous charm, you know, people liked him. A pity he didn't make it home. I tried to look up Eleanor after the war, but no one had any idea where she might be. I wanted her to know how much he cared."

Would it have made a difference if she'd known that in 1916? Aloud, Rutledge said, "Have you kept any of his letters?"

"Regrettably, no. I needn't tell you how it was in the

trenches. Paper was the first to rot in the rain and the mud—nothing lasted very long, not even boots. And what the weather didn't get, the rats did. Stinking bastards!" It was said unemotionally. The rats had become so fierce and so common that not even a heavy shelling rid the trenches of them. You got used to them.

Rutledge nodded. "If you can tell me how to find the house, I'll be on my way."

"I'll do that if you'll come and have lunch with me. My wife's in Edinburgh for the week, and I'm damned tired of my own company!"

THE HOUSE STOOD in a street of houses that had well-kept gardens and a remarkable view of the hills. Two nursemaids with prams passed him as he stepped out of the car, deep in earnest conversation while their charges slept. Rutledge studied number fourteen for a time, then went to the door of number fifteen. But no one appeared to be at home. He tried number thirteen, and an elderly woman opened the door, peering at him over the top of her spectacles, the silver chain attached to them almost the same color as her hair.

"Yes?" She looked him up and down. "If you're here to see Barbara, I'm afraid she's out."

"Inspector Rutledge, Scotland Yard," he told her. "Can you give me a few minutes of your time? I'm interested in the Burns house. At number fourteen."

"Inspector, are you? Why should anyone in London care about the Burns house? It hasn't been lived in since poor Robbie's death."

"Yes, that's what I'm told. He died in France. Do you remember when?"

"In the spring of 1916!" she retorted as if he had doubted her mental alertness. "It's my legs that are giving out, young man, not my brain!"

"I meant no offense, Mrs.—"

"The auld biddy—" Hamish interjected.

"Raeburn. Robbie used to tease me about that. Burns and Raeburn, he said. A better name for a law firm than Burns, Grant, Grant, and Fraser." She stepped back. "Do come in! I can't stand here the morning long."

He followed her into a sitting room cluttered with glass bells covering specimens of dead animals. Giant fish and heads of deer decorated the walls. She caught his eye and said, "My late husband liked to kill things. Birds, red deer, fish—never understood it myself, but there you are. That chair, over there, if you please. I can hear you better. Barbara—my niece—calls it barbaric. But I suppose I've grown used to seeing them. That's a particularly fine fox, you know. I'm told several of the birds are nice as well."

Hamish said, "I wonder who killed her husband?"

Catching the eye of a snarling lynx, Rutledge took the chair Mrs. Raeburn indicated. After a moment, he said, "I've just come from speaking with Mr. Fraser. He tells me Captain Burns had given you a key before he went away to France."

"Mr. Fraser is wrong. Captain Burns gave me the key in 1912, when he joined the practice. I was to let in the painters and carpenters. After they'd finished, he told me to keep it in the event more work had to be done."

"Did he have guests often?"

"At first he did. His fiancée and her family came to dinner any number of times. After the war started, there was less entertaining. But he came home when he could and sometimes brought friends."

"Do you recall hearing the name Eleanor Gray?"

"He was in mourning. His fiancée died unexpectedly in late 1915. There was never any other young lady. The Captain never said anything to *me* about another young lady!"

"Fellow officers, then," Rutledge amended hastily.

"Oh, yes, he sometimes offered them the house. There was a blind officer who stayed for a month. And a flier with severe burns on the face and hands. Better off dead, if you ask me. And one or two others on leave, with no place of their own."

"Was there an officer here—just about the time word came that Captain Burns was a casualty? I believe he might have brought a woman with him."

"There was an officer about that time. From London. I can't tell you his name. But he came alone, arriving quite late. That's why I remember him."

"Because he came later than expected?"

"No, no. He woke me out of a sound sleep, all but knocking the door down. It was raining, and he was wet through. I handed him the key, then slammed the door shut against the wind. But I watched from the window to see he got in all right. The lock is sometimes stiff in bad weather. I'd have known if he'd had a woman with him, wouldn't I? I'd have seen her go in with him!"

"How long did he stay at the Burns house?"

"He was to stay a week, and left after two days."

"Did he tell you why he was leaving?"

"I didn't ask. He brought back the key and thanked me. But it had rained every day. I suppose he found that depressing."

"How was he wounded? Shoulder? Leg?"

"Sometimes it isn't possible to tell, and I never care to ask. He was very brown. I did ask about that. He'd served in Palestine, he said."

"Was he Scots?"

"Yes. He told me he was English, but he was Scots."

"Would you recognize him if you were to see him again?"

She shook her head. "I expect I wouldn't. He didn't have a remarkable face." She studied Rutledge, pushing her spectacles up on her nose. "You do. I'd remember meeting you."

Rutledge said, "If you still have the key, would you allow me to go in and look through the house?"

She stared at him suspiciously. "Why should you wish to do that?"

"I'm sorry. I'm not at liberty to say."

"Oh, very well. Come along. But I warn you, I can't stand on my feet while you take your time about it!"

She went off to fetch the key, and led him to a gate in the middle of the low hedge between the two properties. He looked at the house carefully as they made their way around back. If the bedrooms were on this side, Mrs. Raeburn might well know who had come to stay here. But if they were on the other side—

Mrs. Raeburn unlocked the garden door and bade him wipe his feet before he came into the house. He did as he was told, then followed her down a short passage to the kitchen.

As they walked in, Hamish objected, "There's nithing to find here—"

He was right, the house would have been cleaned many times since Eleanor Gray had come here—if indeed she'd come at all. But Rutledge thought now he could guess the reason why she might have wished to. With news of Robbie Burns's death, she had wanted to see the house where he lived. Where she might have lived as his wife. But where would she have gone from here?

Rutledge and Mrs. Raeburn walked from room to room. The dining room, the parlor, a small study. The furnishings were comfortable, with a number of lovely old pieces that Burns must have inherited, and a wonderful mantelpiece in the parlor. Upstairs there were two bedrooms, one on Mrs. Raeburn's side of the house, and one on the other, with a sitting room in between. The far bedroom appeared to be the master bedroom, and Rutledge studied it with particular interest.

It held a large spindle bed, a wardrobe of carved mahogany, a maple desk under the window, several comfortable chairs, and a tall bureau that matched the wardrobe. He went to that and was about to open one of the drawers, but Mrs. Raeburn stopped him.

She didn't hold with police prying into people's lives, and told him so. "Not without a warrant!"

He turned to the bookcase. Law books for the most part. He touched the spines of several novels, a three-volume history of Scotland, and a collection of six works recounting travels to Europe. He pulled one out at random, expecting to hear Mrs. Raeburn scold him. But apparently books were not as intimate as the contents of a drawer.

It was the volume on traveling in Italy, many of the pages still uncut. He put that back and took out one of the law books. *Robert Edward Burns* was inscribed in handsome copperplate on the flyleaf. The novels held nothing of interest, and he moved on to the volume of travels in France. These pages had been cut, and from the way the spine fell open to "Paris," the chapter had been read a number of times. He flicked through the pages, admiring the line drawings of cathedrals, châteaux, and statues, found nothing of interest, and was on the point of closing the book, when something in the margin of one page caught his attention. The chapter heading was for the north of France. What had become, in fact, the battlefields of the war.

There were brief notations here, in a woman's handwriting. He took the book to the window, his back to Mrs. Raeburn, and read one after the other.

Here he was wounded. Ypres had been underlined on the page. *Here he met one of the pipers we found to play for us.* The name of a small village had been marked. It had become an aid station, Rutledge remembered, and finally abandoned because the smell of death had soaked the ground.

Rutledge moved through the chapter. There were a number of other notes here and there, each relating to some personal event the reader had connected with a place in the guide. Small landmarks in the life of a dead man. A retracing of his journey to death.

On the last page of that chapter was another note, in a hand that was shaking. *Here he died.* And then below that, a last, touching line. *I wish I could die too. E.G.*

Eleanor Gray had been here.

Rutledge closed the book with triumph.

She had reached Scotland. The question was, had she ever left it?

23

————◆————

MRS. RAEBURN WAS BECOMING IMPATIENT. RUTLEDGE opened the wardrobe door before she could protest but saw that it was empty. He moved on to the other bedroom, and then the sitting room.

There was no longer anything in the house of a personal nature. A new occupant could move in that afternoon and never have an inkling of the previous owner. His interests or tastes—loves or disappointments—childhood or death. Except for the books, it appeared that the dead man's belongings had long since been removed for storage or a missionary barrel.

Had Eleanor Gray left other small tokens of her presence here that had been swept away unnoticed in the general cleaning?

"It wasna' what she intended," Hamish said softly.

"No," Rutledge answered silently. "And that's very sad."

He added aloud, "Does the fiscal—Mr. Burns—come to stay often?"

"He did when he went through his son's clothes and such, after. I think the house holds too many memories now, and business doesn't often bring him this way. I've a mind to make an offer for it if my niece settles down. I'm not as young as I used to be, and it will be a comfort to have her next door."

"But not in the same house," Hamish said, interpreting the tone of voice.

"I'd hoped she might marry the Captain. But then he went and got himself engaged to someone else. A pity. Still, she died of appendicitis, Julia did. If he'd come home from the war fancy-free, I'd have tried my hand at matchmaking."

They went out the way they'd come in, and while Mrs. Raeburn locked the garden door, Rutledge walked toward the garden.

"It was once quite lovely," Mrs. Raeburn told him, following down the path among the beds. "Now the gardener keeps it up but doesn't go out of his way. But then, who's to see it, I ask you!"

She turned around, a broad hint that it was time for him to accompany her back through the gate.

He went on, ignoring her. It was in fact a lovely garden—peaceful and secluded. A high wall marked the end.

It was Hamish who noticed the bench.

It had been dragged from its low stone dais by the wall and set in the midst of a bed of annuals. It looked out of place here, like a whale stranded on a foreign beach. The dimensions were somehow wrong, and the plants set in around it lacked the symmetry of other beds, as if having to compensate for the awkwardness of the bench.

The gardener's doing—or someone else's?

Mrs. Raeburn, complaining of her legs, had stopped by the sundial. Rutledge called to her, "How long has this bench been set here? It appears to belong over there by the wall."

"How should I know? I never come that far—my legs, you know."

Rutledge squatted on the grass and looked at the soil of

the bed. It was loose, friable. As if it had been dug up each spring and restocked with plants that would grow contentedly in this corner shaded by the wall. There were forget-me-nots and pansies and a pair of small ferns set in a half-moon around the bench. But nothing was planted under the bench.

You wouldn't plant under the bench. . . .

He went to the shed to find a trowel, and Mrs. Raeburn called plaintively, "Have you *finished,* young man?"

"I'm sorry to be a nuisance," he replied. "If you wish to go back through the hedge, I'll come across in five minutes."

She was mumbling something about taking advantage; he could hear her voice retreating even as she did.

It wouldn't take considerable strength to move the bench. It was heavy and cumbersome, but a person could shift it if he or she knew how to "walk" it off the dais and into the bed. And it had rained both days. . . .

The feet were deep into the soil of the bed now, as if the bench had stood there for several seasons. Rutledge used the side of the trowel to scrape away the layer of compost mulch that kept down the weeds. Then he put the tip deep into the ground and lifted the first clump of soil.

It was thick with what he took at first to be roots. And then he saw that he had uncovered a piece of cloth. Clothing, he amended, looking at it closely. No, it was a corner of blanket. No more than two inches by three.

Blankets weren't put in with compost—they didn't decay at the rate of garden clippings and hedge trimmings. An old blanket went into the dustbin.

He dug about under the bench for some time, but the ground yielded nothing more.

Hamish said, "Someone buried a pet here, a cat or a small dog, and moved the bench so that the grave wouldna' be disturbed."

Rutledge, rocking back on his haunches, reluctantly agreed. A pet wrapped in an old blanket . . .

After all, he hadn't wanted to find Eleanor Gray here,

buried in a back garden. It would finish his investigation in
Scotland.

He hadn't wanted to come to Scotland. Now he didn't
want to leave. There was too much still to be done.

RUTLEDGE KEPT HIS promise and met Hugh Fraser for
luncheon. It was a small restaurant that was popular with
the noonday throng of marketgoers, and Fraser apologized
for that. "But if we go to the hotel, a dozen people will stop
by the table, their minds on business."

"My father followed the law. He found it a fascinating
mistress."

Fraser grimaced. "The law is all right. And I've made a
good living. My clients come from all corners of the district,
from Loch Lomond to Callander. I just don't have the same
taste for it I once had. I never got used to watching men die.
France was bad enough, but there we were firing back. The
influenza epidemic was very different. There was a nurse
bending over me, changing the dressing on my arm, and she
collapsed across the bed. The orderlies carried her away like
a sack of onions. Before dawn she was dead. It was like some
damned medieval plague. The men on either side of me
died of it, and seven men in another ward. I remember
priests coming in the night, and not enough orderlies to
bring us water. My father saw two people drop dead in the
street before they could reach home." He laughed without
humor. "You're a damned good listener, did you know that?"

"A professional requirement," Rutledge said lightly.

"I've never talked about it before. The truth is, I couldn't. I'd
survived, you see—even come to terms with losing my arm. I
was ready to go on living. And then this nightmare came out of
nowhere. And I was terribly afraid of dying from it. It shook my
nerve rather badly. I'm only beginning to understand that."

"We all have our nightmares," Rutledge said with more
feeling than he'd intended. "Even when they last into the
daylight."

"Yes, but most people don't wake up in a cold sweat, on the verge of screaming. I've done that a time or two—frightened the hell out of my wife, I can tell you." But his face said it had happened far more often than he cared to admit.

The woman serving tables came to take their order. Fraser leaned back, sipping his wine. Some of the lines in his face smoothed out as he relaxed.

"Find what you were looking for at Robbie's house?" he asked with frank curiosity.

"I may have. It appears—there's no proof, mind you!— that Eleanor Gray came here in 1916, shortly after she heard the news of Captain Burns's death. And she stayed at the house for two nights."

Fraser stared at him. "Old Raeburn—I'm sorry, she's the neighbor, Mrs. Raeburn—never told me that!"

"She didn't know. Eleanor came to Scotland with someone who'd been told which door to knock on to find the key. Therefore a friend of Burns's. Or so we assume. He could have been a friend of Eleanor's, acting on her instructions. Mrs. Raeburn remembers him." Rutledge gave Fraser a brief description of the man, pieced together from what Mrs. Raeburn had told him and a description of the friend who'd come to the Atwood house with Robbie Burns. "Recognize him?"

"Lord, no." After a moment, he added, "Robbie must have met him in London while he was convalescing. Palestine, you say?" He shook his head. "Afraid I never had much to do with that lot. And the first time I was invalided home, I came here, I didn't stay in London. I wonder why Robbie stayed."

"He'd met Eleanor."

"Yes. That probably explains it." Their meal arrived. Rutledge saw that someone in the kitchen had already sliced Fraser's chicken for him, the pieces tidily rearranged so that a left-handed man could spear them with his fork. "He was in hospital for well over a month, you know, then spent another two getting his strength back. It might be possible to discover the names of other patients there at the same time. The house was somewhere in Sussex. Saxhall—Saxwold—some such name."

"Thanks. I'll see what I can learn there."

Fraser put down his fork and reached for his glass. "She must have cared for Robbie," he said. "To come all this way. Sad that they had no future." He quoted lines from one of O. A. Manning's poems. *"We walked away from all that was warm and dear and stood frightened in cold rain where the guns fired, and in the end, we died in pain, the black stinking mud our shroud, embraced at last not by living arms, but by the bones of those who before us died . . ."*

Rutledge recognized the words. But he said only, "Manning understood better than most."

"Yes." Fraser sighed. "Well, when you catch up with Eleanor Gray, if she isn't happily married to someone else by this time, tell her Robbie loved her too. I truly think he did."

"Do you know if Captain Burns kept a dog? A cat?"

"He didn't. He traveled more than most. But his fiancée was fond of King Charles spaniels." He smiled. "Julia would bring them whenever she came, nasty little monsters, always wanting to climb into one's lap. How Robbie put up with them, I don't know! Love is blind, I suppose."

"Did Captain Burns bury one of them in his garden?"

"Good God, how should I know?" Then he grinned. "Killed it, you mean? Robbie must have been sorely tempted a time or two."

RUTLEDGE DROVE EAST out of the Trossachs, through some of the heart of Scottish history.

Many of the soldiers in France had seldom been farther from home than twenty miles in their short lives. Clan battles made for lively conversation among the Highlanders who had long memories for the feuds, ambushes, and massacres that had colored each family tree until the Battle of

Culloden and the Highland Clearances had changed Scotland forever.

The Lowlanders had had a different perspective. Stirling, a great castle on a crag overlooking the Forth, had been a royal residence until James VI had taken himself off to London. Now it was a quiet county town lost in the backwaters of the past. Bannockburn, where the Scots had won their famous victory over the English, was a monument to Robert the Bruce's determination to be free of the southern kingdom that had dominated his country for a lifetime. There were Scots who had only the vaguest notion now where the battle had been fought. Mary Stuart had been born at Linlithgow Palace, on its knoll above the loch. A queen from birth, she'd grown up to become a thorn in the flesh of Elizabeth of England. John Knox had thundered against Mary from the pulpit, and she had finally been forced to abdicate, a pensioner of the English crown. A rough and glorious past, now no more than a footnote in time.

The Highlands had been emptied and the Lowlands had become the poor cousin forgotten by an England with its eyes on Empire, and left to poverty and ignorance. As someone had said, Scotland's greatest wealth, her sons, had bled away to the colonies. Half the Scots under Rutledge's command had had distant cousins in Australia, New Zealand, or Canada.

At Edinburgh, Rutledge turned west. And decided, after some thought and a good deal of comment by Hamish, to go directly to Jedburgh rather than to Duncarrick. To report to the fiscal rather than to Oliver.

He stopped for a quarter of an hour at Melrose, whose ruined abbey held only a shadow of its former beauty. Stretching his legs as he walked through the broken elegance of nave and chancel, Rutledge tried to picture it as the Cistercians had built it. It was an important enough house that the heart of Robert the Bruce had been buried there, brought home from Palestine and lost for a time in Spain.

Melrose had fallen victim to the Border wars that had

burned Duncarrick and Jedburgh and bled half the Marches.

But Hamish remembered only that Field Marshal Haig, commander-in-chief of the British forces during the war, had been born near here. He did not like Haig, and was restless until Rutledge drove on.

IN JEDBURGH, BURNS rose to meet Rutledge but did not offer his hand. "I understand from Oliver that we're ready to go to trial. I could wish that you had been more successful in finding what has become of the Gray woman. This brooch most certainly puts the accused in the glen near the bones that were found, but it would have been helpful to go into court with proof of her identity clearly set out."

"Perhaps before the trial begins that will also be answered to everyone's satisfaction," Rutledge answered pleasantly. "I came here to ask you about an officer who may have known your son. Let me describe him for you." Without waiting for a response, he gave Burns what little information he had.

Burns listened patiently, then said, "That could fit half the British army."

"Half the Army didn't serve in Palestine."

"Yes, yes, I take your point. And you're trying to locate the man who might have driven Miss Gray to Scotland. I'm still not convinced that he knew my son. He might have been a friend of *hers*, have you considered that?"

Rutledge omitted any account of his visit to Craigness. He had a feeling it would not sit well with the fiscal. Instead he replied, "Yes. Either way, I must start with the assumption that both men visited Atwood House in Miss Gray's company. Which makes it seem likely that your son did meet him. My hope now is that one of Captain Burns's other friends might remember him also."

"Most of my son's friends were from his own unit, or men he met on leave." Burns turned and looked out the window of his office. "A good many of them are dead."

"This man was interested in the structure of the Atwood House stables. Medieval stonework."

"In the building trade, then. But an officer, you said."

"Or a student of medieval history."

"A don." He began to list his son's friends, giving their names, their ranks, their pre-war occupations. Rutledge closed his notebook when Burns had finished.

Of the seventeen men Burns could name, nine were dead, three before 1916. Two others had died of wounds. None of them had served in Palestine, and none of them was a builder or a don. "Although as I think about it now, Tom Warren was interested in history. His father had been attached to the embassy in Turkey at one time, and the family had traveled widely in the Near East."

A slim thread, Hamish pointed out as Rutledge took his leave.

It would have to do.

Rutledge drove on to Duncarrick to find a message waiting from Gibson. He had had no success in locating the engraver.

FINDING MAJOR THOMAS S. Warren proved to be easier than Rutledge had expected. A call to the Foreign Office had brought him the name of the father, who had in fact been a diplomat and had come out of retirement during the war to serve as an authority on the Turks.

Thomas Warren was a solicitor in Durham. Nearly in Lady Maude's backyard, as Hamish put it.

Rutledge set out with a box of sandwiches and a flask of tea, courtesy of The Ballantyne, and arrived in Durham before the hotel clerk had come on duty at The Bishop's Arms. A bath and a shave did much for his appearance, but not for the fatigue that was catching up with him.

Durham had been built by fighting bishops, both castle and cathedral sitting on a well-defended bluff above the winding River Wear. On the other hand, one of the earliest names in English literature was buried here: the Venerable Bede. Before the war, Rutledge had had several friends in the town, but they were gone now. It seemed odd to drive through the familiar streets and not call on one of them.

The law firm was in the center of town, second in a row of buildings that were Victorian Gothic, with even a gargoyle or two leering down at passersby. The street was busy, and Rutledge left his motorcar at The Bishop's Arms, walking the few streets to his destination.

An elderly clerk admitted him and asked him to be seated until Mr. Warren was free. Rutledge took one of the high-backed chairs near the hearth and felt weariness wash over him. Hamish was much taken with the pair of grim-faced eighteenth-century portraits that flanked the clerk's desk.

"Hanging judges," he decided, "with no' a verra high opinion of human nature. I canna' see pity nor mercy in their eyes." When Rutledge looked up to study their faces, he was forced to agree.

Thomas Warren was a fair man with an ugly scar across his face, running from the crown of his head into the collar of his shirt. It had healed, but time had not yet smoothed it into a thin white line. It gave him a sinister appearance.

But he greeted Rutledge with courtesy, listened to what he had to say, and answered, "Yes, I knew Rob. He was a good man. But I've never been to Atwood House, I'm afraid. And I didn't serve in Palestine, I was in France. Where else would the Army put a man with some knowledge of Turkish?"

Rutledge laughed. "It was common practice, I'm afraid." Taking out his notebook, he read aloud the list of names that the fiscal had given him. Warren steepled his fingers in front of pursed lips, noting each.

When Rutledge had finished, Warren said, "That's fairly thorough. Offhand I can't think of anyone to add. The first five you named died in France and to my certain knowledge never set foot in the Near East. That puts them out of the running. Morgan has flame-red hair and wouldn't know a barrel vault from a Roman arch, much less anything about medieval stabling. He spent most of the war at sea and the only wound he suffered was a fractured thumb." He shook his head, still finding it hard to believe. "Talbot, Stanton, and Herbert are dark and aren't likely to be in the running. I didn't know Edwards well enough to tell you where he served. Baldridge and Fletcher were artillery, as I remember, and MacPhee was in naval intelligence. What's this about? Why is it so urgent to find these men? I can't see any of them running afoul of the Yard!"

"They haven't. But they may have information we need. We're searching for a woman who is missing and may be dead. Eleanor Gray—"

"Good God!" Warren said, thunderstruck. "I met her once or twice, you know. In London. She and Rob were on their way to some play or other, a benefit for war orphans. She was trying to persuade him to sit down and rest, when I walked up. We had a drink together at intermission. Lovely girl. I remember asking her if she was related to the Grays over by Menton, and she smiled and said she was but indirectly. The next time I saw her, she had lunch with me, and if I've ever met a girl in love, it was Eleanor. Rob deserved happiness. I was glad for them. And I'd not like to think anything has happened to her!"

"We don't know that it has. We've traced her movements from London to a place called Craigness, a small town on the Teith in the Trossachs."

"That's where Rob lived—"

"Yes. She arrived in a rainstorm with a man. They spent two days at the house and then left." Rutledge paused. "We know she was there because she wrote something in the margin of a book that belonged to Burns. It couldn't have been done earlier, she'd just learned he was dead. That narrows the time, you see. And it's possible that she herself was dead by the autumn of 1916. She hasn't been seen since."

Warren said, "Are you telling me you think she killed herself?" He shook his head. "Not Eleanor Gray!"

"She loved him. The last notation in the book was 'I wish I could die too.' "

"Yes, yes, people say that," Warren replied impatiently. "I've heard them say it. But that's a source of comfort, not a decision taken. 'I wish I could die and end this suffering—I wish I could die and not have to think about it any longer.' Then they straighten their backbones and get on with living. And you didn't know Eleanor Gray. She was incredibly vivid, the kind of woman other women never learn to understand. But men do—men always find that zest for life fascinating."

AS HE ROSE to leave, Rutledge gave Tom Warren his card. "If you should think of anything else that might help, please get in touch. You can reach me in Duncarrick, at The Ballantyne."

HE SLEPT FOR nearly ten hours, roused the hotel clerk at midnight in search of food, and then slept another six. The morning he woke up to was gray with clouds, but there was no rain in them.

Hamish, at his shoulder as Rutledge turned north, was arguing the question of Eleanor Gray's feelings for Robert Burns.

"It could ha' been infatuation."

"A handsome man in uniform, the excitement of war. A romance that wouldn't have lasted with the peace." Rutledge was reminded of Jean, who had adored his uniform, then was terrified by the reality of war. He couldn't imagine Eleanor Gray confusing war with romance and excitement. She had seen too many of the wounded—

"And infatuation is more likely to lead to suicide," Hamish persisted.

"Fiona's mother died of a broken heart."

"That was no' the same! She wasted."

"It doesn't matter. If Eleanor was carrying Robert Burns's child, she wouldn't have killed herself. If she wasn't pregnant—then who's to say?"

"It doesna' explain how she came to be in the glen."

"No. And that's a question we still must answer."

THINKING ABOUT ELEANOR Gray, Rutledge turned off the road north and made a detour to Menton.

He came up the sweep of the drive as the sun broke out of clouds and bathed the house in golden light, turning the windows to burnished copper, the stone to warm peach. It was remarkably beautiful. He pulled up to the steps and then walked a little way from them to look up at the house. This was what made David Trevor love the sticks and stones of building. The angles and shapes, the use of light and shadow, the grace and elegance of line.

We have come a long way from stone hovels and mud huts, he thought. In skill and in knowledge. But we still kill. . . .

He went up the steps and rang the bell.

The butler came to answer it and with perfect poise informed him that Lady Maude was not at home today.

Rutledge would have wagered a year's pay that it was a lie.

But he accepted dismissal without demur.

Lady Maude did not wish to see him.

Was she afraid that he had brought her news she couldn't accept? He had a feeling that the quarrel with Eleanor had wounded the mother as well as the daughter who walked away. Love could be terribly hurtful.

HE PULLED INTO Duncarrick in the early hours of evening and parked the motorcar in its usual place. After lifting his luggage out of the boot, Rutledge walked toward the front of the hotel, his mind still on Eleanor Gray.

He ran into Ann Tait as he turned the corner and begged her pardon.

Recognizing the Inspector, she said, "Where have you been, then?"

Setting down his cases, he answered, "I've been in Durham. Where are you going?"

She lifted the hatbox in her hand, its flamboyant ribbon catching the light from the windows. "A delivery. There's to be a christening tomorrow."

He said, "You weren't here in Duncarrick, were you, when those women were murdered out on the western road? In 1912, I think it was?"

"Good heavens, Inspector! *What* women?" She looked alarmed.

"It doesn't matter. I'd been thinking that Duncarrick was a quiet backwater, and someone corrected me, saying that there had been several murders here before the war."

"That's a fine thing to tell me, walking down these streets in the dark!" She was angry with him, her face flushed.

"It was an old crime, and you have nothing to fear. If you like, I'll just set these in the hotel lobby and walk with you."

She wasn't mollified. "And ruin my reputation for good? They'll be whispering behind their hands tomorrow. And I can't afford it!"

He said contritely, "I'm sorry. I thought the murders were common knowledge. I'll walk down the other side of the street and keep an eye on you."

Ann Tait shook her head. "No. I can look after myself." She turned to go and then swung around. "If you mention a word of this to Dorothea MacIntyre and frighten her to death, I'll see that you pay dearly for it!"

"I spoke to you," he said, "because I thought you might give *me* information. It appears that we're both in the dark. But Dorothea MacIntyre won't hear such things from me, I promise you."

She walked away. He watched her for a time, the swing of her shoulders and the straight back. She had confessed to envy of Eleanor Gray. But he thought that the two women were in many ways very much alike. Independent. Willing to make a life for themselves with their own two hands. Hiding behind a brusque shell because it saved them from pain.

White lace gowns with satin sashes and broad-brimmed hats had passed with 1914, along with lawn tennis and picnics on the Thames and a much simpler world. There were thousands of Ann Taits making a living for themselves now, and hundreds of Eleanor Grays looking for a different future. Five years, and a colder, bleaker world of war had reshaped a generation of women as well as men.

As RUTLEDGE STOPPED at the desk to pick up his key, the clerk handed it to him and then reached into a drawer to find a folded sheet with his name on it.

In his room he unfolded it and read the brief lines written on it.

Sergeant Gibson requests that you call him at your earliest convenience.

Rutledge took out his watch and looked at the time. Far too late to find Gibson at the Yard.

He began to unpack, with Hamish rumbling at his back.

It WAS NEARLY ten o'clock the next morning before Rutledge could reach Gibson.

The sergeant said, "It wasn't a piece of cake. But I found the engraver."

"That's very good news," Rutledge applauded. "I'm grateful."

"You won't be," Gibson retorted, "when you hear what I have to say."

The brooch had been engraved in a back street in Glasgow nearly three weeks before it had been "found" in Glencoe. It was a small shop that specialized in buying and selling jewelry. The owner was frequently asked to remove or change the engraving on items left for resale. But he seldom had the opportunity to use his skills on a piece that had no previous markings on it. He had objected when the man who brought in the cairngorm brooch insisted that the work appear older than it was. But the price agreed on helped overcome any qualms he might have had.

"Could the shopkeeper give you a description of the man who brought in the brooch?"

"Better than that. It had to be left and picked up in three days' time. A name had to be put down on the card."

Rutledge felt his spirits soar.

"Tell me. What was it?"

"Alistair McKinstry."

24

———◆———

STUNNED, RUTLEDGE ASKED GIBSON TO REPEAT THE
name. He did.

"I asked for a physical description as well." But the engraver had relied on the name. "He finally told me that the
man was Scots—medium height, medium coloring, medium
build. He might remember more if you confronted him with
McKinstry. Then again, he might not. He wasn't interested in
the man, only the work that he was being paid to do."

Rutledge thanked him and slowly put down the telephone receiver.

He refused to believe it. In the first place, it made no
sense. McKinstry had been Fiona MacDonald's champion
from the very beginning—

Hamish said, "He had access to a key to The Reivers."

Fiona MacDonald had said that McKinstry had probably
seen her wearing her mother's brooch. He must have known
that it existed. And it would take him only a short time to
search Fiona's room for her jewelry.

The brooch had become the final brick in a wall of evidence against her.

But why—?

It made no sense. Rutledge, a seasoned investigator, found it hard to accept. Hard to believe that he had misjudged a man so completely.

He took out his watch. And made a swift decision. His first stop was the police station. But McKinstry wasn't there. Oliver was.

"Where have you been?" he asked jovially. "Still hunting for straws to make bricks?"

"In a way. Look, I'm going back to Glencoe. I want to see the place where the bones were found." It was not something he wanted to do.

"You climbed up there with MacDougal. There couldn't have been much to see. The bones are gone. The place has already been minutely examined by MacDougal's men. A wasted trip, if you ask me."

"I know. Put it down to stubbornness. At any rate, will you give Inspector MacDougal a call and ask him to meet me there? I'd be grateful if he can spare the time."

"All right. If that's what you want." Oliver added, "I'm surprised to see you in Duncarrick again. Any news to give me on Eleanor Gray?"

"Not so far. I've got a list of names to sift through. That can wait until I see the glen again. I'd like to save myself all that trouble."

Intrigued, Oliver said, "You're saying we overlooked something."

"No. I'm saying I might see things differently." He took out his watch, trying to cut the conversation short. "I've got another stop to make before I leave."

Oliver let him go. Rutledge walked back toward the hotel and then went on to the rectory. Mr. Elliot, Dorothea MacIntyre informed him, was out, visiting a parishioner who was ill.

"It's just as well. Do you mind if I step in and leave a message?"

She moved back from the door, blushing, as if she had failed in her duty because she hadn't thought to ask him for a message. He smiled at her. "It won't take long."

He walked past her, and she turned to a small table under the window, producing a sheaf of paper from the single drawer. It was church stationery. Rummaging, she came up with a pen as well, smiling in triumph as she handed it to him. She was almost childlike in her pleasure.

Rutledge scribbled on a sheet, *I came to call this morning but must leave town for a day. If you have time when I return, I'd like to ask you a few questions.* He signed his last name.

Folding the sheet, he handed it to her. Then he said, "Do you know Alistair McKinstry very well?"

"Know him?" She looked frightened.

"Does he attend services at the kirk? Is he a kind man?"

Relieved that Rutledge wanted only general information and had in no way suggested that she might be a particular friend of the constable's, she answered shyly, "Yes, indeed, he attends regularly. And I think he's kind. He's always kind to me."

"Yes, I'm sure he is." He walked to the door. It was time for the question that had really brought him to the rectory. "When you were cared for in your illness by Miss MacCallum and her niece, do you remember a rather pretty cairngorm brooch that Fiona was fond of wearing?"

She frowned, thinking. "I don't recall Fiona wearing a brooch. She never even wore her wedding ring. It hung on a chain around her neck, where she couldn't lose it. I saw it sometimes when she bent down to settle the pillows or bathe my face."

"But not the brooch."

Trying hard to please him, she said earnestly, "But Miss MacCallum had a lovely brooch! There was a pearl in the center. She let me wear it—for courage—when I came to the rectory to be interviewed by Mr. Elliot."

"Did it help?" he asked, unwilling to cut short her brief burst of enthusiasm. She was pretty when her face was lit from within. Fragile and pretty.

But it was the wrong question. Her face fell. "Mr. Elliot recognized it and made me take it off. He said it was unbecoming to ape one's betters."

Hamish swore. Rutledge felt a strong urge to throttle Elliot. It was, he thought, an intentional cruelty. "Did you tell Miss MacCallum what he'd said?"

"Oh, no!" she said, horrified. "I couldn't! I was too embarrassed. I said only that he was very kind."

As she had just told him that Constable McKinstry was very kind.

DRIVING OUT OF Duncarrick, Rutledge was trying to decide how much weight to give to what Dorothea MacIntyre had told him about the brooch. On the whole, he thought, she was honest and without guile. Confronted, as when he'd asked her about McKinstry and Ealasaid MacCallum had asked about her interview with Elliot, she told lies out of a deep-seated fear of provoking anger. The girl wanted so desperately to please. It was her first—and only—need.

Hamish, taking up another matter, said, "I never gave Fiona a ring. I couldna' tie her to me, going off to war. The bracelet was a gift to remember me by, but didna' bind her."

Rutledge had not married Jean in 1914 for the same reason, using the war as an excuse to put off their October wedding. And in the end it had been the right decision. He felt cold now, thinking about living with a woman who hated him—or hated what he had in her eyes become: a broken stranger.

He wondered if Eleanor Gray might have regretted not marrying Robbie Burns when he was home on leave. . . .

There was a woman sitting along the road just by the pele tower. Something about the droop of her shoulders told him she wasn't well.

He searched for a name and came up with it. Mrs. Holden. Her husband was the sheep farmer. . . . Rutledge braked and came to a stop just beside her. "Are you in trouble?" he asked. "Can I take you somewhere?"

She smiled ruefully. "The doctor tells me to walk if I intend to regain my strength. But I don't have the strength to walk. . . ."

"Then let me take you home—or to the doctor, if you'd prefer that."

He got out of the car and helped her up from the low stone she'd found to sit on. Under his hands her shoulders felt frail.

Lifting her into the car, he settled her in the passenger seat. She was white from even that simple exertion.

"I'm so sorry to be such a nuisance!" she said breathlessly. "It's silly of me to overdo my strength and put strangers to such trouble."

Shutting her door, he examined her face. And didn't like what he saw there. "Let me take you into Duncarrick. I think you ought to see your doctor."

After a moment, her eyes closed, she nodded. "Yes. I need to lie down. He'll be glad to let me lie down for a while."

Rutledge backed the car around and said, "Would you like me to find your husband and bring him to you?"

"No, I thank you. He's in Jedburgh today. Dr. Murchison or one of my friends will see that I get home. Talk to me if you will. And just let me listen. It takes my mind off the weakness."

How does a policeman make pleasant conversation with a near-fainting woman? He said, "I've admired the pele tower. The way it was constructed. I understand it's on your property. I'd be interested in hearing its story. What role it played in the days of the Border raids."

She smiled a little. "My father is the person you should have spoken to."

"Did he write a history of Duncarrick?" It was often the retired gentleman or rector who collected the legends and tales passed down by word of mouth for generations and turned them into a chronicle of sorts.

"He never got around to it, I'm afraid."

A few sentences more and he'd exhausted the subject of the tower. Rutledge cast about for a new topic. "The name of the inn we're just passing. The Reivers. I wonder who chose that. Did the MacCallums have riders in their ancestry?" Riders—reivers—raiders, he thought. Euphemisms for the same bloody trade of Border warfare.

Drummond was just coming out of the inn with Ian MacLeod, returning from feeding the cat. The child looked up, eyes shining, and pointed with excitement to the car. Rutledge waved but didn't stop.

Drummond was glaring after him with murder in his face.

The woman, staring ahead with unseeing eyes, bit her lip. She was in no shape to answer his trivial questions.

"Hold on," Rutledge said gently, touching her hands where they lay trembling in her lap. "We're nearly there."

But he had to carry her into Dr. Murchison's office, her head against his shoulder and her body so light, it was like a feather in his arms.

The nurse came to meet him, having seen them arrive. To Mrs. Holden, trying to smile as she apologized for all the trouble she'd caused, she was all warmth and sympathy.

"My dear!" she said, half scolding, half crooning, as though to a child. "Have we overdone our strength again? Come lie down for a bit and then the doctor will take you home again."

She led Rutledge down a passage, not into the sitting room he could just glimpse through a door that stood slightly ajar. Opening another door, she gestured to an elderly sofa that stood under the back windows. While the nurse fetched a pillow, Rutledge settled Mrs. Holden gently among its cushions, then took the light blanket that had been folded across the high back and spread it over her feet and limbs. As the nurse lifted her head and slipped the pillow beneath it, Mrs. Holden smiled. A wavering smile, and rueful as well.

"I'm so sorry—" she began again.

Rutledge took one of her hands and held it in both of his. "Nonsense. Feel better."

He turned and walked out of the room. The nurse, after a word to Mrs. Holden, followed. She thanked the Inspector for being a Good Samaritan and opened the outer door for him.

"Not at all," Rutledge said. "She seems very weak. Is it serious?"

"The doctor feels it isn't. She caught a chill this spring when she undertook the charity bazaar and was left with a cough. She'd had influenza last year, a very serious case, and was slow recovering from that. Dr. Murchison is trying to rebuild her strength. And sometimes she feels well enough to come into town. The influenza took the heart right out of people. A shame, really."

"Yes. A shame." He remembered Hugh Fraser's words. *It was like a medieval plague.* . . .

Turning the motorcar around again, Rutledge drove away from the town once more and headed in the direction of Glencoe.

He made another brief stop in Brae to speak to Mrs. Davison. She asked him for news of Fiona, but as he had nothing cheerful to tell her, he said only, "I assure you, we're doing everything we can."

"Then if it isn't good news, what does bring you back again?"

They were in the parlor, and the boys, happy to see him, were clinging to the arms of his chair while the little girl climbed confidingly into his lap. Mrs. Davison reached out for her, but he said, "No, let her stay. I don't mind."

The child curled herself against his chest and began to play with the fob on his watch chain.

"I need to ask you about some jewelry that Fiona MacDonald owned. A brooch with a large cairngorm in the center—"

She nodded before he could finish his description. "Yes, I

remember it. A lovely piece. She said it was a wedding gift from her father to her mother. She didn't wear it often. She was afraid, playing with the children, that it might be pulled off or lost. She also had a bracelet from her fiancé, which she allowed my daughter to try on when she'd been especially good." She smiled indulgently. "You can see that young as she is, she has a taste for gold."

He looked down at the fair curls catching on his vest buttons. "It's natural," he agreed. "Had her fiancé also given Fiona a ring?"

"She never said anything about it if he had."

Detaching curls from buttons and fingers from the fob, he set the child on her feet and rose. "You've been a great help," he told Mrs. Davison. "Thank you once more."

She must have read something in his voice. She rose but didn't cross the room to the door. Instead she asked, "Is it important, this brooch?"

"It might be," he confessed. "I'm on my way to find that out."

"Then I hope it will be good news!"

On the step he paused and said, "Do you think that Maude Cook was expecting a child when she left Brae?"

"Maude Cook?" Mrs. Davison shook her head. "No, I'm sure she wasn't. There would have been signs."

"Not if she left in her fifth month."

"Well, that's true, I suppose. But when she left Brae, it was to travel to London to be with her husband. He had been invalided home—what would he have said to find her pregnant by another man!"

She stopped. "I had wondered if she had a lover. . . . No, I can't believe it of her. She wouldn't have been able to conceal her condition from Mrs. Kerr. And Mrs. Kerr would have told half of Brae. No. Possible, but not likely," she ended firmly. "Give Fiona my love, will you? And tell her we are praying for her."

"She will be grateful," Rutledge said, and went down the walk to his car.

Hamish scolded, "You've broken your promise again!"

"No. I asked if Mrs. Cook could have had a child. I've put no one in danger!"

"It isna' right to gie a promise and take it back when it suits!"

"It isn't right for Fiona MacDonald to hang," Rutledge retorted grimly.

"Aye, but she doesna' deserve to put her faith in lies."

RUTLEDGE REACHED GLENCOE before Inspector MacDougal got there, and spent the time climbing back to the rocks on the heights.

How had a woman dragged the dead weight of a body up this slope?

How would *he* have done it?

People found extraordinary strength in times of grave danger. It would have taken enormous effort. And time. At night then, when darkness gave the killer a good nine hours in which to accomplish the task.

And if he'd laid the body on a blanket and pulled—

What if the frayed edges of an old blanket had been cut off and hidden under the bench in the Craigness garden? To make a sturdier corner—

Overhead Rutledge heard an eagle scream and, shading his eyes, looked up. He could just see it, circling for altitude, riding the warming air. In the far distance a car was moving in his direction. Rutledge turned and began to walk back down the mountainside.

The sound of pipes came from somewhere, a lonely shepherd passing the time. Too far for Rutledge to pick out the tune. A pibroch, he thought. Very fitting here, where the mountains gave it body and redoubled the drones. He paused to listen.

Something cracked—a shot—echoing and re-echoing against the rock faces on either side of the road.

Instinctively, Rutledge ducked, long years of war making

it a swift reflex action. The stones just behind him spurted, then slid in a trickling spill toward his feet. He swore.

There was no cover here—absolutely none—he was a clear target, easy to pick off—

Where was the man with the rifle!

Crouching, he scanned the opposite slopes and saw no one.

It hadn't been his imagination! He knew the sound of a rifle; it was clear and definitive—

Then, at the top of the ridge across from him, he caught a slight shift of light and shadow and again threw himself to one side.

But this time there was no shot. MacDougal's car was just below, the motor's noise rising to where Rutledge was crouching. Close enough now to hear a rifle—

Rutledge shaded his eyes, looking intently for movement.

But the sniper had vanished, ducking over the opposite ridge, invisible now.

It would be impossible to catch up with him—

Furiously angry, Rutledge wheeled to look for the spent bullet. He combed the area where he was certain he had seen the small slide of rock chips. It must have struck a stone and ricocheted.

He searched carefully—but he never found it.

INSPECTOR MACDOUGAL, GETTING out of his car as Rutledge reached the road again, said, "You're a great man for the climbing!"

"Good exercise," he answered, thinking of Mrs. Holden.

"Better you than me! What is it you're looking for up there, that you need me to act as guide?"

"I've seen all I need to see on the mountain. Now I'd like to find that young girl, Betty Lawlor."

"The one who discovered the brooch. Any particular reason you'd like to speak to her?" MacDougal looked at him speculatively.

Never infringe on another man's turf. It was a cardinal rule Rutledge followed. "Yes. I'd like to hear how she came to have the price of a new pair of shoes."

"As I remember, she said she'd earned them."

"Yes, no doubt she had. I should have asked her how."

"What does that have to do with finding the brooch?"

"It might have been the price of convincing her to turn it in. I find it hard to believe, thinking back on it, that a child as poor as that would come to you to ask if she could keep the brooch."

"I wondered about it, of course. But the family is honest enough. The father's a drunken sod, but the mother is proud as peacocks. And she's taught her children to be honest as far as I can tell. Besides, how in hell's name would anyone know that Betty Lawlor had found a brooch out here in the middle of nowhere? It's far-fetched, Rutledge!" But he shrugged and pointed down the road. "The croft is just before the end of the glen. Shall we take both cars or leave one here?"

Rutledge had no wish to find water in his petrol again. Or a bullet through a tire. "We might as well take both."

"Safe enough here," MacDougal said. "But it's your choice."

He pulled out ahead of Rutledge to lead the way.

Hamish warned, "Watch your back!"

Rutledge said, "No. He won't risk firing again. Not with MacDougal ahead of us. How did anyone know I was here? I told Oliver—"

Anyone could have overheard Oliver's call to MacDougal. Anyone could have asked Oliver, "I saw Rutledge leaving town, where has he gone?"

"And who did Oliver tell?" Hamish said.

"Or I could have been followed to Brae and then here."

"But if he knew and came ahead while you were in Brae, he would have the time to climb."

"I know." Rutledge let it go. There was nothing he could do now.

Sheep were being driven down the road, filling it with white, curly humps that bobbed ahead and then behind, crowding against the two motorcars. He could hear MacDougal shouting to the man to move them on, and the high whistles to the dogs. Moving to lower pastures before the autumn storms came.

Pulling out of them, MacDougal drove on, then turned off the road where an ancient stone croft squatted in the shelter of the hill.

It has only two rooms, Rutledge thought, *and no water that I can see.* Betty Lawlor was poor indeed.

Hamish said, "There'll be a rill close by. Enough for their needs."

A ragged child of about seven popped his head out the door and then went back inside, calling to someone, before coming to stand on the threshold. His eyes were wide as he took in the two motorcars parked in front of him.

MacDougal had gotten out and was crossing the hard-packed dirt of the yard when a man came to meet him. He was of middle height but heavy across the shoulders, and the filthy undershirt he wore was torn across the back. His trousers were held up with string, not braces. The bleary eyes and fleshy nose told the rest of the story.

"Good afternoon, Mr. Lawlor. I've come to have a word with Betty, if you please."

"I thought you might be bringing her back."

"Where's she got to, then? Out with the sheep?"

"She's gone."

"Gone?" MacDougal looked over his shoulder at Rutledge. "Gone where? Look, I want to talk to her. Tell me where she is, and I'll be on my way."

The ravaged face turned puce with anger. "Gone, I telt ye, and gone she is! That's plain as plain! No skin off my backside if she's alive or dead."

A worn woman in a faded dress came to stand at the door behind him. MacDougal took his hat off to her, but she said nothing.

Rutledge said, "What did you do to her, Mr. Lawlor? That made her run away?" He had a feeling that he already knew.

He thought the man was on the verge of apoplexy, he was so angry.

The woman said, "She wouldna' tell him where she got the money for the shoes. He thought he had a right to know. He thought she might have more of it. So he beat her until she couldn't cry. And that night she left."

"I've got every right to that money! I feed and clothe these brats. I keep a roof over their heads. What they have is mine."

"Beat your children again, Lawlor, and I'll haul you in for drunk and disorderly, and keep you in prison until you rot, do you hear me!" MacDougal's voice was cold. "Do you hear me, man!"

"It willna' do any good," his wife said in a tired voice. "When he's like this, he doesna' remember a word."

Lawlor swung a fist in her direction, but she moved away with the ease of long practice.

Rutledge thought of that same fist beating the thin child he'd seen on the mountainside. Whatever Betty had done, she was better off out of here.

"I want her back!" Lawlor was saying now, his voice plaintive. "There's nobody to tend the sheep."

"You should have thought of that before you beat her," MacDougal answered roughly. "Mrs. Lawlor, did your daughter tell you where she earned the money for her shoes?"

She shook her head. "But she's out wi' the sheep noon and night. Who's to say?"

"Whore, that's what she was. Slut. Selling herself, I'll be bound."

"No, she hadn't sold herself, Lawlor. She provided the police with some information they badly needed." Rutledge added, "Mrs. Lawlor, do you know if your daughter has had a piece of jewelry in her possession for some months now? It was a brooch with a cairngorm center."

She laughed. "And how'd she keep something like that where *he* didna' find it? In her *boudoir*? I never saw her with anything more than the bit of dyed yarn she'd twisted into a bracelet for her sister and herself. If you think my Betty had anything like a cairngorm brooch, you're mad."

MacDougal and Rutledge exchanged glances. Rutledge said to her, "My mistake. I must have misunderstood."

MacDougal walked with Rutledge back to his car. The small boy had come outside now and was fingering the bonnet, then running his hand over the smooth leather of the seat. MacDougal was saying, "She had the brooch. Whether her mother saw it or not. It doesn't make a difference to your case."

"The brooch was seen in Glasgow several weeks ago. In the shop of an engraver. Can you believe that Betty Lawlor was the one who took it there?"

"Great God, no one told *me* that! When did Oliver find out?"

"He doesn't know. I'd rather tell him myself. I just learned the news from my sergeant in London." He smiled at the boy and lifted him into the driver's seat, where the child instantly made motor noises and gripped the wheel like a racer. "But it means that most of Betty's story is a lie. She didn't have that brooch for a year or more—nor did she find it on the hillside. My belief is that the person who gave it to her and taught her a story meant to be told to the police also gave her the money to buy shoes. And there was enough extra to help her escape her father and this place. She would have bargained hard. She carried out her part very well indeed. It will be Oliver's headache to track her down to testify at the trial. I've no doubt he'd do it."

"I don't believe it. You're pulling at straws!"

The horn blew. Rutledge and MacDougal winced.

MacDougal went on. "It's no more than speculation. You can't be sure it's the same brooch! No, until there's proof to the contrary, I put my faith in young Betty."

"I think there's enough proof already to put some doubt into a jury's mind." Rutledge waited, then said, "Will you search for her?"

MacDougal gestured to the croft and the parents still standing in the doorway. "And bring her back to this?" He took a deep breath. "I suppose I shall have to. But it won't be easy. Still, there aren't many ways she could have gone from here. Even with her new walking shoes. Inveraray, most likely, where she could beg a lift in a wagon." He turned away, settling his hat back on his head. "I'll let Oliver know when she turns up."

"Thanks." Rutledge said to the boy, "Will you sit there while I turn the crank?"

The child nodded vigorously. Rutledge started the engine and then let him stay for a moment longer to feel the power of the car under him. MacDougal had already turned around in the yard and was heading back the way they'd come. Rutledge lifted the child down.

With a glowing face he said, "I'll have mysel' one of them!"

"I'm sure you will," Rutledge answered.

And then, as if in payment for the special treat, the boy leaned toward him, standing on tiptoe. "There *was* a man with Betty—I saw him. Even though she claimed it was only the sun playing tricks."

"What did he look like?" Rutledge asked quickly, suddenly intent.

The boy backed away, already regretting his confidence. "Fair," he mumbled, and then ran back to the croft door, slipping between his mother's skirts and his father's legs. Disappearing into the house.

Rutledge nodded to the Lawlors, then turned the car around. He had lost his escort back through the glen. But it had been worth it.

25

WARY OF BEING FOLLOWED, RUTLEDGE DIDN'T STAY THE
night in Lanark as he'd intended. The last thing he wanted
to do was lead someone to the small clinic and Dr. Wilson.
Instead he drove some distance beyond the town, then decided to continue to Duncarrick through the night. With
scones, pork pies, and tea he bought at a pub, and Hamish
to keep him awake, he let the smooth sound of the engine
form a backdrop to his thoughts. His headlamps picked out
road signs and the dark fronts of towns and farms as he
mentally went back through all his notes, looking at every
word with a fresh eye.

Well, reasonably fresh, he told himself as he finished the
last of the scones. He stopped several times to stretch his legs
or clear his head, the night air cool on his face and the
moonlight turning the landscape into stark shapes of deep
shadows and brighter patches. It was a far cry from France,
he thought, where the long line of the battlefield had no natural definition, the trees blasted into black fingers of ruined

trunks and the gentle roll of the fields destroyed in the shelling, with man-made twists of wire and humps of shell-tortured earth the only landmarks. A bizarre black-and-gray world where only the scavengers lived.

Except for a lorry or two, a skittering of hares racing across his headlamps, and once a wagon filled with crates of chickens on their way to market, there was less and less traffic on the road as the hours passed.

Hamish said, "Any decent man is at home in his bed!"

But Rutledge was at peace with the night. It was, he thought, a sanctuary of sorts, where there was no one else to overhear the voice in his head or the long conversations that sometimes tricked him into answering aloud.

Nor did he fear that the sniper might try again. In the night even a marksman would find it impossible to shoot at a moving target, a tire or a radiator, to send Rutledge careering into a ditch. But it helped to keep him awake, thinking about that as well.

"It's a foolish man—or a desperate one—shooting at a policeman."

"It was a warning," Rutledge answered. "I've come too close to something. Or to someone. I've breached the outer defenses of a wall of silence."

Hamish said, "It wasna' a woman, to climb that far with a rifle."

"There's no way to be sure of that. But I rather think you're right. I would give much to know when the first cracks appeared in that wall." Rutledge smiled to himself. "I'd take great pleasure in widening them!"

WHEN HE REACHED Duncarrick, he bathed and shaved, went to bed, and slept two hours. Then he went in search of Constable McKinstry.

Rutledge ran him to earth making his rounds, coming back from the east end of town with a clutch of small boys in his wake. Their faces were long, downcast. Truants by the look of them.

McKinstry dropped them off at the school, where a stern school-master had been watching for him. The boys went in through the door with the air of the condemned, dragging their feet.

"Future criminals," McKinstry said, catching sight of Rutledge standing in a shop doorway. "But they're not bad, really, they just have no taste for learning. I probably didn't either at that age. And they're fatherless. It doesn't help."

"It's an excuse they'll hear until they believe it."

"Still, we make allowances." The constable grinned rue-fully. "The headmaster, now, *he* won't." As the grin faded, he added, "I thought you'd finished with us."

"Not finished, no." They turned to walk along together. "Do you remember, when you came to ask Morag if you could speak to me, what you told me about solving crimes in Duncarrick? You said you knew the people, and that that was often the key to finding who had stolen a horse and why—who had killed a lamb and why."

"Yes. It's true—"

"But in Fiona's case, you were at a loss. You couldn't draw on your knowledge of this town to find out who was persecuting her."

"That's right. I don't have the experience to put with the knowledge."

They crossed the square and dodged a milk dray lumbering past. Rutledge said, "I'm working at a disadvantage also. Eleanor Gray is pulling me in one direction, and Fiona MacDonald is pulling me in another. I can't find the link between them. In life, I mean. How they met, why they met, when and where they met." He took a deep breath. "If Fiona didn't murder Eleanor Gray, then whose bones do we have on a mountainside in Glencoe? And if those bones belong to Eleanor Gray, then how did she come to die there in a wilderness four or five months after she arrived in Scotland?"

"The brooch—"

"Yes." Rutledge stopped outside the hotel. "The brooch. It's damning. But it doesn't put a name to the bones, does it? Only to the killer."

McKinstry rubbed his eyes. "I lay awake at night and try to find an answer. Inspector Oliver says she admitted that the thing belonged to her mother. He came to me later and asked if I'd seen Fiona wearing it after she moved here to Duncarrick. *And I can't remember!*"

"Why not?" It was curt, accusing.

"Because I want so badly to remember that I can't be sure it's true. She wore a green dress, I remember that very well. But I can't be sure if she had a scarf at her throat, or that damned brooch! And sometimes she wore her aunt's pin. It wasn't something a man would think was important, and I'm not much with women's clothing anyway. The green dress was wonderful with her eyes. The rose one brought out the darkness of her hair. And in the summer there was a very soft cream-color affair with a wide collar and sprigs of some flower in a print. Lavender, like lilacs or heliotrope. I can't tell you how they were cut or what she wore with them. Or whether she had on that one brooch—" There was anguish in his face.

"Then what did you tell Oliver?"

"I told him the truth—I couldn't remember!"

"You might have lied, for her sake."

"Yes," McKinstry said with heavy sorrow. "I thought of that too. But I'm trained to duty." He started to walk away, then turned around again. "Would *you* lie to save her?" Whatever he saw in Rutledge's face, he continued, "If I have to, I'll change my testimony in the courtroom. I'd hoped—I thought you might have looked into it. But you went away and did nothing. Damning as it was, you did nothing!"

"Oliver made it plain it was none of my business." Rutledge smiled wryly. "And I've been occupied with Eleanor Gray. I told you."

"Yes, well, if the Gray woman is dead, she's well out of it. If she's alive, I wish to God she'd show her face before it's too late."

This time he turned away and kept walking.

Rutledge looked after him. Hamish taunted, "You didna' confront him with what you've learned about yon brooch!"

Passing through the lobby, Rutledge responded silently, "No. It was more useful to see if he'd bring up the brooch—and in what context. Persuasive, was he, do you think?"

"He left it sitting at your door. I wouldna' call that a verra' brave defense of the accused!"

"Well, then, if he didn't put the brooch in the hands of Betty Lawlor, he must have come close to losing his own belief in Fiona's innocence when he heard the story Betty had to tell! He didn't have much to say on the drive back from the glen, and he didn't have much to say just now."

"If he's behind yon business of the brooch, then it was clever of him to make the Yard an ally—as you pointed out the holes in the charges, he set about filling them in!"

Climbing the stairs, Rutledge answered: "Then he shouldn't have given his own name to that Glasgow jeweler! Was it McKinstry who drove Eleanor Gray north?"

"He was in France in 1916."

Rutledge stopped at the head of the stairs. "No. He told Morag that he had met me there. Until now I've had no reason to doubt what he'd said. It will have to be checked."

"He had a verra' good reason to fire at you in the glen. To prevent you from talking to Betty Lawlor."

"That's possible, yes." He opened the door to his room and threw his hat on the chair beside the bed. Crossing to the window, he looked out at the clouds moving in from the west. "I don't know. I'm a better judge of character, I think, than to be taken in by McKinstry—" He shook his head. "I haven't finished it. It may never be finished."

"Your meddling is no' making someone happy."

Rutledge turned from the window and took a deep breath. "If it isn't Fiona who matters, and it isn't the inn, where's the pawn in all of this?"

"The boy."

"Yes," Rutledge said slowly. "The legacy of the dead. Why is that so very important?"

But Hamish had no answer to give him.

RUTLEDGE ATE A hurried lunch and then went to the police station, requesting to see Fiona MacDonald.

Pringle, on duty, protested, "I don't know that I can give you the key, sir! Inspector Oliver says you've finished with this part of the investigation."

"I thought I was," Rutledge said easily. "I have here a list of names, men who might have known Eleanor Gray. We haven't asked Miss MacDonald if any of them mean anything to her. If Oliver complains, send him to me."

Pringle reached behind the desk for the key and handed it over.

Rutledge found Fiona standing, as if she'd been restlessly pacing her cell. Little enough exercise for a woman accustomed to having her days filled with activity at The Reivers. Prisoners often complained about that—the sheer, wasting boredom of waiting for trial.

He shut the door behind him and began by saying, "I saw the child the other day. He had been feeding the cat with Drummond."

"Did he look well? Happy?" she asked anxiously. "I wonder often if he's sleeping properly. Or if he has nightmares—"

"He seemed happy enough." He took out his list of names and slowly read them to her, watching her face. But Fiona shook her head.

"I can't identify any of them. I'm sorry."

Closing his notebook, he said, "Fiona. If you didn't kill the mother of that child—if you're being persecuted for no reason that either of us can put a finger on—then I'm forced to ask myself what there is about that child that threatens someone's peace enough to get at him through harming you."

"How could such a small boy threaten anyone!" she parried, surprised.

"I don't know. But the deeper I go into this mystery of yours, the more certain I am that he's the key."

"He's only a little boy who thought he belonged to me. He doesn't know or care who his real mother was—who his father might have been. And there's no fortune unless he's allowed to inherit The Reivers when I'm—dead."

"But someone does care. For a time I considered the possibility that it had to do with the Gray fortune. Or protecting a family's reputation. Now I'm less convinced. In my judgment, the child's important because no one is sure exactly who he is, and either someone wants that proof—or wants to bury it with you. I'm beginning to think that the hope was, if the police investigated thoroughly enough, they'd find the answer to the question of his mother's identity. And save someone else the trouble of doing so. Or else the court will hang you and save that someone else the trouble of getting rid of you before you speak out."

Something in her eyes told him that he was close to the truth—but not really there. That he still hadn't put his finger on the crux of Fiona's secret.

As if talking to himself, he murmured, "A child who came to light at the wrong time could cheat someone out of an inheritance. Or embarrass a family on the point of contracting an important marriage. Or bring to light a liaison that has been hidden until now." He added after a moment, "Or it might be that someone wants him rather badly but doesn't want to step forward and admit that the boy is hers—or his. If Ian is in an orphanage, he can be adopted properly, without revealing any connection with you or him."

Fiona said carefully, "If I told you the name of Ian's father, you'd find nothing in the knowledge to explain what's happening. He was an ordinary man. A very kind and a very good man. But a very ordinary man."

"If he's dead, then we're left with the mother."

"Why should his mother—who most certainly knew who that child is—fear him in any way?"

"Then why is she protecting him? At the cost of your life?"

"She's dead. She can't protect anyone, not even herself."

Rutledge said, "Let's examine another possibility. That the child is precisely what you say he is—an ordinary child with an ordinary father, threatening no one. That his mother is dead. What if—mind you, this is pure speculation, but hear me out—what if someone *thinks* the boy matters? And removing you from his guardianship is necessary to prevent him from ever being identified. What if someone has been searching for some time for a missing child about Ian's age? And that someone believes, without a shadow of doubt, that he's been found here in Duncarrick."

"You have a wonderful imagination," she said, smiling in spite of herself. "Or have you convinced yourself that the mother of Eleanor Gray is trying to prevent Ian from ruining her family's reputation?"

"Imagination has often been the best and quickest way through a thicket of lies." He made a swift decision and shifted direction. "Whose wedding ring do you wear on a chain around your neck?"

Her face flamed. "Who told you such a thing?"

"Dorothea MacIntyre. She didn't mean to betray you. In the course of describing how well you'd cared for her when she was ill, she spoke of it. She believed it was truly yours."

"It was my grandmother's ring. If I was a married woman, I ought to have a ring. But it was loose, it didn't fit my finger. So I wore it around my neck, telling my aunt that I was afraid it might fall off and be lost. You'll find it at the inn. Unless someone has taken that as well! I put it away when I could no longer call myself Mrs. MacLeod." She looked away. The memory hurt her.

Earnestly, he said, "Won't you tell me which one of my guesses is closest to the truth? Because once I know, I can protect you, I can protect that child."

"But you can't give him back to me when it's over!" It was a cry of anguish. "You've already told me that no matter how this ends, I shall never have him back again."

He looked at her, trying to read her face. "Is that the bargain you're making with me? If I can guarantee that you shall have your child again, you will finally tell me the truth?"

She bit her lip, torn between duty and love and hope.

He had finally found the key to Fiona MacDonald's silence. Something she wanted more than life—even her own life. That child.

Then, to his utter astonishment, she replied, "Will you kill someone for me? Because if you can't, promises will be useless."

She read his answer in his face.

"No. I didn't think you could." There was infinite sorrow in her voice.

He waited, but she said nothing more. No explanation, no self-defense for even asking such a thing of him.

Into the silence he asked, "Do you trust Constable McKinstry?"

Surprised, she said, "Yes. I think I do. Why shouldn't I? He wanted to marry me."

Hamish said, "If he wed her, he'd have custody of the child. Is that what began this business, her refusal?"

"Why didn't you marry him?" Rutledge asked. "Ian would have had a proper father."

"I didn't want to marry. I didn't want to wake up in the morning and find his face on the pillow next to mine. Or anyone else's. I don't love him. I gave my heart away once. I never want to do it again. It hurts too much!"

He thought of Jean. Yes, it hurt far more than it should, to love.

Fiona smoothed her hands together. "Have you ever made a house of playing cards? I used to do it for the Davison children sometimes. It always falls in upon itself. That's my dilemma, Ian Rutledge. How to keep the cards from falling in on themselves. And try as I will, I don't see the way to prevent it. It will be better for my son to grow up hating me or not even remembering my name and face than for the cards to fall in."

"Someone tried to kill me yesterday." The admission was forced out of him. He hadn't intended to say anything. "Someone shot at me and it wasn't by accident. It was a clear line of fire and he missed by very little. A warning perhaps. And I can't fight back because I don't know how! How many lives will you put at risk for your son?"

She winced, then recovered with an effort. "You're a grown man. You can fight back, even against shadows. A small boy can't." Her eyes filled with tears. "I don't want you to die. Any more than I want to die. But it's a risk that I must take. *God help me!*"

RUTLEDGE WALKED BACK to the hotel, depression settling in like a black shroud. He went to the telephone closet and began the long, wearing task of tracing the house that had been a military hospital during the war. Saxhall or Saxwold.

There was no listing for a Saxhall, but there was for Saxwold.

In the next hour, he tried to locate any staff who had served there. Chiefly the matron or doctor in charge. He found one sister, who gave him the name of three more, and the last one pointed him to Elizabeth Andrews.

In another half hour he was speaking to her. She had been the nurse in charge of Saxwold's most seriously wounded men, and was now at a hospital in Cambridge.

Her voice came over the telephone clearly, forceful, with the slight accent of Yorkshire in it.

Rutledge explained what he was after. "I'm looking for anyone who might have been friends with a Captain Robert Burns who was at Saxwold in 1916. He was there for nearly a month, then was released to convalesce in London."

"Ah, yes, I do recall Captain Burns. A very nice man. I heard much later that he'd returned to the Front and been killed. A waste."

"Indeed. There was a woman, Eleanor Gray, who met him either in London or at Saxwold. Do you recall her?"

"I thought you wanted to know who among the wounded was friendly with him! I have no idea who Eleanor Gray is, Inspector. I had little time to waste on visitors. These were seriously wounded men in my care."

"The problem is that I don't know with any certainty whether Eleanor Gray introduced Captain Burns to the man I'm seeking or if she met him through Burns. If she met him through Burns, it might be someone he knew at Saxwold."

"I understand now. Well, since I have no knowledge of this woman, I suggest we begin with the patients. There were a number of critically wounded men at Saxwold at the time, and they seldom mixed with the other patients. Certainly not often enough for a friendship to be formed. Therefore you must be interested in the men who were more or less able to move about or have visitors. If I remember correctly, there were at least twenty of those. Of them I would say that Captain Burns was friendly with three or four."

She gave him names and told him how badly each was wounded. Three had lost limbs. Rutledge discounted them. Mrs. Raeburn had said she couldn't tell how the man at her door had been wounded. The fourth had been blinded.

Trying to begin from another end of the puzzle, Rutledge asked, "Did you have patients from Palestine in Saxwold?"

"There was indeed one man who had served in Palestine. He'd been an intelligence officer, wounded, and sent home. Captured by the Turks, apparently, for he had been severely tortured. We feared more for his mind than his body, I must tell you that. He didn't know who he was and he was by turns raving, silent, or alarmingly alert. Touch him and he was instantly back in captivity, striking out quick as a snake. We kept him in a room upstairs, under the eaves, where he didn't disturb the other patients. Once Captain Burns could move about, he spent a good deal of time with the very ill, writing letters and so forth. The Captain made an effort to include

Major Alexander in his rounds, though the stairs were difficult for a man with a serious back injury."

"Alexander? Do you have a first name?"

"I'm sorry, no. He told me repeatedly that he was called
Zander Holland, but the only name on his tag when he was
brought in was Alexander. Which isn't surprising, we've had
men with no name at all. But as he began to improve, the
Major was transferred to another hospital. I was told later
that he made a full recovery. I was glad to hear it. One of the
specialists who came to look at the burn cases had seen him
in another hospital."

"He'd been burned?"

"Oh, yes, it was part of the torture, you see. Systematic
burning."

Poor devil! Rutledge thought. "You have no record of his
unit?"

"I told you. Once he began recovering, the Army saw fit
to move him."

"Did Alexander keep in touch with Burns? After he was
transferred?"

"I can't answer that. But I doubt it. Captain Burns would have
told me if he'd had news. Whether they met again in London,
I can't say. I wouldn't be at all surprised if the Captain did make a
point of finding him. It was the sort of man he was. He cheered
up a good many people, ill as he was. It was his nature."

But that was all she could give Rutledge on the patient
named Alexander.

He left his telephone number with her. "If you think of
anything else that might be useful, I'd be grateful if you got in
touch."

"I shall, Inspector," she said, and hung up the receiver.

RUTLEDGE SPENT ANOTHER hour talking to people he
knew in the War Office. But he had no luck there. One official told him that he rather thought he remembered the
chap Rutledge was asking about and had heard that he went

to France after he'd been declared fit for return to duty. "But I'm not sure his name was Holland. And the only Alexander I recall was a sergeant-major in the Fusiliers. Tracking your man down will be well nigh impossible without more information, old boy. I haven't time to play hunches. And we have a bloody long list of wounded!"

AT THE HOTEL desk, Rutledge said to the young woman on duty, "Could you tell me, please, if there is anyone in Duncarrick by the name of Alexander? He was an officer in the war. I'd like to look him up if he's here."

"I don't believe there's anyone in town with that name." She frowned prettily, her hands toying with the pen she'd been using.

Hamish said, "He might not live in the town."

But Rutledge was already asking that question.

"I'm sorry. Perhaps you could ask Constable Pringle or Inspector Oliver. They'd know. Or Mr. Elliot, perhaps."

He began with Constable Pringle. Rutledge found him still at his desk and put the question to him. Pringle considered. "There's an Alexander out on the road to Jedburgh. But he wasn't in the war, sir. He's seventy if he's a day."

"Children?"

"Two daughters. That's all I ever heard about. Old maids, both of them."

Another dead end.

RUTLEDGE WENT OUT to walk, restless and angry.

Hamish said, "It's no' your fault!"

"Cold comfort!" he retorted, long strides eating up the distance to The Reivers. He passed it without looking and was well out the western road before turning and walking back to the town. "Fiona sits in that cell, waiting for trial, and there's going to be a conviction. All I needed was a name. They've given me one. If Alexander doesn't live in the neighborhood of Duncarrick, there's no way to find him. *Damn the man!*" But it was useless to damn anyone. There were still other names to track down.

Nearing the main square, Rutledge came across Oliver.

He was not a happy man.

"You've been meddling again! You told me that you were wanting to see the glen. Instead you went to find the Lawlor girl. And she's gone missing!" He made it sound like Rutledge's fault.

"I did see the glen," Rutledge told him. "And someone saw fit to shoot at me while I was there. Who did you tell that I was on my way to Glencoe?"

"What do you mean, someone shot at you?" He glared at Rutledge. "I called Inspector MacDougal as you'd asked. I don't know who might have overheard the call. MacDougal wasn't in his office when I tried from the station. So I waited until after my lunch and called again from the hotel."

From that stuffy telephone closet. Where Oliver, not thinking about it, must have left the door ajar for air. And who had been in the police station on his earlier attempt to reach Glencoe? McKinstry? Pringle?

"Where was McKinstry most of yesterday?"

"It was his day off. You'll have to ask him that."

"There's no way," Hamish pointed out, "to be sure it was the telephone. You could ha' been seen in Brae—or anywhere on the road—and followed."

"And what's this," Oliver went on testily, "about the brooch not being in Betty's hands for a year or more? That's nonsense!"

"I don't think it is." He gave it a split second's thought, then said, "I can tell you the name of a jeweler's shop on a side street in Glasgow. Send McKinstry with the brooch to ask if the owner recognizes it."

Oliver stared at him. "You're trying to tell me that my chief bit of evidence is a *hoax!*"

"No. I'm telling you that it isn't what it seems."

"Well, I won't have it! We've got witnesses to what Betty

Lawlor had to say—yourself included! You'll confirm in the courtroom what she said. Or I'll have you up for perjury!"

Rutledge gave him the name of the jeweler's shop anyway. "Send McKinstry to look into this. It may not be true. If it isn't, I shall retract any objections I have to the brooch as evidence."

Suspiciously: "Why McKinstry?"

"He won't like doing it. But he'll be thorough. For the sake of the accused."

Mollified, Oliver said, "I'll do that, then!" And he stalked off.

Hamish said, "If the constable took the brooch to Glasgow, he'll no' come home and tell Oliver his own name's put to the engraving card!"

"No," Rutledge agreed. "It will be interesting, won't it, to see how he handles such a minefield. If he gives Oliver the right name, he'll be crucified before the Inspector can draw breath. And if he doesn't give the right name, it will make him look worse when the truth does come out."

He walked into the lobby of the hotel. The savory aroma of baked apples and cinnamon reminded him that he'd had no luncheon. There was a rattle of dishes and utensils coming from the dining room, which meant they might be serving still. His stomach growled at the thought.

He was halfway down the passage to find out, when the clerk at the desk called, "Inspector Rutledge? A telephone message just came for you. You're to return the call at your convenience." She reached into the drawer where messages were kept and handed one to him.

Rutledge thanked her and walked on to the dining room, opening the folded sheet as he went.

It was from Durham. The office of a law firm.

He knew who had called him.

Thomas Warren.

ABANDONING LUNCH, RUTLEDGE went to the telephone closet and closed the door behind him.

He got through to Warren straightaway and identified himself.

Warren asked, "Have you had any luck? Finding the man you're after?"

"Not yet. I found a nurse who'd been matron at Saxwold. She gave me another name. Major Alexander. Does it ring any bells?"

"Alexander? 'Fraid it doesn't. No, sorry."

"He was in Palestine. Wounded there and was brought into Saxwold while Burns was a patient."

"No. Perhaps you'll have better luck with this one! I never met the man, but I have been searching for a letter I'd gotten from Rob when he was in London, convalescing. It was on the occasion of my birthday, and he said"—there was a rustle of paper, as if Warren was turning pages—"here it is: '*I found seven people to celebrate your birthday. Eleanor, of course, and a girl James had asked me to look up, and Edwards was there with the Talbots, who were rather grim. The other brother, Howard, is listed as missing, and naturally they fear the worst. Edwards felt they needed cheering up! And I also invited Alex Holden, who lives in Duncarrick, for God's sake, practically next door in Scotland. He was at loose ends, feeling in the mood to celebrate anything. The bone in his leg refuses to mend properly, thanks to the bloody Turks, and he's got another round of surgery to face. We drank to you and to Victory and again to you but lost count after that, and then ate something before we were completely drunk and forgot what was due the absent guest of honor. I set a glass at your empty place*—' Well, you needn't hear the rest. Alex Holden. You can add him to your list."

26

─────◆─────

RUTLEDGE SAT IN THE AIRLESS CLOSET, HIS MIND RAC-ing, Hamish, ahead of him at first, then falling behind as fact after fact dropped into place.

Alex Holden of Duncarrick. Sandy Holden—of Duncarrick—

Alex or Sandy. Short for Alexander. Zander Holland—Major Alexander. The tags on the wounded were sometimes garbled. Or lost—

He had met Sandy Holden, for God's sake, when he first came to Duncarrick—out by the pele tower, with his sheep! And seen him a number of times in the town since. Rutledge said aloud, "I'll give you any odds you like that they're the same man—!"

All this bloody time, the man he'd been searching for had been under his nose.

The fiscal himself hadn't seen fit to give Rutledge that name!

"There's no proof Burns knew the two men had met," Hamish pointed out.

"No. Probably not. But you'd think, wouldn't you, that after he came back to Duncarrick, Holden would have spoken to the fiscal—a simple word of condolence—'I met your son once, at a dinner in London. I was sorry to hear he didn't make it home from France.'"

"Unless he had something to hide—"

"The fact that he'd spent two nights in Captain Burns's house in Craigness? With Eleanor Gray? Who is now missing? Yes—if he had anything to do with her disappearance. Even if he'd simply provided her the money to sail to America."

The airlessness was making his head ache. Rutledge opened the door and went up the stairs to his room, his mind still racing.

McKinstry had claimed that he couldn't put a finger on the writer of the poisonous letters, even though he knew the townspeople like a book. As any constable would. But the local gentry would seldom cross McKinstry's path. An inspector would deal with them. And Holden had come back from France only in the spring of 1919. McKinstry hadn't had time or opportunity in five months to put him in the tidy mental boxes where the constable kept the pulse of Duncarrick.

"You've sent him on a wild-goose chase to Glasgow!" Hamish scolded Rutledge. "About the brooch. Still, it was foolish for Holden to use his name!"

"If Holden was in Palestine, the Army will have a record of it. If Holden was at Saxwold, Elizabeth Andrews will remember him. If Mrs. Raeburn can recognize him after three years, we have him in Craigness."

"But there's no proof Eleanor Gray died there!"

"I know," Rutledge said. "But if Holden took Eleanor there, the chances are he also took her away. And he can tell us where she went after Craigness."

"Mrs. Raeburn never saw her—"

"It was pouring rain that night. Eleanor could have

waited in the car until the worst had passed. By that time, Mrs. Raeburn had gone back to her bed. And there are the notes in the book's margin."

"But no date!" Hamish reminded him.

"In a way, there is a date. It was written after Captain Burns died. She noted that he was dead."

"Where was Holden when you drove to the glen?"

"According to Mrs. Holden, he was in Jedburgh that day."

"Aye, but was he? She couldna' know for certain if the man went where he claimed he was going."

"True enough." Rutledge ran his fingers through his hair. "All right."

"McKinstry said that in this town he kens everyone's business. It's no' impossible for Holden to do the same if he put his mind to it."

"Yes, and I've seen him with Oliver. Any number of times—"

"And Oliver wouldna' see anything wrong in answering questions Holden might ask. He's an upstanding citizen, concerned for the truth."

"All right, it's possible," Rutledge agreed. "But if the bones in the glen couldn't be traced to him—if no one knew whose remains they were—I don't understand why he'd stir up the past by going after Fiona. The timing is wrong too. Well before those bones were connected with either Eleanor Gray or Fiona, someone was persecuting her. Was it Holden? If so, to what end?"

Hamish didn't see it that way. "If he left Eleanor Gray in the glen, dead, he's been afraid for three years that someone might put a name to her. One day."

"No. If he's been this clever, then he wouldn't risk it. . . ."

Rutledge stopped his pacing and swore. "Holden lost all his horses to the war. He's having to start again. But if he could show that he was the father of the boy, and Eleanor Gray was the mother—true or not, it doesn't matter!—Ian MacLeod would be the heir to the trust that should have come to Eleanor Gray. If Holden knew how that trust stood, if Eleanor had talked about it on their long drive north, through the boy he could find himself in possession of a bloody *fortune*—"

He began pacing again, the room seeming to shrink and close in around him. He swung a chair out of his way.

"It might not matter whose bones they are—or whose child Ian MacLeod might really be. What matters is what people are led to believe. And if Fiona MacDonald is hanged for the murder of Eleanor Gray, then the child she'd been raising *has to be the child of Eleanor Gray*. At least in the eyes of the law. And when there is no one left alive to name the boy's true father, Holden has a very clear run! Very civic-minded of him to step reluctantly forward rather than let the child go to an orphanage."

"Aye. He wouldna' want his indiscretion to hurt his wife," Hamish agreed sourly. "That's the way half the town will see it."

"There have always been two standards," Rutledge answered. "People called Fiona a whore, but there's no name for a man who has an illegitimate child."

27

It sounded plausible.

But the police required proof, not speculations, to arrest a man.

And Rutledge had discovered in his first year at the Yard that what was logical about evidence was not always the truth it was pointing to.

"The first step is to find out all I can about Sandy Holden. And Gibson will have to do that from London. Starting with the Army and the Saxwold medical records. And in the meantime, I need a very good excuse to call on the fiscal again!"

Rutledge put in his call to London, setting in motion the search for the past movements of one Alexander Holden since the end of 1915. "I particularly need to know when and for what periods of time he was in England. And see if you can find any trace of a Major Alexander, also at

Saxwold at the right time. But odds are they're one and the same."

Old Bowels, delighted to hear that Rutledge had found a possible solution to the mystery of Eleanor Gray, said expansively, "Well done!"

"We aren't ready to say that Holden's guilty of anything. We can't find any trace of Miss Gray after the spring of 1916. He may have driven her to Scotland and left her anywhere from Berwick to John o'Groats. Alive. And if she's the mother of the child, she didn't die in the spring!"

"Well, bring him in and ask him what he knows. There's enough evidence for that, at least?"

Rutledge thought: If this is a man who survived capture by the Turks, he'll tell us what he wants to tell and nothing else.

THE FISCAL WAS just leaving his office when Rutledge reached Jedburgh. They almost collided in the doorway, the fiscal surprised to see him and stepping back with courtesy. "Inspector. What brings you here?"

"Have you a moment, sir? It's rather important."

"Have you made progress with the list of names I gave you?" Burns reluctantly turned and led Rutledge back to his office. Passing through the reception room, he asked his clerk to bring them tea. "For I shall be missing my own, no doubt!"

Taking the chair behind his desk, he motioned Rutledge to the one across from it. Rutledge sat down. "Now, then. What's this about?" the fiscal demanded.

"I've been trying to find the man who drove Eleanor Gray to Scotland. Connecting her to Fiona MacDonald has not been as successful."

"There's the brooch, man. I should have thought that was sufficient!"

"The brooch connects the accused to the bones found in Glencoe. I'm afraid it has done little to shed further light on whose bones these are."

"We already have a match of height and age, we have the proper timing of the death. We have the fact that Eleanor Gray went missing in the spring of 1916. And you tell me there's the strong possibility that in that spring of 1916 she came to Scotland. To wait out the birth of her child, I should think, where her circumstances did not embarrass her friends and her family."

"Yes. At present I'm hoping to carry matters a step further by tracing Eleanor Gray's movements closer to the time she was delivered." He paused. "If this child is Lady Maude Gray's grandson, it will have repercussions. For her. And for the solicitors who represent her daughter's sizable estate. Lady Maude—" He hesitated. "Lady Maude is a woman of considerable influence and distinguished connections."

"Indeed." The fiscal's clerk brought in the tea with a plate of sandwiches and a packet of biscuits. Rutledge accepted the cup and the sandwich offered him. Burns went on. "I've actually given some thought to the fact that a guilty verdict at the trial will most certainly establish the boy's heritage. It is one of the reasons I've chosen to let him remain where he is for the time being."

"I've been making my way through the list. Did your son have friends here in Jedburgh? I might add one or two names through them."

"The first two names I gave you were local men. As I told you at the time, they're dead and not likely to be involved."

"Did your son have friends in Duncarrick?"

"Robbie went to Harrow, and until the war the majority of his friends were either from there or in the law. He visited Duncarrick a time or two, but I don't recall anyone in particular he might have known there. Better to describe them as my friends. Certainly I'd have told you if I'd known of any connection!"

Hamish agreed with Rutledge: Unless the fiscal was lying, that meant Holden had never mentioned any meeting with Rob Burns in London.

He finished his sandwich and accepted the offer of

another. They were small but very good. The fiscal had already eaten both of his and began to open the packet of biscuits. His appetite was about to be spoiled—

In his mind, Rutledge could hear Fiona's voice saying, "*The father is an ordinary man. Just—an ordinary man . . .*"

Hamish tried to stop him, but he said aloud, "I must tell you, I think that if Eleanor Gray bore a child, there is a very slim chance that the father of her son might be your own. It strikes me that for some leniency shown by the court at her trial, Fiona MacDonald might be persuaded to name the man. I have a strong feeling that she knows who he is. That Eleanor confided in her before she died."

The fiscal frowned ferociously at him. "If my son had been seriously attached to a woman of Eleanor Gray's background, there would not have been a clandestine affair. Robbie would have come directly to me and to Lady Maude and made his intentions clear! He would have done the honorable thing!"

"Forgive me, sir, for being direct. You weren't fighting in the trenches. These were young men who did things out of need and fear that they would never have thought to do in 1914. They loved where they could and when they could, knowing they were going to die. If your son could have settled his affairs before returning to France, I've no doubt he would have. Eleanor wanted very much to study medicine. She may have asked him to wait—"

"Preposterous nonsense!" the fiscal said, glaring at him. "I will hear no more about it! My son was still in mourning for his dead fiancée—"

"You've made an enemy!" Hamish was saying. "It's no' wise—"

"Another excellent reason to wait, I should think," Rutledge said, ignoring Hamish, and then he backed off. "I can't tell you that any of this is true. I do know that friends of your son believed he loved Eleanor Gray as much as she loved him. Young men who served with him, to whom he would never have lied about his feelings. Eleanor and her mother quarreled shortly before her disappearance. The timing indicates it was after your son had returned to the Front but before his death. Perhaps Eleanor told Lady Maude that she wanted to marry a country lawyer, not a title. Lady Maude, however, refuses to discuss the quarrel."

"I will not hear another word! I will not believe that that child in Duncarrick is my son's *bastard*! I don't care who the mother was!"

Like so many bereaved fathers, Fiscal Burns had kept a holy image of his dead son in his heart—the dutiful, honorable young man who had died bravely for King and Country. Reared in another age, believing in other ideals, he could not contemplate the possibility that love had clouded duty in his son's last days. It would be a betrayal of that pure image, born of the child the fiscal had watched grow up to manhood and march off to war. A Tennyson knight in khaki.

"There's no dishonor here. He'd have married Eleanor Gray. But he died before she could tell him she was carrying their child. I cannot, in good conscience, believe otherwise."

Rutledge stood as he finished saying it, then thanked the fiscal for tea before adding almost as an afterthought, "I don't know what will become of that child in Duncarrick. But if he is abandoned by everyone, it will be sad. His bloodlines appear to be impeccable."

As he walked out of Burns's office, disregarding Hamish and the heavy silence he'd left behind him, Rutledge was well pleased with the seeds he'd sown. Turning his car around, he headed back to Duncarrick.

He told himself he'd spiked the guns of Alex Holden. If Lady Maude did come to accept her grandson at the end of Fiona's trial, she'd find herself with two contenders for the boy's father. And there was some safety in numbers.

In DUNCARRICK, RUTLEDGE considered his next move.

If Alex Holden was as clever as it appeared he was, it

would require more than an inspector of police arriving at his door to shake his nerve.

On the other hand . . . single-minded people often were victims of their own intense preoccupations. It was where they were most vulnerable.

It was late the next afternoon before his opportunity came.

Rutledge had lain in wait in the filthy, half-decayed stone pele tower, where he could watch the drive that led to the Holden farm.

When a motorcar came barreling down the drive and turned toward the town, Rutledge could see quite clearly that Holden was alone behind the wheel.

He gingerly climbed out of the tower, brushed himself off, and set out on the long walk in to the farmhouse.

Extensive and attractive gardens had been laid out around it, with trees forming a screen in front of the vast stables that ranged back to the pastures beyond. Jacobean in style, the house had a wide terrace leading to the door and handsome gables rising above the old glass in tall windows. The property had been made more fashionable a hundred years earlier, with lawns and beds and vistas, Rutledge thought, but the core was much older.

He crossed the terrace with long strides and rapped at the door. An elderly woman in a black dress came to answer his knock, and looked at him with a disparaging expression. He realized that there was still straw on his shoulders. Grinning, he said, "I've come to see Mr. Holden. Rutledge is the name."

"Mr. Holden isn't in, I'm afraid. We don't expect him back for another two hours."

"Ah. Then perhaps I might speak with Mrs. Holden." The tone of his voice was pleasant but firm. This was not a request to be rejected.

"She isn't feeling well today, sir."

"Then I shan't keep her long."

The maid invited him into the cool, high-ceilinged hall,

dim after the sunlight on the road. It was Scottish baronial, with banners hanging from the rafters and targes ringed with pistols and dirks and swords, like sunbursts on the stone between the high windows. The furnishings were more comfortable, a long table by the door and a grouping of chairs around the cold hearth that took up half the side wall. The maid asked him to wait there, and Rutledge walked around studying the array of weaponry. It was, he thought, real—not Victorian replicas of lost family heirlooms.

Many of the swords were claymores, the dreaded double-bladed weapon of the Highland Scots, capable of cleaving a fighting man in two. The blades were rough-edged in places, as if they'd met with bone. Battle swords, not dress swords. He moved on to look at the dirks. They were the famous *skean dhus*, the black knife of the Highlander, worn in the cuff of the stocking.

He smiled, looking at them. Not the elegant ones with cairngorms in the hilt and stags carved in the sheath—these weapons were plain and deadly, with horn to fit a man's hand in the handles and blades honed to razor sharpness.

The Scots under his command had taught him how to use them—a London policeman who could wield them now with the best of Mrs. Holden's ancestors. It was, he thought, a commentary on war, that from farmers and sheepmen and workers in the whiskey distilleries a man dedicated to preserving law and order had learned how to kill silently. Not a skill to be proud of . . .

He was studying a collection of flintlocks when the maid returned and led him to a back sitting room, where Mrs. Holden was lying in a chair with her feet on a low stool. She smiled at him and offered her hand as the maid closed the door behind him. "I have to thank you again for rescuing me. Have you come to see how I'm faring?"

"Yes. You look much better."

"I endured a very firm lecture from the doctor. I'm trying to mind his instructions. May I offer you something? Tea? A sherry?"

"Thank you, no. I've come to talk to you about your husband."

Her face flushed with surprise and wariness. "I'm afraid I can't speak for him. Would you care to come another day?"

He smiled reassuringly. "I shan't ask anything he wouldn't feel comfortable telling me himself. He was in the war, I think?"

"Yes. Nearly the entire four years. It was a very long war for him." Something in her face told him it was very long for her as well.

"I'm trying to find anyone who might have served in France with Captain Burns. The fiscal's son. Can you tell me if your husband knew him?"

She seemed relieved. It was a very simple question. "I've met the fiscal myself once or twice at the home of the Chief Constable. But I don't believe I've ever met his son, nor have I ever heard my husband speak of the Captain as a friend. I believe, in fact, that he was killed in France."

"Yes, that's true. I expect my informant was wrong. I was told by a man in Durham that Captain Burns had been acquainted in London with someone from Duncarrick. Both men were recovering from their wounds and they had been out to dine on at least one occasion with friends of Eleanor Gray."

This was a name she knew. "I've been told that she's the woman Miss MacDonald is accused of killing. How sad!" But the words didn't have the right ring to them, as if they were spoken because it was expected of her. Not because of any deep-rooted sympathy.

"How well do you know Miss MacDonald?" he asked.

"Not—I told you before, I hardly knew her. To nod to on the street. To speak to in a shop. That was all." She gestured with her hand, as if inviting him to look at the difference between her home and The Reivers. "We moved in different circles."

"A pity. I've interviewed her often, but I can't seem to break through the wall of silence she's erected around herself. Nor will anyone help me. She will likely hang."

Mrs. Holden smothered a cry.

Hamish called him callous and cruel, but Rutledge had a message he wanted conveyed to Holden. And this was the only way to do it. If Fiona meant nothing to Mrs. Holden, it would not be a lasting hurt.

"Surely—" she began, then stopped.

"I wish I could tell you differently. I wish I could prevent it. There's no hope now. She'll go to trial before the year is out."

She cleared her throat but her voice was still husky. "And the child? What's to become of it?"

"We thought in the beginning that the boy belonged to Eleanor Gray. But new information has come to light. I've traced the mother now—"

She turned very white and he went swiftly to her side, kneeling to take her hand. "Let me call your maid—"

"*No!*" She raised herself a little in her chair, and stared at him. "What do you mean, you've traced the mother?" The urgency in her voice struck him like a blow.

He said slowly, "We have a name. We have located the doctor who delivered the child. We can prove beyond question that the mother survived the birth, and was released from the clinic, where she'd been treated for rather serious complications."

"Gentle God—so much!"

"I'm afraid so."

"Have you told the police? *Have you told Miss MacDonald?*"

"I've told Miss MacDonald. She denies it. But I don't need her confirmation. I have my own." He was no longer interested in conveying messages to anyone. As Hamish rumbled in his head, he kept his eyes on Mrs. Holden. She had come to the end of her strength. But her spirit was undaunted.

Rutledge realized with sudden anger that this woman was not ill. She had been tortured as severely as any suffering her husband had endured at the hands of the Turks. It was there, in her voice, in her face, in the stiff, angular agony of her body. She had been made to choose—

Her hands were shaking, and she buried them in the folds of her sleeves, where he couldn't reach them. *"I don't believe you!"*

"It's true," he said softly. "Do you want to hear the name of the child's mother? Shall I tell you the name of the clinic? Shall I give you the initials on his christening gown? MEMC. Are they yours?"

She began to cry and fished for a handkerchief in her pocket, then pressed it to her eyes. "I'm childless. I feel dreadfully for this dead mother. It's nothing more than any woman would feel—"

He waited. She began, slowly, to find the steel she needed. "You've upset me, I'm afraid. I must apologize. It's the weakness I've suffered since the spring. Perhaps you'd better leave after all. I hope you won't speak of this to my husband. He will only be angry with me for letting you stay when I was feeling ill."

He admired her courage. He admired her strength. But there were other lives hinging on the truth and what he had to do must be done now.

"You *are* Mrs. Cook, aren't you? And the boy is yours. Are you Maude Cook—or Mary Cook—or both? Mrs. Kerr will recognize you, and so will Dr. Wilson."

"No! No. No."

"The child is yours," he repeated. "But your husband believes it's Eleanor Gray's."

She lifted her eyes to stare at him, startled eyes that were wide with shock. As he watched, she bit her lip, a thin line of blood marking the place.

Rutledge said, "And you've allowed him to think that's true."

Her hands reached for him, taking his arms just below his shoulders, holding him with a fierce grip that was a measure of her need. "No—*you don't understand.* He knows it's mine. Dear God, *he knows.* But he can't—he hasn't found out these things you've discovered. He isn't the father, you see! He will never have children by me, I'm ruined, I can't have more. And he hates me for that. He hates Fiona. And most of all, he hates my child. If I ever tell him the truth, even to save Fiona, he will see that the boy is given to us to raise, and then he will take the *greatest pleasure in destroying him*! My husband has powerful friends—the fiscal, the Chief Constable—Inspector Oliver—barristers in Jedburgh and Edinburgh. He can arrange it. He will even claim that he was Eleanor Gray's lover if he has to! Alex will stand there in public and lie to them all, and in the end, they'll let him have his way. The only way that Fiona and I can truly protect Ian is for her to die and the child to be left to the mercy of *strangers*."

IT TOOK HIM a quarter of an hour to calm her down again. She was shaking so badly, Rutledge feared for her, but when he offered to summon Dr. Murchison, she refused to let him. Instead she asked for a sherry, and he found the decanter by the window, poured her a glass, and held it while she sipped it.

A little color came back into her face. The shaking stopped. But she was beginning to think clearly again too. Rutledge asked once more about the doctor.

"No, I mustn't call him just now. He'll see I've been crying and demand to know why I was so upset. He'll tell Alex. And Alex will question Margaret—our maid. You must leave here and I shall say to my husband that you came to ask after my health because you'd found me ill by the pele tower and were concerned."

"Will he believe you?"

"I don't know." She took a deep breath. "Yes. I'll make him believe me. I haven't any choice. He has held this thing over my head for months now. Since he came home in the spring. And I take the greatest pleasure in *not* breaking. But sometimes—sometimes the strain is so great, I can hardly breathe. My chest hurts with it."

"How could he have found out? About the boy?"

"When I had the influenza, the doctor must have told him I'd borne a child. Or when I had the chill, I might have said something in my sleep. I was feverish, I sometimes woke crying out for—for someone. Alex is very clever; he began to see that I had—that there was something I hadn't told him. How he connected all this with Fiona, I don't know. We'd been so very careful! But once his suspicions were aroused, I wouldn't put it past him to go to the inn of an evening and search the family quarters. Who was there to see when Fiona tended bar! There was a christening gown. It had been my grandmother's. Or perhaps he saw my face when I looked at Ian. So I stopped making excuses to pass The Reivers."

"That still isn't strong enough—"

"Yes. You don't know him. He's very clever, I tell you! It started when he began asking me where I was in 1916 when he called from London to say he was sent home to recover from wounds. I wasn't here, you see—and I wasn't here when he called to tell me he was being sent on to France. Over and over he'd ask where I was, what I was doing, who I was with—until my very silence answered him! It was after that that he must have learned somehow that I'd borne a child. He would bring me small gifts—a blue baby's shawl. A small rattle for a teething child. A rocking horse he said he'd found in Edinburgh and knew I'd like. The servants thought it was a loving promise of children, when I was better. But I can't have any more children! The nurse who bathed me— the doctor—*someone must have told him there was a child*!"

Rutledge shook his head. "He must have discovered something. Did you meet Fiona? Was there any communication between you?"

"We met at night sometimes, at the pele tower. But after Alex came home, we stopped. Drummond—I don't know, he's very loyal to me and my family. He wouldn't have told anyone what he knew. Drummond brought me home, you see, from Lanark, when I was well enough to travel. But his sister was jealous of Fiona. Sometimes jealous people see more clearly. And Alex is a master at finding out secrets. He was trained to spy."

"The persecution of Fiona was a test?"

"The anonymous letters? At first, yes. To make me tell him what he wanted to know. But I wouldn't, and it escalated. He spread lies to Mr. Elliot and to Oliver—to the fiscal and other influential people, for all I know—until they came to believe that they'd thought of it themselves! When McKinstry didn't search the stables, it was Alex who persuaded Inspector Oliver to go back. He reminded him of those old murders, before the war, that hadn't been solved. That pricked Oliver's pride. Alex *knew* the Jacobite bones must be hidden somewhere—he'd come across an old story about them in some of my father's papers. That was to be the end of it, but by that time, Inspector Oliver was rabid to find a body. And throughout the whole ordeal, Alex would come home and tell me what he had been doing that day to make Fiona's life unbearable. And watch me, until I could crawl off somewhere and hide my anguish!"

"Mrs. Holden. How did your husband come to know Eleanor Gray?"

"I'm not sure that he ever did. I've never heard him speak of her at all."

"There's some evidence that he could well be the man who drove her north, just after Captain Burns died. If he did, he may have been the last person to see her alive. I'd come to believe that he was after the boy because young Ian might inherit Eleanor's fortune once it was established that he was her child."

"He *knows* Ian is mine—it's revenge that drives him, not money!" she cried. And then pressed her fingers against her eyes as if they ached. "I haven't the strength to worry about this Gray woman too. I have enough sorrows already." She looked out the window. "I should never have given my child life. I went to Glasgow once, did you know? Fiona took me. To a place where abortions were done. Never mind how I found out about it, another poor, desperate woman had gone there and later confided in me. But I couldn't go through with it. I loved Ian's father, you see. In spite of my fear of being found out, I *loved* his father. . . ." She lay back, her eyes shut. "I love him still. . . ."

Hamish said somberly, "Holden is driving her into her grave—she's likely to die before Fiona's trial! Does he no' ken the risk he's taking?"

I don't think he does, Rutledge answered silently. *It would spoil his game if his wife died prematurely. He wants the name of her lover, and he wants his wife to see that she's caused an innocent woman to die a fearful death. Damn the man!*

But contrary to what Mrs. Holden had said, Rutledge believed Holden had known that Eleanor Gray's body lay in Glencoe. He might even have been clever enough to see how useful it could be. A remarkably tidy way of punishing Fiona and ridding himself of the past. The problem was, this was going to be bloody difficult to prove!

He stood up. "What do you want me to do, Mrs. Holden? I can't bring your husband in and charge him—there's only your word against his that he's responsible for what happened to Fiona MacDonald. People would believe *him* if he told them your health is frail and that your mind has been affected by it."

"There must be a way to stop him! You—I can't go on like this! I can't live with Fiona's life on my conscience, and I can't buy it back without destroying my child! I have come to hate Alex—but he's the albatross around my neck, and I cannot be freed from it."

"Will you kill someone for me?"

He heard Fiona's voice quite clearly in his head.

"Tell me—did you live in Brae before your son was born?"

She nodded. "I was desperately in love. He—Ian's father—was in Glasgow for some time and we met when we could. I was happy. I had closed the house here—with the horses gone and the servants leaving, it was an excuse."

"And the initials on the christening gown?"

"My maiden name. I was born Madelyn Elizabeth Marjorie Coulton. But I was afraid to use it in Brae or the clinic. Because, you see, he'd gone back to sea and not long afterward was killed." She stopped, let her voice steady once more. "He died and I had a baby on the way. I stayed in Brae as long as I dared, hiding the pregnancy as best I could. Then I took a hotel room in Glasgow for a time before going to the clinic. There was nowhere else that I dared to have the child. If Alex had died, of course, I'd have claimed that Ian was his. But Alex was alive and I couldn't risk brazening it out. If I hadn't met Fiona—if she hadn't been willing to take the child as her own—I would have killed us both. The boy and myself."

28

---◆---

RUTLEDGE LEFT MRS. HOLDEN WITH SOME APPREHEN-
sion—concerned for her—afraid that when Alexander
Holden walked back into his house, his suspicions would be
aroused by something in her face. It wouldn't take him long to
discover that Rutledge had been there. He was too intelligent
not to know why. Mrs. Holden was very fragile. What would
he do? Bully her—or find a new, unexpected strength in her?

"Whatever he does," Hamish said, "it's no' possible to stop
him. You canna' go to Oliver until you hear what London's
learned about Holden! You canna' go to the fiscal without
proof. This is Holden's ground, he'll ken what to do—"

"There may be a way to distract him." Rutledge had
nearly reached his motorcar, concealed well out of sight of
the Holden property. He pulled it to the head of the drive,
where Holden couldn't pass him.

Then he waited. With infinite patience. Even Hamish
stood the long watch in silence. They had shared such
watches many times in the trenches—there was almost that

same comfortable sense of companionship. Almost—but not quite.

It was nearly dusk when Holden came. The long shadows of the autumn day had given way to clouds, and the first sprinkles of rain.

The lights of Holden's car picked out the dark shape of his own, and slowed.

Holden called sharply, "What's happened?"

Rutledge replied, "I've come to speak to you. Your maid told me you were out, and I waited."

"For God's sake, why didn't you wait at the house?"

"Because I didn't want your wife or your servants to hear what I've got to say." He gestured around them at the dark road and the dark drive. "We have a little privacy here." The sprinkles turned to the first heavy drops.

Holden looked for hidden ears before turning back. "Then say what you have to, and let us both get in out of this rain!"

"I traced you to Craigness, Holden. To Rob Burns's house. I found written proof there that Eleanor Gray had come north with you that night in 1916 when it rained so hard. She waited in the car until the worst had passed before coming in. And Mrs. Raeburn didn't see her. You left with her—and Eleanor Gray disappeared. Did you kill her? Did you drag her body on a blanket up the slopes of the mountainside in Glencoe and leave her for the jackals and the ravens?"

Holden said, "Don't be an idiot! I never knew Captain Burns. His father will tell you that. And my wife!"

"It won't matter what they say. You've left a trail behind you. And I've uncovered it. You thought, trained as you were, that you were skilled at deception. But I can bring witnesses who remember your face and who can place you in Saxwold, in London, in Craigness, and even in Glencoe. Unimportant people you thought we'd never be clever enough to find. There's other proof. I'll have it soon. It's a loosely woven net at present—but it will tighten."

The car's lamps were fully on Rutledge's face, but they

cast macabre black shadows on Holden's. There was no way to read his eyes. His hands, on the wheel, were white-knuckled. Rutledge watched them. If they moved—

Hamish said, "Is there a weapon in his car?"

I don't know, Rutledge answered silently. He could feel the tensing of his body. A sitting target, pinned by the light. Holden had tried to shoot him once—

"Save your wife the disgrace of seeing you brought in by Inspector Oliver's men. Tell me what happened to Eleanor Gray."

It was meant rhetorically, but to his immense surprise, Holden did.

"I've nothing to be ashamed of. She wanted to find passage to the States. There was nothing to keep her here, she said. I drove her as far as Glasgow, and then went back to London on my own. I don't know what became of her after that. And I didn't see any point in telling Inspector Oliver about it. That was in the spring, and they tell me she died in late summer."

"You're a very accomplished liar. But you aren't dealing with Turks now. Or with Inspector Oliver. Your name carries no weight in London. The Yard is handling Eleanor Gray's death, not Duncarrick." Rutledge's voice was cold.

Holden turned his head away, looking around them, trying to see beyond his headlamps. Satisfied at last, he turned back.

"You won't believe me if I tell you the truth. No one will." He lifted a hand to wipe the rain from his face. "Damn it, come to the house!"

"No. Your wife is ill. I won't put her through this. Tell me here—or at the Duncarrick police station."

"You're a bloody stubborn man, did you know that? Eleanor Gray spent the night in Rob's bed, which I thought rather macabre, but I couldn't have cared less. I was so tired from driving that I fell asleep in the guest room almost at once. Heavily asleep. I don't even remember closing my eyes. I must have been snoring. Or she might have felt ill, I don't know. I woke with a start, and in the darkness sensed rather than saw someone bending over me." He turned away again, the shadows on his face shifting and changing. "The Army had taught me how to kill. Fast and silently. My hands had found her neck before I'd even realized where I was or who was in the house with me. By the time I was awake enough to find a light, she was dead. I had to clean the carpet, and I was all for burying her in the garden. I even moved the bench so it would cover the grave. But the rain was coming down in buckets, I was afraid it would wash her out before the morning. So I got her into the back of the car, pulled a blanket and some of my clothes over her, and went through the house to find anything she might have left. The next morning as soon as the neighbor was up and about, I returned the key and drove off."

"Where is Eleanor Gray now?"

"On that damned mountain in Glencoe! Where else? Or she was. I never dreamed— It was damned bad luck that Oliver was so good at his job, wasn't it?"

Hamish growled a warning as Holden lifted a hand, but it was only to wipe his face again.

Rutledge said, "If her death was an accident, why didn't you call the police straightaway, or a doctor?"

"She was professionally killed, man. Not a mark on her, except where my fingers found the spot on the back of her neck! Her mother is one of the richest women in England. Do you think Lady Maude would have believed me? She'd have seen to it that I hanged! I'd had a violent history at Saxwold, and the next hospital as well, and the Army was glad to send me off to France for cannon fodder. Look, I nearly killed a nurse once when she came up behind me unexpectedly. I had my hands on her throat before she could even scream. They thought I was out of my head. But I wasn't. I'd lived too long with danger, and it was a reflex to strike first. Like a snake. They were ready to pack me off to an asylum with the shell-shocked men and leave me to rot!"

Rutledge involuntarily shuddered. With men like him— "How did you know the rocks were there—on the mountainside? They aren't easily seen from the road."

"My father took me there sometimes as a boy. He was obsessed with tales of betrayal and murder." He pushed his rain-matted hair out of his eyes. "My father would have made a bloody Highlander if he hadn't been born in Carlisle. He collected all those weapons you see in the hall, buying them up all over Scotland. It gave him a sense of history. I put them up when I married Madelyn. It was something from my own past. The rest of the house was hers."

He looked at Rutledge for a long while, ignoring the rain. The patience of the hunter, waiting for the rabbit to break cover. But Rutledge was patient, too, and as skilled. Holden said at last, "You know the truth now. What do you think you should do about it?" When Rutledge didn't respond, he continued, "I don't intend to be railroaded into a sentence of death by Lady Maude and her lawyers. She was a distant and uncaring mother according to Eleanor, but she'll raise heaven and earth to see me dead once she's told I killed her daughter." There was cold menace in the calm voice. "If I were you, I'd go back to London and let the MacDonald woman go to trial and pray that she's acquitted. What is she to you, after all!"

What, indeed? Rutledge didn't know the answer to that himself. He sat there feeling the rain soaking through his shirt to the skin, and fought his anger.

"Don't threaten me!" he told Holden.

"Call it a friendly warning, Inspector. But keep in mind the fact that I could walk into The Ballantyne or anywhere else you believed yourself safe, and you'd be dead before you heard me come through the door. You can bank on that." He put his car into gear again. "I didn't intend to kill Eleanor Gray. And I won't hang for it."

The lights swung in the darkness, turning the slanting rain to silver. And Holden smiled at Rutledge before the car disappeared down the drive, a black shadow against the stark brightness of its lamps.

ALL THE WAY to the hotel, Hamish's voice pounded in Rutledge's head, demanding to know how much he believed of what Holden had said.

Rutledge was wet through, cold, and very tired. But he said, "The man's an accomplished liar—that's what he was trained to do in the war. Still, I have a feeling he told me the truth about killing Eleanor Gray. That's the pity—she went north with a man she considered a friend, and safe. Whatever Eleanor did that night in Craigness, whether it was waking him out of a sound sleep or in some way making him angry with her, she died for it. And if he killed her the way he described, there wouldn't have been any marks on the body that the coroner would have been able to identify two years later."

Rutledge took a deep breath, feeling his anger drain away.

Eleanor Gray was dead, she couldn't contradict Holden's account of how it happened. He might even rally enough support to get away with it.

Hamish agreed. "He said it himself—a snake. Quick to strike."

The nurse, Elizabeth Andrews, had called him that too. "London will give me the rest of the evidence I need to present to the fiscal, but a good lawyer will twist it into whatever shape Holden devises. A jury will never convict him. They'll believe him where they would never have believed Fiona. We shall have to make him betray himself."

"He won't betray himself. He didna' betray himself when the Turks tortured him."

"I'll find a way." There was grim determination in Rutledge's voice.

THE NEXT MORNING Rutledge awoke to lowering skies and more rain, sweeping in gray sheets along the streets and rattling like stones against his windows. A depressing day.

Unable to sleep after he'd turned off his light, he'd lain awake trying to find a solution to the dilemma he faced. Hamish, playing devil's advocate, seemed to relish pointing out that most of his answers wouldn't work.

You couldn't frighten a man like Holden. You couldn't make him come to you. If he'd survived torture . . .

Then what did he want? What was it that Holden valued most?

His wife had made that clear. His revenge. He wanted Fiona to hang and his wife to know that she'd had the power to save her.

Rutledge lay in his bed, forearm resting across his forehead, and thought it out from start to finish.

Hamish said, "This way willna' work either. He can claim he was trying to protect his wife."

"Yes. He can say that. Oliver might believe him. But it's worth a try."

"It's too damned risky!"

"I can take care of myself!"

Hamish laughed. "In the dark, there's nothing you can do. You havena' his experience, man!"

"I crawled through No Man's Land that night in '15 and took out that hidden machine-gun post. They never heard me coming."

"It's no' the same!"

He got up, dressed, and went down for breakfast.

THEY LET HIM in to see Fiona. He told Oliver and Pringle that he was leaving Duncarrick and wanted to appeal one last time to the conscience of the accused.

When he walked into the cell, he said, "I've come to say good-bye." But he had his finger in front of his lips, signaling her to be silent. "Before I go, I must appeal to you one last time . . . for the sake of Lady Maude Gray and her daughter. . . ."

In the passage outside the door he could hear Oliver's footsteps receding. Rutledge came to Fiona and took her hands. "I know who Mrs. Cook is," he said softly. "I've spoken with her."

"No, that's impossible—!"

"Fiona, just listen to me. There isn't much time. I know what her husband is trying to do to her. And to you. You're a scapegoat. Tethered to a charge of murder—he's going to destroy Madelyn Holden through you and watch her die of shame. What you don't know is that he also killed Eleanor Gray. Those bones on the mountainside *are* hers. The ones that Oliver found. And Holden will kill again. It's too easy for him. He'll kill that child, too, but it won't be fast or merciful."

"I've protected Ian—"

"I know what you've done. But Mrs. Holden is being frightened to death. Do you understand me? She's battered every day by that man's suspicions and doubts and anger. When I lifted her to carry her into Dr. Murchison's office after she'd fainted, she was so thin, I was afraid of hurting her!"

"I thought—I was *sure* he'd never touch her!"

"He hasn't. Not physically. He torments her instead, day after day. He's sapping her courage, and one day she'll want to die. And then she will die. By her own hand."

"Don't tell me these things, I can't bear it!" she cried.

"You need to hear the truth, all of it. From start to finish."

He gave her all the information he had. Trusting her.

She listened in silence, without asking questions, nodding from time to time as she understood where he was going. Accepting every word, trusting him in her turn.

When he'd finished, he said, "Wait until late this afternoon. After I've left for London. Summon Inspector Oliver. Tell him you want to speak to Mr. Elliot and the Chief Constable. Tell *them* that you don't want to die. That you can prove that Ian's mother is still alive. Tell them that the truth is hidden in The Reivers, and if Fiscal Burns will come in person tomorrow, you'll take them there and give them your proof."

"They'll want to go straightaway—"

"No, they'll have to speak to the fiscal. If need be, let them think you're hoping to catch a glimpse of the boy."

She shook her head. "No. I won't tell them that. I won't use Ian!"

"You must make your story plausible, Fiona. I want Holden to be told what's happening. I want him to believe it. It's the only way to make Oliver and the rest recognize how they've been used." He added, "There's one last thing. Mrs. Holden didn't tell me the father's name. And I didn't press her. But now I need it. It's the one crucial piece of information I don't have."

She said, "It's not my place—"

"Fiona—" He stopped, then went on. "Holden is extraordinarily clever and he will turn everything to his advantage, finding some way to destroy that child. We must get Ian MacLeod out of Duncarrick, out of reach. Tomorrow."

"His father is dead—he can't help you!"

"It doesn't matter! Even a dead man's name makes a child safer. Mrs. Holden has no family, but Ian's father might."

She bit her lip. Finally, struggling with her own conscience and fearful of his, she said, "Will you swear to me— on your honor—that you won't tell anyone unless you have to?" He nodded. "He was a naval officer. His name was Trevor."

Rutledge felt his heart turn over. "No."

"You wanted to know—"

"I—*Ross* Trevor? Are you very sure, Fiona? That Ian is his child?"

She was frightened. "I should never have told you—I knew it was wrong!"

"No. It—it's good news. I'm glad for him." There had been nothing of Ross in the child's face— Except for the eyes, Rutledge realized suddenly. Those changeable eyes. "I'm glad for him—" he said again. But what about David Trevor? Would he, like the fiscal, refuse to accept his son's decision to love another man's wife?

It was Hamish who reminded Rutledge that the man who mourned his son so deeply would have to grow used to this news. But Morag would love the child. For Morag mourned too.

"You have sworn!" Fiona was pleading, confused by his sudden uncertainty.

"I'll keep my word." But he must persuade Mrs. Holden to find David Trevor once Alex Holden went to trial.

"You've forgotten Fiona—" Hamish railed. "You promised to see that the child was given back to *her!*"

Rutledge could read the despair in her face. She also knew what she had lost. Not her trial, but her son.

No, Mrs. Holden and David Trevor would see that she was never alone again—

But Hamish refused to be mollified. He said, "How many promises will ye break?"

Rutledge leaned forward, kissing her cheek. "Fiona—it will be all right."

She didn't move. Her face wrung his heart. She said forlornly, "Will it? I wish I could be as sure."

29

OLIVER BADE RUTLEDGE FAREWELL AND WISHED HIM A
safe drive back to London. "Although I don't know what
you're to tell Lady Maude Gray."

"The truth. What I know about it." But not the part
Holden had played.

"Well, then, she ought to be glad to learn what's become
of her daughter. You can tell her, we'll see that the accused is
punished for what she's done."

Rutledge shook his hand, walked back through the
downpour to the hotel, and notified the Ballantyne staff to
draw up his bill. Then he began to pack.

It was shortly after luncheon that he drove out of
Duncarrick. He let the motorcar stand in the street in the
rain, for all the world to see, his luggage in the back and a
hamper of food on the seat next to him.

Ann Tait, worried about her geraniums drowning in
their pots, paused to look down the street at his car, then
hurried back into her shop.

Mr. Elliot, coming back from calling on a parishioner, stopped to ask if he was leaving.

"Yes," Rutledge replied. "I've finished my business here."

"You left a message with my housekeeper that you wished to speak with me." His black umbrella glistened with raindrops, and the sleeves of his coat were damp.

"I found the information elsewhere. I'm glad I didn't disturb you."

"I wish you Godspeed, then."

Rutledge thanked the minister and went around to turn the crank, drying his hand on his trouser leg before reaching for it.

HE DROVE SOME miles out of town, then found himself a quiet spot in a small copse of very wet trees where the motorcar was nearly invisible from the road.

It would be a long wait. It might even be a useless one. But he was prepared to be patient. And to endure another soaking.

BY NIGHTFALL RUTLEDGE had completed his notes, setting out his entire investigation—when and with whom he had talked, what he had been told and by whom—each step in the long chain and the conclusions he had reached. Then he set the notebook under the dash, well out of the rain. He had also eaten the sandwiches, and nearly finished the tea. He wished for more to fight the raw chill.

He waited another hour, then got out and cranked the engine. The rain had let up a little. Still, it took him nearly half an hour to reach the western edge of Duncarrick, avoiding the main streets and the more traveled roads. He arrived at his destination reasonably sure he hadn't been seen. Few people were out on such a wretched night.

Rutledge left the motorcar hidden deep in the shadows of the pele tower, well out of sight. Then he walked the rest of the way, his shoes heavy with water.

Hamish, restless in his head, was a low rumble like thunder. Like the guns in France, which haunted both of them still.

Some twenty minutes later, moving quietly and keeping to the shadows, he reached The Reivers. Wet and cold, he stood silently in the doorway of the stables and waited to see if anyone had noticed him slipping across the yard. But the windows of houses that overlooked the inn yard were either dark or had had their shades pulled.

Rutledge had considered summoning Drummond as an ally, then decided it was far from certain just where Drummond's loyalties lay. Feeling to be certain that his torch was still in his pocket, he crossed quickly to the back of the inn and found a window that he was able to force open with his knife.

A London burglar, he thought, pleased, couldn't have done it better—or more quietly.

Climbing in, he let himself down gingerly, then reached up to refasten the sash as best he could. Satisfied that the window wouldn't attract attention on a night like this, he bent to remove his shoes. They felt heavy, waterlogged.

Something stirred in the darkness, and he jerked away from it, prepared to defend himself.

But it was only Clarence, her light mew of greeting lost in the frantic beating of his heart.

Stooping, he rubbed her back, then let his eyes grow accustomed to the darkness before moving on.

He found himself in the small back room that had been used as storage for the kitchen. A stack of wooden boxes stood there, and he cut a strip from the top of one to reinforce his temporary patch on the window frame. He also found some towels in a drawer and used them to wipe his wet face and his hair. His stocking feet were reasonably dry, and he was grateful for that.

Moving slowly, cautiously, Rutledge made his way through the inn. In each room he paused, his eyes alert, his ears tuned to the merest sound. The silence was heavy, even shutting out the sound of the rain, and the white blur that was Clarence had already gone ahead of him, disappearing around a door. The kitchen. The bar. The inn parlor.

Rutledge came to the stairs, and after listening intently went up them softly, his stocking feet close to the outer edge of the treads, where there would be the least chance of a sound as his weight settled on the old wood.

There was no one in the room upstairs that belonged to Fiona.

He moved around it with care, checking behind the door and in every corner, even lifting the curtain around her clothes before looking under the bed. The floorboard, his questing hands told him, was still in place.

No one had been here. He was fairly certain of that. The question was, would someone come in the night? This night? Another night? Not at all . . .

It was a long watch. His shoulders grew tired, and his eyes burned from staring into the darkness. His clothes began to dry from the warmth of his body. His ears, picking up the creaks and moans of an old building, tried to place each one. Later, moving quietly to the window, he looked out into the street. But there was no one about. The rain, heavy and growing chilly as the wind picked up, had kept most people at home. There was only one umbrella moving down the street, shining in the light spilled out from windows.

If Holden had come here and found the christening gown with the telltale initials—if he had come again to take away the brooch—surely he would come now—

There was a *chink!* from somewhere in the house. The cat?

Rutledge was very still now, no longer waiting, feeling instead the adrenaline surge of danger. His breathing grew deeper, steadying him.

Rutledge had no illusions about Holden. He would kill . . . given the need.

Nothing. No one stirred in the bar below. No one came up the stairs.

Another quarter of an hour passed.

Suddenly he could feel the cool rush of air and smell the dampness of the rain. Someone had opened a door. Then it was closed again.

He waited, drifting silently behind the curtain surrounding Fiona's clothes. The faint scent of her perfume reached him, evoking her image.

But no one came up the stairs.

He waited, and in the end decided to go closer to the stairway, where sounds from below would be magnified.

Moving to the top of them, he listened again. And then in the silence a soft footfall reached his ear.

It was too late to go back to where he'd been.

He moved back a very little, opening the stairs to whoever was climbing them with such stealth. After a few seconds he could—he thought—make out the dark shape coming toward him. The stairwell, like a pit, yawned into stygian darkness. But the shape moved . . . breathed. He could hear the quick, shallow breaths, the carefully placed feet on the steps. . . .

Rutledge stood where he was, letting it reach him. Go past him—

It went into the child's room, out of his line of vision, and was there for some minutes. Rutledge could hear the clothes chest open and after a time close. And then it was coming toward him again, something white grasped in front of it. Without seeing Rutledge in the deep shadows, it made for the head of the stairs.

And then Rutledge acted, moving from the balls of his feet, taking full advantage of the element of surprise, catching his quarry from behind, pinning the arms hard to the sides before he realized that it wasn't a man he held in his grip but a woman.

Dear God!

"I'll see you dead before I let you finish this." Her voice was husky, low. And breaking free while he was still absorbing the unexpected shock, his grip loosened, she lifted her arm.

He saw the flash of a knife and spun away.

She came after him, raising it again. Determined. He caught her wrist, and the thinness told him who it was.

"Mrs. Holden? It's *Rutledge*!" He spoke quietly, the words no more than a hiss. But she gasped, and said, "Oh, no!" in horror.

He moved closer to her, whispering, "What are you doing here?"

"He told me there was proof at The Reivers. He said he was coming to find it. I thought he meant the christening gown— But he had promised Oliver and the Chief Constable to have a drink with them first. So I came ahead, to stop him."

She pressed something into his hands. He felt the cold steel of a dagger and the warmth of the hilt where her fingers had been. "It's sharp," she warned. "I was going to kill him with it. You must take it. You must kill him for me! If you won't, I shall!"

"Mrs. Holden, you must go. Please! How in the name of God did you get in here without a *key*?"

"But I've had a key. Fiona gave me one after her aunt died. A precaution, if anything went wrong and I needed to reach Ian."

"Then give it to me and go. I'll see it's returned tomorrow!"

"Will you kill him?" she asked, her voice trembling.

"Not if I can help it."

"You have the dirk. It was my father's! If you won't do it for me, do it for Fiona!"

And then she was gone, moving down the steps with the same silent care she'd used coming up them.

His heart still racing, Rutledge took a long breath. Then he listened. Somewhere a door opened and closed quietly. The only sign of it was the brief rush of cold, damp air. She was gone.

He went back into the bedroom. Something brushed past his leg, and this time he knew it was the cat. He bent to touch her, and she wrapped herself around his calf. He pushed her away then, afraid that the loud rumble of her purr would mask the other sounds he was waiting to hear. She went off, and he heard the small *plunk!* as her body leapt onto the bed.

There was a soft cry—

It came from the bar, and he stood where he was, tense and poised to move fast.

A decoy? To draw out anyone hidden in the darkness? Hamish was warning him to stay where he was—

Or had Holden run into his wife in the street?

There was nothing Rutledge could do but find out.

He went to the stairwell and listened, but heard nothing.

He began to move down, one step at a time. Swift—but sure.

At the bottom, he paused again. The cat had come down after him, and he tried to see if she had heard something he hadn't. But she sat down on her haunches when he stopped. Her eyes were on his face.

He had left all the doors open behind him when he had come up the stairs. Now that served him well.

Moving quietly, he worked his way back to the bar.

And stumbled over something on the floor, nearly pitching forward, catching himself in time on the edge of the bar.

Reaching down, Rutledge groped at his feet, and touched hair. A woman's soft hair. There was a white patch beside her. The christening gown—

He found her throat and searched for a pulse.

There was none.

Gentle God! Holden had killed his wife—

Anger swept him, following on the heels of shock.

He remembered what Holden had told him in the rain the previous night: that there was nowhere Rutledge could consider himself safe. It was true.

Rutledge got slowly to his feet, every nerve ending alive. Eyes sweeping the black shadows. All his training in France rushing back—

He was here—but where? Rutledge could feel him like a second skin.

The cat's sharp hiss warned him. There was a blindingly bright flash, a deafening report, and he was already dropping. Not fast enough this time. Something spun him half around, slamming into his chest.

He had been hit—

He knew the drill. It had happened before. Shock. Numbness. And then the pain.

Almost in the same instant, he acted, instinct already guiding hand and brain, throwing the dirk—aiming for the place he'd seen the flash of powder.

The Scots under his command had taught him well. The harsh intake of breath told him he'd hit his mark. Something fell heavily, taking a bar stool over with it. The clatter was appalling. And then silence.

Rutledge moved toward it, his own breathing uneven. Whoever it was still had a pistol—

He reached out, felt heavy, immovable flesh, and instinctively flinched.

There was no sound except for his own breathing—

Fumbling, he turned on his torch and looked down into the dead face of Alexander Holden. The knife, protruding from his throat, had severed the artery. There was a great deal of blood. Staining the scrubbed floor. Rutledge stared at it. Black and red, where the torch picked it out.

He realized he was no longer thinking clearly.

Rutledge told himself, *Fiona will have to explain—or they'll find my notebook—London knows about Holden too—*

He remembered the torch in his hand, staring down at it, then turning it off. *Why did he have to kill her—why couldn't Madelyn Holden have lived—*

I wanted to save her. Most of all I wanted to save Fiona—

His breathing was harsh now, and his chest felt like fire. *I'm bleeding,* he told himself. *And there's nowhere to go for help.*

He didn't want to think about Fiona. She belonged to Hamish. She always would. . . .

He found a chair and half fell, half slumped in it.

Hamish had been yelling at him, roaring in his ear. Or was it the sound of his own blood?

He couldn't tell.

From somewhere he could hear the sounds of the pipes. They were faint, and then stronger. Coming toward him.

Rutledge knew what they were playing. He'd heard it too many times not to recognize it at once.

It was "The Flowers of the Forest." The lament for the dead. He had heard it played for every dead Scot under his command. He'd heard the pipes skirling into battle, he'd heard them grieve. This was a dirge for the dying.

He was dying.

Hamish was like a trumpet in his head. "You will no' die. Do you hear me? *You willna' die!*"

"You're already dead, Corporal. You can't stop me." Rutledge was finding it hard to concentrate.

"You willna' die! I willna' let you die!"

The sound of the pipes had begun to fade. Rutledge thought, *The funeral is over—they've buried Hamish. Hamish is dead, and I'm to blame—I've killed him.* But where had this chair come from? They didn't have chairs at the Front—

The fire in his chest was smothering him.

He could feel Hamish taking hold of him.

It was what Rutledge had feared for such a long time that now he was grateful for the dark so that he didn't have to look up and see the dreaded face bending over him. He said to Hamish, "It's too late. I'm dead. You can't touch me now. I'm free of you—"

"YOU SHALL NOT DIE!"

30

IN THE LAMPLIT DRUMMOND PARLOR, THE TICKING OF the mantel clock competed with the soft patter of rain beyond the lacy curtains and glass panes that shut out the night. The soothing quiet was broken only by the dry rustle of the Edinburgh paper Drummond was reading and the regular *click* of his sister's ivory knitting needles. It was late, the child already asleep, the clock's hands nearly touching half past the hour of eleven.

A sound, heavily muffled but unmistakable, brought Drummond to his feet, the newspaper flying in all directions.

A shot—

He waited, but only for an instant. The image in his mind sent him headlong out into the small hallway. Brushing past the mirrored hat stand, he flung open the outer door and plunged into the rain, running hard.

His sister, calling his name, reached the door he'd left standing wide and leaned out, demanding to know what he thought he was doing.

Over his shoulder he shouted, "Go back inside, woman!"

But at the door of The Reivers, Drummond stopped, putting out his hand cautiously to touch the latch.

He'd seen her only that morning, she'd surely do nothing so rash—it wouldn't save Fiona—

The latch lifted, and his heart began to thud.

She had the other key—

Kicking off his shoes, he swung the door open, tensed for whatever stood behind it. *What if there were the two of them here—what if she had shot him? They'd hang her too!*

Nothing happened. There was nothing in the darkness.

He listened intently, begging the silence to talk to him, to tell him if one person—or two—had come here. . . .

No sound except for his own breathing, and the blowing of the rain against his back. The wind was picking up a little; he could feel it across his shoulders.

Making his way into the entry, he moved forward one step at a time, soft-footed in his stocking feet. The hair on the back of his neck standing on end, his eyes wide against the pitch-blackness, concentrating on the stairs just ahead of him.

But it wasn't dark enough here—

Another step. On his wet skin he could feel the air from the open door that led from the family's quarters into the side of the bar.

It had been closed before—he'd closed it when he fed the white cat.

Stretching out his hand, he could feel the frame of the door. Moving cautiously, he leaned forward to stare into the bar.

For an instant he thought he heard a word spoken softly.

A white smudge on the floor at the far end of the bar— The cat, then.

He took another step, unsure where the voice had come from, and in the same instant, his toe nudged something blocking the threshold, immovable, nearly tripping him up.

Startled, Drummond dropped swiftly to his knees, praying hard now.

"Don't let it be her—please, God—"

His fingers found the rough fabric of a man's overcoat.

A sudden gust of wind and rain blew into the open doorway behind him, shaking him, crouched and defenseless there. He flinched away.

Even as he realized that it was only the rain, his heart seemed to choke him, rising in his throat like a stone.

He reached for the coat again, found an arm—the warm blood soaking a shoulder—a face. Trying hard to find a pulse, he thought, *She* has *shot him—not herself.*

But his fingers touched the blade and then the handle of a knife instead. Protruding grotesquely from the throat.

Someone spoke.

Drummond jerked to his feet, and then saw in the pale square of light from a window that someone sat in a chair twenty feet away.

"Madelyn?" Drummond called softly, unconsciously using her given name as he'd done when she was a child. "What's been done, then? Are you hurt?"

His voice seemed to roar through the stillness of the room.

The slumped figure in the chair didn't answer.

Reading the awkward angle of the one shoulder he could see, Drummond hurried forward, right hand outstretched as if to ward off a blow.

The figure didn't move. Drummond leaned down to touch the shoulder, and the head fell back. In the pale light, Drummond made out Rutledge's profile.

His eyes were open—dark patches in a bone-white face—

Drummond, startled, fumbled for Rutledge's throat, fingers slipping beneath the collar.

A pulse, faint, erratic. His hands moved down the front of Rutledge's coat, where the white shirt was black with wet blood.

Shot, then, and barely alive. They'd all but killed each other—

Relief flooded through him, so sudden and wild, he felt light-headed with it. But not her. She was safe.

He bent to snatch up the crumpled white cloth he could just make out beyond Rutledge's feet, and too late realized that it was gripped in hands that were soft, long-fingered. A woman's—

Drummond began to pray again, raggedly and disjointedly, pleas tumbling over each other in his head. His hands ran over the body, the shoulder, the face, the silken hair.

He sprang to his feet, made his way to the lamp that was always kept on the bar, found it, and managed to light it on the second try.

Its gold-and-blue flame leapt up so brightly, he was blinded.

And then his gaze moved beyond the glass chimney and he saw the carnage all too clearly.

Holden, in the doorway. A pistol still clutched in his right hand, a *skean dhu* piercing his throat, projecting at an odd angle from front and back, cutting the great artery as cleanly as butter. Drummond whistled softly.

Rutledge, in the chair. Shot and barely alive, head forward now, his eyes closed.

And Madelyn Holden, lying almost at the Londoner's feet, what appeared to be a child's lacy christening gown still strained to her breast.

The men were soaked in their own blood.

There was none on her—

Drummond went to her, kneeling beside her, lifting her into his arms, crooning to her as a mother would croon to an ill child.

But the weight of her body, without buoyancy and life, the open eyes that didn't focus on his face, told him the truth.

A surge of primeval pain ripped through Drummond, and he cried her name again, pulling her against his chest, bending his head over her, rocking her body with his, shaking with tremors that broke into deep, harsh sobs.

And he nearly missed the words.

He'd forgotten the man in the chair. Looking up, he realized that Rutledge must have spoken. But not to him.

Hardly words, more a murmur. "The pipes have stopped—"

Here was the only one left alive to tell him what had been done in this dark room—

Tears wet on his face, Drummond gently lowered Madelyn Holden's body to the floor again, stumbled to his feet, and went to Rutledge.

The pulse in his throat was no more than a thread now, the breath so shallow, it seemed not to exist.

"You shall not die!" Drummond thundered in unconscious echo of Hamish's voice. "Not here! Not till I've finished with you—!"

He curled his arms under Rutledge's shoulders and then his knees, grunting as he lifted the unresisting weight.

Muscles straining, Drummond made his way to the door, stepping uncaring over Holden.

Tommy Braddock stood just outside, a large black umbrella over his head. The rain had subsided, but a cold wind blew, whipping the skirts of the coat he'd thrown on over his nightclothes.

"What the hell—" he exclaimed as Drummond stepped out into the drizzle, a man's body gripped in his arms.

"Keep the rain off him!" Drummond ordered. "My house. Then the doctor. Bring him back as soon's you can!"

Braddock slammed the inn door shut behind them and tilted the umbrella over the burden Drummond carried, recognizing the man from London and swearing in surprise under his breath. But one look at Drummond's face and he said nothing, keeping pace as best he could.

Drummond paid no heed, concentrating on walking back the way he'd come barely ten minutes before. "You'll live. Do you hear me?" he said once to Rutledge.

Ahead they could see the house door wide open and Drummond's sister leaning out into the wet night, a lamp in her hand. The flame danced and shifted, then burned stark and straight.

He saw it, a beacon, his grief so heavy that the flame seemed to flicker through his tears.

If Holden had killed Madelyn, Drummond promised himself that he would come back to The Reivers this same night and cut out the bastard's heart.

"You shall not die!" Drummond silently repeated the words in cadence with each step, a malediction—and a benison.

He moved strongly, steadily, toward the light.

If you enjoyed Charles Todd's LEGACY OF THE DEAD, you will not want to miss any of the superb mysteries in the series. Look for A TEST OF WILLS, WINGS OF FIRE, and SEARCH THE DARK at your favorite bookseller's.

And turn the page for a tantalizing preview of Charles Todd's newest mystery, WATCHERS OF TIME, coming in hardcover from Bantam Books in October 2001!

WATCHERS
OF TIME

by

CHARLES TODD

SEPTEMBER 1919

OSTERLEY

DR. STEPHENSON TURNED AWAY FROM THE BED WHERE the dying man lay breathing so lightly the blanket over his thin chest barely stirred. His bony, restless fingers plucking at the edge of the wool were the only signs of life and awareness. Twice the young woman sitting on the bed beside him had tried to still them, covering them with her own, but his hand picked up the silent tatoo again, like a drummer remembering his place, as soon as she released it. He had already frayed an inch of the binding. She gave up and sat back, sighing.

His face was grooved by illness, and a stubble of beard emphasized the lines, like a rough landscape of suffering below the still-weathered skin of forehead and nose. Shaggy gray eyebrows hung heavily over the sunken lids. Age weighed him down, but there was a certain strength there as well, as if life had made him fight for all he had, and he had not forgotten the battles.

Catching the eyes of the man's sons, who were standing on the far side of the bed, faces in shadows cast by the scarf draped over the lamp's shade, the doctor nodded toward the window across the room, out of earshot of the patient. The young woman looked up as they walked away but stayed where she was. She didn't want to hear what was being whispered.

Another gust of wind swept the front of the house, and rain was driven heavily against the panes, rattling them. The storm had stalled, as they sometimes did here along the coast, reluctant to move inland and lose itself in the hilly terrain there. For three hours or more it had hovered over the village, flailing everyone and everything out in the open.

The older of the two brothers bent his head to hear better as Stephenson said softly, "He's moving comfortably and peacefully toward the end. There's nothing more I can do. But he might wish to have Mr. Sims here? And I should think your sister would be comforted as well."

Mr. Sims was the vicar.

The younger brother answered, "Yes. I'll go for him then." He went quietly across the room to the door. The scarf that shaded the lamp by the bed riffled as he passed, and the light flashed once across his face. There were wet trails of tears on his cheeks.

His sister reached out and briefly took his rough hand.

The other brother sighed. "He's had a long life, Pa has. But not that long. Sixty-four. We'd thought he'd be with us another five—ten years. His own father lived to just past eighty. And Uncle Tad's young for seventy-six." He shook his head.

"Your Uncle Thadeus has the constitution of an ox," Stephenson agreed. "He may well outlive your grandfather's years. But your father's heart has given out, and his body must follow." He studied Martin Baker's face, noting the lines of worry and sleeplessness. Hetty Baldwin, his housekeeper's daughter, was getting a good man in Martin, the doctor told himself. Much like Herbert in character—God-fearing, with strong ties to his family and a fierce sense of duty. It was a sound match. "Everything happens in God's own time, you know. Even this. And it's a kindness that he won't linger." He spoke the words as comfort, then lifted his chin toward the bed. "Look, see if you can persuade Elly to rest a little. She's hardly stirred form his side since yesterday morning. We'll call her if there's any—urgency. She will only wear herself into collapse, driving herself like this."

"I've tried, to no avail." He turned toward the window, pulling aside the shade a little to look out. Rain ran down the glass in rivulets, pushed against the house by the wind. A filthy night, he thought. A fitting night for death to come . . . He dropped the shade back in place and said to Dr. Stephenson, "There's naught to be done to make it easier on her?"

"I'll leave something. A sleeping draught. Give it to Elly in a glass of water, when your father is gone. And, Martin—see that Fred doesn't insist on being one of the pallbearers. That shoulder of his is not fully healed, and the socket will never be as strong as it was. He's not out of the woods yet. He could still lose the arm if he's not careful. The army surgeons can't work miracles without a little help!"

"I'll remember."

"Good man!" A clap on Martin's shoulder for comfort, and then Stephenson walked back to the bed. He reached down and touched Elly's hands, folded tightly in her lap. They were cold, shaking. "Your father is comfortable. He would want you to be the same. Let Martin fetch you a shawl, at least."

She nodded, unable to say anything. The gray head on the pillow moved, first to the right, and then toward the left. His eyes opened, focused on his daughter's face, and he said in a gravelly voice, "I want a priest."

The doctor leaned down and said reassuringly, "Yes, Fred has just gone to fetch Mr. Sims."

"I want a priest!" the old man repeated querulously.

"He's coming, Papa!" Elly said, fighting her tears. "Can you hear me? He'll be here very soon—"

"Priest," her father demanded. "*Not* vicar."

"Herbert," the doctor said soothingly, "let me lift you while Elly gives you a little water—"

The dark eyes shifted to the doctor's face. "I want a priest," he said very clearly this time, refusing to be distracted.

The bedroom door opened and Fred was ushering in the vicar. "I met him on his way here," he said. "Coming to see if we had need of him."

Mr. Sims was taller than Fred, thinner, and not much older. "I've been sitting with Mrs. Quarles, and thought it best to call on you before going home," he explained. Herbert Baker had taken all day to die. Most of the town knew the end was near, a matter of hours at best. Sims had stopped in twice before.

Sims reached out to touch Elly's arm, saying easily, "Ellen, do you think you could find a cup of tea for us? We could use the warmth on such a wet night."

She flushed shyly. "Tea? Oh—yes. I've just to put the kettle on."

Smoothing the blanket over her father, she got up, reluctantly leaving the room. Sims took the place on the bed that she'd vacated and squarely met the eyes of the dying man. "You're a fortunate man, Herbert Baker. You were married to a good woman—a fine wife and mother. Both your sons survived the war, and have work. Elly is a lovely girl. God has been kind to you."

"Thank'ee, vicar, and I'll have you say a prayer for me after the priest goes!"

The vicar looked up at Martin, then said, "Dr. Stephenson?"

"He's been asking for a priest. Just now, before you came in. I don't know why—"

Fred said, "Father James is the only priest in Osterley. He's a *Catholic*—"

"That's right—he's the one!" the dying man said with more will than strength. Something in the depths of his eyes flared with hope.

Martin said, "If that's what he wants, humor him, then. Fred, go and see if Father James will come here." Fred hesitated, glancing uneasily at the vicar, as if he'd just been asked to commit heresy. But Mr. Sims nodded encouragement, and he went out the door.

Martin said, "You'll stay?" to Sims.

From the bed came the single word, "Stay." The lined face was exhausted, as if speaking was a greater effort than he could manage.

Sims said, "I'll go to the kitchen, then. From the look of her, Ellen is more in need of that tea than I am!" Rising from the bed, he said to Herbert Baker, "I'll be within call. Never fear." His smile was reassuring.

Herbert nodded, and closed his eyes. The wind had dropped again and the rain lost some of its strength. On the roof overhead it seemed to fall softly, now, with a summer patter.

Dr. Stephenson said quietly to Sims, "He's sound enough in his mind. But dying men often have whims like this. Best to humor him!"

"Yes. I knew a man in the war who wanted to be buried with his little dog. Only he didn't have a dog. But when they came to bury him, his arms were folded across his chest as if he'd held one as he died. Strange comfort, but who are we to question?"

He went out the door, shutting it quietly behind him. There were voices on the stairs. Sims speaking to Ellen. And then they went down together.

The room was silent. Martin watched his father for a time, and then said anxiously to Stephenson, "It'll be an easy passing?"

"As easy as any. His heart will stop. And his breathing will follow. He will be asleep, long before that. I didn't expect him to wake at all. I thought he'd reached the last stage."

Herbert, roused by their voices, said, "Is the priest here, then?"

"Not yet, Papa," Martin answered, lowering himself gently to sit on the bed next to him. "Fred's gone to fetch him." He gripped his father's hands, unable to say anything, a plain man with few graces. But the warmth of his fingers seemed to give a measure of peace to the dying man. Martin cleared his throat hoarsely, warmed in his turn.

The silence lengthened. After nearly a quarter of an hour, Fred came in, bringing a short and balding man of middle age in his wake. Father James greeted Stephenson with a nod and came to shake Martin's outstretched hand. His fingers were cold from the night air. "I understand your father has been asking for a priest," he said, his face showing only concern.

"I don't know *why*, Father—"

"Nor does it matter. I'll speak to him, then, shall I?" It was a question asked gracefully, setting Martin at his ease. The priest turned quietly to bend over the bed. After a moment he said, "Mr. Baker? Herbert? It's Father James. What can I do to help you?"

Baker opened his eyes, seemed to have trouble focusing them, then blinked as he looked up at the white clerical collar, clearly visible against the black cloth. "Father James, is it?"

"Yes." As a thin, trembling hand came out from under the blanket, Father James reached for it and the claw seemed to lock onto his.

"Send them away!" Herbert Baker said. "Just you and me."

Father James looked across at the dying man's two sons and then at Dr. Stephenson. They walked to the door, opened it, and went out, their shoes loud on the wide boards of the passage, then moving together down the stairs.

Father James, waiting until they were well out of earshot, looked around to collect some impression of this man lying in the bed waiting for death to come. He knew who the Bakers were, but had never exchanged more than a word or two with any of them.

It was a big room set under the eaves, with simple but sturdy furnishings, and a worn carpet on the floor. Someone had painted watercolors of the sea and framed them for hanging. An amateur's hand, the sunrises and ships vigorous, but showing an untrained eye. The family had taken pride in them, to put them here. The single window faced the street, the shade pulled against the night and the curtains drawn across it.

So many houses in Osterley had this same air of working class austerity, Father James thought. The years of prosperity lay in the past—well before Herbert Baker's time. No one starved, but people worked hard for their bread.

As the priest turned back to the bed, he saw the woman's photograph on the table beside it. The soft whisper of the rain faded, then revived as a squall, the wind sending a gust of drafts into the house and making the lamp dance to its tune. Baker's wife? She had died before the war, as he recalled, and this must have been taken some ten years before that. The daughter—Ellen?—looked much like her. The same dark hair and sweet face, staring at the camera with trusting and expectant eyes.

He sat down gently on the bed's edge, where Ellen and the vicar had sat before him, and said in the voice that was his greatest gift as a priest, deep and steadfast, "I'm here. We are alone in the sight of God. In the name of the Father, the Son, and the Holy Spirit, tell me how I may serve you?"

HALF AN HOUR later, Father James walked down the stairs of the Baker house, and found the family, the doctor, and the vicar waiting for him in the small, very Victorian parlor. Tea had been brought, and poured, but the cups were still more than half full, sitting forgotten. Wind rattled the shutters, a theatrical announcement of his appearance.

Every face had turned toward the priest, their eyes pinning him in the doorway, concern mixed with weariness and not a little curiosity in their expressions. He cleared his throat and said to the family, "Your father is resting quietly now. He has asked me to reassure you that he wishes to be buried in accordance with his own beliefs, with Mr. Sims officiating. I have served him by giving him a little comfort. If he should require me again, you've only to let me know. And now, if you'll forgive me, I must go. It is late—"

He was offered refreshment, he was offered the gratitude of the grieving family. Prevailed upon by Mr. Sims, he sat down and drank a cup of lukewarm tea, out of kindness. Dr. Stephenson, watching his face, was struck by the lines of tension about the eyes, putting it down to the awkwardness of being in an unfamiliar household among strangers not of his faith. The two of them, doctor and priest, had shared many long watches together over the years, and Stephenson had always found him a strong and dependable ally in the business of offering peace to the dying and solace to the survivors. Even so, the face of death was never commonplace. One learned to accept, that was all.

Father James behaved with sympathetic courtesy toward Herbert Baker's children, that deep voice bringing a measure of comfort to Ellen, as it had to her father. Fred and Martin, both slack-faced with exhaustion, appeared to find a renewal of strength in his assurance that Herbert Baker had made his peace with his God and had not changed his faith. Simple men, they couldn't fathom their father's odd behavior, and were half embarrassed by it. Father James, understanding that, said only, "Your father was not frivolous. At the end, we are all in need of God's grace, like a child before his father. I'm some years older than the vicar. Perhaps to a man of Herbert Baker's age, it mattered." He smiled across the tea table at the vicar.

The vicar looked up. Tansy, the liver-and-white spaniel sitting by his chair, patiently waited for Sims's fingers to resume scratching behind the curly ears. The vicar said, almost diffidently, "In the war it was the same. They were so young, most of them. But old in experience that I couldn't match. I sent more than a few of them along to the Methodist chaplain, who was closer to their fathers' age than I was. That seemed to be the best thing to do for them." Then he turned the conversation, adding to Father James, "You must be thanking God that this weather held until after your Autumn Fete at St. Anne's. It was a blessing . . ."

Ellen said, "Martin went with Hetty to the bazaar. He brought me a brush for Tansy, and a new lead." A smile lit her pale face, and then faltered. "Papa was well enough to go last year."

"So he was," the vicar answered. "He has been a rock of strength each spring at Holy Trinity too. I took pleasure in working with him."

As soon as it was decently possible, Father James rose and took his leave. Martin Baker politely escorted him to the door and thanked him again. He stepped out into the night. The rain had dropped off, and there was only the wind to keep him company on his long walk home.

Dr. Stephenson, climbing the stairs once more, found that the priest was right; Herbert Baker seemed to be resting quietly, slowly losing his grip on life.

In the small hours of the night, the man died peacefully, his family gathered about him. His daughter Ellen sobbed quietly and his two sons watched in anguish as he drew several short, uncertain breaths, and then stopped breathing, only a thin sigh passing his lips. The vicar, by his side, prayed for Herbert Baker's soul as the sigh faded.

THE FUNERAL WAS well attended, and Herbert Baker, coachman by trade, was sent to his eternal rest with the good will of a village that had known him to be an honest and plain-speaking man with no vices and no outstanding talents, except perhaps for loyalty.

A WEEK AFTER the funeral, Dr. Stephenson returned to his surgery late one afternoon to find Father James just walking out the door.

"Well met!" Stephenson exclaimed. "Come in, let me pour myself a drink, and I shall be at your service. First babies are not to be hurried! This one kept its mother and me awake all of the night and well into the afternoon, and I've missed my breakfast, my lunch, and my usual hours." He led the way back through the doorway, down the passage and into his private office. It smelled of wax and disinfectant, a blend that Father James found to be a sneeze-maker. He dragged out his handkerchief, sneezed heartily three times, and grinned lopsidedly at Stephenson.

"You should hear me when they've waxed the pews and the confessional at St. Anne's! The blessing is, I'm not bothered by incense."

The office was small, painted a pleasing shade of blue, and offered three chairs for visitors as well as the more comfortable old leather one behind the doctor's broad wooden desk. Dr. Stephenson settled into that, and Father James took his accustomed place in the ancient wingback. The priest said as Stephenson lifted the bottle of sherry and offered it to him, "No, thank you. I've another call to make, and she's temperance mad. I'll lose my reputation if I reek of good sherry."

Stephenson grinned. "How does she manage communion wine, then?"

"It's consecrated, and the evil of the grape has been taken out."

The doctor chuckled, then poured his own glass. "Yes, well, the mind is a wonderful thing, wonderful."

"It's about the mind I've come," Father James said slowly.

"Oh, yes?" Stephenson sipped his sherry with relish, letting it warm him.

"I'd like to ask you if Herbert Baker was in full control of his faculties, when he called me to him on his deathbed."

"Baker? Yes, well, that was an odd business, I daresay. But he was dying of congestive heart failure, and his mind was, as far as I could tell, clear to the end of consciousness. Any reason why you feel it might not have been?" His voice lifted on a query. Stephenson was a man who liked his own life and that of his patients as tidy as possible.

"No," the priest said. "On the other hand, I'm seldom asked to second-guess Mr. Sims's parishioners. Or he mine, for that matter. It was curious, and I found myself wondering about it afterward. Baker most certainly *appeared* in full control, though understandably weak. Still, you never know."

"Which reminds me," Stephenson said, turning the subject to something on his own mind. "There's one of your flock I do want to talk about. Mrs. Witherspoon. She's been refusing to take her pills again, and I'm—er—hanged if I can understand it."

The priest smiled. "There's a challenge for you. At a guess, I'd say that when she feels a little stronger, she's convinced she doesn't need them. Then she feels unwell again and quickly takes two to make up for it. A good-hearted woman, but not overly blessed with common sense. If I were you, I'd have a talk with her husband. She pays more heed to what he says than to anyone else. The sun shines out of Mr. Witherspoon, in her view."

The ironmonger was the most lugubrious man in Osterley. Stephenson laughed. "The eye of the beholder. Well, there's a thought. The woman will make herself seriously ill if she doesn't heed someone!" He looked at his wine, golden in the little glass. "I had a patient once who swore that sherry was Spanish sunlight caught in a bottle. Never been to Spain myself, I'm hard pressed to escape for a few hours in Yarmouth. But there's most certainly medicinal magic in it." He finished the wine and then said, "How are those triplets of yours?"

Father James beamed. They were his sister's children and lived some distance away. "Thriving. Mary is coping, with the help of two nuns I found for her, and every member of the family they can dragoon into service. I've done my own turn, walking the floor at night. I expect those boys will be holy terrors by the time they're eight. Their father was something of a devil himself at twelve!"

"Aren't we all? But responsibility comes soon enough."

The priest's face changed subtly. "It does. I'll be on my way, then. Get some rest—you look as if you could use it!"

Watching him out the door, Stephenson had the curious feeling that Father James should take his own advice.

NEARLY TWO WEEKS had passed since the funeral. Stephenson, rested and busy, had long since put Herbert Baker out of his mind when he took his wife to visit friends.

It was a dinner party like a dozen others the doctor attended with some relish whenever he could. There were eight couples, and he'd known all of them for years. Comfortable with each other, sharing a common history, they had found in each other a companionship that had few boundaries. Stephenson could count most of them as his patients, and his wife had sat on committees of one sort or another with every one of the women— church bazaars, flower arrangements, food baskets for the poor, spring fetes, charity cases, visiting the sick, welcoming newcomers to Osterley, and generally forming an ad-hoc social group that was as small as it was select.

He couldn't have said afterward how the subject arose. Someone asked a question, another guest expanded on it, and a wife raised a laugh by adding her own views. Stephenson found himself picking up the thread, and the next thing he knew, he was telling the story of a dying patient who had wanted to hedge his bets in the next life by seeing both the vicar and the priest.

One of the guests leaned forward. "Was that old Baker? My wife mentioned she'd seen Father James walking out of Baker's front door in a pouring rain, saying good-bye to young Martin on the step. I told her she must have been mistaken— Baker was sexton for seventeen years at Holy Trinity!"

George Handley said, "Had the right idea, though, didn't he? Who was it that said Paris was worth a Mass?"

That dissolved into an argument over whether it was Henry

IV and progressed to a recital of the opening lines of "The Vicar of Bray." Herbert Baker had been forgotten once more.

IT WAS LATE in the evening on the second of October when Father James returned to the Victorian Gothic house that served as St. Anne's rectory. He let himself in through the unlocked kitchen door, grateful for the lamp still burning on the small table by the window, and sniffed appreciatively at the scent of bacon. His dinner, dry but certainly still edible, was sitting on an oven rack in a covered dish. He lifted the cover. There were onions too, and what appeared to be a scotch egg.

His housekeeper, Mrs. Wainer, had—as always—remembered that the body needed nurturing as well as the soul. He could feel the saliva flow in his mouth. Onions were his greatest love.

Father James set the lid in place and closed the oven door. Tired from a long vigil by a very ill parishioner, he stretched his shoulders as he straightened his back. The chair by the bed had been too low, and his muscles had cramped. But the man had lived, thank God. His family needed him.

He went down the passage that led past the parlor and the small music room that he had converted into a parish office. In the darkness he moved with the ease of long familiarity. As he reached the hall by the front door, he could hear the clock in the parlor cock itself to strike the hour, the *whirr* of the gears a soft sound that stopped him, one hand on the newel post at the foot of the stairs.

The clear golden chimes always reminded him of the house where he had grown up—the clock had come from there—and the laughter of his mother and father, sharing the reading of a book as the children sprawled at their feet. It had been a nightly ritual just before bedtime, and it was something he himself, celibate and alone, missed. Mark had died in the war, killed on the Somme, and Judith had died of the influenza, taking her unborn child with her. But Sarah had brought her triplets alive into the world, and he looked forward to the day when their rowdy spirits and lively voices would brighten the silence of the old rectory. Sarah had already promised them for a week each year, though they were not yet three months old. He smiled to himself at the thought. Mrs. Wainer, bless her, would probably quit in disgust.

As the chimes echoed into silence, he went on up the stairs to his study on the first floor. The lamp on the desk wasn't lit, but one in his bedroom was burning, a low flame that guided his movements. He went through the bedroom door to put his case and coat away, and then wash his hands before dinner.

Coming back into the dark study, he failed to see the shadow that stood immobile in the deeper shadows beside his private altar. The gold chain on the priest's chest gleamed in the moonlight pouring through the windows. Noticing that the draperies hadn't been drawn, Father James crossed the room to pull them to, reaching high over his head to move the heavy velvet across the wooden rod. The first pair were only half shut when the shadow stepped out directly behind the priest. In the figure's hand was the heavy crucifix that had always stood on the altar between a slender pair of candlesticks. It was lifted high, and the base of the cross brought down with stunning force, straight into the bald head that seemed, in this light, to be tonsured and unnaturally white.

A target that was so clear it seemed to draw a sigh from the priest. He began to crumple, like old clothes falling to the floor. The crucifix was lifted again, the base flashing in the pale light as it descended a second time. As the priest hit the carpet with an ugly *thump*, the bloody scalp was struck a third time.

Then, with efficient grace, the shadow stepped back, dropped the crucifix from a gloved hand, and set about silently, swiftly, wrecking the room.

THE POLICE, SUMMONED the next morning by a distraught Mrs. Wainer, took note of the food left untouched in the oven, of the black blood pooled beneath the priest's head there by the window, and the state of the room: the paper-strewn floor and the scattered contents of the desk drawers. They examined the tin box that lay upside down and pried open with scissors, emptied of parish funds. And came to the conclusion that Father James, returning home unexpectedly, had been attacked by someone he'd disturbed in the midst of a burglary.

Not a target, a victim.

He'd heard a noise in the house, they said, discovered there was an intruder upstairs, and gone to the window to summon help. The alarmed thief, hiding in the bedroom just behind the study, had picked up the first weapon that came to hand—the crucifix—and struck Father James from behind. In his terror he'd hit the priest again, and then fled, leaving the kitchen door standing wide, the money from the box in his pocket. Muddy shoe prints near the lilac bush showed a worn heel, a tear in the sole near the toe. A poor man, then, and desperate.

The house next door, usually filled with three generations of family, had stood empty last night. They had traveled to West Sherham to attend a party in honor of the eldest son's engagement. But had Father James known that? They would surely have come to his call—or at the very least, glimpsed the fleeing murderer and hurried to investigate. Not that it would have saved the priest.

The townspeople of Osterley, whether members of St. Anne's, Holy Trinity, or no church at all, were shocked and horrified. Mr. Sims, trying to minister to his flock as well as the priest's, until the Bishop could send someone else down from Norwich, heard the same litany over and over again. "He was such a good, caring man! He'd have helped whoever it was, given them the money, done his best for them—*there was no need to kill him!*"

But Mr. Sims thought, There *was* need, if Father James had seen the face of the man invading his home and threatening him with the crucifix from his own altar. Recognition was knowledge—and there were some who might be afraid that even the compassion of a priest had its limits.

Fear was seldom ruled by reason; it reacted to danger first and logic afterward. The first blow was surely fear—the succeeding blows could have been fear, or could have been cunning. How was anyone to know, until the killer had been found?

Sims tried not to look into the eyes of the people of Osterley and speculate. But he found himself doing it. Human nature was human nature.

The war had taught Sims that frightened men did whatever they had to do to stay alive. And in the trenches killing had become a natural reaction to peril. He wondered if the priest's attacker was an unemployed soldier, one so desperate that he'd felt no compunction about taking life. And then scolded himself for such unchristian speculation.

All the same, how far would the few pounds stolen from the rectory go? How long before empty pockets drove the killer to strike again?

That night—for the first time since he'd come to Osterley—Mr. Sims locked his doors. The vicarage stood behind a high wall in an expanse of wooded lawn, old trees that had always been his pride and given him a sense of continuity with those who had served Holy Trinity before him. Now it seemed isolated and secretive, hidden away and intolerably vulnerable.

He told himself it was merely a precaution, to lock his doors.

In fact, he was coming to terms with the unexpected discovery that the Cloth, which had always seemed his armor and his shield, was neither, and that a man of God was no safer than any other householder.

ABOUT THE AUTHOR

Charles Todd is the author of *A Test of Wills,*
Wings of Fire, and *Search the Dark.* He lives on the
East Coast, where he is at work on the next book
in the Ian Rutledge series, *Watchers of Time.*

BANTAM MYSTERY COLLECTION

MC 6/01